C000137100

Gissing and the City

NEWNES SIXPENNY COPYRIGHT NOVELS

NEW
GRUB STREET

GEORGE GISSING

Gissing and the City

Cultural Crisis and the Making of Books in Late Victorian England

Edited, and with an Introduction by

John Spiers

Senior Research Fellow,
Institute of English Studies,
University of London

Visiting Professor,
School of Humanities, Social Sciences and Law,
University of Glamorgan

Published in association with the Institute of English Studies, School of Advanced Study, University of London.

First published 2006 by
PALGRAVE MACMILLAN
Houndmills, Basingstoke, Hampshire RG21 6XS and
175 Fifth Avenue, New York, N.Y. 10010
Companies and representatives throughout the world

PALGRAVE MACMILLAN is the global academic imprint of the Palgrave
Macmillan division of St. Martin's Press, LLC and of Palgrave Macmillan Ltd.
Macmillan® is a registered trademark in the United States, United Kingdom
and other countries. Palgrave is a registered trademark in the European
Union and other countries.

ISBN-13: 978–1–4039–9772–2 hardback
ISBN-10: 1–4039–9772–1 hardback

This book is printed on paper suitable for recycling and made from fully
managed and sustained forest sources.

A catalogue record for this book is available from the British Library.

Library of Congress Cataloging-in-Publication Data
Gissing and the city : cultural crisis and the making of books in late Victorian
   England / edited, and with an introduction by John Spiers.
      p.   cm.
   Includes bibliographical references.
   ISBN 1–4039–9772–1 (cloth)
   1. Gissing, George, 1857–1903—Knowledge—London
(England) 2. Gissing, George, 1857–1903—Homes and
haunts—England—London. 3. Novelists, English—Homes and
haunts—England—London. 4. London (England)—Intellectual
life—19th century. 5. London (England)—In literature. 6. City and
town life in literature. I. Spiers, John, 1941–
   PR4717.G53 2005
   823′.8—dc22
                                                            2005051453

10   9   8   7   6   5   4   3   2   1
15 14 13 12 11 10 09 08 07 06

Printed and bound in Great Britain by
Antony Rowe Ltd, Chippenham and Eastbourne

For Christopher Terrance Spiers (1943–2005)

Life is mostly froth and bubble,
Two things stand like stone;
KINDNESS in another's trouble,
COURAGE in your own.

– Adam Lindsay Gordon

Contents

List of Figures

Acknowledgements

Gissing's works have two chief attractions: they compel because of the ideas they present, and the art they embody. London, its vitality and perplexity, pervades his work. And so it was especially appropriate that the Centenary conference to commemorate his death (which occured on 28 December 1903) was held at the Institute of English Studies at the University of London, in association with the School of Humanities, Social Sciences and Law at the University of Glamorgan. The Institute is in the heartland of the Gissing territory, a few yards from the British Museum and from Gissing's homes in Colville Place, Gower Place, and Huntley Street. I am especially indebted to Professor Warwick Gould, Director of the Institute of English Studies, for facilitating the success of the Centenary conference in July 2003 on 'Gissing and the City', and for all his encouragement and advice. The papers published here are based on contributions made to that event, and have been developed from those papers. It is striking to note the international interest in Gissing. The conference was attended by 88 scholars, who heard 31 papers. The participants were from the UK, Canada, France, Greece, Israel, Italy, The Netherlands, Sweden, the USA, and Japan – where there is a large following, with many of Gissing's books in print.

Dr. Sally Ledger and Dr. Michael Baron of Birkbeck College, University of London, both gave me every support in planning the conference, as did my colleagues and friends: Professor Michael Connolly, Director of the School of Humanities, Social Sciences and Law at the University of Glamorgan; Professor Pierre Coustillas of the University of Lille and Hélène Coustillas and Dr. Bouwe Postmus of the University of Amsterdam. I am grateful to the anonymous and perceptive reader who advised Palgrave. My warm thanks to Paula Kennedy, Helen Craine, and Satishna Gokuldas of Palgrave Macmillan. I owe much, too, to my beloved wife Leigh, who first suggested that a conference should be convened in London to mark the centenary of Gissing's death, and who (as ever) gave me a great deal of guidance. The contributors to the book have, too, been delightful colleagues.

J.S. Twyford, Sussex
1 March 2005

Notes on Contributors

Lara Baker Whelan is Acting Director, Center for Teaching Excellence, and Assistant Professor of English, Rhetoric and Writing at Berry College, Mt. Berry, USA. Her scholarly work on Victorian literature has appeared in *Genre* and *Mosaic*; she is currently at work on a book dealing with depictions of the suburbs in mid-Victorian literature. She has also published in the area of composition studies and computers, as well as the narrative theory of interactive fiction.

Meaghan Clarke is Lecturer, Leverhulme Special Research Fellow in the History of Art at University of Sussex, UK. She is the author of *Critical Voices: Women and Art Criticism in Britain 1880–1905* (Ashgate, 2005). Her current project entitled 'The Writing of Art History: Gender, Modernity and Professionalization' examines the construction of the discipline at the end of the nineteenth century.

Pierre Coustillas is Emeritus Professor of English at the University of Lille, France. His best-known publications concern George Gissing, whose significance and originality have been re-evaluated as a result of his dedication and scholarly work since the early 1960s. Outside the field of Gissing studies his volumes and articles have been diversely devoted to Conrad, Kipling, Hardy, George Moore, and Jack London. His latest book is *George Gissing: The Definitive Bibliography* (Rivendale Press, 2005).

Richard Dennis is Reader in Geography at University College London, UK. His research focuses on the social and cultural geography of late nineteenth- and early twentieth-century cities. He has contributed essays on London to *The Times History of London* and the *Cambridge Urban History of Britain*, and is currently completing a book on *Cities in Modernity*, exploring modes of representation and modern sites in London, New York, and Toronto, 1850–1930. He is an associate editor of the *Journal of Urban History*.

Elizabeth F. Evans is Professor of English at the University of Wisconsin-Madison, USA. Her dissertation, *Liminal London: Women in Urban Spaces of British Fiction, 1880 to 1930*, explores intersections of gender, space, and modernity in works by George Gissing, Amy Levy, Henry James, H. G. Wells, Virginia Woolf, and Dorothy Richardson.

John Halperin is Centennial Professor of English at Vanderbilt University, USA.

Mary Hammond is Lecturer in English at Middlesex University, UK. Her research interests lie in the area of nineteenth- and early twentieth-century print culture, reception, and readership studies, and she has published widely in these areas.

Christine Huguet is Senior Lecturer at the University of Lille in the north of France. She has written a doctoral thesis on George Moore's *Esther Waters* and contributed articles on Victorian and Edwardian fiction, on the picaresque heritage and the *Don Quixote* tradition in British literature. She is currently working on the fiction of Charles Dickens and George Gissing.

Simon J. James is Lecturer in Victorian Literature in the Department of English Studies at the University of Durham, UK. He is the author of *Unsettled Accounts: Money and Narrative Form in George Gissing* (Anthem, 2003), essays in the collections *A Garland for Gissing* (Rodopi, 2001) and *George Gissing: Voices of the Unclassed* (Ashgate, 2005), and articles on H.G. Wells and Charles Dickens. He has also edited Volume 2 of *The Collected Works of George Gissing, Charles Dickens: A Critical Study*, and four H.G. Wells novels in Penguin Classics.

Emma Liggins is Lecturer in English at Edge Hill College of Higher Education, Ormskirk, UK. She has just completed George Gissing, *The Working Woman and Urban Culture* (Ashgate, 2005). She also has written a chapter on Gissing and Margaret Harkness in Louise Jackson and Krista Cowman (Eds) *Women and Work Culture, 1850–1950* (Ashgate, 2005).

Scott McCracken is Professor of English at University of Keele, UK. His book *Masculinities, Modernist Fiction and the Urban Public Sphere* will be forthcoming with Manchester University Press in 2006. He is co-editor of *new formations*.

Josephine A. McQuail is Professor of English at Tennessee Technical University, USA, where she has taught for 15 years. Her interests include the Romantic period, especially William Blake and the visual arts, and the Victorian period, especially George Gissing. She took a 3-month sabbatical in London, where she researched the origins of the Royal Academy. At the time of working, she was involved in researching the Tennessee community of Rugby, founded by Thomas Hughes, where Gissing's best friend Eduard Bertz served as a librarian for a short time. She has published on topics including William Blake and mysticism, Blake and children's literature, Blake and Allen Ginsberg, and on the Victorian travel writer, Ethel Brilliana

Tweedie. At the time of writing she was serving as Executive Director of the North-east Modern Language Association.

Margaret E. Mitchell is Assistant Professor of English at the State University of West Georgia, USA. Her work has appeared in *Studies in the Novel, Women's Studies: An Interdisciplinary Journal*, and elsewhere. She is also the coeditor of the journal *Lit: Literature Interpretation Theory*.

Bouwe Postmus is Lecturer in English at University of Amsterdam, The Netherlands. He is a regular contributor to *The Gissing Journal* and published *George Gissing's American Notebook: Notes–G. R. G. – 1877* (1993); *The Poetry of George Gissing* (1995); *George Gissing's Memorandum Book: A Novelist's Notebook, 1895–1902* (1997); *An Exile's Cunning: Some Private Papers of George Gissing* (1999); he edited *A Garland for Gissing* (2001), the conference papers of the first International Gissing Conference at Amsterdam in 1999, which he organised. He was a member of the advisory committee of the second Gissing Conference in London in 2003.

John Sloan is Fellow and Tutor in English, Harris Manchester College, Oxford, and CUF Lecturer, Oxford University, UK. His books include: *George Gissing: The Cultural Challenge* (Macmillan, 1989); *John Davidson: First of the Moderns, A Literary Biography* (Clarendon Press, 1995), and *Oscar Wilde* (Oxford University Press, 2003).

John Spiers was trained at the University of Sussex as a social historian. He organised the National Book League exhibition, 'The Rediscovery of George Gissing', in London in 1971, and co-authored the published guide. He also organised the Gissing centenary conference at the IES in 2003. In 1969 he founded the scholarly publishing firm The Harvester Press, commissioning the publication of Gissing's Diary and re-publishing 20 of his books. He is now a Senior Research Fellow at the Institute of English Studies, University of London – working in publishing and cultural history – and a Visiting Professor in the School of Humanities at the University of Glamorgan. He is President of The Gissing Foundation, a Trustee of The Ruskin Foundation and a Visiting Fellow in the Ruskin Programme at the University of Lancaster. He is also the author of three books on health-care philosophy and practice. He has held a number of senior public appointments in this field, including an advisory role in the Cabinet Office.

Luisa Villa is Professor Associate, Faculty of Modern Languages at University of Geneva, Switzerland. She has published extensively on late Victorian–early Modernist literature, and is author of books on Henry James (*Esperienza e memoria*, 1989), George Eliot (*Riscrivendo il* *conflitto*, 1994) and *ressentiment* in English fiction at the turn of the century (*Figure del risentimento*, 1997). Together with Marco Pustianaz she has recently edited *Maschilità decadenti, La lunga fin-de-siècle* (Sestante/Bergamo U.P. 2004).

Laura Vorachek is Instructor, Department of English at the University of Alabama, USA.

Introduction: Why does Gissing Matter?

John Spiers

Framework and approaches

Every writer lives at least three lives. First, by publishing work as a creative, cultural intervention, and to try to impose some kind of shape on things. Second, as a symptom of that culture and context, that historical moment into which – and within which – they intervene. Third is a personal struggle to live a real life amidst commercial realities. Gissing was thus both a product and a producer of his times. And, just as J.M.W. Turner changed the way we look at skies and their 'reality' and John Ruskin how we view Venice, Gissing is one of those who has shaped how we see and experience 'the city'. Gissing usually offered a reasoned view of city, culture, and context, even though his personal feelings frequently took him in a different direction. The inter-play between reason and emotion shapes, enriches, and yet embeds uncertainties in his work, and is often the basis of his creative ambiguities.

He wrote about deeply important, passionate matters. Notably, he sought to give a literary form to the often disorienting, fragmented experience of the big city. He captures many essences and ambiguities of his historical moment. He does so in the solitude of authorship yet amidst the tumult and alluring repulsion of London. He offered a wide-ranging curiosity, meticulous observation, and an idiosyncratic creative intelligence concerning the apparently illimitable London he saw and imagined. In doing so, he captured a particular view of London's complexity, images, places, spaces, and experiences. He did so both as a personal and artistic exploration, and to reach an audience and earn a living. He wrote at a time when social investigation and experience, occupations and social position, institutions and conventions were themselves newly questioned. He thus offers a personal vision, a psychological account, a documentary, and a mythic and devouring London, yet one full of opportunity. This was for him a lived, flesh, and blood experience. And, unlike Mr Micawber, he usually thought that nothing would turn up; or, if it did, that it would be for the worst.

Gissing's works offer the city itself as the epic text of modernity. If the past always has a pattern, the most powerful understandings which these new essays offer of Gissing's time, chance, work, and place are the repeated emphases on the contradictions, ambiguities, and unresolved and perennial issues of modern culture. These – still with us today – became very explicit in the new urbanised world and they constantly appear in Gissing's 'writing self'. He can thus be seen as part of the late Victorian revolt which included Morris, Ruskin, Wilde, and the ever-present echo of Carlyle. He questions the fundamentals of cultural value and their determination, notably of how meaning is produced, and in what does value inhere. His novels reflect a profound contemporary crisis of cultural shock in asking and answering. They show an acute awareness of unprecedented transformations at a time of both technological and intellectual tumult, expanding audiences, democratic shifts, and sharp alterations in the conditions (and scale) of literary production. He is associated with 'meaning' and analysis of the lives of women; of commerce and book markets; with suburban life, and especially the lives of the poor; and with the relationships between ideas and art, education and individual potential. Gissing is a key figure in 'writing' both the city and the masses. As John Carey has written, 'Gissing seems, in fact, to have been the earliest English writer to formulate the intellectuals' case against mass culture, and reformulated it so thoroughly that nothing essential has been added to it since. One reason for reading Gissing is that he allows us to watch the superstitions that dominate our idea of "culture" to take shape' (Carey, 1992, pp. 93–4).

Gissing and the City focusses us on the relationships between his works and the cultural, historical and social context, and on how we construct and consider these. These relationships embrace both those of aestheticians and literary critics, and those of book historians who focus on publisher, production, the reader, and the act of reading as a cultural practice. Here, there is more than one essential act – not only writing and reading, but production and publication. Gissing offers a 'reading' of shifts in contemporary publishing, trade structures, and the literary market place. So, too, of the decay of the provincial press, the augmented power of the London reviewer, the wider influence of advertisement, and the new co-ordination of these forces generating between them (Gissing thought) a concentrated, impersonalising, vulgarising culture alien to art. These cultural interactions included new technological developments, changes in the educational system, new social and political movements, shifts in urban geography and class formations, new patterns of leisure, and dynamic notions of time and space. Much of this was summed up in the notion of a growing consumer culture. Here, the city was a crucial context. Gissing also offers a notable account of the conditions of ordinary life – for the working- and the middle-classes – and of changes in cultural and economic conditions such as those in transport, housing, and work.

What Gissing *means* – and what he *should* have meant – is the source of significant debate. Here we face questions about the emergence of 'culture' itself as a critical idea; scrutiny of the origins of our present world; queries on the nature of change over time; interrogations on the nature of nature itself; and reflections on what we mean by order and what we mean by disorder. In terms of literature and cultural production, the issues with which Gissing was concerned include the nature of imagination, the nature of 'representation', the nature of writing (and of book-making, and its increasing intensity and velocity), the conditions of authorship and the nature and pursuit of a literary career. These problems include what it 'means' to 'consume' a book. Each of these issues is encapsulated in the analysis of the cultural and economic role of the city, its images and impacts, and of the new mass consumer society. Here Jason Epstein, the innovative twentieth-century American publisher, made an important point (reflected elsewhere in economist Jane Jacobs's work) about the relationships between authors and the City: 'Books are written everywhere but they have always needed the complex cultures of great cities in which to reverberate' (Epstein, 2001; Jacobs, 1961, 1969, 1984).

As Donald Olsen said (echoing Max Weber), 'The justification for great cities is that they both encourage and embody excellence. It is their function to be better than other cities and to attract individuals and institutions that are similarly "better"' (Olsen, 1976, pp. 13–20). It was in the newly urbanised world that people confronted the complex tasks that made it possible for large numbers to live together in a rapidly changing urban environment where there were, as the urban historian H.J. Dyos noted, 'not merely growing numbers, but changing attitudes, movements, structures, images', and an urban culture that rose without a historical tradition which might explain it (Dyos, in Hennock, 1973, p. v). Indeed, as E.P. Hennock has said, 'The social implications of urbanisation form one of the great themes of modern British history' (Hennock, 1973, p. 3). In Gissing's time there had been no successful precedent to which to turn. And, by the twentieth century, the newly urbanised environment had been transplanted globally, and with fewer national characteristics than fundamental human ones. Deborah Parsons, too, noted that it was the evolving, open city which enabled women to enter man-made space, offer displacing values, enjoy the city of spectacle and consumption, and which offered 'the necessary conditions for women's greater access to public urban space' (Parsons, 2000, p. 82). Thus, a new female, independent, and specifically urban lifestyle – the 'New Woman' – emerged in work, home, sexuality, education, employment, leisure and politics, consumption, and the arts in this permeable, adaptive society of opportunity and freedom – as Nancy Lord finds in *In The Year of Jubilee* (1894).

Luisa Villa shows, in a paper of exceptional richness and originality, that Gissing's ambivalent attitude towards modernity, his paradoxical London, was on the one hand strictly compartmentalised, and on the other dynamic and open to progressive change. It was a London which included the challenging and carnivalesque crowd – as both overtly political and as mass consumer – and where individual desire is unleashed/emancipated/ commodified/empowered, as she suggests. Villa considers the representation and images of the crowd, the carnival, 'the masses', and the crisis of authority these represented, alongside the new commodity culture.

Gissing sought to participate in and understand what was going on around him, to represent and bring into focus underlying structures and to explore these in imaginative fiction. His is a city of ambivalent modernity in which his work is necessarily embedded. He understood that things – specificities – reveal principles. By focussing on what was small, humble, taken for granted, his fiction teases out underlying philosophies, choices, prejudices, and causes. He shows that the commonest things, the most ordinary details, are the most important things. For these have a history, a politics, a prismatic meaning concerning power and potentials, class, ethnicity, and gender. They have cultural resonance, consensual order, and clout. They are crucial clues to social change, as the social anthropologist Margaret Visser has shown (Visser, 1997, pp. xvii–xxii).

London was seen by many Victorian investigators as a city divided geographically and on class lines: the glittering west; and the growling, despairing, threatening east. There were other perspectives, too, which offered conceptual oppositions: the city as encounter and connection, or the city of personal loss; the city as spectacle, or of individual suffering; the city as the gendered product of the male gaze, or of new female possibility; the city with femaleness as an experienced obstacle, with gender the unavoidable central issue in reform debate; the city within which we see the recovery or re-invention of active female possibility and opportunity, as subject and observer rather than as object and observed, of vocation and achievement. As Deborah Epstein Nord notes, it was, indeed, flux itself which enabled the city to become '...Elizabeth Dalloway's sense of possibility and...Woolf's recognition that for women, yet to come the city might be a locus of expansion and emancipation, that, even as others compare them to hyacinths and early dawn, they might nonetheless become explorers and adventurers' (Nord, 1995, p. 248).

Gissing and ambiguities

Gissing – notably, because of *New Grub Street* (1891) – has a key place in the definition of the history of the nineteenth-century book. His working-life coincided with the shift from the circulating libraries' monopoly of the book market – which he disliked – for the middle-class reader to new patterns of book-buying and reading, journalism, literature, and authorship – with much of which he was also exceedingly uncomfortable. The key cultural question here was (and is) what was ominous and what was opportune for the individual author, the reader, and the wider society? For example, were the changes in culture and in publishing and the making of books – which has to combine both art and trade – positive, creative, democratic, and life-enhancing, or were they destructive of a 'high' culture which should be maintained even if, in many senses, this left out the 'masses'? Was consumerism a destructive 'commodification' of the masses, or an opportunity for a better standard of life for all? And, indeed, were (and are) people to be seen as 'the mass', commodified and alienated, or as potentially self-responsible individuals with the latency to be released into individual freedom, self-sufficiency, and self-expression – by education, by politics, by mutuality and self-organisation, by art and literature, by rising living standards, by an enhanced sense of self within a community? In these terms, which historical developments do we rue or relish? How, too, did (and does) gender constrain or warp, disable or equip participation?

These cultural and personal ambiguities and choices are more than visible in Gissing's literary representations and language. They are, indeed, the source of many of his own ambiguities, creative challenges, and difficulties. He reflected acutely modern ambivalences, which shaped (and sometimes mis-shaped, in social fantasy and illusory solutions) his fiction. These perennial ambiguities embrace many of the moral and creative dilemmas of the modern author, as well as how to live by literature and how to make books. Gissing posed the struggles of the self and psyche in a new urban space which was in some senses repellent and yet full of opportunity. He reflects profound ambiguities: the allure and the shock of new, complex, crowded, and ever-shifting urban spaces; the challenge, in Matthew Arnold's terms, of 'culture' or 'anarchy'; the transformation of built London, yet its persistent class character; the opportunities and compromises of new markets; the identity, diversification, democratic (and, to some, destructive) impact of new forces; changing concepts of public and private space; and the overriding question of what is the genuine source of progressive change, posed by Marxist critics like Raymond Williams (Williams, 1973) and by contrasting modern cultural critics like Isaiah Berlin, Gertrude Himmelfarb and Virginia Postrel (Berlin, 1969; Himmelfarb, 1973, 1984; Postrel, 1998). These two traditions concern two different concepts of order, or two different kinds of optimism. They concern values in the urban and industrial context – for example, in the politics of the workplace – which Gissing described. These issues fundamentally focus three problems: the idea of 'progress' in history, the creation and distribution of wealth, and, indeed, the existence of industrial civilisation itself. These wide-ranging choices concern whether industrial entrepeneurship, risk-taking courage and drive (for example, in building the railways, an immense and complex undertaking); the organisation of production, investment, incentive and competition, individual and society-wide material gain – including freedom of movement, better food, health care, lighting, leisure, labour-saving devices, and access to the optical lense for reading as well as the social disruption and the dislocation of individual lives implicit in industrialisation – are to be welcomed or warned against and resisted. And how are gains and losses – for example, whether more people have benefited than suffered from industrialisation – to be accounted, balanced, and interpreted in the assessment of both personal and historical outcomes?

In these terms, the chapters in this book may be seen as engaging with large philosophical questions and the meanings of Gissing's fiction and the literary, cultural, historical, and sociological context of his work as well as its imaginative, idiosyncratic curiosity concerning human perceptions and human uses of the landscape and the experiences of his characters. This engages with the history of 'high', 'popular', and 'mass' culture, the industrial production of cultural forms, and the relationships between the production, consumption, and reception of them. Notably, on literary representation: what does a novel do, and how does it do it; and on fruitfulness and expla-nation: where does it lead us? Each of these problems is addressed in the light of new work on the City itself as a new urban experience. This offered to writers a newly fluid publishing context with its many new opportunities, its advancing and receding social forms, and its changing audiences. Walter Sickert urged us to study 'gross material facts'. And Gissing was indifferent to little that mattered in his time. He discovered for himself Berlin's precept, too, that you cannot have everything, and have to make choices (Berlin, 1969).

Gissing's topics include power, pretence, idealism, empire and imperial expansion, education and self-education, every aspect of urban life, practical help, the cultures of charity and philanthropy, and the craft of the writer. Suspicious of the virtues of the present and the 'spirit of the age', he engages with the complicated relationships and connections between class, money, marriage, social status, and self-respect. He particularly shows how class, money, prejudice, and expectations shape the relations of the sexes. Gissing, like George Moore (notably in *A Mummer's Wife*), says much about what is called 'the marriage market'. He is often viewed in the context of the male gaze. This is now more challenged than at any time in history. He focussed on women and their nature and status in private, public, and professional spaces. Several contributors explore these issues. For example, Meaghan Clarke focusses on art galleries as cultural prisms, where there arose the question of who owned 'the gaze' in the gallery – the observer or the observed, the consumer or the consumed.

Paradigms, narratives, and 'the uncertainty of modernity'

Gissing's city is both a physical and a spiritual landscape. It enables him to highlight serious, moral and psychological considerations. The essays here re-examine the issues with which his fiction is concerned in terms of the dominant paradigms (and abstractions) of explanation which have been influentially deployed in situating Gissing and his achievement, and by reference to the City. Thus, the book reflects traditional (or 'great tradition') critiques (including mystical connoisseurship) which have privileged the individual 'subject' in history; feminism, and gender studies, focussed on the experience and exercise of power and on the experience of 'marginality'; Marxism, looking forward to 'inevitable' revolutionary class struggle; various grammars of cultural theory and critical differentiation – notably the ideas about power of Michel Foucault, and the deconstruction approach associated with Jacques Derrida and the *Annales* school of *histoire totale* (or structures and *mentalites*).

In addressing the bigger picture which these 'projects' form (and the roles and presuppositions they fulfil), academia has offered critical or dialectical categories which propose competing 'correct' 'meanings'. These are informed by explicit – often termed 'central' – assumptions, moral, political, and social positions. They situate literary works in various functionalist frameworks. Critics have focussed on a considerable cluster of binary opposites: elite/popular; high/low; hegemonic/marginal; consumer/consumed; subject/object; passive/active; theory/praxis; universal/gendered; the work/the culture; the fixed-self/ideological illusion; culturally authorised/unauthorised; possession of cultural capital/lack of; male/female; masculine 'presence'/feminine 'absence'; voice/silence; text/gap; presence/presence of an absence; centre/margin; right/left; good/evil; self/other; nature/culture; history/her story. Contributors in this collection suggest that the fuller picture is often more elusive, more nuanced, more perplexing than the command (and commands) of categories imply. The essays in this book thus offer a range of critical methods concerning the controverted 'narratives' which treat the complexities, the similes, the energies, the precisions – as well as the evasions and absences – of Gissing's imaginative works. For example, Scott McCracken re-engages with the city in Gissing in terms of 'the uncertainty of modernity'. He discovers a different, strange, more exotic London than the dismal town most often associated with Gissing. And he finds a more playful, ironic, modernist Gissing, at work in the city as a dreamscape, highlighting the emergent commodity culture of his time. How Gissing has been received in a century of criticism is assessed, too, by Pierre Coustillas in a wide-ranging and expert essay.

Pictures of London

Gissing is especially identified with London – which was, according to Henry James, the 'most complete compendium of the world'. Gissing is associated with particular metaphors and images of London (Matthiesen and Murdock, 1947, p. 28). As David Glover has said, 'London is a strangely fractured presence in Gissing's work' (Glover, in Postmus, 2001, p. 149). 'London' exists as different constructs in our different minds, offering different possibilities, identities, representations, and problems – including the 'relationships' between 'fact' and 'fiction'. Or, as W.M. Thackeray said in *Lovel The Widower* (1860), 'though it is all true, there is not a word of truth in it'. Here, Gilles Deleuze advises, 'this is why art is so important: it "invents" the lies that raise falsehood to this highest affirmative power' (Deleuze, 1989, p. 146).

For many contemporaries the Victorian city was the confusing locale of contrasts and ambiguities: of improvement and expiation, of seduction and sensation, of moral danger and sexual opportunity, of mass poverty and new hope. It was, in Judith Walkowitz's term, the 'city of dreadful delight' (Walkowitz, 1992), including its role as the city of opportunity. All these aspects inform and frame the fundamental elements of subjectivity – 'nature', 'art' and 'culture'. When we focus on an author and a place – as Gillian Tindall has pointed out – we enquire, too, about 'the literary uses to which places are put, the meanings they are made to bear, the roles they play when they are re-created in fiction, the psychological journeys for which they are the destinations' (Tindall, 1991, p. 9). As she says, 'these physical settings, these real places... are essentially put to use as metaphors, emblems or examples for ideas that transcend that particular time and place. In them, a local habitation and a name are given to perennial human preoccupations, and it is in the peculiar tension between the timeless and the specific that much of the force of the novel lies' (Tindall, 1991, p. 10).

Deborah Parsons has shown that the urban writer is not only a figure within a city, but also *the producer* of a city: 'The writer adds other maps to the city atlas; those of social interaction but also of myth, memory, fantasy, and desire.' Thus, a text to be read, a city to be traversed, and a city where 'forms of perception, experience, and communication are predicated on the "body" and "soul" of the city'. This urban map is significantly influential 'in the very structures of social and mental daily life' (Parsons, 2000, p. 1). In terms of Gissing's urban preoccupations, our contributors ask what is the meaning of city spaces – public places, work places, social spaces, private places – the city streets themselves, and their literary presentations? How were these spaces defined, represented, produced, negotiated, and consumed? What were the relationships between different kinds of spaces – 'architectural, spectacular, performative and lived'? (Driver and Gilbert, 1999, p. 8).

The peripatetic craftsman

Gissing was a meticulous and impeccable researcher, and this was crucial to his art, as Bouwe Postmus shows. Like Dickens before him, and Arthur Symons in his own time, he was a peripatetic wanderer in East and West, amidst often indeterminate, legitimate and illegitimate, social spaces. He gave his daytime and night-time to careful scrutiny, often during incessant and lengthy walks through or secret London, and the countryside, too. To this extent, he reflected one important contemporary fictional method, of imaginative writing rooted in meticulously observed experience. This is seen in Zola's Second Empire fiction, in E.A. Poe's *The Mystery of Mme Roger*, in Wilkie Collins's *The Moonstone*, in Charles Reade's plots which often derived from newspaper cuttings. Gissing sought documentary evidence, which he carefully noted and retained, and which he re-fashioned in imaginative literature. This fractured and recast the reader's notions about what constituted 'reality'. He utilises the physical landscape (as well as the idioms and rhythms of everyday speech) as the background for both thought and action. Postmus shows how Gissing's observations and his studies relate to his art and the fusing and minting of his imaginative processes, the sedulous cultivation of the craftsman in himself, how he actually set about writing, the intimate details of the '*actual* pen-work', in Arnold Bennett's phrase.

Cultural processes in art and society

One key starting point is to understand the selective, ordering, and critical processes of the artist. The essays in this book ask directly or indirectly what are Gissing's 'meanings' – for example, the meaning of his 'male artistic "gaze"' – in terms of the literary and cultural geography of the late Victorian city? On one level this is concerned with the 'cultural work' performed by a text. On another it is concerned with the nature of creative order itself – and of how it arises or is derived. An important aspect concerns, too, different concepts of the city, its imagery, and how the reader sees the world. Is the city in 'chaos', or are its apparent confusions a reflection of an underlying, non-hierarchical, creative order? On the basis of which values is it to be judged? For example, by those of hierarchy and control by Webbian 'experts' (who 'know' best our best interests, better than we do ourselves). Or by the alternative 'harmony' offering a creative order of new potentials which come from an apparent disorder but which is itself enriching? Many modern literary critics write of the swarming 'chaos' of the city – implying waste, profligacy, and destruction – linking this idea to 'the nature of capitalist transition'. Here, Raymond Williams has offered a Marxist account which situates the city at the centre of capitalist global control, and of 'the utilitarian reduction of all social relationships to a crude moneyed order'. He insists on 'the long process of choice between economic advantage and other ideas of value', and on 'a social dissolution in the very process of aggregation'. He discusses, too, the ambiguities of capitalism, which increased wealth but distributed it unevenly, and which 'depended' on overseas exploitation (Williams, 1973, pp. 35–6, 61, 82, 216, 289–306).

A cultural critic like Virginia Postrel offers an entirely different perspective (Postrel, 1998). Here we find a huge divide. By her reading of society we might say that the changes in the making of books in Gissing's time were an aspect of a major historical, literary, and cultural question – perhaps one of the most important of such questions – concerning whether the industrial revolution and urbanisation were a catastrophe or a blessing. These two conceptual possibilities represent powerful opposing cultural and political images because they represent distinct and contrary ways of looking at the world, at people, at human nature, and at cultural possibilities. The first presents London as a morally blighted, doom-laden and devouring hell of rootless and Babylonic confusion, of harshly unnecessary suffering, the certain consequence of capitalist industrialisation and urbanisation, a symptom not a success. The second offers the idea of the city as the place of dynamic growth, of opportunity and surprises, of incessant renewal – of new choices, necessary trade-offs, new social mobility, changes in family life and in gender-specific roles, social and economic investment and education. All this amidst the apparent chaos which is itself a special kind of creative, organic, adaptive order, as Postrel argues. The choice is between the statist and the dynamist view. The statist believes that technology enslaves us, that economic and market changes make us insecure, that popular culture coarsens us, that consumerism despoils the environment, and that the forces of change must be disciplined (usually by bureaucracy and by a Webbian elite). The dynamist supposes that unplanned trial-and-error in an open society supports creativity and enterprise, and brings the benefits of unpredictable discoveries as the key to human betterment for all. The choice concerns two conflicting views of progress, and of the nature and sources of order in a self-organised society. It is between two views of the nature of life, of human potential, of who can learn to choose, and of who will make the trade-offs which are unavoidable in every life, by whom and on whose behalf. The issue here is who decides? And *who decides* who decides?

Clearly, even in prosperous Victorian cities many – even those with a regular income – lived precariously, despite enjoying a higher standard of living than their grandparents, as Charles Booth and Seebohm Rowntree showed (Booth, 1892; Rowntree, 1901). Everyone knew their pawnbroker. Many in the lower classes were paralysed by the depressed condition of much of the fabric of the slums, encapsulating misery and degradation. My own grandfather was born in an East London workhouse, where his own grandmother and two sisters (of 13 children) had died. Yet economist Jane Jacobs suggests that a key to the informal, urban, creative order is to ask why does economic activity increase, or decrease, and how do the connections work? Or, what is wealth, and how does it arise? So in reading Gissing – with his slum studies, his critique of money-grubbing vulgarians, and of those whom Thackeray (in *Vanity Fair*) called 'turtle-fed tradesmen' – we need to ponder whether cities create poverty or prosperity. Jane Jacobs suggests that the fundamental question is not how economic life *ought* to work, but how it does and has worked. She shows that *all* developing economic life depends on city economies, and that *all* expanding economic life depends on working links *with* cities (Jacobs, 1986, 2002). Developing economies have three master characteristics: economic life becomes more urbanised; as city trade expands it sparks other cities into life; increased quantities of goods and services are produced, and become available for import-replacing, thus generating further development. On this view, unlike the images offered in many literary and counter-cultural presentations, cities are problems of *organised* (not dis-organised) complexity. They – and their distribution of goods and services, their proffering of opportunities – are essential to improve living standards. They offer an open-ended adaptive heartland of improvisation which contrasts with 'expert' master plans of various kinds. And they require us to live with the ragged edges, and to manage these as best we can, on behalf of ourselves and others.

The alternative idea of catastrophe depends on two kinds of analysis: Marxist economic interpretation, and the subjectivity and interpretive force of an imaginary landscape to which Gissing is a significant contributor. His is the echo of John Martin's apocalyptic, cataclysmic perspectives of hell (in Milton's *Pandemonium*, for example), and of the accounts of Blake, Hogarth, Fielding, Carlyle, Wordsworth, Gaskell, the darker side of the later Dickens, Mayhew, Greenwood, Doré, and Jerrold. Wordsworth was concerned with the 'dissolute city', and Tennyson, in *Locksley Hall*, haunted by the visions of hungry squalor in the new city slums, where 'among the glooming alleys Progress halts on palsied feet'. John Ruskin, too, in the *Crown of Wild Olive* wrote of 'that great soul city of London – rattling, growing, smoking, stinking – a ghastly heap of fermenting brickwork, pouring out poison at every pore...'. This image of the city has had wide ramifications in the critical (chiefly Marxist) interpretation of modern society. And, as H.J. Dyos said, 'London invited more sharply divided opinions, more deep-seated ambivalence than any other city or town in Victorian England' (Dyos, in Cannadine and Reeder, 1985, p. 82). In the modern period the 'bleak age' orthodoxy was powerfully argued, too, notably by Arnold Toynbee in his *Lectures on the Industrial Revolution in England* (1884), and re-iterated by the Webbs, by J.L. and B. Hammond, by J.B. Priestley's *English Journey* (1934), and by E.P. Thompson's *The Making of the English Working Class* (1963) (Weaver, Boon, and Thompson, each in Taylor and Wolff, 2004; Thompson, 1963; Weaver, 1997). These latter interpretations crucially relied on the theoretical analyses offered by Engels, which appear to have been deeply flawed. As Andrew Sanders, a literary critic with a sophisticated historical understanding, has stressed, the 24-year-old Rhinelander 'had little real experience of large cities, and even less appreciation of how a complex metropolis like London actually functioned' (Sanders, 2003, p. 116).

Sanders recently wrote – as Gissing understood – that:

> The stark contrast between the standard of living enjoyed by the rich and
> the dire condition of the desperately poor in London was obvious to any
> observer, but so were the many social gradations which lay between
> these extremes, gradations which embraced both the modestly rich and
> the middlingly poor. It has since been estimated that, although four out
> of five inhabitants of mid-Victorian London were either manual workers,
> or the dependants of manual workers, in 1841 only one in five of these
> workers was employed in an industry that had been radically changed by
> the effects of the industrial revolution. Such workers exceeded a third of
> the workforce only in Lancashire. London was not Lancashire, nor was
> its economy rural. Given its distinctive history and geography, and given
> its complex demography and its political influence, the population of the
> capital, and the employment patterns of Londoners, posed quite distinctive
> questions to those Victorian commentators who attempted to make
> sense of them. (Sanders, 2003, pp. 116–17)

This view is backed up by the historian Theodore Hoppen's influential study
of *The Mid-Victorian Generation 1846–1886* (Hoppen, 1998, pp. 56–9).

The view of the industrial revolution as a sudden and disastrous discon-
tinuity which immiserated the newly urbanised and thus degraded the
nation depends on theoretical assumptions about class struggle that are
central to Marxist criticism. Yet the resulting view of urban life has been
contradicted by such major economists and cultural historians as Clapham,
R.M. Hartwell, and Gertrude Himmelfarb (Clapham, 1926; Taylor, 1975;
Cannadine, 1984; Schwarz, 1992; Coleman, 1992; Himmelfarb, 1973, 1984,
Rogers, in Taylor and Wolff, 2004). It nevertheless remains a key part of the
framing in which writers like Gissing are read and recommended. However,
this historical view of a 'dismal tale' appears to have overlooked or
discounted long-term economic and social cycles and changes in material
life which reached beyond Gissing's generation. It is now rejected by a new
and current generation of demythologising historians who offer a different
idea about how ideas, economy, and culture interact. For these, by contrast
with what Simon Schama called 'penitential histories' and Geoffrey Blainey
dubbed the 'black arm-band historians', industrialisation and urbanisation
are regarded as a necessity and a blessing, not least for the poorer (Blainey,
1993, pp. 10–15; Schama, 1995, p. 13). One such revisionist, Helen Rogers,
recently wrote that 'Intellectual historians have also begun to free themselves from the "mind forg'd manacles" of the Industrial Revolution...'
(Rogers, in Taylor and Wolff, 2004). So have economists, notably writers like
Charles F. Sabel and Jacobs (Sabel, 1982; Jacobs, 1961, 1969, 1984). These
offer the City as opportunity, as the essential locale of social and individual
development, as *the* key to an economy reliant on adaptive discovery and

emulation and which raises all boats. That it is cities, too, which achieve the best concentration in the arts, politics, economics and civilisation. Here, every idea, invention, talent, attitude is tested against every other, with the good ideas successfully adopted, in a process of continuous adaptation. It is a global pattern.

Jacobs urges that cities are the vital economic generators of diversity, prolific incubators of new ideas; the homes of niches and of immense numbers and ranges of small and creative enterprises (Jacobs, 1984). This is an unconscious, unplannable, unpredictably intricate and diverse economic co-operation which interweaves human patterns and mingled uses, and which relies on the inter-dependence (and the fluidity) of classes. They are brought together, not divided, by the city. The urban experience is indeed, on this view, not chaos, but 'a complex form of order akin to order typical of all living things, in which instabilities build up ... followed by corrections, both the instabilities and the corrections being the very stuff of life processes themselves' (Jacobs, 1984, pp. 144–5). It offers an underlying, dynamic, highly developed form of order. This is only possible on a large scale in cities, with so many people close together, containing so many different tastes, skills, wishes, supplies 'and bees in their bonnets'. Cities which lose this dynamism collapse. Economies without such cities do so, too (Jacobs, 1961, p. 147). On this view, standards for the working class dramatically improved overall, and the lower middle class, rather than being subsumed into an immiserated working class, in fact grew in numbers and became highly influential in terms of manners, mores, and attitudes – not least concerning 'a belief in respectability, merit competition, money, hierarchy, privacy and success' (Hoppen, 1998, p. 46).

Here we have to deal with many contradictions, as we read Gissing. One is that, as Foucault argued, modernity included the evolution of a disciplined society which itself curtails individual freedom by 'systems of surveillance' (Foucault, 1991). This coincided with both qualitative and quantitative gains in terms of living standards, life-chances, and longevity in all classes (despite continued class differentials). Higher living standards were created by new markets, and by the profits of Empire. There was, too, more leisure, although the British Holidays With Pay Act dates only from 1938. Urban growth impacted on many aspects of life. Housing stocks grew and changed, as population increased. By no means all of these new houses were built for the middle classes. Demand for goods and services was fuelled, too, by the process of urbanisation. Even though there were significant regional and sectoral variations in incomes, both wages and salaries were in general rising sharply in the third quarter of the century. They continued to rise, if more slowly and erratically, for the rest of the century. Falling prices, too, helped to raise living standards. Between 1874 and 1896 prices fell by about 40 per cent. Income tax statistics show that the salaried middle classes did well, but that the living standards of the population *as a whole* rose – if the consumption of goods and the lengthening of life expectation is any guide. Rising incomes prompted both new demand and new expectations. New industrial techniques, too, reduced costs and distributed innovations more widely (Mathias, 1967; Mitchell and Deane, 1971; Fraser, 1981; Adburgham, 1989; Rappaport, 2000).

In the long view looking back from 2005 to 1903 we can see that modern-isation, innovation, and social re-structuring did generate a widespread elevation of living standards for the mass of the population. W. Hamish Fraser has said of these changes in living standards, consumption and revolution in retailing that 'In spite of problems and setbacks for many and the persistence of deep-seated poverty, for most people the late nineteenth-century brought a real improvement in living standards. The British people were able to concern themselves with more than mere subsistence; they had a surplus to spend on more and better food, on a wider range of clothing, on more elaborate furnishing for their homes and on a greater variety of leisure pursuits. For the first time people had a *choice* of how and where to spend their money' (Fraser, 1981, p. ix). These were part of a transformation of the *world* economy in these decades. A key – perhaps the only key – has been to lift people of all classes up the social and economic gradient. And, as the literary critic K.K. Ruthven observed, 'Most working-class people would much rather become middle class than classless...' (Ruthven, 1984, p. 27). These, of course, are all key issues about cultural meaning. They are, too, historical issues concerning how a larger population could have been supported *without* an industrial revolution, and how housed without urbanisation.

The cultural historian Lynn Hunt has emphasised that cultural meaning is itself a text to be read. The practice of history is itself a process of text creating, of 'seeing', of giving form to subjects. These assembling choices themselves have social and political implications: 'The deciphering of meaning, then, rather than the inference of causal laws of explanation, is taken to be the central task of cultural history, just as it was posed by [Clifford] Geertz to be the central task of cultural anthropology' (Geertz, 1973; Hunt, 1989, pp. 12–13). Hunt stresses that Foucault, too, described his version of history as one that 'disturbs what was previously considered immobile;...fragments what was thought unified;...shows the heterogeneity of what was imagined consistent with itself' (Megill, 1985, pp. 234–5).

The critics, and images of the city

Even if all this were to be so in the longer run, it was bewildering in the short run. London's unprecedented vastness was, as Sanders noted, one which was commonly met – for example, by the French critic Hippolyte Taine in 1860 – 'with a gasp that intermingles wonder with horror' (Sanders, 2003, p. 115). By 1800 its population had passed one million. By 1860 it was three million – the largest city by far which the world had ever known. By

Gissing's death in 1903 it held close to 10 million people. In 1801 only 17 per cent of the population of England and Wales lived in towns of more than 20,000 inhabitants. By 1911 that figure has risen to 60 per cent. The population became increasingly urbanised, and the towns became larger (Hennock, 1973, p. 1). In this context, as Sanders says, 'Essentially, London *needed* to be interpreted, but how it was interpreted depended on the sharpness and the quality of the axe that any given observer was grinding' (Sanders, 2003, p. 115).

As we have seen, two key questions are *what kind of a problem the city is* and *which ways to think about this are useful?* Gissing helps us to consider these two focal but often fudged questions. Ultimately, these concern reaching a view about a social, cultural, and economic balance sheet and the dimensions of accounting. One context for examining Gissing's meanings concerns the source of all the wealth – and he writes a good deal about money, as Simon James has stressed (James, 2003). Here we again confront ambiguities: the ambiguity of industry as the price and the provider of prosperity, and of slum development; the Victorian and Edwardian increase in affluence for all classes, but with extremes of living and housing standards; over-crowding, but falling death rates due to medical advances; greater re-distribution, but continued (and necessary, because dynamic?) contrast; increased democracy, but poor education and the 'vulgarity' of consumerism (but with better housing, clothing, medicine, food, and drink); and different conceptions of culture and of opportunity. Ambiguously, too, an apparently improving world was soon to experience two World Wars, the inter-war slump, unprecedented state-sponsored mass murder, and environmental damage which has queried (or re-inforced?) the traditional goal of economic development, and the power of adaptation to cope.

From realism to egoism

Gissing shared a widely held view among the Victorian intelligentsia that the road they felt themselves to be travelling was both dangerous and ugly. In *The Crown of Life* (1899) he is explicit: 'The brute force of money; the negation of the individual – these, the evils of our time, found their supreme expression in the City of London.' However, gradually retreating into a Paterian subjectivity, Gissing avoided taking a practical part in what Diana Maltz dubbed 'missionary aestheticism' and the Ruskinian ennoblement of working people (Maltz, in Postmus, 2001). John Halperin argues that in addition Gissing was an early ecologist who believed that commerce devastated nature – another key issue in reaching a balanced view about industrialisation. Mary Hammond – re-examining his modernity – suggests that we need to reappraise the received image and dimensions of Gissing as the glum presenter of the alienated individual, the doomed writer, and the embattled self. Gissing as the exemplar of the creative dilemmas of the alienated modern author in an urbanised world of literary pulp traditionally holds the ground. Yet his ambivalence about London – and his representation of it – is more complex, more nuanced, and more intriguing, as she shows. We now know, too, that despite Gissing's own difficulties, popular editions of good books sold in vast numbers, and the publishing industry itself became increasingly sophisticated, multi-layered, international, and alert to the new democracy (Altick, 1957; Rose, 2001).

Gissing's overall answer to social problems, both for men and for women, was the development of the self and a commitment to the truths of art. As Hammond shows, he moved from realism to egoism, and to intensely personal relationships with time and space, notably in *The Private Papers of Henry Ryecroft* (1903) – Gissing's expression of the English rural ideal. This personal development (which was moral, artistic, and political) saw him abandon the political and social for the individual and the autonomous. She argues that he turned away from mediocrity, democracy, and consumerism towards the inner life of the artist, but that this itself had modernist dimensions. Emma Liggins suggests, too, that in this sense he deserves a more secure place as a modernist. Tindall has pointed out that he made a remarkable advance, since *New Grub Street* (1891) is the novel which shifts fiction away from the theme of the individual versus circumstances towards the modern image of the individual grappling with himself (Tindall, 1974, p. 157). Gissing achieved this, too, as Hammond shows, without the distancing languages of modernist writers. He was committed to artistic principles – to the pattern and artistic effect – rather than to a 'class' theory and point of view in the conflict between labour and capital. In this sense, he shared the notion expressed by Heidegger that art is inaugural, expressing the basic truth of being, bringing a pre-existing truth into public light (Heidegger, 1971, p. 77).

The anxieties which Gissing expresses about his time and place contrasted, too, with the pride and excitement in the march of intellect, the wonder and admiration, the zest for the new, and the surging march of time that many others like Arnold Bennett felt. Unrepelled, the highly disciplined Staffordshire outsider spoke of the spirit of the age with an undiminished zest for 'the age of improvement', with a fascination and a new sense of becoming.

London, the changing labyrinth

London, meanwhile, was a city of constant change. The pressures on living centrally were eased by new transport for both middle classes and the poor. But access mattered, and given the high cost of land the environment was built upwards as well as outwards. How and where the people were housed, and how domestic life was conducted, was changing rapidly. Two of the most important developments were upwards (blocks of flats) and outwards (suburbia). Both involved continued class differentiation, slum clearance, and the development of purpose-built zones and styles. All this was to accommodate different class, work, and living needs. Gissing, alert as ever to change, gives both flats and suburbs a significant place. Richard Dennis analyses key themes in the physical and cultural evolution of the block of flats and its usage and literary representation. He offers new insights into 'home', marginality, modern 'simplicity', what he calls promiscuous spaces, and the gendering of flats. Both he and Lara Baker Whelan examine Gissing's literary representations and those of Charles Booth and others with regard to place. Dennis examines a key aspect of the role of community in relation to urban space. For the first time, a small group of late Victorian middle-class women could afford to live on their earnings outside marriage – as Vicinus (1985) has shown. They came to live in flats, streets, houses, rooms (often, lonely rooms), garrets and 'barracks', new model buildings – like Farringdon Road buildings. Gissing shows us the details of city life in unyielding, concrete form. Flats were also part of the rise of new possibilities for women. They made it possible for unmarried middle-class women (like Beatrice Webb and her cousin the novelist Margaret Harkness) to navigate the city on their own, settling in flats, exploring the possibility of an unchaperoned social and economic independence, many seeking political, economic, and social power, as Dennis describes (Vicinus, 1985; Davidoff, 1986; Nord, 1995; Rappaport, 2000).

Location was an important subject for Gissing because class signals and class structure were expressed in physical terms. These signals are sometimes lost to modern readers, for places and possibilities have much altered, as have class relations. However, where people met, where they went, how they occupied themselves, where they lived and worked all concern the novelist of circumstances. One of the most important contributors to large-scale urbanisation were the railways – combined with the electric telegraph. The power of transforming technology exerted huge forces for change. The increase in the circulation of capital, too, impacted on every aspect of the built environment and on every facet of geography, psychology, intellect, education, and emotion. Technical innovation changed how space was thought of, used, and organised. The railway both simultaneously annihilated space *and* compartmentalised it. Christine Huguet shows, in a close reading of the novels and Gissing's short stories, that the Thames, like the railway, was both a highway and a class divider.

One major issue dramatised by the railway concerned the potentials of women. Here, a new female mobility and railway travel was a major new threat to the male. New railway travel enabled the female body to move, but within powerful impersonal and cultural constraints. Single women, for example, constituted a large proportion of Thomas Cook's early clientele. But they constituted many kinds of sexual and economic threat. As Margaret Visser has said, 'There is an ancient insistence in our culture that women ought to be pure, and that this involves *not moving around*. Women stay at home; they are there for roving males to return to. Mobility in women is therefore disconcerting and probably expressive of promiscuity.' (Visser, 1997, p. 1).

Gissing, mass culture, and the production of books

Gissing was more concerned with art than with instrumentality. He was a writer who sought to write for the cultivated class. He matters because he is an author seemingly specifically generated in part by opposition to mass culture, and to the changing structure of the making of books. He supported himself by his writing, as he did his passion for the classical world and for European travel. Yet, as Pierre Coustillas and Colin Partridge say, 'Most of his novels of the 1880s and early 1890s (to 1892 with *Born in Exile*) involved him in more or less open warfare with publishers, publishers' readers, editors or critics' (Coustillas and Partridge, 1972, pp. 1, 3). His relations with his publishers are now receiving detailed scrutiny, notably by Fred Nesta whose important book-length study is awaited. [Nesta, 2004a,b]. Gissing's was, of course, one man's view of cultural crisis, of the conflict he saw between art (and artistic conscience) and a commerce which he believed to be both corrupt and corrupting, negating the individual and the culture. He felt that he spoke for the cultured minority, who saw themselves going into the margin, who were no longer leading cultural debate as a recognised, respected, cultivated minority. Gissing, indeed, felt himself caught within a growing mass commodity culture – the 'convergence of economics and aesthetics' in the *fin de siècle* which Regenia Gagnier has analysed (Gagnier, in Ledger and McCracken, 1995).

London in the 1890s was at the centre of a new, vast, global communications industry. This was extending and increasing in both pace and reach, and thus of cheapness. It was evolving what Adrian Poole has called 'a total industrialisation of writing' (Poole, 1975, p. 142). The technological innovations of printing, the telegraph, and new concentrations of capital were all in motion, in new mass markets. New publishers and entrepreneurs confronted a new domestic market for the elementary educated population. The elite literary world was challenged, both with new opportunities and with a crisis in its assumptions about itself. Here, Gissing is one guide (as Bennett and H.G. Wells are others) to the changing relationship of the writer and society, and the role of literature, journalism, and new media, in a shifting world which saw the rise of the 'ordinary' reader. Gissing shows us changes and diversification in readership, the power of advertising, the mutually reinforcing role of publishers, booksellers, editors, reviewers, and literary agents. He exemplifies – whilst he resists – changes in ownership and distribution in an altered world where writers like Marie Corelli and Hall Caine triumphed yet at the same time new publishers like William Heinemann and A.H. Bullen nurtured minority writers.

Gissing's work offers an enquiry into possibilities – such as the potential of education for all – many of which Gissing himself denied. Gissing exemplifies, too – in the struggle of one culture against another – what could not happen in literary relations, what could not succeed, what could not be changed by hard work alone. He focusses attention on the activities of cultural intermediaries (publishers, libraries, printers, distributors, reviewers, newspaper proprietors, and entrepreneurs), on consumers and on the differing cultural choices to be made. Here John Carey has urged, persuasively, that the questions are more open than Gissing suggests: 'The idea that popular writing might have "literary value" is not entertained. It is assumed, too, that writing for a mass readership is easy. Anyone, or certainly any intellectual, could do it if he chose to debase himself' (Carey, 1992, p. 108).

Peter McDonald has written of writers that 'the first task of any literary analysis is not to interpret their meaning, but to reconstruct their predicament' (McDonald, 1997, p. 13). As he shows, this task is to reconstruct the particular structure of what Foucault – who assumed that power *is* intellectual – called 'the field of possibilities'. These were represented by rival or different communications structures. One challenge is to assess (and perhaps to balance) 'the field', 'the life', and 'the work'. McDonald, deploying the analysis offered by Pierre Bourdieu, speaks of a fundamental opposition in the literary culture of Gissing's time, between 'the sub-field of restricted production' (which Gissing *consciously* chose to occupy) and 'the sub-field of large-scale production' (which Gissing despised), which set a hierarchical structure. The two fields – separately occupied by what McDonald calls the cultural context of 'the purists' and 'the profiteers' – were characterised by different capital structures, audience size, publishing and marketing strategies. This fundamental divide represents a pivotal division over values, and the principles of evaluation. It has determined the evolution (and assessment) of these particular structures, and concerns bedrock issues of competence, judgement, and the nature of art (Bourdieu, 1990, 1993; McDonald, 1997, pp. 13–124).

McDonald shows that

> The agents in the 'sub-field of restricted production' [– or, in our terms, Gissing as an aestheticist] – act according to the principles of legitimacy specific to the literary field. They measure value primarily, if not exclusively, in aesthetic terms; they concern themselves chiefly with the particular demands, traditions, and excellences of their craft; they respect only the opinion of peers or accredited connoisseurs and critics; and they deem legitimate only those rewards, like peer recognition, which affect one's status within the field itself. (McDonald, 1997, pp. 13–14)

Thus, the purist Gissing of 'The Hope of Pessimism', of art for art's sake, his refusal to pursue multiple careers, his withdrawal from politics and his hesitations about journalism, his rejection of potential supplementary income (Gissing, in Coustillas, 1970). Yet the expanding market for reading matter and the multiplying numbers of outlets for writers offered new opportunities by which to maintain himself without being dependant on a patron or on one institution. But Gissing shied away from this widening access, for writers and for readers, and from allied educational and democratic changes. Later in his career – facing tightening economic realities in an increasingly complex market shaped by George Newnes, Alfred Harmsworth (later, Lord Northcliffe), W.T. Stead, and W.F. Tillotson, who pioneered new styles, formats, and journalistic techniques with innovative flair (Jackson, 2001) – Gissing (like Conrad) dabbled in the alternative which Wells and Bennett (of the next generation) fully embraced. They, too, believed that the working classes were evolving. Gissing did not. Gissing believed, with Conrad, that the literary elect which he sought to join should have exclusive control over literary value, and that the only legitimate goal of his life was to secure a literary reputation with his peers and with posterity (McDonald, 1997, pp. 30–2). As *New Grub Street* shows, the enemy included the encroaching commercial, political, journalistic, and other socio-economic interests influencing reading, editorial selection, publication, distribution, and payment and marginalising the 'real' 'man of letters'. Yet these culturally transforming forces generated a new reading public, although one that Gissing believed incapable of aesthetic appreciation.

Gissing's major statement concerning these issues is *New Grub Street*. This is one of the greatest of urban novels, not least for its representation of these choices. It offers a special summation of the literary market place as he saw it, and the Victorian world transformation to the brand-new consumer world. The novel is unrivalled as an examination of the writer's life, of the writing and publishing process, and of one influential view of the changing relations in cultural power between author and publisher, author and audience. It dramatises what Gissing saw as a key cultural choice: the surrender of individual judgement to the demands of the commercial leadership of a new mass, democratic reading public. It encompasses the social conflict between the claims of free and autonomous selfhood ('artistic integrity') and the controls of the market place. But it is more complex than this single focus, if unrealistic in its romanticism. Certainly, Gissing does not, in the terms of Raymond Williams, critique the existing relations of literary production and broader industrial development from a socialist point of view. Instead, he offers a complex, expansive, specific, and sharply characterised novel. Yet from the socialist perspective, as Howard, Lucas, and Goode argued, Gissing's 'vision is limited by the absence of...an awareness of the nature of social change. This means he is never completely certain whether he is offering a fixed metaphysical image or a changeable historical one...and [he had] an inability to sort out whether his own alienation is from the social system or the rest of humanity' (Howard, Lucas, and

Goode, 1966, p. 4). However, 'you can relate even the confusion to the actualities of a changed historical situation in which the available accounts of social change could only be seen as evasions' (Howard, Lucas, and Goode, 1966, p. 4). Gissing is often accused of adhering to no social theory. And, as Korg noted, too, 'Gissing's indecision about metaphysical questions is the ultimate source of his indecision about social and economic questions' (Korg, 1963, pp. 136, 177; Korg, in Coustillas, 1968, pp. 64–79). However, an explicit commitment to politics may have hindered rather than helped him. As Adorno said, 'A successful work is not one which resolves contradictions in a spurious harmony, but one which expresses the idea of harmony negatively by embodying the contradictions, pure and uncompressed, in its innermost structure' (Adorno, 1967, p. 32).

On one level, Gissing's challenges ask us to consider what did books mean in terms of who read them and what effect did they have. On another, how did Gissing – as one producer – live, work, and pursue his relationships with publishers? Who did he presume were his readers, and what readings took place? What role did he, they, and booksellers, publishers, and reviewers play as cultural and economic agents? This cluster of questions – what Roger Chartier called the triangular relationship between the text as conceived by the author, as printed by the publisher, and as read (or heard) by the reader – asks us to explore the social context of reading Gissing, and of how he related to (and was shaped by?) his audience, the new media, booksellers, and his peers. These recognitions in Gissing's work help us see more clearly the *issues* of culture and social choices, of the fragmentation of social and intellectual life, of what one of our contributors, John Sloan, has called 'the whole problem of contemplative freedom and intellectual privilege', as they do, too, of book history and of textuality, of symbolic value and material production, of book trade relationships and cultural legitimacy (Sloan, 1989, p. 13). Gissing's fictions undermine the claims of single-dimension and tribalist answers, even if he adopts what Sloan calls a 'potentially disabling combination of Arnoldian humanist education and low-class marginality', and is 'unable, because of the division of fact and value, to theorise his *malaise*' (Sloan, 1989, pp. 30, 58).

Gissing and the 'woman' question

Several contributors stress gender relations, and gender as a category of analysis – concerning how both male and female character, potentials, and achievement are defined and considered. Gissing explored the often contradictory roles played by women, and he says much about what is called 'the marriage market' and of the woman who tried 'to balance three problematic areas: sexuality, spirituality, and power', in Martha Vicinus's words, and who sought 'significant work, emotionally satisfying friendships, and a morally charged freedom' (Vicinus, 1985). *The Odd Women* continues to attract particular attention in the women's movement, and this despite its bold dismissal of female potential as regards education and – despite Gissing's intuitions and sensitivities – the many very unattractive female personalities he offers. However, he was fully aware of the key crises concerning the relationships between home and work, and definitions of male and female identity, sexual lifestyles, economic situation and work, status, opportunity, and influence. These were observed in terms of both relationships and their frontiers, including the use of private and public space – the home, place of work, street, music hall, department store, art gallery, discussion club, political or literary society, religious movement, tea shop, railway system, and so on.

Again, Gissing draws attention to the dilemmas and the new social questions that new choices presented to women, notably in what Sally Ledger called 'the reconstruction of masculinities, feminism and empire... and the relationship between nascent modernism and late-twentieth-century postmodernism' (Ledger, in Ledger and McCracken, 1995, p. 1). Josephine McQuail shows that Gissing was both an advocate for women's rights and a misogynist. His conclusion, in *The Odd Women* and *In the Year of Jubilee*, is that there can be no real independence for women without self-responsibility, self-discipline, and self-knowledge. Yet this is necessarily threatening, and sexual. Here, railways are always significant locales. George Eliot, in *Middlemarch*, warned that 'Women both old and young regarded travelling by train as presumptuous and dangerous.' But this was published in 1871–72, and the view changed rapidly. To Gissing, however, railways remained another aspect of an ambivalent underworld, although one scene of female emancipation. Some of Gissing's pivotal scenes occur on steam railways, and on the new Metropolitan District Railway opened in 1868. These offered many different kinds of movement, new social and sexual opportunities. They enabled many new links, just as they confronted Gissing with new and ambiguous paradoxes. For example, the new ease of travel was taken up by the masses. W.M. Thackeray thought that the new train had so changed daily life that the railway embankment was like a wall that divided past and present. Gissing's interest in travel, in transport systems (and, in particular, railways and their class system) opens up pivotal issues of class, sexuality, and gender, as McQuail shows.

Liggins examines the complex nature of the generalised restrictions on women's lives in terms of class as well as of femininity. She shows that the restrictions on the working-girl's occupation of public space cannot be understood separately from the questions of her marital status and the work culture which severely limited free movement and time-off. Laura Vorachek addresses the 'vexed question' of Gissing's own feminism, and his self-contradictions as his ideas changed. She considers the New Woman's increased autonomy and sexual freedom in terms of the pursuit of a professional musical career which intrudes into masculine definitions of appropriate occupations – as illustrated by Alma Frothingham in *The Whirlpool* (1897). And she explores contemporary sources on the key question of the relationship between gender and genius, of women's intellectual and artistic capabilities – the controverted issue of why have there been no great women artists, famously explored by Linda Nochlin (Nochlin, 1994).

Margaret Mitchell is concerned with the imagined possibilities of the city, especially concerning gender and the negotiation of public and private space, which raise issues concerning the limitations on selfhood in a crowded city. She examines 'the ideological work' which gender performs in the novels, notably in helping to re-shape both individual lives and the city itself. Mitchell sees these changes as central to the resolution of social conflicts. Her context is two extremes of Victorian feminity – the domestic angel and the prostitute. Gender is central to all possibilities, especially for the re-structuring (or increased permeability) of class. She explores how the city can impose rigid boundaries on life, and the conventions of gender which shape identity. She also examines how the city, too, can offer a kind of freedom which 'has profound implications for gender and for social progress in general' Elizabeth F. Evans focusses on the shop-girl who sought more independence, and who was herself emblematic of several roles and of several moral anxieties. Gissing and his contemporaries were ambivalent about shop-girl freedom, for they represent 'both modern life's ominous commodification and women's dangerous new accessibility to public spaces'. This is another area in which Gissing examines class confusion, ambiguity in terms of sexual respectability, and a de-stabilising threat.

Meaghan Clarke, an art historian, is similarly concerned with the wide question of the city, its spaces, and the relationship of middle-class women to those spaces. These issues concern who possesses the world, and the role and function of cultural philanthropy in bringing art to the unclassed. Clarke enquires into the ways in which art was used to legitimise the actions of women and to widen their boundaries. Her analysis of women and journalism (which was seen as an alternative to the other arts and the professions) in the 1890s examines the real woman on Grub Street – especially real-life women art journalists, whose work has been missing from accounts of the city. She shows the development of this work as a career, and the conditions for the production of art writing. Women art journalists fitted into the fictional and the factual definitions of the New Woman, and they contributed to these shifting and ambiguous definitions. Their lives also query the stereotypes of the 'New Woman', for the women art critics she studies rarely identified with this 'media construction'.

By this enquiry Clarke offers another context – the changes in the London art world which parallel changes in the literary culture – by which to consider the issues which Gissing's work represents. For example, the role and influence of unfavourable attitudes towards career women; gendered-definitions of income and status, conservative re-inscriptions of sexual roles. Clarke highlights the role of art and access to the interior public space of the art gallery, where women were both the observer and the observed, and where the positive, creative (and subversive) role of the masquerade evolved as a method for self-presentation for the woman who was not a courtesan (though often mistaken for one) in a modern city of spectacle. Such women could be feared as well as fashionable. Clarke offers an altern-ative reading of Victorian public space, re-integrating the work and writing of women as art writers within the history of modernity. She thus confirms Parsons' comment on the woman 'as an increasingly autonomous and observing presence' (Parsons, 2000, p. 43).

Defining meaning

William Morris (like Ruskin) defined 'meaning' as 'the invention and imagination which forms the soul of this art', but he had little patience with aestheticism. Instead he emphasised social purpose (Morris, 1910–15, pp. 100–1). Gissing, who endorsed the first but ultimately shied away from the second, never-theless asked key questions about the nature of literary labour and about society and the individual. For example, under what conditions is individual culture possible? And whose? In social life, how is personal self-development, self-responsibility, and mutuality to be encouraged in an otherwise unequal and economically harsh world? This awkward, shy idealist, this self-doubting and unfashionable provincial, this often impractical and usually intransigent artist who stood shy of manifestoes, was perhaps wiser and more practical than he seemed in clearly outlining dilemmas, testing ambiguities, being uncertain about certainty, and being suspicious of 'grand narratives'.

Mary Hammond, in her rich and multi-faceted essay, suggested a fruitful re-assessment of modernism, its roots, its treatment of the City, and of how Gissing should be read within it. Dr. Hammond reads Gissing alongside the proto-modernists. He was, too, complex, ironical, and often in more than one mind. In intriguing ways, he 'retreats' politically yet 'advances' artistically. As Dr. Hammond shows, his revulsion at London's scenes, sights, spaces, and smells co-existed with 'an undeniable fascination with modernity's greatest achievement, the city . . . ' He is much more than a key if confusing figure in the 'Late Victorian Revolt'. He is a primary contributor to the modernist frame of mind.

The essays gathered here are all valuable enquiries into these significant issues, promoted by concern for what Gissing means as well as by study of his 'Fortunes, Misfortunes, Uprisings (and) Downfallings' (to borrow from *Nicholas Nickleby*). He embodies in his writing his own assumptions about human behaviour and society. These necessarily affect both the questions which he asks and the answers he finds. He addressed perennial, deeply disturbing, threatening, genuinely perplexing, and still unresolved questions. Indeed, as Isaiah Berlin has suggested, many of the answers offered in our contemporary society are incommensurable (Berlin, 1969). It is no surprise that Gissing, like many, was uncertain and sometimes self-contradictory. Simon James, in his important recent book, wrote that 'While deeply morally engaged, even at times opinionated, Gissing's work is so structured that its meanings should not be read as closed. If resistance to the monologic determinations of received wisdom is a characteristic of great literary writing, then Gissing deserves perhaps a more prominent place in the canon of Victorian fiction than he has occupied up to now' (James, 2003, p. 148).

Gissing was concerned, like the historian, with searching for causes and explanations, trying to understand *why* things happened, and presenting human choices and voices in vivid characters and indelible scenes. His work is a clear reminder of the significant choices that all writers make in terms of the approaches we adopt towards our subjects, our unstated values, the premises with which we begin, and thus the questions we ask and 'answer'. Here, Gissing is a prismatic and a significant figure, inevitably and even necessarily and constructively full of contradictions and ambiguous 'meanings'. This may be in good part why, a century after his death, his work and personality has not 'gone down to the tongueless silence of the dreamless dust' (Holland, 2004, p. 323). He was, beyond all and above all, a man of literature and of art. And he resists confinement in a bell-jar.

Bibliography

Adburgham, Alison, *Shops and Shopping, 1800–1914: Where and in What Manner the Well-dressed Englishwoman Bought Her Clothes* (London: Barrie & Jenkins, 1964; second edition, 1989).

Adorno, Theodor W., *Prisms* (London: Spearman, 1967).

Altick, Richard D., *The English Common Reader: A Social History of the Mass Reading Public 1800–1900* (Chicago: University of Chicago Press, 1957).

Benjamin, Walter, 'The Work of Art in the Age of Mechanical Reproduction', in Arendt, Hannah, ed., *Illuminations* (London: Jonathan Cape, 1970).

Berlin, Isaiah, *Four Essays on Liberty* (Oxford: Oxford University Press, 1969).

Blainey, Geoffrey, 'Drawing up a Balance sheet of our History', *Quadrant*, Vol. 37, No. 7–8, July–August 1993, pp. 10–15.

Boon, Timothy, 'Industrialisation and catastrophe: The Victorian economy in British film documentary, 1930–50', in Taylor, Mike and Wolff, Michael, eds, *The Victorians Since 1901. Histories, Representations and Revisions* (Manchester: Manchester University Press, 2004).

Booth, Charles, *Life and Labour of the People in London* (London: Macmillan, 1892).

Bourdieu, Pierre, *In Other Worlds: Essays Towards a Reflexive Sociology* (Cambridge: Polity Press, 1990), trans. Matthew Adamson.

——, *The Field of Cultural Production* (Cambridge: Polity Press, 1993), trans. Randal Johnson.

Bowlby, Rachel, *Just Looking. Consumer Culture in Dreiser, Gissing and Zola* (New York and London: Methuen, 1985).

Cannadine, David, 'The present and the past in the English Industrial Revolution', *Past and Present*, 103, 1984, pp. 131–42.

Carey, John, *The Intellectuals and the Masses. Pride and Prejudice among the Literary Intelligentsia 1880–1939* (London: Faber and Faber, 1992).

Chialant, Maria Teresa, 'The feminisation of the city in Gissing's fiction: The Streetwalker, the flaneuse, the shopgirl', in Postmus, B., ed., *A Garland for Gissing* (Amsterdam: Rodopi, 2001).

Clapham, J.H., *An Economic History of Modern Britain. The Early Railway Age, 1820–1850* (Cambridge: Cambridge University Press, 1926).

Coleman, D.C., *Myth, History, and the Industrial Revolution* (London: Hambledon Press, 1992).

Coustillas, Pierre and Partridge, Colin, eds, *Gissing: The Critical Heritage* (London: Routledge & Kegan Paul, 1972).

Cross, Nigel, *The Common Writer. Life in Nineteenth-Century Grub Street* (Cambridge: Cambridge University Press, 1985).

Darnton, Robert, 'What is the history of books?', in Darnton, Robert, *The Kiss of Lamourette. Reflections in Cultural History* (New York: W.W. Norton, 1990).

Davidoff, Leonora, *The Best Circles: Society, Etiquette and the Season* (London: Croom Helm, 1986).

Deleuze, Gilles, 'The Powers of the False', in *Cinema 2: The Time-Image* (1985) (London: Athlone Press, 1989), trans. Tomlinson, Hugh and Galeta, Robert.

Driver, Felix and Gilbert, David, eds, *Imperial Cities. Landscape, Display and Identity* (Manchester: Manchester University Press, 1999).

Dyos, H.J., 'Greater and Greater London: Metropolis and Provinces in the Nineteenth and Twentieth Centuries', in Cannadine, David and Reeder, David, eds, *Exploring the Urban Past* (Cambridge: Cambridge University Press, 1985).

Epstein, Jason, *Book Business. Publishing Past Present and Future* (New York: W.W. Norton, 2001.

Foucault, Michel, 'What is an author?' in *Language, Counter-Memory, Practise* (New York: Harper & Row, 1975), ed. and intro. by Bouchar, Donald F.

——, *Discipline and Punish. The Birth of the Prison* (Harmondsworth, Penguin, 1991; trans. *From Surveillance et punir: naissance de la prison* (Paris, Gallimard, 1975).

Fraser, W. Hamish, *The Coming of the Mass Market, 1850–1914* (London & Basingstoke, Macmillan, 1981).

Freeman, Michael, *Railways and the Victorian Imagination* (New Haven and London: Yale University Press, 1999).

Gagnier, Regenia, 'Is *Market Society* the Fin *of History*', in Ledger, Sally, and McCracken, Scott, eds, *Cultural Politics in the Fin De Siècle* (Cambridge: Cambridge University Press, 1995).

Geertz, Clifford, *The Interpretation of Cultures* (New York: Basic Books, 1973).

Gissing, George, 'The Hope of Pessimism' (1882, unpublished), in Coustillas, Pierre, *George Gissing: Essays and Fiction* (Baltimore: Johns Hopkins University Press, 1970).

Glover, David, ' "This spectacle of a world's wonder": Commercial culture and urban space in Gissing's *In The Year of Jubilee*', in Postmus, B., ed., *op. cit.*

Grylls, David, 'George Gissing and Biographical Criticism', *English Literature in Transition*, Vol. 32 (1989), No. 4, pp. 454–70.

Hamilton, Jill, *Thomas Cook: The Holiday-Maker* (Stroud, Gloucs.: Sutton Publishing, 2004).

Hayek, Friedrich, *The Constitution of Liberty* (London: Routledge & Kegan Paul, 1960).

Heidegger, Martin, 'Der Ursprung des Kunstwerkes', Holstered (Frankfurt, 1972), trans. Hofstadter, A., as 'The Origin of the Work of Art', in *Poetry, Language, Thought* (New York, 1971).

Hennock, E.P., *Fit and Proper Persons, Ideal and Reality in Nineteenth-Century Urban Government* (London, Edward Arnold, 1973).

Himmelfarb, Gertrude, 'The Culture of Poverty', in Dyos, H.J. and Wolff, Michael, eds, *The Victorian City* (London: Routledge & Kegan Paul, 1973), Vol. 1.
——, *The Idea of Poverty. England in the Early Industrial Age* (New York: Alfred A. Knopf, 1984).
Hobson, Dominic, *The National Wealth. Who Gets What in Britain* (London: HarperCollins, 1999).
Holland, Max, *The Kennedy Assassination Tapes* (New York: Alfred A. Knopf, 2004).
Hoppen, Theodore K., *The Mid-Victorian Generation 1846–1886* (Oxford: Oxford University Press, 1998).
Howard, D., Lucas, J. and Goode, J., *Tradition and Tolerance in Nineteenth Century Fiction* (London: Methuen, 1966).
Hunt, Lynn, ed., *The New Cultural History* (Berkeley, CA.: University of California Press, 1989).
Jacobs, Jane, *Cities and the Wealth of Nations* (1984; Harmondsworth: Penguin, 1986).
——, *The Death and Life of Great American Cities* (1961; New York: Random House, 2002).
——, *The Economy of Cities* (New York: Random House, 1969).
Jackson, Kate, *George Newnes and the New Journalism in Britain, 1880–1910* (Aldershot: Ashgate, 2001).
James, Simon J., *Unsettled Accounts. Money and Narrative in the Novels of George Gissing* (London: Anthem Press, 2003).
Keating, Peter, *The Haunted Study. A Social History of the English Novel, 1875–1914* (London: Secker & Warburg, 1989).
Kent, Christopher, 'Victorian studies in North America', in Taylor, M. and Wolff, M., eds, *op. cit.*
Kern, Stephen, *The Culture of Time and Space 1880–1918* (Cambridge, Mass.: Harvard University Press, 1983; 2003 ed. with new preface).
Korg, Jacob, *George Gissing, A Critical Biography* (Seattle, Washington: University of Washington Press, 1963).
——, 'Division of Purpose in George Gissing', in Coustillas, Pierre, ed., *Collected Articles on George Gissing* (London: Frank Cass, 1968).
Ledger, Sally and McCracken, Scott, eds, *Cultural Politics in the Fin De Siècle* (Cambridge: Cambridge University Press, 1995).
Ledger, Sally, *The New Woman: Fiction and Feminism at the Fin de Siècle* (Manchester: Manchester University Press, 1997).
Liggins, Emma Jane, 'Idiot Heroines and Worthless Women? Gissing's 1890s Fiction and Female Independence', in Postmus, B., ed., *op. cit.*
McCracken, Scott, '*Postmodernism*, a chance to *reread*?', in Ledger, Sally and McCracken, Scott, eds, *op. cit.*
McDonald, Peter D., *British Literary Culture and Publishing Practice 1880–1914* (Cambridge: Cambridge University Press, 1997).
Maltz, Diana, 'Gissing as thwarted aesthete', in Postmus, B., ed., *op. cit.*
Mathias, Peter, *Retailing Revolution. A History of Multiple retailing in the Food Trades Based Upon the Allied Suppliers Group of Companies* (London: Longmans, 1967).
Matthiesen, F.O. and Murdock, K.B., eds, *The Notebooks of Henry James* (New York: Oxford University Press, 1947).
Megill, Allan, *Prophets of Extremity: Nietzsche, Heidegger, Foucault, Derrida* (Berkeley, CA.: University of California Press, 1985).
Mitchell, B.R. and Deane, Phyllis, *Abstract of British Historical Statistics* (Cambridge: Cambridge University Press, 1971 edition).
Morris, William, *The Collected Works of William Morris* (London: Longmans, Green 1910–15).

Nead, Lynda, *Myths of Sexuality. Representations of Women in Victorian Britain* (Oxford: Oxford University Press, 1988).

——, *Victorian Babylon. People, Streets and Images in Nineteenth century London* (New Haven: Yale University Press, 2000).

Nesta, Fred, 'The Thyrza Contract and Two Unpublished Letters,', *Gissing Journal*, Vol. XL, No. 1, January 2004a, pp. 35–42.

——, 'George Gissing, International Copyright and Late Victorian Publishing', *Gissing Journal*, Vol. XL, No. 4, October 2004b, pp. 13–19.

Nochlin, Linda, 'Why are there no great women artists?' (first published 1971) in *Women Art and Power: And Other Essays* (London: Thames & Hudson, 1994).

Nord, Deborah Epstein, *Apprenticeship of Beatrice Webb* (Ithaca, NY: Cornell University Press, 1985).

——, *Walking the Victorian Streets. Women, Representation, and the City* (Ithaca, NY: Cornell University Press, 1995).

Nozick, Robert, *Anarchy, State and Utopia* (Oxford: Basil Blackwell, 1974).

Olsen, Donald, J., *The Growth of Victorian London* (London: B.T. Batsford, 1976).

Parsons, Deborah L., *Streetwalking the Metropolis. Women, The City and Modernity* (Oxford: Oxford University Press, 2000).

Poole, Adrian, *Gissing in Context* (London: Macmillan, 1975).

Postmus, Bouwe, ed., *A Garland for Gissing* (Amsterdam: Rodopi, 2001).

Postrel, Virginia, *The Future and Its Enemies. The Growing Conflict Over Creativity, Enterprise and Progress* (New York: The Free Press, 1998).

Price, Richard, *British Society 1680–1880. Dynamism, Containment and Change* (Cambridge: Cambridge University Press, 1999).

Rappaport, Erica Diane, *Shopping for Pleasure. Women in the Making of London's West End* (Princeton: Princeton University Press, 2000).

Rogers, Helen, 'Victorian studies in the UK', in Taylor, M. and Wolff, M., eds, *op. cit.*

Rose, Jonathan, *The Intellectual Life of the British Working Classes* (New Haven and London: Yale University Press, 2001).

Rowntree, B. Seebohm, *Poverty, A Study of Town Life* (London: Macmillan & Co. Ltd., 1901).

Ruthven, K.K., *Critical Assumptions* (Cambridge: Cambridge University Press, 1979).

——, *Feminist Literary Studies: An Introduction* (Cambridge: Cambridge University Press: 1984).

——, *Faking Literature* (Cambridge: Cambridge University Press, 2001).

Sabel, Charles F., *Work and Politics* (Cambridge: Cambridge University Press, 1982).

Sanders, Andrew, *Charles Dickens* (Oxford: Oxford University Press, 2003).

Schama, Simon, *Landscape and Memory* (London: HarperCollins, 1995).

Schwarz, L.D., *London in the Age of Industrialisation* (Cambridge: Cambridge University Press, 1992).

Selig, Robert L., 'A sad heart at the late-Victorian Culture market. George Gissing's *In the Year of Jubilee*' in *Studies in English Literature, 1500–1900*, Autumn 1969, pp. 703–20.

Sloan, John, *George Gissing: The Cultural Challenge* (London: Macmillan, 1989).

Stubbs, Patricia, *Women and Fiction. Feminism and the Novel 1880–1920* (Brighton: The Harvester Press, 1979).

Taylor, A.J., ed., *The Standard of Living in Britain in the Industrial Revolution* (London: Methuen, 1975).

Taylor, Mike and Wolff, Michael, eds, *The Victorians Since 1901. Histories, Representations and Revisions* (Manchester: Manchester University Press, 2004).

Thompson, E.P., *The Making of the English Working Class* (London: Gollancz, 1963).

Thompson, James, 'The BBC and the Victorians', in Taylor, M. and Wolff, M., eds, *op. cit.*

Tindall, Gillian, *The Born Exile, George Gissing* (London: Maurice Temple Smith, 1974).

——, *Countries of The Mind. The Meaning of Place to Writers* (London: The Hogarth Press, 1991).

Vicinus, Martha, *Independent Women. Work and Community for Single Women 1850–1920* (Chicago: University of Chicago Press, 1985).

Visser, Margaret, *The Way We Are. The Astonishing Anthropology of Everyday Life* (New York: Kodansha International, 1997).

Walker, Lynne, 'Vistas of Pleasure: Women consumers of urban space in the West End of London 1850–1900' in Campbell Orr, Clarissa, ed., *Women in the Victorian Art World* (Manchester: Manchester University Press, 1995).

Walkowitz, Judith, *City of Dreadful Delight: Narratives of Sexual Danger in Late-Victorian London* (Chicago: Chicago University Press, 1992).

Weaver, Stewart, 'The bleak age: J.H. Clapham, the Hammonds and the standard of living in Victorian Britain', in Taylor, M. and Wolff, M., eds, *op. cit.*

——, *The Hammonds. A Marriage in History* (Stanford, CA: Stanford University Press, 1997.

Williams, Raymond, *The Country and The City* (London: Chatto & Windus, 1973).

Winter, James, *London's Teeming Streets 1830–1914* (London: Routledge, 1998).

1

New Woman on Grub Street: Art in the City

Meaghan Clarke

In *The Common Writer: Life in Nineteenth Century Grub Street* Nigel Cross drew parallels between Gissing's novel, *New Grub Street*, and real-life counterparts (1985). The five characters he considers are all male: Jasper Milvain, Alfred Yule, Edwin Reardon, Harold Biffen and Whelpdale. The women writing on New Grub Street are left out of Cross's case studies. However, one does not have to look far for real-life women art journalists. For example, the real-life figure Cross identifies as the counterpart to Milvain, Wilfrid Meynell, was married to the extraordinarily prolific art critic and poet Alice Meynell.

Real-life women art journalists occupied a range of positions and identities that overlapped *New Grub Street*'s Marian Yule and Jasper Milvain. The majority established their careers 'under the dome' that Marian detested. They also shared commonalities with the superfluous women of *The Odd Women*, they frequented the same spaces – such as the Burlington – and journalism offered a new career avenue for 'odd' women. Like journalism and, one might argue, because of journalism, the London art world was undergoing an intensive popularization during the 1880s and 1890s. Not only was the round of the galleries part of the social circuit, required of both old and new money, but it was reaching a far broader audience on the pages of the rapidly expanding newspaper and periodical press. The exhibition spaces of the metropole offered a plethora of opportunities for art writers to observe and record. This chapter will consider the role of women art journalists in London during the late nineteenth century. More specifically, I will first address the conditions for the production of art writing based on the experiences of three women: Alice Meynell, Florence Fenwick Miller and Elizabeth Robins Pennell.[1] In the second section of the chapter, I will consider the journalistic contributions of these three women on art in the city, ranging from 'modern' developments in art, to the Royal Academy in Burlington House, and philanthropic projects in the East End.

Writing women

Unfavourable attitudes towards career women remained prevalent in the periodical press, further substantiated by the scientific currency of craniometry, anthropometry and eugenics, and their use in conservative reinscriptions of sexual roles; hence marriage was continually put forth as the ultimate goal for daughters (Bland, 1995, pp. 76–7). This attitude was countered by the social economist and friend of Gissing, Clara Collet, who asserted that women ought to pursue work which allows them to be self-supporting and added that 'to expect one hundred women to devote their energies to attracting fifty men seems slightly ridiculous' (Collet, 1892, p. 551). Indeed, as Deborah Epstein Nord has noted, the 1880s was a period in which a generation of middle-class women, born in the 1850s and 1860s, lived with social and economic independence (Nord, 1995, p. 181), and women journalists were among this group that achieved professional recognition.

In *New Grub Street* it becomes clear that the place to make a profitable living is journalism not novel-writing. In *Journals and Journalism*, Alice Meynell's husband (writing under the pen-name John Oldcastle) commented that there were 'not a few' women who had made a name for themselves in periodical literature (Oldcastle, 1880, p. 16). In 1893 and 1894, the *Lady's Pictorial* published a series on 'Lady Journalists', with the idea that journalism was a suitable profession for ladies that had 'happily long passed from the vague and uncertain region of theory into that of successfully accomplished fact'. No longer restricted to the vagaries of fashion or movements in frivolous circles, women journalists had won success writing on art and literature, philanthropic efforts, political and social achievements, foreign travel and exploration of great cities (1893, p. 734). In a similar vein, the journalist Margaret Bateson encouraged woman to enter the field due to its egalitarianism, 'if proof was needed of the good fellowship that exists, it is found in the absolute equality of treatment meted out to both sexes by the Institute of Journalists' (Bateson, 1906, 125–8). Nevertheless, although in 1892 W.T. Stead contended that in the profession as a whole there was little sex prejudice, he also patronizingly recommended that women be admonished as freely as men because 'women need it more than anything else'; to 'spare the rod spoils the child' and 'women can bear spoiling quite as little as any child' (1892, p. 12). The Institute of Journalists initially remained dominated by men, but a separate Society for Women Journalists was founded in 1895 with the objective to unite women journalists for mutual protection and advancement. Art critics were well represented in the society. Alice Meynell was president in 1898, and other critics such as Gertrude Campbell and Julia Cartwright were among the members. By the 1890s, women art journalists had been depicted in *Punch*, and even the art press acknowledged the presence of women among its ranks in print, thereby validating their position within the profession.

In practical terms, art journalism did not present the same difficulties for women writers as reporting on, for example, crime or the public sphere of politics. To begin with, galleries were available during the daytime and were accessible to those middle-class women traversing the metropole in growing numbers. Lynne Walker has mapped out the rapid increase in women's presence in the public spaces of the West End in the late nineteenth century; women in the workforce, particularly journalists, utilized public transport and the streets and entered public buildings. Women were present at exhibition openings and press days in the West End, as is evidenced by their reviews in the press. Walker argues that the presence and autonomy of women in the West End 'made spaces for real change through the develop-ment of a public ideology for women' (Walker, 1995, p. 9). Articles and books advising women journalists offer a fractured and contradictory version of occupational standards; yet these dissonances evinced and effected changing opportunities for women journalists.

By definition women art critics during this period were not 'men of letters'; unlike John Ruskin they did not acquire that title nor its sage-like status. On the contrary, like Jasper Milvain's description of the new 'trade', many women art critics were strategists; they juggled numerous freelance art reviews and articles, and the placement of these was closely linked with editorial and artist contacts. Just as Milvain could reel off how much he had earned each day, Alice Meynell recorded the earnings from each paragraph, article and book in her account book. The pay scales were, however, not gender-neutral. Wilfred Meynell was paid twice Alice Meynell's rate for *Daily Chronicle* paragraphs (Meynell, 1947, p. 7). Women art writers negoti-ated independent positions and financial success, despite constraints on their access to education and employment, by formulating alternative methodologies for articulating artistic discourse. The majority of women art critics did not restrict their writing to art, but wrote on other topics for periodicals as well as novels, prose and poetry, as exemplified by Meynell. Many women also negotiated gender restrictions by writing specifically for women as did Florence Fenwick Miller.

Women art journalists fit variously into the fictional and factual defi-nitions of the New Woman, and indeed they contributed to these shifting definitions through their writing. However, as Talia Schaffer cogently observes, women rarely identified themselves with the 'New Woman' stereotype prevalent in the press, and the lifestyles of women art critics likewise indicate the instability of this media construction (Schaffer, 2001, pp. 39–53).

Art in the city

At the end of the century, debates around the 'modern' in art were rife in the press. Some critics repeatedly demanded a reorganization of British art's oldest surviving institution, the Royal Academy. William Frith's painting of a *Private View at the Royal Academy 1881* (1882) depicts the heady mixture of artists and critics – President Frederic Leighton in the centre and Oscar Wilde to the right. It was this popular jam-packed space that Gissing described to his brother a year later in 1882, 'The Academy was glorious, only so tremendously crowded that it was difficult to get near the pictures' (Mattheisen, Young and Coustillas, 1991, p. 81).

The gallery was already a space where women went – it was in the Burlington where Monica in the *Odd Woman* was found with Everard Barfoot by her jealous husband Widdowson. The Burlington was frequented by many women including the absent/present Alice Meynell continuously preparing anonymous and signed reviews for/by her 'Jasper Milvain' editor husband. If any woman journalist epitomizes the new journalistic methods decried by Gissing it is Meynell. In her articles and reviews she skipped across artist cliques and exhibitions rather than allying herself with a particular artistic approach, and in so doing effected a consistently remunerative publishing strategy. However, perhaps more interestingly, rather than iterating accepted art historical teleologies that pit the traditional against the avant-garde, her texts articulate an overlapping panoply of artists and shows.

Not surprisingly to those in the 'know', the pages of *Merry England* and the *Weekly Register* often praised the work of the battle artist Elizabeth Butler, Meynell's sister. The sisters' correspondence evidenced their symbiotic relationship, attending to minutiae such as the exact positioning of Butler's painting at the Burlington, as well as the wording of reviews, and arrangements with periodical publishers and dealers. However, Meynell did not restrict her attendance to the traditional academic venues preferred by her sister, but also journeyed to the exhibitions of the French-influenced New English Art Club whose members explicitly rejected studio-based academic painting. Indeed it was Meynell who was credited with introducing the *plein air* Newlyn School to the mainstream art world in the *Art Journal* (1889). However, her penchant for light over 'make-believe' narratives had already been expressed in an extraordinarily early article that compared the work of contemporary British artists unfavourably with that of Degas and Monet. She labelled Degas as both 'realist' and 'impressionist' explaining,

> But in fact there is an essential unity in the aims of impressionary art and naturalistic literature, inasmuch as both proclaim a complete denial of the ideal ... no artist has ever gone further in his refusal of beauty or the ideal. (1882, pp. 80–1)

Pictures like Degas's *l'Absinthe* would later attract huge criticism in London for the prurience of their subject matter, but here Meynell is explicitly linking such pictures with the aims of naturalistic literature. What Meynell is appealing to here is realism in the sense of a representation of social reality, a definition of realism having more in common with literary realism than pictorial naturalism. What makes Meynell's contemporary interpretation of Degas therefore particularly interesting was that she offered through the comparison with naturalistic literature a reading of his work to an audience incredibly uneasy with the unpleasant and unsightly element of impressionist work. Degas' 'realistic' depictions of modern life were later studied and admired by the London Impressionists, specifically Walter Sickert. Not only have both Gissing and Sickert been popularly associated with 'Jack the Ripper', but it is the paintings of the latter artist that are most suggestive of Gissing's descriptions of the darker side of London.

More recently scholars have indeed suggested a wider relationship between impressionism and 'realism' in Gissing's impressions of atmosphere. Xavier Baron posits Gissing's essay 'On Battersea Bridge' at this conjunction, suggesting that Gissing was aware of Whistler's impressionist interpretations of the city, conjoining 'impressionistic details as a means of combining the dynamics of artistic perception with the particulars of realistic observation' (Baron, 2000, p. 117). However, art writing at the time reveals unease with the latter mode of viewing, whereas the former offered a more saleable label for modern art particularly for figures such as Whistler. For example, Elizabeth Robins Pennell asked in a review of his 1892 Goupil retrospective, 'what are most of Mr. Whistler's Nocturnes but impressions of the river?' (1892, pp. 280–1). Pennell was amongst a group of New Critics advocating 'modern' art; associated with the New English Art Club, the band included George Moore, R.A.M. Stevenson, D.S. MacColl and Walter Sickert (Stokes, 1989; Gruetzner Robins, 1995, 2000). Like Meynell, her reviews reveal the tensions around notions of impressionism and 'realism' in the London art world. French Impressionist work was shown in London in conjunction with New English Art Club exhibitions. In the *Star*, Pennell praised the exhibition of work by Monet and Degas; of a piece by the latter artist she wrote, 'the unflinching realism, will reveal to those who have never seen them before the source of much of Mr. Steer's and Mr. Sickert's inspiration, and the first cause for their interest in the music halls of London' (1891, p. 4). As Anna Gruetzner Robins points out, in the 1890s it was still these images of underworld London and Paris that received hostile responses in the press (1995, p. 96).

This great discomfort with art when it depicted the city, particularly images of women, such as *l'Absinthe*, opens up a wider question of the city, its spaces and the relationship of middle-class women such as Pennell, Meynell and Fenwick Miller to those spaces. Discussions of public space in the nineteenth-century city have been dominated by the Baudelairean *flâneur* and his acute powers of observation,'if waist-lines have been raised and skirts become fuller, you may be sure that from a long way off his eagle's eye will have detected it' (1863, p. 401). More recent scholarship offers us a redefinition of the *flaneuse* as female observer, and Maria Theresa

Chialant identifies Gissing's walking women as transgressive 'nomadic subjects' (Parsons, 2000; Chialant, 2001). As Lynda Nead has argued, what the Baudelairean account tends to exclude is

> the presence of all kinds of women on the city streets; women who were not necessarily prostitutes... but women of all classes and identities tracing paths and lives in the spaces of the city. Nor were these women necessarily passive victims of a voracious male gaze, but they can be imagined as women who enjoyed and participated in the 'ocular economy' of the city; they were women who looked at and returned the gazes of passers-by. (Nead, 2000, p. 71)

Nead therefore advocates an approach which 'challenges orthodoxies of modernity and their Baudelairean typologies such as the *flâneur* and the whore and reintegrates women of the middle classes within the history of modernity' (2000, p. 9). Although missing from theoretical accounts of the city, the writings of women art journalists help to explore this alternative reading of Victorian public space. Art writers held a unique position in that not only did they travel from their homes to galleries, studios and exhibitions in the West End and beyond, but also they recorded their visual engagement with the city in the rapidly expanding print media. Art criticism offered a formalized structure for the gaze, and one that was being increasingly professionalized.

Public spaces were not limited to city streets, for the art gallery afforded women journalists another kind of – interior – public space where they were both observers and observed. In 1884 Gissing visited that other late Victorian edifice to high culture, the Grosvenor Gallery, and could not resist reporting to his sister the interpretations of his fellow-patrons, 'I stood before a splendid picture of Aphrodite swimming on the waves I heard a little girl say to her mother: "Who's that mamma?" And her mother replied, passing on – "Oh, a goddess, my dear – that's all." I put up my opera glass to hide my face' (Mattheisen, Young and Coustillas, 1991, p. 202). *Punch* similarly mocked the appearance-conscious lady patron and viewer, yet for the Grosvenor Gallery the epitome of elite culture, women artists and women patrons were integral to the aesthetic publics who spelt the Grosvenor's success (Newall, 1995). Colleen Denney contends that what makes the Grosvenor distinctive is that works were given special consideration, rather than crammed in to mimic the department store (2000, p. 217). The Grosvenor facilitated a longer look – attending to aesthetics and luxury in a space away from the street. The interventions of women art critics in this 'ocular economy' demonstrate that women in the art gallery were both owners and objects of the gaze, observers and observed, consumers and consumed.

Florence Fenwick Miller, author of the 'Ladies' Column' in the *Illustrated London News*, shows the ambiguous nature of women's place in the galleries and their relationship to the gaze through her detailing of the costumes worn by female visitors to London Exhibitions. Louise Jopling exhibited 30 paintings at the Grosvenor between 1877 and 1890, and her studio showings were a high point in Fenwick Miller's art season. In 1888 Fenwick Miller noted,

> Here, in Mrs. Jopling's Studio...are at one moment four well-known literary ladies and two pretty actresses one of them charming Miss Norreys, in a softly-draped gown of brown cloth, with a cape to match, relieved by a vest of pink crêpe, and a big brown velvet hat above her red-gold hair. (Miller, 1888, p. 356)

On the one hand, in her attention here to feminine fashion and appearance, Fenwick Miller might seem to be simply appropriating the gaze of the male *flâneur*, reaffirming the status of women spectators and artists as objects of that gaze. Yet one has to understand these columns and Fenwick Miller's commentary on them in the context of her own agenda of advancing the cause of women artists, such as Jopling. Hence the appearance and paintings of Jopling are repeatedly presented to her reading public, as Fenwick Miller signals the importance of Jopling's participation in the ritualized season of public performances and by extension her qualifications for election to the Royal Academy. Superficially these fashion diaries seem to position women with respect to the art gallery as a space of leisure and consumption, yet in fact the agenda that Fenwick Miller is keen to articulate with respect to women artists and the Royal Academy betrays an increasing tension around the status of women in the gallery as a *professional* space.

This contrast between the city as a space of leisure or consumption and as a professional space is also found in the work of Elizabeth Robins Pennell. Pennell described her pattern of movement around the city reviewing exhibitions in the 1890s as follows:

> Journalism has led me into pleasant places but never by the path of idleness. Rare has been the month of May that has not found me in Paris, not for the sunshine and gaiety that draw the tourist to it in that gay sunlit season, but for the industrious days, with my eyes and catalogue and note-book, in the *Salons*....Even in London when I might have passed for the idlest stroller along Bond Street or Piccadilly...oftener than not I have been bound for a gallery somewhere with the prospect of long hours' writing...the result...duly appeared in the long columns of many a paper, in the long articles of many a magazine. (1916, p. 19–20)

In her trajectory around the city Pennell might have been mistaken for a *flaneuse*, but in fact maintained a peripatetic pace in search of copy.

Moreover, Pennell's movements were not confined to the galleries of the West End, for Pennell, like Gissing, ventured beyond the glamour of Bond Street galleries to Whitechapel and Mile End. Diana Maltz has recently traced the development of Gissing's disdain for Aestheticism's practical claims to social improvement (2000). This disdain was shared by Pennell who investigated the philanthropic projects, bringing art to the working classes at Samuel and Henrietta Barnett's St Jude's at Whitechapel, and Walter Besant's People's Palace at Mile End. Like the Royal Academy and the Grosvenor Gallery, the East End exhibition openings quickly became yet another event in the already crowded social calendar of the London art world. Attendance was very high and the openings became obligatory for those in the 'know', managing to combine two trendy pastimes for West Enders: 'slumming it' and a private view. However, in contrast to the West End, here the gaze of the female art critic crosses into the realm of tourist and/or ethnographer. As scholars have demonstrated, for women travellers this intersection of class, ethnicity and gender effects a criss-crossing of visuality that reinforced and resisted existing codes of femininity and cultural superiority. It was the transformation of this space into a venue for the fashionable upper- and middle-classes that partially incited the wrath of Pennell. In the *Nation* she questioned whether St Jude's and the People's Palace attracted 'the class for which they are intended' (Pennell, 1888b), prompting an angry letter to the editor from none other than Walter Besant. 'Permit me to say the whole of the audience on Sunday morning, almost without exception, consists of genuine workmen. The men in corduroys...are not the sort of men for whom the Palace is designed. They are the lower class, the men who hang about bars and drink all their wages' (Besant, 1888). However, the class bias of the exhibitions was not Pennell's only complaint. Another debate was around the type of spiritually uplifting art that was being exhibited in the East End and its accompanying interpretation. For *The Century* Pennell reported on responses of 'workmen' to a St Jude's exhibition where Burne-Jones' *The Mill* had an extended catalogue entry explaining its deeper meaning, 'In the quiet hush of the evening, an old mill, its busy days work over, its wheel at rest, stands reflected in the stream. Pigeons settle down to rest, and while the men refresh themselves in the water, after the days toil, the girls dance gravely to the music'...: 'Where's the bloody mill?' asked the to-be-reformed British workman. Another, greeted it with, 'There ain't no dress improvers wanted there' (Pennell, 1888a, p. 455). Other reporters were on the lookout for art in action, civilizing, refining and working miracles on visitors, but in contrast, Pennell's motive was to demonstrate the futility of employing 'Burne-Jonesy mythicism' for ministering purposes (Pennell, 1888a, p. 456).

At the beginning of *New Grub Street* Jasper Milvain delivers an exposition of professional journalism to his sisters: 'your successful man of letters is your skilful tradesman. He thinks first and foremost of markets'. Unlike

Milvain's foil, Reardon, many skilful trades*women* went 'to work with magazines and newspapers and foreign publishers, all sorts of people'. The art writing of Meynell, Fenwick Miller and Pennell suggests a dynamic and shifting visual culture in Gissing's London; as art (re)viewers they made visible a diversity of visions of modernity both inside and outside metropolitan London.

Note

1. See M. Clarke, *Critical Voices: Women Writing Art Criticism in Britain 1880–1905* (Aldershot: Ashgate, 2005) for case studies of these women.

Bibliography

Baron, Xavier. 'Impressionist London in the Novels of George Gissing,' in *Lineages of the Novel: Essays in Honour of Raimund Borgmeier*, eds Bernhard Reitz and Eckart Voigts-Virchow (Trier: WVT Wissenschaftlicher Verlag Trier, 2000).

Bateson, Margaret. *Professional Women Upon Their Professions* (London: Horace Cox, 1906).

Baudelaire, Charles. 'The Painter of Modern Life,' (1863) *Selected Writings on Art and Artists* introduced by Patrick Edward Charvet (Harmondsworth: Penguin, 1972, p. 401).

Besant, Walter. 'The People's Palace,' *Nation* (28 June 1888), p. 526.

Bland, Lucy. *Banishing the Beast: English Feminism and Sexual Morality 1885–1914* (London: Penguin, 1995).

Chialant, Maria Theresa. 'The Feminization of the City in Gissing's Fiction: The Streetwalker, the *Flâneuse*, the Shopgirl,' in *A Garland for Gissing*, ed., Bouwe Postmus (Amsterdam, NYC: Rodopi, 2001) pp. 52–65.

Collet, Clara. 'Prospects of Marriage for Women,' *Nineteenth Century* (April 1892), p. 551.

Cross, Nigel. *The Common Writer: Life in Nineteenth-Century Grub Street* (Cambridge: Cambridge University Press, 1985).

Denney, Colleen. *At the Temple of Art: The Grosvenor Gallery 1877–1890*. London: Associated University Presses, 2000).

Epstein Nord, Deborah. *Walking the Victorian Streets: Women Representation and the City* (Ithaca and London: Cornell University Press, 1995).

Gissing, George. in *New Grub Street*, ed. Bernard Bergonzi (Harmondsworth: Penguin,1968).

——. *Odd Women* (London: Lawrence and Bullen, 1893).

Gruetzner Robins, Anna. 'The London Impressionists at the Goupil Gallery; Modernist Strategies and Modern Life,' *Impressionism in Britain* (Barbican Art Gallery: Yale University Press, 1995), pp. 87–96.

Gruetzner Robins ed., Walter Sickert: *The Complete Writings on Art* (Oxford: Oxford University Press, 2000).

Joyce, Simon. 'Castles in the Air: The People's Palace, Cultural Reformism, and the East End Working Class,' *Victorian Studies* (Summer 1996), pp. 513–538.

Koven, Seth. 'The Whitechapel Picture Exhibitions and the Politics of Seeing,' in *Histories, Discourses and Spectacles*, eds Daniel J. Sherman and Irit Rogoff (London: Routledge, 1994), pp. 22–48.

'Lady Journalists,' *Lady's Pictorial* (11 November 1893), p. 734.

Maltz, Diana. 'Practical Aesthetics and Decadent Rationale in Gissing,' *Victorian Literature and Culture* (Vol. 28, 2000), pp. 55–71.

——. 'George Gissing as Thwarted Aesthete,' in *A Garland for Gissing*, ed., Bouwe Postmus (Amsterdam, NYC: Rodopi, 2001), pp. 203–213.

Mattheisen, Paul F., Arthur C. Young and Pierre Coustillas eds. *The Collected Letters of George Gissing*, Vol. 2, 1881–1885 (Athens: Ohio University Press, 1991), p. 82.

Meynell, Alice. 'Pictures from the Hill Collection,' *Magazine of Art* (1882), pp. 80–81.

Meynell, Sir Francis. *Catalogue of the Alice Meynell Centenary Exhibition* (1947).

Miller, Florence Fenwick. 'Ladies' Page' *ILN* (7 April 1888), p. 356.

Nead, Lynda. *Victorian Babylon: People, Streets and Images in Nineteenth-Century London* (New Haven and London: Yale University Press, 2000), p. 71.

Newall, Christopher. *Grosvenor Gallery Exhibitions: Change and Culture in the Victorian Art World* (Cambridge: Cambridge University Press, 1995), p. 23.

Oldcastle, John. *Journals and Journalism with a Guide for Literary Beginners* (London: Field and Tuer, 1880).

Parsons, Deborah. *Streetwalking the Metropolis: Women, the City and Modernity* (Oxford: Oxford University Press, 2000).

Pennell, E.R. 'English Faith in Art,' *Century* (April 1888), p. 455.

Pennell, N.N. 'East End Missions,' *Nation* (28 April 1888), p. 340.

Pennell, A.U. 'The New English Art Club,' *Star* (30 November 1891), p. 4.

Pennell, N.N. 'Mr. Whistler's Triumph,' *Nation* (14 April 1892), pp. 280–281.

——. *Nights: Rome, Venice in the Aesthetic Eighties; London, Paris in the Fighting Nineties* (London, Philadelphia: J.P. Lippincott, 1916).

Robins Pennell, Elizabeth 'Around London by Bicycle,' *Harper's New Monthly Magazine* (September 1897), pp. 489–510.

Schaffer, Talia. 'Nothing but Foolscap and Ink,' *The New Woman in fiction and in fact: fin de siècle feminisms*, eds Angelique Richardson and Chris Willis (Houndmills, Basingstoke; New York: Palgrave), 2001.

Stead, W.T. 'Young Women and Journalism,' *Young Woman* (October 1892), p. 12.

Stokes, John. *In the Nineties* (New York: Harvester Wheatsheaf, 1989), p. 34.

Walker, Lynne. 'Vistas of pleasure: Women consumers of urban space in the West End of London 1850–1900,' in *Women in the Victorian Art World*, ed. Clarissa Campbell Orr (Manchester: Manchester University Press, 1995), pp. 70–85.

Weiner, Deborah E.B. 'The People's Palace: An Image for East London in the 1880s,' in *Metropolis London: Histories and Representation since 1800*, eds David Feldman and Gareth Stedman Jones (London: Routledge, 1989), p. 46.

Wilson, Shelagh. 'The highest art for the lowest people': The Whitechapel and other philanthropic art galleries, 1877–1901,' *Governing Cultures: Art Institutions in Victorian London*, eds Paul Barlow and Colin Trodd (Aldershot: Ashgate, 2000), pp. 172–186.

2

Buildings, Residences, and Mansions: George Gissing's 'prejudice against flats'

Richard Dennis

> I used to have a prejudice agst. Flats, but I see that it came of insufficient knowledge, like most prejudices. In a wilderness like London, it is vastly better even than a house of one's own. No rates & taxes, one door which shuts in everything, a large, well-lighted common staircase, &, lastly, a location in a neighbourhood where the rent of a house would be extravagant. The privacy is absolute. I have not yet passed two people in going in & out. You put your name on the door, &, if you like, also have it put up on a sort of index at the foot of the staircase.
>
> – *Letters*, 2, p. 279

Gissing's letter to his brother – dated 28 December 1884, six days after moving to 7K, Cornwall Residences, the flat that was to be his base for the following six years – was matched by more domestic but equally enthusiastic sentiments in letters to his sisters. To Ellen he delighted over his flat's furnishings including 'real Chippendale' chairs, 'heavy dark curtains, with brass chains to loop them up, & behind them white curtains, supported by red silk bands' and 'a round table, with handsome red cloth' (*Letters*, 2, p. 280). To Margaret, by now six weeks into his tenancy: 'I am admirably quartered here, feeling I have a home for the first time in my life.... I have frequent visitors, who all exclaim about my comfort' (*Letters*, 2, pp. 291–2).

But his enthusiasm was short-lived. Less then eight months after moving in, he complained to his brother: 'I live a very hermit's life; weeks pass & I do not exchange three words with a soul.... I pay an enormous rent for the privilege of living in a barracks' (*Letters*, 2, p. 337).

By the time of *The Private Papers of Henry Ryecroft*, Gissing's – or, at least, Ryecroft's – antipathy to flats had reached fever pitch:

> I should like to add to the Litany a new petition: 'For all inhabitants of great towns, and especially for all such as dwell in lodgings, boarding-houses, flats, or any other sordid substitute for Home which need or foolishness may have contrived'. (*Ryecroft*, p. 8)

Flats had become the enemy of Englishness, the end of 'the old English sense of comfort'. 'There can be no home without the sense of permanence, and without home there is no civilization – as England will discover when the greater part of her population have become flat-inhabiting nomads' (*Ryecroft*, pp. 256, 260). Yet, in late Victorian Britain, most occupants of suburban and rural villas and cottages rented or leased their dwellings on terms far less secure than the successive 3-year leases by which Gissing occupied 7K (Daunton, 1987). There is some irony in the fact that Gissing's tenancy of 7K lasted just over 6 years, far longer than his occupancy of houses in Exeter, Epsom and Dorking, and following on from the previous seven and a quarter years in London, in which he had lived at 14 different addresses.

Architectural perspectives

In the mid-1870s the reality of domestic life in London had been exposed most authoritatively by the architects, T. Roger Smith and William H. White, in a paper to the Society for the Encouragement of the Arts in which they reiterated the claim made 20 years earlier that 'three-fourths of London houses were lodging-houses – that is to say, houses in which two or more families or groups extemporise residences in a building constructed for the accommodation of a single one' (Smith and White, 1876, p. 156).

Given the necessity for many people to live centrally, and the high cost of land in central London, it was surely better to erect purpose-built flats, each with its own sanitary facilities and soundproof walls, rather than perpetuate the system of subdividing town-houses for purposes for which they were unfit. White developed their argument further in a paper to the Royal Institute of British Architects, of which he was soon to become Secretary. White had lived in apartments in Paris for several years during the 1860s, and in the 1870s occupied rooms in Covent Garden. He had ample practical experience of the advantages and disadvantages of flats and lodgings, and played down the differences between the horizontal flat and the vertical house, stressing the need for the same separation of functions in the former as in the latter and celebrating the privacy that a self-contained flat facilitated, equivalent to that of a house occupied by only one family, and far superior to the promiscuous use of space in a shared dwelling. White avoided using the word 'flat' as much as possible, concluding that his proposals would offer 'not barracks, taverns, or co-operative hotels, but – purely and simply – homes', a sentiment close to Gissing's heart expressed in a built form that experience led him to abhor (White, 1877, p. 1170).

White was more architectural commentator than practising architect (Felstead *et al.*, 1993, p. 987; *The Times*, 22 October 1896, p. 3). Someone with more practical experience of designing flats was Frederick Eales, the son in the architectural practice of C. Eales & Son (Felstead *et al.*, 1993, pp. 273–4). In a paper to the Architectural Association in 1884, Eales discussed how to lay out flats clearly separating different functions – bedrooms, reception rooms, and 'the kitchen and servants' part'. He rejected separate staircases for servants, which might facilitate misbehaviour and the spread of gossip beyond the control of their employers, much as was reputed to occur in communal servants' quarters associated with apartment houses in Paris (and scandalously exposed in Zola's *Pot-Bouille*); rather, he proposed dumb-waiters so that coal and groceries could be hoisted up to flats on upper levels without tradesmen having to use the main stairs. Nor did he like the idea of resident concierges, preferring simple in-out signs in each entrance hall, elaborating on the arrangement Gissing described at Cornwall Residences. In these ways, convenience could be combined with domestic privacy (*Building News* 46, 1884, pp. 360–3; *The Builder* 46, 1884, pp. 351–3, 386).

I have discussed White's and Eales' advocacy of flat-living, not only because they were the most prominent writers and speakers on the subject in the 1870s and 1880s, but also because Eales was the architect, and White a resident from 1881 until his death in 1896, of the real block of flats in which, in *The Whirlpool* (1897), Gissing placed Hugh and Sibyl Carnaby: Oxford and Cambridge Mansions.[1]

Flats in Gissing's novels

Gissing situated several of his characters in purpose-built flats, as opposed to rooms or lodgings. In *New Grub Street* Edwin and Amy Reardon begin married life in what was Gissing's own flat on the edge of Regent's Park. In *The Odd Women* (p. 118) Mrs Luke Widdowson, 'a handsome widow of only eight-and-thirty', occupies a flat in Victoria Street. By the late 1880s, when Gissing set his story, Victoria Street, newly laid out in the 1850s, was lined by blocks of mansion flats, the closest that London had yet come to a Haussmannesque apartment-lined boulevard (Tarn, 1974; Watson, 1993). Elsewhere in the same novel, two bachelors, Bevis and Barfoot, occupy separate flats in the same block in Bayswater. Beatrice French takes a 'bachelor's flat' in Brixton (*Jubilee*, pp. 212, 274–5); Lord Polperro has a flat in Lowndes Mansions, Sloane Street (*Town Traveller*, p. 144); and Will Warburton occupies 'a flat on the fourth floor of the many-tenanted building hard by Chelsea Bridge' (*Warburton*, p. 5). Farther down the social spectrum are the 'large new block' in Fulham 'of the kind known as model

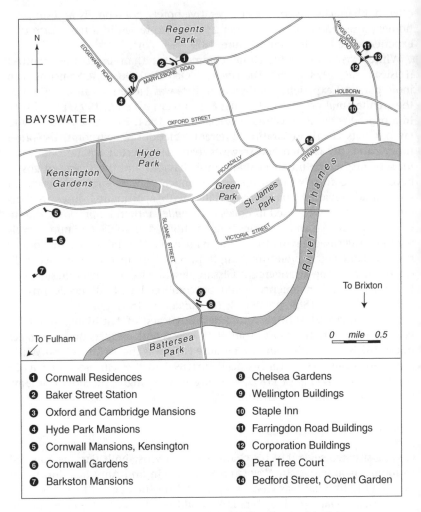

Figure 2.1 Gissing's London, showing locations referred to in this chapter

lodging-houses' where Ida Starr has a two-roomed tenement in *The Unclassed* (pp. 158–9), and the Farringdon Road Buildings to which the Hewett family move during the course of *The Nether World* (Figure 2.1).

I have identified five main themes running through Gissing's writing about flats; no doubt there are others:

Home?

Could a flat ever be a 'home'? After attending his friend's wedding, Barfoot 'had no inclination to go home, if the empty flat could be dignified with such a name' (*Odd Women*, p. 125). In similar vein, for Hugh Carnaby, reluctantly back in London after travelling the world, 'in Oxford and Cambridge Mansions it cost him a great effort to pretend to be at home' (*Whirlpool*, p. 184). On the downward spiral into poverty, Reardon denigrates his and Amy's flat near Regent's Park: 'Compare what we call our home with that of rich people.' But later, from the perspective of rooms in Islington, their flat had been 'home-like' (*New Grub Street*, pp. 232, 282). For Ida Starr, in her model dwelling:

> It's like having a house of my own. I see nothing of the other people in the building, and feel independent.... I pay only three-and-sixpence a week, and so long as I can earn that, I'm sure at all events of a home, where I can be happy or miserable, as I please. (*Unclassed*, p. 159)

Likewise, for the Hewetts, compared to their previous residence in a basement in King's Cross Road, their shared flat in Farringdon Road Buildings constituted 'much more satisfactory quarters'. The flat was on the fifth floor – 'a bit high up, but that don't matter much' (*Nether World*, pp. 199, 245). It seems that the poor could appreciate their flats as 'home' much more easily than the rich.

Marginality

Many of Gissing's flat-dwellers live on the top floor (as Gissing did himself in Cornwall Residences). The Hewetts were on the top floor of Farringdon Road Buildings; and in her Fulham model dwellings 'Ida's number was up at the very top' (*Unclassed*, p. 158). Warburton lived on or immediately below the top floor of his block in Chelsea,[2] and the Reardons, too, were on the top floor of their block. These were pre-penthouse times and there were no lifts in any of these buildings; living at the top meant cheapness and marginality, not wealth and power. Nevertheless, there were some advantages:

> The noise from the street was diminished at this height; no possible tramplers could establish themselves above your head; the air was bound to be purer than that of inferior strata; finally, one had the flat roof whereon to sit or expatiate in sunny weather. (*New Grub Street*, p. 76)

The necessity of ascending or descending several flights of, usually, bare stone stairs could also be used to powerful dramatic effect. On Alma's and Harvey's arrival at Oxford and Cambridge Mansions for their critical meeting with the Carnabys at the end of *The Whirlpool*, Alma first 'found the ascent too much for her'. Harvey urged rest 'But Alma hastened upwards' (pp. 438–9). And at the end of the confrontation,

She rose without help, and walked to a mirror, at which she arranged her dress. Harvey opened the door, and found all quiet. He led her *through* the passage, *out* into the common staircase, and *down* into the street. (p. 443, my emphases)

When the Reardons first argue about Edwin's inability to finish writing his latest novel, there is a ritual, processional quality about the way he 'took his hat and stick and descended the eight flights of stone steps, and walked in the darkness round the outer circle of Regent's Park'; and as Amy listens out for his return, 'Yes, a footstep, briskly mounting the stone stairs. Not like that of the postman. A visitor, perhaps, to the other flat on the top-most landing. But the final pause was in this direction, and then came a sharp rat-tat at the door.' Amy opens the door to find Jasper Milvain with 'his urban silk hat' (*New Grub Street*, pp. 86, 100).

The illusion of modern simplicity

Several female characters enthuse about the modernity and simplicity of life in flats; they perceive flats as a solution to the servant problem; but in practice they stuff their flats full of junk and they continue to have problems with servants. For Mrs Frothingham, in *The Whirlpool*, 'Everything is so easy; things go so smoothly. Just one servant, who can't make mistakes, because there's next to nothing to do. No wonder people are taking to flats' (p. 107). In practice even one good servant was hard to find, as Bevis observed in conversation with Monica:

A place like this must seem to you to be very unhomelike....I suppose it's a retrograde step in civilization. Servants are decidedly of that opinion; we have a great difficulty in getting them to stay here. The reason seems to me that they miss the congenial gossip of the area door. (*Odd Women*, p. 206)

This was a viewpoint that contradicted the fear of moralists that there was *too much* scope for gossip among the servants of adjacent flats. Other servants, like Warburton's Mrs Hopper, were non-resident: 'she came at stated hours' (*Warburton*, p. 7), much like Gissing's own servant, Mrs King, at Cornwall Residences. The Reardons have a 'maid-servant, recently emancipated from the Board school', who 'came at half-past seven each morning, and remained until two o'clock' (*New Grub Street*, p. 77). While it is hard to find out about such employees, the census for Cornwall Residences enumerated several *resident* teenage domestics: in both 1881 and 1891 there were two 15-year-old general servants living in households in Cornwall Residences, with several more aged 16–19.[3] In Oxford and Cambridge Mansions, the Carnabys appear to have several staff: on Alma's first visit she observes 'a small page, very smartly equipped'; later, there are references to 'the servant', 'the maid-servant', 'the housemaid', 'a servant', and 'the same servant' (which might be taken to imply that there was more than one) (*Whirlpool*, pp. 177, 232, 269, 296, 311, 318). At the real Oxford and Cambridge Mansions, in 1891, 11 households had no live-in servants, 35 had 1, 14 had 2, and 2 households had 3 resident servants each.[4]

If flats did not put an end to the 'servant problem', neither were they associated with simplicity. While Ida Starr had 'nothing in the way of furniture beyond the most indispensable articles' (*Unclassed*, p. 158), and the Hewetts, thanks to Sidney Kirkwood's philanthropy, benefited from the basics of simple living – 'Oil-cloth on the floor, a blind at the window, a bedstead, a table, a chest of drawers' (*Nether World*, p. 200) – most middle-class flats in Gissing's novels embody the vulgarity of their occupants. Beatrice French's flat in Brixton displayed 'as much fashionable upholstery and bric-à-brac as could be squeezed into the narrow space' (*Jubilee*, p. 275). In Mrs Luke Widdowson's more lavish flat in Victoria, 'Costly and beautiful things superabounded; perfume soothed the air.' Mrs Widdowson displayed a 'taste for modern exuberance in domestic adornment' (*Odd Women*, pp. 117–18). Much the same could be said about the Carnabys' flat in Oxford and Cambridge Mansions: 'Here was no demonstration of the simple life; things beautiful and luxurious filled all available space, and indeed over-filled it' (*Whirlpool*, p. 172). When Alma revisits the flat later in the novel she finds that 'The drawing-room was changed; it had been refurnished, and looked even more luxurious than formerly' (p. 414), an observation that seems to confirm the amorality of flat-dwellers: how could Sibyl go on consuming and accumulating while her husband was in prison?

Promiscuous spaces

Flats were dishonest spaces associated with intrigue. Beatrice acknowledged the smallness of her bedroom, 'adding archly, "But I sleep single." ' Her sister was less sure: 'She lives alone in a flat, and has men to spend every evening with her; it's disgraceful' (*Jubilee*, pp. 275, 319). For Mrs Luke Widdowson, wealthy but craving a title, the principal function of her flat was to catch eligible men: 'her flat in Victoria Street attracted a hetero-geneous cluster of pleasure-seekers and fortune-hunters, among them one or two vagrant members of the younger aristocracy. She lived at the utmost pace compatible with technical virtue' (*Odd Women*, p. 118). When Monica visits the Bevises, she finds (Mr) Bevis on his own, with not even a servant to act as chaperone. Gissing comments that:

> As regards social propriety, a flat differs in many respects from a house. In an ordinary drawing-room, it could scarcely have mattered if Bevis enter-tained her for a short space until his sisters' arrival; but in this little set of rooms it was doubtfully permissible for her to sit *tête-à-tête* with a young man, under any excuse. (p. 206)[5]

The problem of flats, as noted earlier, was how to separate activities which 'ought' to be kept apart. This was compounded in a small flat, like the Reardons, where, when Edwin was using the front room as his study, Amy was obliged to receive visitors in the kitchen-cum-dining-room-cum-parlour:

> and then the servant had to be disposed of by sending her into the bedroom to take care of Willie. Privacy, in the strict sense, was impossible, for the servant might listen at the door (one room led out of the other) to all the conversation that went on. (*New Grub Street*, p. 165)

Among families with lower expectations, it was easier to rearrange the space. The Eagles squeeze themselves into one room, 'so encumbered with furniture that not more than eight or ten square feet of floor can have been available for movement' (*Nether World*, p. 241). John Hewett and his young son sleep in the second (middle) room, where the family also take their meals, and the two young Hewett girls occupy the third room. When Clara arrives she has to share with her much younger sisters, although her father phrases things the other way round: 'Clara – shall you mind Amy and Annie comin' to sleep here? If you'd rather, we'll manage it somehow else' (p. 244). In practice, Clara stayed in the third room most of the time: she and Mrs Eagles 'scarcely saw more of each other than if they had lived in different tenements on the same staircase' (p. 273).

It was not only the layout and uses of rooms within flats but the organisation of 'common parts' which added to a sense of duplicity. This is most evident in *The Odd Women*, when the private detective hired by Monica's husband does not bother to follow her into the Bayswater block of flats a second time but assumes she is going to visit Barfoot because he has previously observed her knocking on the door of Barfoot's flat. In fact, she is visiting Bevis, and had only previously knocked on Barfoot's door when she was afraid that she might be observed at the door to Bevis's flat. Confident that Barfoot was not at home, she had known it was safe to knock on his door (*Odd Women*, pp. 246–8)!

The gendering of flats

Flats are part of the threat posed by women's liberation, whether women in their own flats (Beatrice French, Mrs Widdowson, Sibyl Carnaby – it really is her flat, not Hugh's); women reacting to having to live in a less than perfect flat (Clara Hewett, Amy Reardon); or women visiting men in flats (Monica Widdowson). The least feminised of Gissing's flats is Will Warburton's. Male characters who live alone in flats treat them in much the same way that Tarrant in *In The Year of Jubilee* or Earwaker in *Born in Exile* use their rooms in Staple Inn. When Earwaker resolves to live in his 'chambers' at Staple Inn for the rest of his life, he explains that 'The new flats are insufferable. How can one live sandwiched between a music-hall singer and a female politician?' (*Born in Exile*, p. 345). This perhaps reflects Gissing's own experience of the mixture of people to be found in Cornwall Residences where, in 1891 (just after Gissing's departure), female heads included 12 'living on own means' (in 1881 their equivalents had been recorded as 'annuitants' and 'railway shareholders'), and also an actress, two singers, two teachers, and the manageress of a milliner's shop.

'Those Farringdon Road Buildings'

Most of the flats Gissing mentions remain anonymous. Brixton, Bayswater, Chelsea, and Victoria had numerous blocks of flats by the 1880s. But Oxford and Cambridge Mansions and Farringdon Road Buildings were both real buildings and, as an urban geographer, I cannot help speculating why Gissing chose these particular buildings. For the remainder of this chapter, therefore, I will concentrate on these two sets of buildings and also on Gissing's own flat in Cornwall Residences. Was he simply transferring his own experience of flat-living onto other buildings, and what might he (and his readers) have known about Farringdon Road Buildings, Oxford and Cambridge Mansions, and the neighbourhoods in which they were situated?

Gissing could not have failed to notice Farringdon Road Buildings on his visits to Clerkenwell while researching for *The Nether World*. They had been erected in 1874 by the Metropolitan Association for Improving the Dwellings of the Industrious Classes, one of the oldest philanthropic housing agencies in London (Tarn, 1973, pp. 97–8). As a series of five parallel blocks at right angles to the street, their layout was more visible to the outsider than either Corporation Buildings just across the street, where the courtyard was hidden from view and the mass of housing was tempered by a continuous row of shops at ground-floor level and elaborate iron balconies, or the Peabody estate at Pear Tree Court just to the south, one of the Cross Act slum clearance sites which the Peabody Trust acquired from the Metropolitan Board of Works in 1879.[6] Corporation Buildings were too old for Gissing's purposes – they dated from 1865 – and too unlike the barrack- or workhouse-style architecture that characterised many model dwellings, while the Peabody estate was too new, completed only in 1884, after the period in which most of the novel was set. Moreover, it is unlikely that the Peabody Trust would have allowed the Eagles and the Hewetts to share one flat. In fact, the 1891 census returns indicate an absence of sharing among unrelated households, even in Farringdon Road Buildings. Of 247 households, three took in one 'lodger' each, one included a 'boarder', and three more accommodated a total of four 'visitors'. There were certainly some three-generational (children–parents–grandparents) households, and some nephews and nieces among the residents, but for the most part, each flat housed a nuclear family.[7]

The Eagles–Hewett household comprised initially six and later (when Clara returned) seven people, living in three rooms on the fifth floor. Their rent would have been about 7s per week. John Hewett's wages were 25s per week (*The Builder* 32, 1874, pp. 1003–4; *Nether World*, p. 199), several shillings above Charles Booth's poverty line of 21s per week for a family with two children. The Hewetts were not among the poorest of the poor, and in this respect they resembled their neighbours: the Buildings were shaded in the fourth of seven classes – 'mixed, some comfortable, others poor' – on the 1889 edition of Charles Booth's poverty map (Reeder, 1987).

Seven people in three rooms was spot on the average for Farringdon Road Buildings, which in 1891 accommodated 1230 persons in 524 rooms (2.35 persons per room), although this average disguised a reality in which some flats were underoccupied and others grossly overcrowded: up to 6 people in 1 room, 12 in 3 rooms. What especially stands out is the number of small children: 339 aged 0–9, of whom 33 were less than 12 months old. Between parallel blocks, each 67 feet high, were 'spacious area[s]' 20 feet wide which served as playgrounds (*The Builder* 32, 1874, p. 393). Imagine the high-pitched noise that must have echoed around these canyons. No wonder that 'The yells of children at play in the courtyard tortured [Clara's] nerves' (*Nether World*, p. 274).

Farringdon Road Buildings were noted for their semi-private balconies, shared between pairs of flats on each landing. The balconies were commended by their architect as places where small children could play under the watchful eyes of parents or older siblings, and where cultivation and display of flowers could aid the conversion of 'dwellings' into 'homes'; but they were disparaged by critics who lamented the loss of light and ventilation to sculleries and toilets set back in the shade created by overhanging balconies, and who also feared disputes between neighbours over the use of shared space (*Building News* 27, 1874, p. 652; *The Builder* 32, 1874, p. 1056; *The Builder* 34, 1876, pp. 583–4) (Figure 2.2). This comparatively private character of the Farringdon Road Buildings' balconies contrasts with a popular image of tenement staircases and balconies overflowing with 'groups of gossiping women' (Ryan, 1990, pp. 225–6) and makes it more plausible to imagine Clara contemplating suicide: 'Had not this place tempted other people before now?' (*Nether World*, p. 275). However, it is also clear that Gissing assumed the balcony *was* on the public staircase, as it was in most blocks of model dwellings, such as those built by the Improved Industrial Dwellings Company (Tarn, 1968). For Gissing, Clara's privacy and isolation was a consequence of living at the top of the building, where the only passing traffic would have been the occasional housewife on her way to or from the roof to hang out or retrieve her washing.

For the most part, contemporaries praised the Farringdon Road Buildings. Twenty years after they opened, they still attracted the commendation of

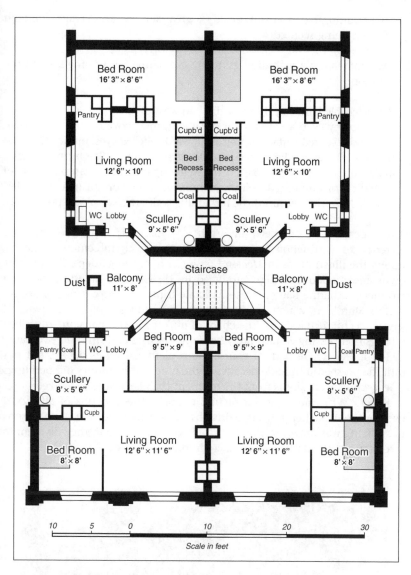

Figure 2.2 Farringdon Road Buildings: Floor plans; redrawn from plans in *The Builder* 32 (December 1874) and Bowmaker (1895)

housing reformer, Edward Bowmaker (1895, p. 94), who explained that the 'through passages and staircases':

> materially assist ventilation and admirably provide for isolation.... The w.c. is entered from the lobby, each tenant having separate accommodation.

This building has been financially a great success, an average dividend of 6 p.c. being secured.

Yet we remember the buildings today primarily for Gissing's damning description:

> What terrible barracks, those Farringdon Road Buildings! Vast, sheer walls, unbroken by even an attempt at ornament; row above row of windows in the mud-coloured surface, upwards, upwards, lifeless eyes, murky openings that tell of bareness, disorder, comfortlessness within.... Pass by in the night, and strain imagination to picture the weltering mass of human weariness, of bestiality, of unmerited dolour, of hopeless hope, of crushed surrender, tumbled together within those forbidding walls. (*Nether World*, pp. 273–4)

This evocation of 'modern deformity'[8] remarkably prefigures another reference to Farringdon Road Buildings in the architectural literature. Among the illustrations in *Modern Housing*, a hymn to garden suburbs, new towns and moder*nist* design produced in 1934 by the American housing reformer, Catherine Bauer, is a remarkable triptych, 'Three Kinds of Metropolitan Slum', in which Farringdon Road Buildings appear sandwiched between 'central chaos' and 'the chaos of uncontrolled expansion', described in terms that Gissing would surely have endorsed: 'a built-in slum'. To Bauer (1934, p. 14), 'There had, of course, been plenty of slums before, but not until the prosperous middle decades of the nineteenth century did buildings appear which were slums from the moment the plans were conceived or set on paper.' Why Bauer (or her picture editor) settled on this of all model dwellings to make her point remains obscure – perhaps for the same reasons that Gissing was drawn to them. In their geometric rigour, they do seem to have been a particularly dispiriting environment (Figure 2.3).

Figure 2.3   Farringdon Road Buildings (from a contempory illustration, source unknown, previously reproduced in C. Bauer, *Modern Housing*)

'Aristocratic flats'

Oxford and Cambridge Mansions also attracted some notable illustrations. The flats were erected in stages between 1879 and 1882, to be followed during 1883 and 1884 by the even more luxurious Hyde Park Mansions.[9] *The Builder* (44, 1883, p. 144) published a perspective illustration, remarkable for playing down the buildings' modernity, emphasising their architectural eclecticism and their domesticity, and eliminating the most distinctive feature, the acute angle on the corner of Marylebone Road and Lisson Street (now Old Marylebone Road and Transept Street). A later illustration, in an advertising brochure of c.1910–12, gives a completely different view, almost too desperate to stress the building's enduring modernity.[10] But *The Builder* certainly, if unintentionally, captured the pretentiousness and fussiness of decorative detail which made Oxford and Cambridge Mansions an appropriate home for the Carnabys. The 'workings' of the flats are best illustrated by some later plans, produced in the 1930s, which differentiate between 'drawing room', 'dining room', 'best bedroom' and what, by then, was a 'morning room' beyond the kitchen but which, in the 1880s, would have been the maid's bedroom (Figure 2.4).[11] In this way Eales had attempted to implement his ideas about segregating different activities and different classes, though he thought it preferable to exclude some people, such as children, altogether: 'It was most disagreeable to be always meeting them on the stairs' (*The Builder* 46, 1884, p. 386). Fortunately, most residents of Oxford and Cambridge Mansions were childless, just like the Carnabys. Only 5 per cent of the Mansions' population were aged 0–9 in 1891, compared to 28 per cent of inhabitants in Farringdon Road Buildings.

The Carnabys had just returned from Honolulu and Queensland. The residents of Oxford and Cambridge Mansions in 1891 counted Jamaica, Tasmania, Calcutta, the Punjab, Cairo, Cape Colony, Buffalo, and Niagara among their places of birth. European birthplaces also featured prominently: Denmark, Holland, Rotterdam, Oporto, Paris, Dresden, Augsburg, Hamburg, Luxembourg, Belgium, and Boulogne. Among a population barely 200-strong (including servants), this was a substantial colonial and continental representation, the more so since it omits people like William H. White, whose birthplace was in Sussex despite his experience of life in Paris and Bengal.

Even more than at Cornwall Residences, there was an impressive number of female-headed households in the Mansions: 46 per cent in 1891. Most female heads were older than the 'new women' of Gissing's stories or of his own acquaintance, like Edith Sichel, who lived in an even grander flat in Barkston Mansions, Earl's Court (*Letters*, 4, p. 138; *Diary*, p. 170). In 1891 the only female heads with occupations listed in the census were a 26-year-old 'vocalist' and a 52-year-old 'journalist'. By 1901

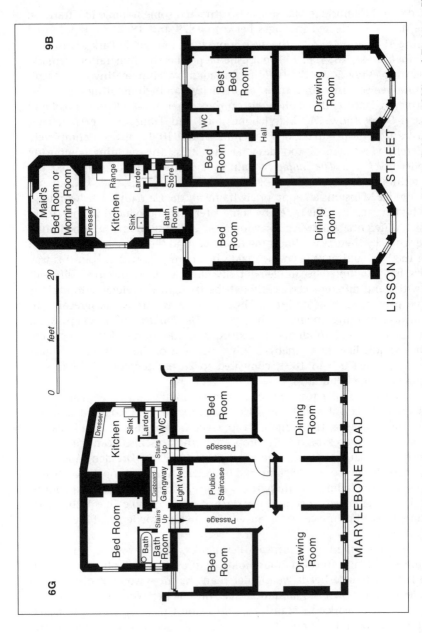

Figure 2.4 Oxford and Cambridge Mansions: Floor plans; based on information in *The Builder* 44 (February 1883) and Drainage Plans (c.1927), Westminster Archives Centre

the occupations of eight female heads were recorded, including 'hair specialist', 'private secretary', 'court dressmaker', 'theological bookseller', 'certified hospital nurse', and – especially pertinent to the theme of *The Whirlpool* – three professional musicians.[12]

Gissing would have been familiar with Oxford and Cambridge Mansions from his six years in Cornwall Residences. His regular route to cafes on Edgware Road, and his occasional visits to restaurants in Chapel Street, would have taken him close to, if not directly past, the flats (*Diary*, pp. 29, 142, 144, 151). In August 1889 he dined in Chapel Street with his sister, Margaret, prior to their departure for the Channel Islands. Two months later, Gissing wrote to tell her that 'Next week I am to make the acquaintance of a family of Roberts's friends, – some people who live in one of the aristocratic flats I showed you near Edgware Road. They have a Shaksperian reading society' (*Diary*, p. 160; *Letters*, 4, p. 129). These were the Fennessys, who lived at 6E, Hyde Park Mansions, one of the grandest flats in the whole complex.

'A place of extraordinary gloom'

By comparison with Farringdon Road Buildings and Oxford and Cambridge Mansions, there are few historical references to Cornwall Residences apart from those provided by Gissing himself or by Roberts in *The Private Life of Henry Maitland*.[13] They were erected in stages, as a succession of 'houses' much as Oxford and Cambridge Mansions were, between 1872 and 1875, on the sliver of land left between the Metropolitan Railway's Baker Street Station and the Nash terraces facing onto Regent's Park.[14] Gissing's flat, 7K, was on the top floor of no. 7, erected between March and July 1872. The builder, Nicholas Fabyan Daw, retained ownership at least as late as 1895, but by 1908 the buildings had been acquired by the Metropolitan Railway and, in an inter-war expansion of the station, the southernmost 'houses' were demolished to make way for Chiltern Court, luxury flats whose first occupants included both Arnold Bennett and H.G. Wells (Jackson, 1986).

As originally built, two flats opened off each staircase on each floor. A plan survives for Flat 9D, dated 1932–33, when the Metropolitan Railway was planning to convert each suite into two bed-sitters, and it is possible to match the pre-alteration version to the descriptions of 7K in Gissing's letters and of the Reardons' flat in *New Grub Street*: three rooms, a kitchen/dining-room and scullery at the back of the flat, a bedroom at the front which opened into the kitchen, and a front room (used by Reardon as his study) which opened off the entrance passage (Figure 2.5).[15] Roberts (1958, p. 60) noted that Maitland's flat 'had at least two rooms and a kitchen. Yet it was a place of extraordinary gloom, and its back windows overlooked the roaring steam engines of the Metropolitan Railway.' This was some exaggeration: no doubt, from Gissing's top-floor vantage-point it was possible to look down

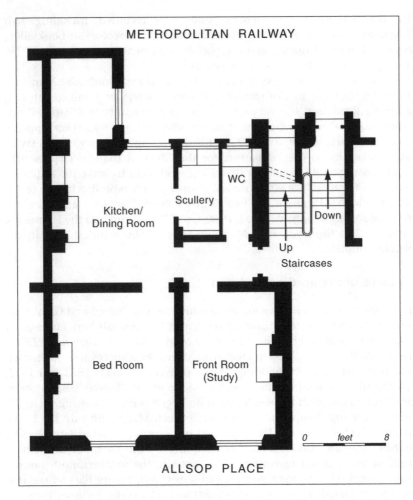

Figure 2.5 Cornwall Resisdences: Floor plan; based on information in Drainage Plans (1933), Westminster Archives Centre

into the station, but there was space for another building between the back of Cornwall Residences and the railway tracks. Nonetheless, Gissing himself acknowledged how 'Everybody draws attention to the fact that the fumes of Baker Street Station must be poisonous, & I daresay there is something in that' (*Letters*, 3, p. 189). James Gaussen, who lodged with Gissing for several months in 1885, and whose mother had arranged its rental in the first place, recalled (but some 70 years later) the absence of a bathroom and the 'dimly lit stone staircases', which led him to 'fancy this must have been one of the first Artisans' Flats built' (Curtis, 1976, p. 4). Alfred Gissing's reference to 'a flat roof immediately above him, upon which he sometimes sat of a summer evening' (Coustillas and Petremand, 1994, p. 11) reinforces the impression of model dwellings (where flat roofs were used to hang out washing to dry). Yet while the description resembles Farringdon Road Buildings or an Improved Industrial Dwellings Company estate, neither the rent nor the characteristics of the tenants suggested artisanal status.

At Cornwall Residences, Gissing's male neighbours included a Catholic priest, retired army officers, a Royal Navy captain, barristers, solicitors, secretaries and clerks, a composer, various travellers and agents, but hardly anybody directly engaged in 'trade'. By comparison, at Farringdon Road Buildings almost everybody was working class, from general labourers and a sewer-sweeper to an artisan élite of printers, bookbinders, and instrument makers. Three clerks at Farringdon Road Buildings (among a total of 207 male heads whose occupations were recorded) were all simply 'clerks', but at Cornwall Residences clerical workers mostly held specific appointments: 'MP's secretary', 'banker's clerk', 'hospital secretary', 'clerk HM Patent Office'.[16]

Gissing's rent at 7K was £10 per quarter, equivalent to just over 15 shillings per week, or roughly twice the rent of three rooms in Farringdon Road Buildings (*Letters* 2, p. 272).[17] This matches the difference in rateable values – Gissing's flat was rated at £22, while 3-roomed flats in Farringdon Road Buildings were mostly rated at £12–13.[18] By comparison, the rateable value of the Fennessys' flat in Hyde Park Mansions was £84, and rateable values at Oxford and Cambridge Mansions were mostly between £40 and £80, implying rents of £75–150 per annum. When Gissing contemplated letting his own flat, furnished, he asked for '60 guineas a year, – very little too' (*Letters* 3, p. 244). By contrast, in April 1894, furnished flats to let in Hyde Park Mansions were being advertised at 4½ guineas per week for 4 bedrooms, dining room and drawing room, and an apparently extortionate '10 guineas per week or £300 a year' for 'a lofty and light ground floor SUITE', with the same number of rooms. Similar sized flats elsewhere on Marylebone Road were offered at 3½ guineas and 5 guineas per week (furnished), or £120 per annum unfurnished for a 4-year lease for a 4-bedroom flat 'approached by lift' and £150 per annum for 'a capital 1st floor suite, fitted with electric light'.[19]

'Buildings – Mansions – Flats – Residences – Dwellings'

Even if Cornwall Residences was already far from the 'model dwellings' end of the market, management aspired to a higher status: 'Amusing piece of flunkeyism. Tonight comes a circular from Lane [the manager], informing me that henceforth "Cornwall Residences" will be "Cornwall Mansions"' (*Letters*, 3, p. 228). Despite Gissing's disdain for the new name, and his continued use of 'Residences' in letters to family and close friends, he was not above using 'Mansions' when writing to people he wished to impress, such as Edith Sichel (*Letters*, 4, pp. 113, 127). The choice of title was critical in class-conscious late Victorian London. *The Builder* (36, 1878, pp. 31–2) entitled one essay '"Buildings" – "Mansions" – "Flats" – "Residences" – "Dwellings"'. In E.M. Forster's *Howards End* (1983, pp. 59–61, 67–8) the Wilcoxes take a suite in 'Wickham Mansions' while Leonard Bast occupies a 'semi-basement' in 'Block B' of a group of South London dwellings. 'Buildings' invariably signified philanthropic or council housing, whereas 'mansions' were private, middle and upper class. But there was a constant upward pressure on terminology, as 'mansions' was adopted by down-market speculative builders, in much the same way that 'park' became the label for every aspirant suburban estate. There were two more Cornwall Mansions, both in Kensington; one a group of genuine if rather vulgar 'mansions' – houses not flats – the other a block of luxury flats (similar to Hyde Park Mansions).[20] When the latter were about to open, residents of the former, 'finding that the word is now applied to less than ultra-select blocks of residences,... petitioned the Kensington Council to change the name to Cornwall-place' (*Daily Chronicle*, 17 June 1901). The author of a 1905 guide to flats concluded that 'the word "Mansion" has long ceased to convey the idea of a mansion, and when "Gardens" are referred to, few people expect to see a garden' (Perks, 1905, p. 204). The block in which *Will Warburton* begins was clearly the real Chelsea Gardens (and at this stage Warburton was sufficiently well-off to afford a comfortable mansion flat), yet Chelsea Gardens was merely one of the grander developments of the Improved Industrial Dwellings Company, the largest of the '5 per cent' model dwellings companies. But the blocks facing onto Ranelagh Gardens were only part of the company's estate at Chelsea Bridge. Go round the back and you find the parallel, but more modestly labelled Wellington Buildings.[21]

Conclusion

In this essay, I have tried to 'go round the back' of some of the buildings that Gissing wrote about. It is a remarkable coincidence that he should have chosen to position his characters in two of the best documented blocks of flats in late Victorian London. I am left with the sense that Gissing did transfer his own experience of living in Cornwall Residences onto his account of Farringdon Road Buildings. Yet while many of the flats in both buildings were three-roomed, approached up bare, stone staircases, their social and demographic environments could not have been more different. At Cornwall Residences 40 per cent of households were headed by women, at Farringdon Road 15 per cent. At Cornwall Residences, there were between two and three residents per flat, at Farringdon Road Buildings, more than five, and in three-roomed flats, more than six. At Cornwall Residences there were hardly any children; at Farringdon Road Buildings there were children everywhere. The figures for Cornwall Residences may have been diminished by the absence of some residents on Census Day, away on business, staying with friends or family, or even at another home in the country. But that in itself emphasises the difference between the two buildings, one occupied by a cosmopolitan population able to come and go, to escape the London heat or the London fog, the other 'confined to barracks'.

One last set of statistics is worth contemplating, for it returns us to the perception that flat-dwellers were 'nomads' or transients. It is hard to track the mobility of Farringdon Road Buildings residents. Unlike mansion-flat occupants, their names never appeared in directories. Fortunately, ratebooks for the area were well maintained, and names of male householders also appear in electoral registers. Taking a time period roughly comparable with the time Gissing spent in Cornwall Residences (1884–91), we find that about one in eight of males on the electoral roll for Farringdon Road Buildings in 1884 were still at the same address in 1891 while as many again had moved flats but remained within the Buildings. In total, just over a quarter were still to be found somewhere on the estate seven years on. By comparison, less than one in five household heads in the 1891 census for Oxford and Cambridge Mansions had been there seven years earlier, and fewer than one in ten heads at Cornwall Residences had remained as long.

It may be objected that Farringdon Road Buildings was a sufficiently large estate to offer opportunities for moving between flats whereas, if mansion-flat tenants decided to move, they had little choice but to go elsewhere. Indeed, at least two of the first residents of Oxford and Cambridge Mansions had moved from Cornwall Residences.[22] Nevertheless, the consequence was that the population of the model dwellings was rather more stable than that of the mansion flats. The numbers who moved flats within the estate imply a potential for community that contradicts Gissing's damning indictment of 'those Farringdon Road Buildings'. Moreover, Ryecroft's condemnation of 'flat-inhabiting nomads' perhaps reflects Gissing's experience of an unusually nomadic set of neighbours in Cornwall Residences. Yet these differences do also confirm the fears and hopes of contemporaries. Model dwellings were meant to 'fix' their inhabitants, to put an end to 'flitting' from one 'rookery' to the next, the kind of behaviour so graphically depicted in *The Nether World*. Residents of model dwellings were supposed to be *less* transient than their poverty-stricken neighbours. But residents of mansion flats were thought to be *more* transient than their middle-class neighbours, so flats were perceived as threatening the geographical as well as the social stability of middle-class metropolitan society. A model dwelling could, in time, become a 'home'; a middle-class flat could not.

As for Gissing's personal 'prejudice against flats'? Flat-living represented metropolitan life in its purest, most concentrated form, in which there is most potential for social intercourse and most probability of social isolation. It is unsurprising that a man of Gissing's sensitivity, who longed to escape London yet depended on the place for his inspiration, could never be comfortable anywhere for very long. He confessed his ideal in a letter to Eduard Bertz, written soon after Gissing's second marriage and move to Exeter:

> This matter of a dwelling-place is very troublesome for people in our position; we are for ever at the mercy of ignoble creatures, & are forced to live in their hateful proximity. Surely there ought to be *Colleges* for unmarried intellectual men (or even for married of small means,) where we could dwell much as students do at the University. . . . Who will advocate 'Literary Homes'? (*Letters*, 4, p. 288)

Gissing's ideal residence was not so very far from being a flat, a serviced flat to be sure, in a community of like-minded people who would know when to be quiet and when to be sociable, a block of bachelor flats, with no Beatrice Frenches claiming bachelor status, no Amy Reardons or Sibyl Carnabys disrupting the status quo, with a man-servant supplanting or at least supplementing the Mrs Hoppers. It seems that at least part of Gissing's 'prejudice against flats' was rooted in, not his prejudice against, but certainly his discomfort with, women.[23]

Notes

1. Kelly's Directories indicate that White moved from 23 Bedford Street, Covent Garden, to 8B, Oxford and Cambridge Mansions, some time in 1881. For Eales' association with both Oxford and Cambridge Mansions and neighbouring Hyde Park Mansions, see *The Builder*, 44 (1883), pp. 140, 144–5; 45 (1883), p. 144; 49 (1885), p. 532.
2. The real 'Chelsea Gardens' which occupies the site specified by Gissing is a mixture of five- and six-storey buildings, so Warburton was, at the very least, within one floor of the top.
3. Census enumerators' books, RG11/157, 42–5 (1881), RG12/101, 73–6 (1891). 'Cornwall Residences' became 'Cornwall Mansions' in July 1888 but, like Gissing, I have chosen to use its original title.
4. Census enumerators' books, RG12/99, 94–8 (1891). For further analysis, see Dennis (2001).
5. Compare Edith Wharton's observation (1974, p. 27) about Mrs Mingott's domestic arrangements, 'which recalled scenes in French fiction, and architectural incentives to immorality such as the simple American had never dreamed of'.
6. On Corporation Buildings, see *The Builder*, 23 (1865), p. 484; *The Times*, 10 March 1866; on Pear Tree Court, see Peabody Trust Annual Reports for 1879, 1883, 1884: London Metropolitan Archives (LMA).
7. Census enumerators' books, RG12/225, 71–94 (1891).
8. Gissing's phrase for the redeveloped area south of Farringdon Road Buildings (*Nether World*, p. 280) seems equally appropriate for the Buildings themselves.
9. District Surveyor's Returns, St Marylebone North, 1879–82: LMA MBW 1683, 100, 1709. Of the 12 'houses' comprising Oxford and Cambridge Mansions,

nos 3–7 were occupied by Census Day in April 1881; all 12 were listed as occupied in Kelly's Directory for 1883 (compiled in late 1882).

10. Consolidated London Properties Ltd, *Residential Flats and Chambers to Let* (c.1912), brochure in Westminster Archives Centre (WAC).
11. Drainage Plans for Oxford and Cambridge Mansions, various flats and dates (1935–38), WAC.
12. For 1901 census, see RG13/115, 39–42.
13. There is a brief, and somewhat confusing, mention in Perks (1905, p. 27), giving the erroneous impression that Cornwall Residences, Clarence Gate and Cornwall Mansions, near Baker Street Station, 'built about 1872', were different buildings.
14. District Surveyor's Returns, St Marylebone North, 1871–74, LMA MBW 1619, 1626, 1634, 1642; Marylebone Ratebooks, 1875–1895, WAC.
15. Drainage Plan for 9D Cornwall Mansions, WAC.
16. Gissing refers several times in his letters to the popular composer, Procida Bucalossi, who lived in the flat beneath him. On Census Day, 1891, Flats 7A–D, 7J and 7L were all unoccupied. Gissing's successors at 7K were a 42-year-old solicitor and his wife. Presumably this was the man who subsequently committed suicide, as Gissing learnt from the manager of the flats (*Diary*, p. 314). The Royal Navy captain was Charles Gissing, 'a pleasant fellow' (*Diary*, p. 232).
17. In addition, Gissing paid Mrs King 2/6 per week (later increased to 4/- and then 5/-) to attend for two hours daily to do his cleaning (*Letters*, 2, pp. 292, 358; 3, p. 213).
18. Ratebooks for Farringdon Road in Islington Archives.
19. '*Flatland' Register of Flats* . . . (April 1894), advertising brochure in Museum of London. Note the convention of advertising unfurnished in pounds, but furnished flats in guineas.
20. Gissing must have known about the élite Cornwall Mansions, since they formed part of Cornwall Gardens where Lady Revill had her London home in *Sleeping Fires* (1895).
21. Chelsea Gardens and Wellington Buildings were erected in 1878. The former comprised 104 flats of between 4 and 6 rooms; the latter had 151 flats, mostly 3 or 4 rooms. In other words, many of the flats owned by a limited dividend, '5 per cent' company, were larger than Gissing's flat at Cornwall Residences.
22. Captain James Le Messurier and Miss Mary Phillpotts, both resident in 3, Oxford and Cambridge Mansions in 1881 were listed in the London Court Directory for 1881 (reflecting their address in late 1880) as resident at 13 Allsop Place (the official postal address of Cornwall Residences).
23. I am grateful to The Drawing Office, Department of Geography, University College London, for their preparation of the illustrations to this chapter.

Bibliography

Bauer, C. *Modern Housing* (Boston MA: Houghton Mifflin, 1934).

Bowmaker, E. *The Housing of the Working Classes* (London: Methuen, 1895).

Coustillas, P. ed., *London and the Life of Literature in Late Victorian England: The Diary of George Gissing, Novelist* (Hassocks: The Harvester Press, 1978).

Coustillas, P. and Petremand, X. 'London homes and haunts of George Gissing: An unpublished essay by A.C. Gissing', *The Gissing Journal*, 30 (2) (1994) 1–14.

Curtis, A. 'Gissing and the Gaussens: Some unpublished documents', *The Gissing Newsletter*, 12 (4) (1976) 1–6.

Daunton, M.J. *A Property-Owning Democracy? Housing in Britain* (London: Faber and Faber, 1987).

Dennis, R. 'Reconciling geographies, representing modernities' in Black, I.S. and Butlin, R.A., eds, *Place, Culture and Identity* (Quebec: Laval University Press, 2001), pp. 17–43.

Felstead, A., Franklin, J. and Pinfield, L. *Directory of British Architects 1834–1900* (London: Mansell, 1993).

Forster, E.M. *Howards End* (Harmondsworth: Penguin, 1983) (orig. 1910).

Gissing, G. *The Nether World* (London: Everyman, 1973) (orig. 1889).

——. *New Grub Street* (Harmondsworth: Penguin, 1968) (orig. 1891).

——. *Born in Exile* (London: Everyman, 1993) (orig. 1892).

——. *The Odd Women* (London: Virago, 1980) (orig. 1893).

——. *In The Year of Jubilee* (London: Everyman, 1994) (orig. 1894).

——. *The Unclassed* (Hassocks: The Harvester Press, 1976) (orig. 1884, 1895).

——. *The Whirlpool* (London: Hogarth Press, 1984) (orig. 1897).

——. *The Town Traveller* (London: Methuen, 1956) (orig. 1898).

——. *The Private Papers of Henry Ryecroft* (Brighton: The Harvester Press, 1982) (orig. 1903).

——. *Will Warburton* (London: Hogarth Press, 1985) (orig. 1905).

Jackson, A.A. *London's Metropolitan Railway* (Newton Abbot: David and Charles, 1986).

Perks, S. *Residential Flats of All Classes* (London: Batsford, 1905).

Mattheisen, P.F., Young, A.C. and Coustillas, P., eds, *The Collected Letters of George Gissing* (Athens, Ohio: Ohio University Press, 1991–3).

Reeder, D., ed., *Charles Booth's Descriptive Map of London Poverty 1889* (London: London Topographical Society, 1987).

Roberts, M. *The Private Life of Henry Maitland* (London: Richards Press, 1958) (orig. 1912, 1923).

Ryan, P.F.W. 'From London tenement to London mansion' in *Edwardian London Volume 4* (London: Village Press, 1990), pp. 224–30, reprinted from Sims, G.R. (ed.) *Living London* (London: Cassell, 1902).

Smith, T.R. and White, W.H. 'Model dwellings for the rich', *The British Architect and Northern Engineer*, 5 (1876) 156–8.

Tarn, J.N. 'The Improved Industrial Dwellings Co.', *Transactions of the London and Middlesex Archaeological Society*, 22 (1968) 43–59.

Tarn, J.N. 'French flats for the English in nineteenth-century London' in Sutcliffe, A. (ed) *Multi-Storey Living* (London: Croom Helm, 1974), pp. 19–40.

Tarn, J.N. *Five Per Cent Philanthropy* (Cambridge: Cambridge University Press, 1973).

Watson, I. *Westminster and Pimlico Past* (London: Historical Publications, 1993).

Wharton, E. *The Age of Innocence* (Harmondsworth: Penguin, 1974) (orig. 1920).

White, W.H. 'Middle-class houses in Paris and central London', *The Builder*, 35 (1877) 1166–70.

3
Gissing's *Saturnalia*: Urban Crowds, Carnivalesque Subversion and the Crisis of Paternal Authority

Luisa Villa

Visions of the city, visions of the crowd

The writing of this chapter was provoked, first of all, by the perception of the excitement and energy that Gissing's prose repeatedly exhibits in conjunction with descriptions of contemporary urban malaise as epitomised by unruly urban multitudes. Such excitement and energy deeply conflict with the censorious slant of Gissing's crowd scenes, and, in so doing, they inevitably bring to the forefront the question of the author's ambivalent attitude towards modernity, the 'paradox' – as William Greenslade (2001, p. 271) so aptly put it – of a novelist who 'write[s] so memorably about what he affects to despise'.

One way of approaching this ambivalence, while specifically connecting it to urban spaces and urban crowds, is provided by two well-known critics and by their deeply contrasting visions of the late Victorian metropolis: John Goode's 'London', rigidly mapped by the processes of urban zoning, where 'space is structured to guarantee the divisions on which it rests' (Goode, 1978, p. 99), and Judith Walkowitz's 'city of dreadful delight', where 'marginalized groups – working men and women of all classes – repeatedly spilled over and out of their ascribed, bounded roles, costumes and locales into the public streets and the wrong parts of the town, engaged on missions of their own' (Walkowitz, 1994, p. 41). Such different images of the city – one strictly departmentalized, the other more dynamic and open to progressive change – have been variously deployed by critics while reading Gissing's urban fiction, and can therefore be taken as authoritative reminders of the conflicting aspects of modernity that impinged upon his narrative imagination. *They* made his London into precisely the paradoxical place it is – a place where women can move about more freely and marginal subjects acquire a new visibility, while at the same time impalpable boundaries (such as those John Goode so forcibly underscored in his reading of *Thyrza* or *The Nether World*) and impersonal norms shape and constrain that newly acquired freedom.[1] Such is the double bind of *fin de siècle* urban modernity, as should be preliminarily brought to mind while tackling Gissing's crowds. Mobs invading public spaces, momentarily erasing distinctions and bridging social distances, stand for the democratic pull which opens up and reconfigures the urban public sphere towards the end of the century. Thus they starkly contrast and significantly disrupt the tendency of Gissing's fiction to reflect and naturalise the processes of urban zoning and urban segregation which were inherent in the transformation of London and which his highly pronounced historical consciousness was all too ready to recognise and inscribe in his fictional topography.

The focus on urban crowds, however, allows for a further, diachronical contextualisation of Gissing's paradoxical attitude within the specific tradition of discursive representation of crowds, as developed in the course of the century from the Romantics (Wordsworth, De Quincey), through prominent Victorian essayists (Carlyle, Bagehot) and social novelists (Dickens, Gaskell, Charlotte Brontë, George Eliot), up to theorists working in the field of nascent scientific sociology, such as Sighele and Fournial, Le Bon and Tarde.[2] It has already been noted that Gissing's crowd scenes belong to this large textual corpus: indeed, they seem to share its characteristic attitudes, first and foremost the idea that 'the crowd produces a peculiarly damaging mode of equality, reducing everyone to its own vulgar level of homogeneity' (Glover, 2001, pp. 140–1). What I intend to underscore in the present chapter is the positive potential inherent in the image of crowds, the way they body forth the very allure of modernity, with its promise of emancipation, its Utopian yearnings, its outrageously excessive desires. As Robert Nye (1995, p. 43) underscores, there are indeed two competing traditions among theorists of the crowd: 'one negative, hyperrationalist and politically conservative, the other sympathetic, committed to exploring non-logical processes and imbued with the spirit of rebellion'. The latter would be taken up later on by the avant-garde and by such radical continental anti-parliamentarians as Sighele and Sorel as well as by social thinkers like Canetti, who saw in the raw, barbarous forces released by the crowd a potential for political and moral regeneration. But one does not need to look forward to the twentieth century to catch a glimpse of such an alternative tradition: it is enough to go back to the arch-conservative Le Bon. Censorious as he undoubtedly was, he did not fail to acknowledge, and even appreciate, the revolutionary potential of the crowd: 'When the structure of a civilization is rotten, it is always the masses that bring about its downfall' (Le Bon, 1982, p. xviii).

Of course, Gissing never really endorsed this idea of the crowd. A lower-middle-class writer socially located 'in the world of the single room set against the chaos and inhospitality of the street' (Walkowitz, 1994, p. 38), he was bound to distrust all ecstatic experiences of emancipation from the boundaries of the individual self, and to be repelled by the metropolitan spectacle of crowds which might exhilarate a less conflictual *flâneur*.

However, he does seem to have tapped some of their tumultuous energies, and – in his own oblique way – shared some of their 'spirit of rebellion'. To put it as John Plotz would: like many a nineteenth-century man of letters, Gissing seems to have benefited from the challenging presence of the crowd, whose pressure mobilised, stretched and revitalised resources of style and rhetoric.[3] Alarmed as he often is by the crowd's 'democratic' tendency to threaten the social hierarchies and/or to weaken and debase its members' individuality, the bourgeois intellectual is, on the other hand, susceptible to derive from the spectacle of the crowd an intensification of his own sense of self.

It must be added that, by the time Gissing came to try his hand at the representation of urban crowds, their overtly political connotation (their traditional affinity with class struggle, which had been paramount to the novelists of the previous generation) was complemented by their emerging profile as mass-consumers within the new commodity culture. Gissing's fiction was not slow to record this very innovative aspect of late Victorian modernity. To effect its representation, though, he seems to have felt he had to hark back to the past, resorting to the ancient Saturnalian pattern of festive inversion, which is not in itself a wholly neutral medium, devoid of perturbing socio-political implications. With the notable exception of the riotous multitude in *Demos* (1886), all his main crowd scenes – the market-place of Whitecross Street in *Workers in the Dawn* (1880), the Bank Holiday in *The Nether World* (1889), the Jubilee night in *In the Year of Jubilee* (1894) and the New Year's Eve episode in *The Town Traveller* (1898) – are festive and apolitical. Here, crowds appear to be only temporarily emancipated from the constraints of everyday life, and are engrossed in the act of consumption – of their leisure, first of all – following a pattern of carnivalesque release and subsequent disciplinarian re-containment. As argued by Stallybrass and White, disorder appeals to the middle-class observer for a variety of reasons, and carnivalesque indulgence has not necessarily to do with an interest in their potential for progressive social transformation. However, while studying Gissing's ambivalent attraction for scenes of urban disorder I have come to feel that there is indeed, in his fiction, an affinity between carnivalesque mobs and 'sharpened political antagonism' (Stallybrass and White, 1986, p. 14). The latter is always to be construed, in Gissing, as a form of radical individualism. No matter how repressed and conflictual, the individual's demand for freedom ends up by being intensified in conjunction with the spectacle of the crowd. That is to say, Gissing's crowds seem to (provisionally) authorise the individual's yearning to unfettered self-realisation, together with his/her restlessness under the pressure to conform exerted by economic necessity and/or family obligations.

Hence my general contention that carnivalesque moments of subversion strategically highlight, in Gissing, the late Victorian crisis of paternal authority. Gissing's plots predicate such a crisis on his fictional young people's attempts to exceed the social and psychological boundaries forced onto them by the patriarchal order of society – an order which, at the fin de siècle, seemed to be dangerously threatened by subversive modernity, with its democratic unleashing of individual desires. Both the Bank Holiday in *The Nether World* and the Jubilee Night in *In the Year of Jubilee* are, it seems to me, evidence of this.[4]

The Bank Holiday

Gissing's awareness of the widespread presence of a carnivalesque pattern of festive release – or 'discharge', as Naomi Schor (1978, p. 85) would call it – and disciplinarian re-containment in his fiction becomes explicit in *The Nether World*, where the crowd scene is included in a chapter specifically entitled 'Io Saturnalia!'. Here, as we know, the story is told of how Robert Hewett and his young bride Pennyloaf celebrate their wedding, spending a festive day among the crowds at the Crystal Palace. The analogy with the ancient Roman feast – when servants were exceptionally allowed to wear the freeman's 'pileus' – foregrounds the question of usurpation of roles and spaces (the 'democratic' erasure of differences) which is the key factor in Gissing's representation of urban crowds. The use of Latin in the title, as well as a number of cultured references in the chapter, is a symptom of the narrator's need to emphasise his detachment from the lower orders of society, whose vulgar but energetic vitality and indifference to *etiquette*, regulations, and laws both attract and repel the middle-class spectator. The mob is unhappily impervious to artistic as well as natural beauty, and the narrator is keen to show he is an altogether different kettle of fish by setting an alternative standard of educated sensitivity:

> Away in the west yonder the heavens are afire with sunset, but at that we do not care to look; never in our lives did we regard it. [...] Here under the glass roof stand white forms of undraped men and women – casts of antique statues – but we care as little for the glory of art as for that of nature [...]. (Gissing, 1992, p. 110)

In order to do so, however, he has joined in the gregarious 'we' of the crowd, thereby mixing himself with it and adhering, by way of an ironic mimesis, to the limitations of its (uncouth) perspective. In a novel where – it has been noted (Sloan, 1989, pp. 77–8) – the complicity between narrator and implied reader is based on the distancing of 'them' ('the poor') as objects of external observation, the very exceptional use of a first-person plural lumping provisionally together the middle-class spectator and the working-class crowd may be read as an index of Gissing's own vacillation in the face of the vulgar but liberating 'Saturnalia'.

This ambivalent attitude pervades the text in the form of a tension affecting its spatial dimension. There is no doubt that the overall impression given by the scene is one of euphoric expansion through the internal barriers which cut across and organise urban space: the 'perpetual rush of people for the trains to the "Paliss"' (Gissing, 1992, p. 105), the lack of 'distinction between "classes"' on the trains ('get in where you like, where you can') (Ibid., p. 112), the impotence of the police in the face of rampant disorder ('There was no question of making arrests; it was the night of Bank-holiday, and the capacity of police cells is limited') (Ibidem), and the general unholy mix of sounds, voices and bodies ('universal is the protecting arm') (Ibid., p. 110) do suggest that people are moving about with unusual freedom. On the other hand, it is true that the Crystal Palace is a location set apart for popular entertainment, and that its invasion by the working classes is inscribed in the compulsory map of urban segrega-tion. Such a map is only superficially perturbed by the excesses of the Bank Holiday, which will soon be over and, with remarkable harshness, will re-deliver the protagonists to their routinised, servile abjection – their festive clothes reduced to rags (as if to underscore that servants cannot wear the 'pileus' for more than a single day), their faces scratched and bruised, and all around them, the usual squalor: 'An hour later noises of a familiar kind sounded beneath the window. A woman's voice was raised in the fury of mad drunkenness, and a man answered her with threats and blows. "That's mother," sobbed Pennyloaf' (Ibid., p. 113).

It is interesting to note that such a brutal conclusion to the Bank Holiday foreshadows the outcome of the two parallel stories of disobedience to the father's will which figure prominently in the novel, and significantly inter-sect with the representation of urban disorder. Not only does the carnival scene coincide with the celebration of Bob's wedding, which is highly deplored by his father; it closely follows the narration of the final rift between Clara and Mr Hewett. Intergenerational tension is, indeed, crucial to *The Nether World*, and is best narrativised through Clara who articulates the desire to leave the Clerkenwell ghetto, and does temporarily realise it. Clara's ambition of social mobility is pitted against the unwritten laws of urban segregation, which make it 'normal' to stay where you belong, and 'pathological' (Ibid., p. 78) to indulge your selfish self. Thus, out of her attempt at self-assertion, she gets vitriol, and a new imprisonment at Crouch End. Needless to say, Bob's decision to ignore his father's wish, and marry 'poor Pennyloaf' – which brings into view Gissing's own *penchant* for declassing sexual transgression – does not fare any better.

The violence with which Gissing's plot castigates young people who disobey their father is – I would argue – a necessary corollary of the 'very specific zoning' (Goode, 1978, p. 107) of the novel. No doubt unhappiness is meted out also to those who practise virtuous renunciation; but the harshness of the punishment envisaged for those who rebel significantly contributes to the painful extremism of *The Nether World*. The more the text takes the logics of urban segmentation as an indisputable fact, and the more it conforms to its unwritten law, the more resentfully it ends up by inveighing against its injustice. In this sense, the bitterness with which the narrator contemplates 'the great review of the People' (Gissing, 1992, p. 109) on the summer Bank Holiday may be read as stemming from the inauthentic quality of the freedom granted to the multitudes. What is carnival, after all, if not the servants' holiday? A temporary suspension of the limitations and constraints of everyday life, a preordained licence routinised by the calendar, and marked by the very same abjections (the same servile passions, the same rivalries, the same greeds, the same miseries) which make up everyday life? No wonder a total destruction of the existing order of things is invoked as the prerequisite for a different and more harmonious festival:

> For, work as you will, there is no chance of a new and better world until the old be utterly destroyed. Destroy, sweep away, prepare the ground; then shall music the holy, music the civilizer, breathe over the renewed earth, and with Orphean magic raise in perfect beauty the towers of the City of Man (Ibid., p. 109).

Here, the (very unusual) iconoclastic fury of Gissing's narrator seems to feed off the same overwhelming yearnings which animate the modern crowd – yearnings which the Bank Holiday provisionally releases, and concomitantly re-contains within the pattern of a permissive (but by no means free) proletarian vacation. Therefore, though the festive crowd is an object of scorn and vituperation, there seems to hover behind this scene the idea of a different multitude – a truly unchained one, capable of erasing ('Destroy, sweep away, prepare the ground') the inhuman order of the city, as appears irrevocably given in the novel. Though strenuously kept at bay by the conservative, classicist stance, such a crowd infuses the narrator's tirade with some of its 'boundless energy and liability to intoxication' (Nye, 1995, p. 42).

The Jubilee

Within the Gissing canon, *In the Year of Jubilee* may be construed as representing the polar opposite to *The Nether World* and at the same time its close rewriting. Like its predecessor, the 1894 novel is no doubt preoccupied with the metropolitan topography, namely with the specific fact of the growing suburbia and its segregating effects on middle-class women; but it relents considerably on the rigidity of the city's internal boundaries, and greatly softens the stringency with which patriarchal law is applied. The way the Jubilee novel tackles intergenerational tensions and their encroachments upon the freedom of the young is strongly reminiscent of *The Nether World*. Here too we have a family triad made up by a father (as inefficient disciplinarian), a daughter (desirous to escape her imprisonment in a prescribed area of the city map, ready to disobey, and as a consequence plunged into a new, more radical state of physical and psychological constraint) and a son (dragged by his juvenile passions towards a declassing marriage, and destined to an untimely death). The dislocation of this plot into a different social milieu, characterised by a relative economic prosperity, allows for a new emphasis on questions related to consumption and superfluity (Goode, 1978, pp. 164–5; Sloan, 1989, p. 130), which replace the (senseless) production and bare struggle to survive foregrounded by the earlier novel. Hence the centrality of issues like mass consumption, advertising and spectacle – the spectacle, above all, which the crowd itself provides for its own entertainment. The festive multitude gathered out in the streets on the evening of Jubilee day is not there to catch a glimpse of the Queen, but – as Nancy says – 'to see the people and the illuminations' (Gissing, 1994, p. 26).

What is more striking, then, in the 'carnivalesque' crowd scene of the Jubilee novel is that it does not really seem to stand out as a moment of suspension of servile everyday life. Much rather, it simply seems to bring into fuller view the very essence of the experience of modernity. At the culmination of the 'Age of Progress' it coincides with a weakening of exterior class distinctions, a general permissiveness and a universal injunction to desire, that is to imitate the upper classes in the (once elitist) practices of conspicuous consumption of goods, services, and 'culture'. The provisional exchange of clothes between servants and masters, and the temporary suspension of prohibitions – which were the key to the ancient Saturnalia – seem to have turned into the norm for modern urban subjectivity. The festive ethos of consumption seems to have replaced the workday ethos of ascetic production, and the transgressions of the father's law (a law based on decorum, sobriety, sense of duty, and of differences) seem to be no transgressions at all within this brand-new order of the city. Here, sons and daughters feel encouraged to ignore their father's old-fashioned appeal to domestic pieties; and to challenge traditional forms of social control is not – as with Clara Hewett – to be 'pathological', and therefore bound to break one's wings against 'the bars of the real' (Schreiner, 1883, p. 291); much rather, it means to put oneself 'into complete accord with the spirit of [the] time' (Ibid., p. 82), joining the festive crowds and losing oneself in them. Indeed, the crowds themselves hardly seem to have preserved any of their antagonistic spirit to law and order: they are 'carelessly obedient' to police pickets, they tamely walk along prescribed routes, and '[b]ut for an occasional bellow of hilarious blackguardism, or for a song uplifted by strident voices, or a cheer at some flaring symbol which pleased the passers, there was little noise; only a thud, thud of footfalls, and the low, unvarying sound that suggested some huge beast purring to itself in stupid contentment' (Ibid., p. 58).

This lack of resisting antagonism on the part of the Jubilee crowd, and its new 'all class' inclusiveness,[5] is connected with the general softening of Gissing's *parti pris* against the urban mob, and his ability in this novel to put himself, so to speak, within the crowd, while keeping censoriously out of it. He does so by allowing himself (and his readers) to sympathise with his female protagonist, to see the crowd through her eyes and to experience the appeal it exerts on those who, like her, bring to it their own desire for freedom and emotional intensity. Nancy, and the reader with her, enjoys the tumult, the sheer fact of being hustled by the 'profane public' (Ibid., p. 52), and the pleasures of anonymity once she gets rid of the insufferable Mr Barmby and can lose herself in the thick of the throng: 'She had escaped to enjoy herself, and the sense of freedom soon overcame anxieties. No one observed her solitary state; she was one of millions [...]' (Ibid., p. 58). Of course, since at the same time the narrator is out of the crowd, and shares the father's opinion that to join the Jubilee celebration is 'to mix with the rag-tag and bobtail' (Ibid., p. 33), the novel also gives us a more traditional, conservative perspective on Nancy's experience, recording it as a de-individualising and de-classing event. It is a swamping of her heterogeneity (as Le Bon would have it) by vulgar homogeneity (Le Bon, 1896, p. 8), wherein 'her emotions' are reduced to 'those of any shop-girl let loose' and the 'culture to which she laid claim evanesced in this atmosphere of exhalations' (Gissing, 1994, p. 58).

The tension and reciprocal interdependence between the 'massifying' experience of Jubilee Night ('to mingle with the limitless crowd as one of its units, borne in whatsoever direction') (Ibid., p. 54) and the euphoric intensification of the sense of individual freedom is yet another aspect of the ambivalence inherent in the nineteenth-century discourse of the crowd. The distinction of *In the Year of Jubilee* rests in its sophisticated emplotting of such a connection. Nancy's paradoxical experience of an enhanced sense of self gained through self-dispersion in the crowd is premised to more radical challenges to patriarchal law, a more uninhibited desire of self-assertion ('Abundant privilege; no obligation. A reference of all things to her sovereign will and pleasure') (Ibid., p. 82) which no longer has to do with books and culture, but seems to draw upon the energies of the crowd: 'She wanted to live in the present, to enjoy her youth. An evening like that she had spent in the huge crowd [...] was worth whole oceans of "culture"' (Ibid., p. 83). This jubilating sense of self-expansion finds its climax in the scene of the excursion onto the Monument. Here Gissing seems to catch the impact of the 'vision of London's immensity' (Ibid., p. 87) on the imagination of those subjects who felt newly empowered by late Victorian social transformation:

As soon as she had recovered from the first impression, this spectacle of a world's wonder served only to exhilarate her; she was not awed by what she looked upon. In her conceit of self-importance, she stood there, above the battling millions of men, proof against mystery and dread, untouched by the voices of the past, and in the present seeing only common things, though from an odd point of view. Here her senses seemed to make literal the assumption by which her mind had always been directed: that she – Nancy Lord – was the mid point of the universe. No humility awoke in her; she felt the stirring of envies, avidities, unvowable passions, and let them flourish unrebuked. (Ibid., p. 88)

It is true that the story that follows will show that Nancy's was indeed a 'conceit of self-importance' – a regressive narcissistic delusion of omnipotence, which naively ignored the limits set by patriarchal society to middle-class women's freedom. This, however, does not totally undermine the strength of this scene. The net of lies, humiliations, and constraints wherein Nancy will be caught as a consequence of her will to independence never looks like an inevitable punishment for her acts of disobedience; much rather, it looks like the (despicable) outcome of the resistance of a residual patriarchal order, which, setting itself against the 'spirit of the time', opposes women's full citizenship by petty legal devices (wills and codicils, as in the story of Casaubon and Dorothea). Mr Lord's illness, which surfaces after the fatal Jubilee celebrations, reflects the erosion of paternal authority by democratic modernity; and only very mildly does his death – which follows Nancy's sea holiday and sexual indulgence – evoke guilt and those constraints of feeling that elsewhere in Gissing act as internalised substitutes for weakened patriarchal obligation. This does not imply that Gissing's heroine is devoid of psychological depth and conflict. But, as suits a novel eminently engrossed in the modern freedom to consume (experiences, spectacles, commodities), her inner conflict has to do with a bifurcation of desire, and with ineffable questions of taste. Like any shop-girl, Nancy inclines to indulge in the pleasures of the crowd (and sex), but like any self-respecting decently educated young lady, she will prove more susceptible to Tarrant's distinction and pedigree (to the charms, Bourdieu would say, of his cultural capital), than to the upstart exuberance of Luckworth Crewe – the man of the crowd with a special gift for commerce and advertising, the prototype of new metropolitan entrepreneurship, and of fledgling massified welfare.

By way of conclusion

In more than one sense, *In the Year of Jubilee* represents the culmination of Gissing's fictional investigation of metropolitan life. Here, more than anywhere else, Gissing seems to have taken up the challenge that ambivalent modernity made to the literary imagination, facing both its unpleasant aspects ('The process of cultural deformation and degeneration, of engulfing advertising and speculative building...') (Greenslade, 2001, p. 277) and its most emancipating implications. The latter are rarely emphasised in Gissing's works, and in the Jubilee novel they enjoy the limelight through the text's willingness to share Nancy's viewpoint, her perception of the crowd and her participation in its 'vulgar' excitements.

It is well known that Gissing did not carry on in this vein: in the following novel – *The Whirlpool* (1897), the last of his 'major phase' – his capacity to empathise with middle-class women attracted by the energetic bustle of the metropolis is minimal, and there is no recognition of the new margins of individual freedom offered by urban modernity. The crowd is a vapid audience shaped by advertising and fawned on by the press; its favour is coveted by vain young ladies; and London has turned into a senseless vortex of gossip, rivalries, intrigues, cheating, hysteria, and even physical violence. From this wholly negative vision of the city sprung – among other things – some further 'minor' fictions of urban life. The first, *The Town Traveller* (1898), remarkable for its comic vein, contains Gissing's last *Saturnalia*.

In this novel, the London whirlpool with its dreadful-yet-attractive energies is represented, and somehow 'distanced' (Goode, 1978, p. 195), through the point of view of the lower orders of society. These do not coincide with the suffering working class of *The Nether World*, depressed by diminished professional opportunities and rigidly confined to the Clerkenwell ghetto; they include, rather, people employed in the tertiary sector (commercial travellers, shopkeepers, waiters, petty clerks, and attractive young 'ladies' enlisted in the industry of entertainment) destined to a perpetual, solitary migration from one employment to another, from one rented room to another, and from one quarter to another in the huge, labyrinthine metropolis. This state of universal uprootedness and potential anarchy – where families are dispersed, and fathers are either missing or, like Mr Spark, have 'long resigned all semblance of paternal authority' (Gissing, 1992, p. 58) – does not seem to induce any modernist anxiety in the narrator, or in his characters. Apparently, it is the socio-economic location of the latter, which makes them, by and large, beneficiaries of the consumer boom round the turn of the century, which sustains the optimistic view of modern urban life displayed by the novel.

As for the 'romantic' adventure which *The Town Traveller* sportively foregrounds, it is made possible by the very social and topographical structure of the metropolis, with its multiple, distinct, yet occasionally permeable worlds and its perennially incipient crowds – a structure that allows for anonymity, sudden disappearances and fortuitous encounters. All this generates a *quasi* detective story pivoting on the elusive Mr Clover/Lord Polperro, and culminating in Gissing's last crowd scene, wherein it is not the sons and daughters, but the (missing) father himself who shows an affinity with the unruly festive mob flooding the streets on New Year's Eve. A carnivalesque paternal *persona* who liked 'the liberty of the plebeian status, and sought it under disguises' (Ibid., p. 199), the drunken, demented Polperro plunges merrily into the thick of the throng ('Let's go into the crowd [...] I like a crowd.') (Ibid., p. 251), and gets trampled to death.

Tendentially Gissing's fathers are not to be trusted as efficient enforcers of discipline.[6] And indeed, in the face of the modern erosion of the economic and ideological basis for their authority, it was vain to pit them against the turmoil of the crowd. This irreverent Bacchic ending, making short work of the elderly Dionysus, seems therefore appropriate enough.

Notes

1. One good example of such new impersonal normativity is represented by timetables. Lynn Hapgood (2000, p. 305) has underscored how the increased freedom of physical movement, granted by new and cheaper means of transport, was paralleled on the one hand by decreased social mobility, and on the other by the general subjection to the pressures of the timetable: 'London's vast size could now be reckoned in minutes and the timing of peoples' movements predicted.'

2. My main reference for an outline of the late nineteenth-century crowd theory is Jaap van Ginneken, 1991, while for the representation of crowds in nineteenth-century literature see Plotz, 2000, Visser, 1994, as well as Benjamin's seminal reflections in his famous Baudelaire work (1968).

3. Within Plotz's stimulating perspective, the literary representation of modern urban crowds figures as their 'antithesis' (an attempt to contain them, to interpret them, to draw a lesson out of them, to impose on them some sort of order); and, on the other hand, it is, mimetically, its 'double' – a 'double' which comes into being by feeding off the crowd's frightening-but-seductive energy. Plotz's argument provides a new critical approach to the productive ambivalence which pits the modern individual against the crowd.

4. In analysing the two novels and their crowd scenes I partly enlarge upon some observations I made in my book-length study on *ressentiment* in late Victorian fiction (Villa, 1997), where I tried to show how the dynamics of *ressentiment* and carnivalesque patterns of release and recontainment are widespread in Gissing's fiction, and play a crucial role in the shaping of his plots, as well as in the construction of his characters. The present chapter is an extract from a much longer article in Italian, which tries to cover, and make sense of, all main crowd scenes in Gissing's novels (Villa, 2004).

5. This 'all class' inclusiveness was a characteristic of *fin de siècle* crowds in Britain, and – apart from the 1887 and 1897 Jubilees – will be apparent in other significant public events, such as *Tennyson's funeral* (1892) or *Mafeking Night's celebrations* (1900). To the spectacle provided by the crowds on the former occasion attention has been drawn by Stephen Arata (1999, p. 56), while the significant middle-class component in the popular celebrations for the liberation of Mafeking has been underscored by Paula Krebs (1999, pp. 12–14).

6. In Gissing, if fathers are there at all – which is hardly ever the case, especially when sons are concerned – they rarely patrol the borders of respectability; as often as not they themselves rather flirt with crime and metropolitan chaos. The crucial example here is Edward Golding, the dying father presiding over the market-place scene which opens *Workers in the Dawn*: an alcoholic, a thief, a decadent drifter in the city of dreadful night and even more dreadful crowded promiscuity. There were of course obvious biographical reasons why Gissing's fathers should not figure as reliable disciplinarians, but, as Scott McCracken (2004) points out in an interesting essay on 'fathering the *fin de siècle*', the missing or weak father is

typical of much avant-garde fiction of the time. This is indeed a case where biographical plots significantly intersect, and support, the larger shared experience of an intellectual and artistic generation.

Bibliography

Arata, S. '1897', in Tucker, H.F., ed., *A Companion to Victorian Literature and Culture* (Oxford: Blackwell, 1999).

Benjamin, W. 'On Some Motifs in Baudelaire', in *Illuminations*, ed. Arendt, A. (New York: Schocken Books, 1968).

Gissing, G. *The Town Traveller*, 1898 (Brighton: The Harvester Press, 1982).

——. *The Nether World*, 1889 (Oxford: Oxford University Press, 1992).

——. *In the Year of Jubilee*, 1894 (London: Dent, 1994).

Glover, D. ' "This spectacle of the world's wonder": Commercial culture and urban space in Gissing's *In the Year of Jubilee*', in Postmus, B., ed., *A Garland for Gissing* (Amsterdam-New York: Rodopi, 2001).

Goode, J. *George Gissing: Ideology and Fiction* (London: Vision Press, 1978).

Greenslade, W. 'Writing against Himself: Gissing and the Lure of Modernity in *In the Year of Jubilee*', in Postmus, B., ed., *A Garland for Gissing, op. cit.*

Hapgood, L. 'The Literature of the Suburbs: Versions of Repression in the Novels of George Gissing, Arthur Conan Doyle and William Pett Ridge, 1890–1899', *Journal of Victorian Culture* 5 (2000) 287–310.

Krebs, P. *Gender, Race and the Writing of Empire: Public Discourse and the Boer War* (Cambridge: Cambridge University Press, 1999).

Le Bon, G. *The Crowd: A Study of the Popular Mind*, 1896 (English trans. Atlanta: Cherokee Publishing Company, 1982).

McCracken, S. 'La paternità della fine secolo', in Pustianaz, M. and Villa, L., eds, *Maschilità decadenti. La lunga fin de siècle* (Bergamo: Sestante/Bergamo University Press, 2004).

Nye, R. 'Savage Crowds, Modernism and Modern Politics', in Barkan, E. and Bush, R., eds, *Prehistories of the Future: The Primitivist Project and the Culture of Modernism* (Stanford: Stanford University Press, 1995).

Plotz, J. *The Crowd: British Literature and Public Politics* (Berkeley and Los Angeles: University of California Press, 2000).

Schor, N. *Zola's Crowds* (Baltimore and London: Johns Hopkins University Press, 1978).

Schreiner, O. *The Story of an African Farm*, 1883 (Harmondsworth: Penguin Classics, 1986).

Sloan, J. *George Gissing: The Cultural Challenge* (London: Macmillan, 1989).

Stallybrass, P. and A. White *The Politics and Poetics of Transgression* (London: Methuen, 1986).

van Ginneken, J. *Crowds, Psychology and Politics 1871–1899* (Cambridge: Cambridge University Press, 1991).

Visser, N. 'Roaring Beasts and Raging Floods: The Representation of Political Crowds in the Nineteenth Century British Novel', *Modern Language Review*, 89 (April 1994) 289–317.

Villa, L. *Figure del risentimento. Aspetti della costruzione del soggetto nella narrativa inglese ai margini della 'decadenza'* (Pisa: ETS, 1997).

——. 'Gissing, le folle e la modernità urbana: trasgressione, carnevale e crisi dell'autorità paterna', *Nuova corrente*, 51 (2004) 127–64.

Walkowitz, J. *City of Dreadful Delight: Narratives of Sexual Danger in Late-Victorian London* (London: Virago, 1994).

4
Gissing, Literary Bohemia, and the Metropolitan Circle

John Sloan

George Gissing's biographers and critics, beginning with Morley Roberts, have frequently commented on his romantic attachment to the myth of 'la vie de Bohème'. Gillian Tindall, writing with no-nonsense Britishness, as well as with a woman's eye to the matter, went so far as to attribute the depth of Gissing's attraction to his first wife, Nell Harrison, to 'a desire to create the de Musset-Murger idyll...this cloud-cuckoo-land of love-in-a-garret in his own life' (Tindall, 1974, p. 76). Among critics, Pierre Coustillas has noted more positively that in taking up the theme of artistic bohemia, Gissing, together with George du Maurier and Oscar Wilde, looked with sympathy into the wider intellectual ambitions of the artist's life (Coustillas, 1986, p. 130). It is this wider intellectual ambition that I wish to consider. The aim will be to show that in spite of Gissing's sentimental attachment to the idea of Bohemian freedom and non-conformity, his fictions reveal not only the necessary doubleness of the genuine Bohemian, but also the dangers of the little circle that provides Bohemia with its sense of community and difference. Important in this context is the recognition of the ways in which the idea of literary Bohemia emerged in England, and of Gissing's formative place within this.

It is worth reminding ourselves that the cradle of artistic bohemia was metropolitan Paris of the Second Empire with its cheap lodging houses, its café society, and its revolutionary cultural and intellectual traditions. Students and work-girls, artists and their models were brought together in an atmosphere that seemed free from older social conventions. The crowded proximity of Parisian life provided paradoxically the spaces of anonymity and freedom from familial ties that allowed romantic redefinition of the self and the possibility of new, often transient contacts and relationships (Wilson, 2000, p. 28). The result was a gradual blurring of the distinction between those who lived unconventional life-styles and social nomads – in France, 'La Boheme' originally signified simply a gypsy. Henri Murger, who gave literary expression to Bohemia in his *Scenes de la vie de Bohème*, believed that 'Bohemia neither exists nor can exist anywhere but in Paris' (Murger, 1908, p. xxi).

As Gissing was aware, Thackeray introduced the new sense of the word into English. In Thackeray's novel *The Adventures of Philip* (1861), his newly christened Bohemia of 'billiard-rooms, oysters ... of pulls on the river' (Ch. 5) and 'plenteous pocket-money' (Ch. 7) suggests a land of batchelor leisure, clubbiness, and cushioned ease far removed from the struggling Bohemians of Murger's Rue des Martyrs. Male clubbiness which formed the adhesive of British Bohemia was essentially an escapist, recreational Bohemia lacking in effect the genuine literary and intellectual intercourse of French café society. Indeed, in London's Fleet Street, sexual segregation was maintained with the opening of a separate club for women journalists in the 1890s (Mitchell, 1992, p. 109). Daniel Nutt's attempt to bring the flavour of Parisian life to London when he opened the Café Royal in London's Regent Street prompted Beerbohm Tree to remark famously: 'If you want to see English people at their most English, go to the Café Royal where they are trying their hardest to be French' (Deghy and Waterhouse, 1955, p. 109). George Saintsbury, writing on Henry Murger in 1878, made no bones about his view of English Bohemia when he wrote: 'To put the thing briefly, the Bohemian ideal in France is not unlike Chatterton; the Bohemian ideal of at least some Englishmen bears a strong resemblance to Dick Swiveller' (Saintsbury, 1878, p. 231). As a declared enemy of the English brand of Bohemia, and also of the new wave of decadent 'tavern haunting *fainéantise*' of the 1870s, Saintsbury praised 'the burden of sadness' and 'note of warning' in Murger's work (Saintsbury, 1878, p. 249).

Gissing's view of Murger's 'la vie de Bohème' corresponds in some key points to Saintsbury's. An entry in Gissing's *Commonplace Book* similarly celebrates 'the sad note' in Murger 'who knew what poverty meant' (Korg, 1962, p. 35). In identifying Thackeray as the closest English equivalent to Murger, Gissing comments on the complete absence of this note of sadness in Thackeray, and on the sharp difference between Thackeray's sentimental portrait of Fanny Bolton and the *grisettes* of Murger and de Musset (Korg, 1962, p. 31). It was a gap in English literature that Gissing clearly set out to fill.

Some of the close parallels between Gissing's work and European fictions of 'la vie de Bohème' have been noted by other critics – the shades of Murger in the unconventional relationship between Osmond Waymark and Ida Starr in *The Unclassed*, for example (Maltz, 2001, p. 10). It was clearly literary recognition rather than chance or personal taste alone that attracted Gabrielle Fleury to *New Grub Street*. However, the differences in Gissing's version of Bohemia reveal the social and intellectual boundaries of the bohemian ideal in England. Significantly, Gissing does not set out to disguise the prudery and inhibitions of nineteenth-century metropolitan London. Bohemia anglicized in Chelsea or the Strand was not one that allowed unmarried men to live openly *en menage* (Price, 1914, p. 33). Metropolitan London was as great a melting pot as Paris, and appeared to offer the same opportunity for anonymity and romantic relationships. Returning from Westbourne Park in 1881 to his old stamping ground around Tottenham Court Road and the British Museum, Gissing himself observed that 'lodgers here in London generally live in utter unconsciousness of one another's ways & works' (Mattheisen, Young, Coustillas, 1991, p. 57). Yet London landladies and neighbours kept moral watch on the comings and goings of lodgers and tenants, retaining the inhibiting mores of the old towns and villages and a sharp divide between the respectable and the disreputable.

Gissing does in fact go much further in frankness than Thackeray, creating in Ida Starr an imaginative counter-image to his dissatisfied conception of the 'English girl' in whom, he wrote in his *Commonplace Book*, 'first conscience, & secondly stupidity' kept from 'the kind of "romantic liaison" glorified by Murger and George Sand' (Korg, 1962, p. 35). The result is arguably much less of a male fantasy version of real womanhood than, for instance, his contemporary George Moore's naif Gwennie Lloyd, who takes off her clothes for art in the sensational *A Modern Lover* (1883), or Morley Robert's prim *grisette*, Mary Morris, in his self-consciously bohemian novel, *In Low Relief* (1890). But the liaison between Waymark, the self-declared 'bohemian' (Ch. 6), and Ida Starr, with her spirited 'independence of judgment' (Ch. 14), must remain clandestine, and Harriet Smales's entrapment of Julian Casti into marriage, incredible as it seems to some of today's readers, is made possible because of the impropriety of his foolishly agreeing to visit her alone in her room.

Another odd feature of Gissing's struggling Bohemians is their devotion to classical literature and culture. Waymark's non-conformity, his 'joy in outraging what are called the proprieties' (Ch. 7), finds paradoxical expression in the form of coffee evenings listening to his friend Casti's classically inspired verses. Intellectually, one might argue, Gissing's bohemians, unlike their French counterparts, do not achieve a self-conscious separation from the academicism and classicism that continued to dominate culture in both countries in the nineteenth century. Indeed, their reverence for classicism leads in the end to a renunciation of politics and radicalism, or, in the word Gissing uses, 'combat'.

Admittedly, Bohemia as a reservoir of radical energy has always seemed apolitical to some. V.S. Pritchett, with evident impatience with twentieth-century Bloomsbury, has argued that 'what Bohemia really did to artists and writers in the long run was ... to isolate them from society' (Pritchett, 1946, p. 201). Theirs is, so to speak, a picturesque, isolationist stance. Condemnation of the cult of Bohemia as a form of escapism, nurturing reaction and inaction has been characteristic of the political left from Marx onwards. Yet in France at least, Bohemia was also identified with political radicalism, and particularly with the part played by students and artists in nurturing anti-establishment feeling following the failure of the Revolution of 1848, and again after the defeat of the socialist-inspired Paris Commune in 1871. The second-generation Bohemia of Verlaine and the anarchist Symbolist movement flourished in the 1870s, as the first had done in the 1850s, as an aesthetic counterpart to bourgeois life.

Gissing's bohemian 'unclassed' heroes are also seen in the context of radical, social and political upheavals – in *Workers in the Dawn*, the republican hopes in England in the 1870s, and in *The Unclassed*, the challenge to old-fashioned Liberalism in the period prior to the limited extension of franchise in 1884, the year the novel appeared. Yet the pattern of development in Gissing's heroes from politics to aesthetics, combat to detachment, has all the appearance of a cultural and spiritual withdrawal. Like George Saintsbury in the article already cited, Gissing looked uneasily upon the flamboyant tendencies that characterized 'Les Dernières Bohèmes' of his generation, which by the 1880s included Wilde's provative brand of anarchist symbolist aesthetics. Gissing and indeed his hero Waymark display the more shadowy tendencies of the English type of *flaneur*, 'haunting the underworld of the working classes' as 'a social investigator', rather than given to conspicuous display (Parsons, 2000, p. 20). In turning back to Murger and the first-generation Bohemia of the 1840s and 1850s, Gissing, it might be argued, identified with their less abrasive artistic, apolitical ideals. Indeed, Roberts records Gissing's belief that the whole of Murger sprang from the chapter in Balzac's *Lost Illusions* (*Illusions Perdues*) in which the poet-hero Lucien de Lubempre 'writes and sings drinking songs with tears beside his dead mistress, Coralie' (Roberts, 1958, p. 176). From this one might conclude that Gissing, like many since, viewed Bohemia mainly in picturesque, artistic rather than social, political terms.

Yet what is in fact striking in Gissing's presentation of bohemian rebellion is his recognition, derived from Murger, of the value and necessity of doubleness. Murger's celebration of doubleness emerges in the context of his distinction in his 1851 Preface to *Scènes de la Vie de Bohème* between the 'amateurs' and the 'dreamers' on the one side, and on the other side the 'true Bohemians' who are able 'to live in duplicate, to keep one life for the poet in them – the dreamer that dwells on the mountain heights where choirs of inspired voices sing together – and another for the laborour that contrives to provide daily bread.' This 'double life', according to Murger, is 'almost always carried on in strong and well-balanced natures' (Murger, 1908, p. xxiii). Murger has a tough edge that belies his seeming sentimentality. Baudelaire noted the 'bitter raillery' ('*amère gauserrie*') with which Murger speaks of Bohemia (Baudelaire [1880], p. 3; see also Seigal, 1986, p. 118). Indeed the attempted separation of Bohemia and genuine art by anti-bourgeois writers from Flaubert and Baudelaire through to Zola and Rimbaud does not conceal their own ambiguous relation to it.

An uncertain sense of distance from and attraction to Bohemia can also be said to characterize Gissing's life and work. In devising an unexpected legacy for Henry Ryecroft in rural Exeter, for example, Gissing constructs a utopian dream or myth of autonomy and distance from Bohemian London and the squalid penny-pinching miseries of literature as trade. Yet, as John Goode has argued, the diaries fail to provide a coherent or consistent viewpoint. In particular, Goode points to the 'uncontained energies' which punctuate the 'inert detachment' of the work's structure (Goode, 1978, p. 48). This is very striking in the 'Spring' and 'Autumn' sections. In celebrating his perfect and ordered bourgeois domesticity, Ryecroft remembers his London years with bitterness and derision. The keynote is that of Murger transferred to English fiction. At the same time Ryecroft's recollections of struggling and starving authorship, of garret life and coffee stalls, and books found in second-hand stalls around the Tottenham Court Road are charged with a heroic nostalgia that feeds the myth of literary Bohemia and the hero as man of letters. *The Private Papers of Henry Ryecroft* was one of the most popular and successful of Gissing's works in his lifetime for that reason, particularly with bookmen and literati. The diary itself constitutes a reassertion of past artistic ambition at the point at which Ryecroft declares that his life is over. Ryecroft has bade farewell to authorship, but he continues to write his 'private papers'. They are not intended for publication, but his friend and editor recognises in them a literary design and purpose. The contradiction that compels the work, in other words, lies in the continuing claims of the past that Ryecroft seeks to deny.

Among Gissing's earlier exponential characters, Waymark demonstrates doubleness in an extreme form in his combined role as rent-collector for the capitalist Woodstock, and would-be combative novelist who burns the midnight oil. His double nature is mirrored in Ida Starr, the prostitute with a cherished ideal of selfhood. Rather than indicating any insincerity or dishonesty, their attempt to live out the seeming contradiction of bourgeois and bohemian instincts, of inner freedom and outer realities, marks them out as strong, well-balanced natures. Waymark's opposite is Casti, the weak ineffectual dreamer, unable in the end to combine the demands of domestic life and circumstances with the life of the poet. The pattern of success and failure here closely follows the distinction made by Murger between the 'dreamer' and the 'true Bohemian'.

In his characterisation of Waymark, Gissing resists the polarization of bohemian and bourgeois that would obscure the interconnection between these seemingly oppositional terms. In particular, Gissing recognises that Bohemia is not a space outside bourgeois life, but, as Jerrold Seigal has argued, 'the expression of a conflict . . . at its very heart' (Seigal, 1986, p. 10). In Gissing, that conflict engages both artistic integrity and economic necessity, the desire for intellectual freedom and the need for community and acceptance. Waymark's ambiguous 'unclassment', his reluctance to take up a stable and limiting social identity, is characteristic of Bohemia. Indeed, in so far as Waymark's situation mirrors Gissing's own, it calls into question Michael Collie's identification of Gissing's 'real self' with a hidden, 'repressed' bohemianism beneath a conventional, detached public persona (Collie, 1977, p. 9).

In the final volume of the original three-volume edition of *The Unclassed*, Waymark partially retracts his separation of politics and art, social enthusiasm and artistic detachment, in the reawakening of his 'old desire' to write 'something savage': 'After all, perhaps art for art's sake was not the final stage of his development. Art, yes; but combat at the same time. The two things are not so incompatible as some would have us think.' Waymark's sense of a connection between aesthetics and politics, of art as a latent power base of radical energies and feelings cuts across the conventional Arnoldian opposition between politics and aesthetics that shapes much nineteenth-century thought and fiction. In George Moore's *A Modern Lover*, for example, the hero Lewis Seymour abandons his garret life as a struggling painter for society and politics. Gissing too, in *Workers in the Dawn* (1880), shows Golding being eaten away from within by the seemingly irreconcilable pull of politics and aesthetics, while in *Thyrza* (1887) the conflict is externalized in the opposing characters of 'The Idealist' Egremont, the Arnoldian missionary of culture, and the Dalmaine, the practical Parliamentarian. But in *The Unclassed* at least, Waymark's strength and independence lie in his bohemian resistance to such a split or categorization. In the passage quoted above, the shift from past to present tense ('the two things are not so incompatible as some would have us think') suggests that this is also Gissing's view. It marks the point at which the bohemian spirit feels the stirrings of a genuine avant-gardeism, and wider intellectual ambitions, and in the case of a writer like Gissing, the beginnings of modernity.

From this point of view, Fredric Jameson is probably right when he argues of Gissing and his 'intellectual' protagonists that 'the author of *New Grub Street* does not understand the "alienation" of such intellectuals in the Romantic terms of the *poète maudit* struggling against the philistine masters of a business society, nor even in the Mallarméan terms of the structural alienation inherent in writing and linguistic production' (Jameson, 1981, p. 200). Gissing demonstrates in striking ways the anomalous dependence on traditional forms of the lower-class radical intellectual of the English type. Gissing's resistance to the reality of ordinary life, including existing forms of art, is restricted. His avant-gardeism, within the forms of literary realism, is limited to a double-edged irony, a capacity to look on both sides and see the weaknesses of both. His attachments are academic rather than progressively intellectual. Yet for all his classicism, conservative class instincts, and recurrent dreams of economic independence and cultured ease, Gissing and his 'unclassed' heroes nevertheless belong within the broader social phenomenon of romantic individualism and resistance to everyday reality that provided Bohemia and related avant-garde movements with many of their recruits.

Although Gissing continued to examine the relationship between the bohemian dissident or outsider and the social and economic establishment in his novels after *The Unclassed*, he did not again place the 'strong, well-balanced' nature at the centre of the action. In *Born in Exile*, for example, Godwin Peak is unable to sustain the strain of his peculiar double life when he deserts his friends and literary London with the aim of secretly marrying into the old rural upper-class social order. Ryecroft is provided with a means of escape from Bohemia. Perhaps only Nancy Lord, secret novelist and working mother in *In the Year of Jubilee*, has to fight for both her soul and body, and in facing the challenge breaks down the diametric opposition between Villadom and Bohemia. More generally the pattern of success and failure in Gissing's fiction polarizes into the neurotic and the venal, with the burnouts trapped in the cul-de-sac of their idealism, and the sell-outs adapting opportunistically to social conventions and the demands of the market. This pattern is most evident in Gissing's greatest novel, *New Grub Street*, where we have a straightforward battle between art and trade. Reardon dreams his way back to poverty and the garret as the only authentic life, while Milvain with minimum literary talent insinuates his way to the centre of a coterie of flatterers and admirers. Neither proves capable of greatness. Again, Gissing takes his cue from Murger who compares the battle in the artistic world to war, in that 'all the fame goes to the leaders', while the rank and file are rewarded with only a few lines or 'end in obscurity...laid away from life in a winding-sheet of indifference'. Like Murger, Gissing looks down with affection and also with irony 'into the underworld, where the obscure toilers are striving' (Murger, 1908, p. xxiv).

Gissing's ironies are directed not only against the delusions and ambitions of youth, but also against the psychology of the coterie. The *petit cénacle* or 'little circle' has always played an important part in the life of Bohemia, offering a point of identity and independence of society based on interests and ideals rather than on kinship. In Gissing's own life, the metropolis provided an opportunity to avoid his family. He preferred the company of those who shared his literary interests, like the German émigré, Eduard Bertz, and the globe-trotting Morley Roberts, to the uncomfortable proximity of his London relatives. His real-life bohemian friendships are mirrored with affectionate nostalgia in the Waymark-Casti and Reardon-Biffen scenes in *The Unclassed* and *New Grub Street*. Yet Gissing generally shied away from the closer intimacies and the seductions of the closed circle or coterie whose purpose for the individual was often recognition and admiration in a lonely metropolitan world. Gissing's lifelong friendship with Bertz was maintained through correspondence rather than proximity, the two having grown apart intellectually when to Gissing's amazement Bertz 'drifted over to the religious revivalists' and joined the Salvation Army (Mattheisen, Young, Coustillas, 1991, p. 155). The more sociable Gissing of the later successful years has in this respect sometimes been exaggerated.

He dropped his association with Roberts and the so-called 'Quadrilaterals' after only a month, and his attendance at the Omar Kayyam Club dinners in the later 1890s was occasional and eventually rather lukewarm. He never had any great faith in what he called ' "societies" ... for whatever purpose' (Mattheisen, Young, Coustillas, 1992, p. 147). His was, as Nigel Cross has noted, 'one of the most reclusive lives in the history of authorship' (Cross, 1985, p. 224).

The problem for Gissing was not the forced homogeneity and conviviality that was often the style of recreational Bohemia. Rather, in recognising that the closed corporation was inside as well as outside commercial culture, Gissing was wary of any group that might serve as a false measure of worth. At the point where the coterie and the literary market place intersected, Gissing recognised that the inner circle could also sometimes serve as a sinister centre of influence and rivalry. This is shown in *New Grub Street* in the *cénacle* of 'old companions' that gather at Alfred Yule's side when the rumour goes round that he will be offered the editorship of *The Study*. The circle gloats over Yule's plan to take up the poisoned pen against his hated rival, Fadge, 'with scornful laughter, with boisterous satire, with shouted irony, with fierce invective' (Ch. 8). The 'coming man' Jasper Reardon demonstrates the connivances of the literary market place which consists of social networking and a cynical use of his column space to flatter those in positions of influence. Although there appears to be a kind of redemption and genuine disinterestedness in his article praising 'The Novels of Edwin Reardon', Milvain's article also appears to feed the colourful myth of the writer who has sacrificed life for his art, commodifying the myth in a way that flatters his own and his reader's sense of their cultured inner selves.

We see the commodification of the Bohemian myth in striking form in *The Whirlpool* (1897) in which the would-be Bohemian girl Alma Frothingham is flattered and taken up by a variety of coteries. Before her marriage to Harvey Rolfe, Cyril Redgrave attempts to convert her anti-conventional impulses to his own hedonistic version of sexual Bohemia. 'There is a convention of unconventionality: poor quarters, hard life, stinted pleasures – all that kind of thing ... There's no harm in poverty that doesn't last too long' (Ch. 8). This is Redgrave's warning to her against the notion that 'easy circumstances were not favourable to artistic ambition'. Alma's brief career as a professional musician demonstrates in textbook fashion 'the psychology' of the art world described as far back as 1841 in Charles Roehm's *Physiologie du commerce des arts* which attempts to account for the changing relations of artistic production brought about by the shift from patronage to a buyer's market:

> In order to be in fashion ... to be in vogue, you have to be known. If you don't have real merit, but are conniving, you can manage to extort a momentary vogue: you will be flattered by a coterie of journalists, or you

will have the talent to insinuate yourself into the good graces of some high and powerful amateur whose protection will have influence on your reputation as an eminent man. (Quoted, Brown, 1985, p. 10)

Alma finds her 'powerful amateur' in Putney's Mrs Raynor Mann, the 'patroness of musicians'. At the same time, her promotional agent Felix Dymes invests substantial effort and money to secure her flattering notices in the popular press. In the end, neither Alma's talent nor personality are equal to the 'puffery', but the irony of the story is not so much that she has failed as a performer but that she has failed as a 'star' capable of keeping the publicity bandwagon rolling and the show on the road. *The Whirlpool* has certain features in common with the less realistic *Trilby* (1894) which can be read as a metaphor for the marketing of artistic Bohemia in which the mediocre and even talentless may be promoted and mesmerised by a new breed of entrepreneurial Svengalis.

It is a measure of Gissing's irony that Alma's struggle against conventionality should be played out against the institution of the male club which George Moore scornfully declared had originated with the villa and the circulating library from the 'Housewife by Respectability' (Moore, 1937, p. 114). Harvey Rolfe, with his inherited 'competency' and membership of the Metropolitan Club, represents a version of escapist, recreational Bohemia as a place of reaction and inaction. It is Alma who struggles to reconcile Villadom and Bohemia, conventional needs and anti-conventional impulses, the claims of self-expression and the crushing restraints of middle-class womanhood – children, servants, the suburban home. There is nothing strong or well-balanced in Gissing's neurasthenic heroine; but neither is there an offered alternative in Harvey Rolfe to the perceived debasements and extensions of modern metropolitan life. In Harvey Rolfe, as later in Henry Ryecroft, Gissing places ironically his own conservative tendencies and bourgeois dreams of material well-being.

Gissing himself remained an anti-bourgeois bourgeois, too traditional in his education and instincts to embrace the progressive aspects of new aestheticism, as Wilde was to do, or recognise the potential of the coterie as an oppositional intellectual coalition in the new expanding market place. Yet there is strength as well as pathos in Gissing's maintained stance of spiritual, and even physical isolation. In this respect at least, Gissing's situation corresponds closely to Ryecroft's where Ryecroft declares:

Most men who go through a hard time in their youth are supported by companionship. London has no *pays latin*, but hungry beginners in literature have generally their suitable comrades, garreteers in the Tottenham Court Road district, or in unredeemed Chelsea; they make their little *vie de Bohème*, and are consciously proud of it. Of my position, the peculiarity was that I never belonged to any cluster; I shrank from casual acquaintances, and through the grim years, had but one friend with whom I held converse. It was never my instinct to look for help, to seek favour for advancement; whatever step I gained was gained by my own strength... The truth is that I never learnt to regard myself as a 'member of society'. (Spring, VIII)

Ryecroft's declared distance from consolatory communities and coteries is matched by his declared indifference to contemporary notice: 'For the work of man's mind there is one test, and one alone, the judgment of generations yet unborn' (Spring, I). In Gissing's ironic accolade to starving and struggling authorship, and in his maintained irony towards recreational Bohemia, the description 'bourgeois Bohemian' fits him well (Collie, 1977, p. 9), not in the sense of his harbouring a repressed inner self, but in terms of a courageous doubleness and independence that consisted, with some success as it turned out, of living, and, in his own mind, writing for posterity.

Bibliography

Baudelaire, Charles, 'Préface' to Leon Cladel, *Les Martyrs Ridicules: Roman Parisien* (Bruxelles: Henry Kistemaeckers [1880]).

Brown, Marilyn R., *Gypsies and Other Bohemians: The Myth of the Artist in Nineteenth-Century France* (Ann Arbor, Michigan: UMI Research Press, 1985).

Collie, Michael, *George Gissing: A Biography* (Folkestone: Dawson, 1977).

Coustillas, Pierre, 'The Light that Failed': Of Artistic Bohemia and Self Revelation', *English Literature in Transition*, 29, 2 (1986) 127–39.

Cross, Nigel, *The Common Writer: Life in Nineteenth-Century Grub Street* (Cambridge: Cambridge University Press, 1985).

Deghy, Guy and Waterhouse, Keith, *Café Royal: Ninety Years of Bohemia* (London: Hutchinson, 1955).

Goode, John, *George Gissing: Ideology and Fiction* (London: Vision Press, 1978).

Jameson, Fredric, *The Political Unconscious: Narrative as a Socially Symbolic Act* (London: Methuen, 1981).

Korg, Jacob, ed., *George Gissing's Commonplace Book* (New York: New York Public Library, 1962).

Maltz, Diana, 'Bohemian Bo(a)rders: Queer Friendlly Gissing', *Gissing Journal*, 37, 4 (2001) 7–28.

Mattheisen, Paul F., Young, Arthur C., and Pierre Coustillas, eds, *The Collected Letters of George Gissing*, Vol. I (Athens, Ohio: Ohio University Press, 1991); Vol. II (Athens, Ohio: Ohio University Press, 1992).

Mitchell, Sally, 'Career for Girl: Writing Trash', *Victorian Periodical Review*, XXV, 3 (1992) 109–13.

Moore, George, *Confessions of a Young Man*, Ebony Edition (London: Heinemann, 1937).

Murger, Henri, 'Preface', *The Latin Quarter* (*Scenes de la Vie de Bohème*) trans. Ellen Marriage and John Selwyn, with an introduction by Arthur Symons (London: Greening, 1908).

Parsons, Deborah L., *Streetwalking the Metropolis: Women, The City, and Modernity* (Oxford: Oxford University Press, 2000).

Price, Julius M., *My Bohemian Days in London* (London: T. Werner Laurie, 1914).

Pritchett, V.S., *The Living Novel* (London: Chatto & Windus, 1946).

Roberts, Morley, *The Private Life of Henry Maitland* (London: Richards Press, 1958).

Saintsbury, George, 'Henry Murger', *Fortnightly*, XXX, August (1878) 231–49.

Seigal, Jerrold, *Bohemian Paris: Culture, Politics, and the Boundaries of Bourgeois Life 1830–1930* (New York: Viking, 1986).

Tindall, Gillian, *The Born Exile: George Gissing* (London: Temple Smith, 1974).

Wilson, Elizabeth, *Bohemians: The Glamorous Outcasts* (London and New York: I.B. Tauris, 2000).

5

Between Dreamworlds and Real Worlds: Gissing's London

Scott McCracken

I want to begin with an image of the city with which you will all be familiar, the Angel Islington at the opening of Chapter IV of *The Nether World*:

> Here was the wonted crowd of loiterers and the press of people waiting for tramcar or omnibus – east, west, south, or north; newsboys eager to get rid of their latest batch, were crying as usual, 'Ech-ow! Exteree speciul! Ech-ow! Steendard!' and brass band was blaring out its saddest strain of merry dance-music. The lights gleamed dismally in the rain-puddles and the wet pavement. With the wind came whiffs of tobacco and odours of the drinking-bar. (Gissing, 1974, p. 30)

And I want to follow that image, as representative of Gissing's city, through a particular tradition of Gissing criticism, left-wing critics like Raymond Williams, John Goode and Fredric Jameson, in some ways his strangest promoters. I am afraid this means that, for about half of this lecture, you will have to accompany me on a long march through the key Marxist critics of Gissing in the twentieth century. The march complete, I want to ask: why is it that tradition, in the urgency of its need to establish Gissing as a kind of realist, has ignored the phantasmagoric in his texts? An illumination that, after the belated translation of Walter Benjamin's *Arcades Project* into English, becomes difficult to justify. *The Arcades Project*, I will suggest, opens up a different perspective on Gissing's London as a kaleidoscope of different experiences and states of consciousness. Even the short passage just quoted is replete with the material structures, the technologies, the architectures that construct a city of dreamworlds: mass communication in the shape of the evening newspaper; popular music, in the brass band; city lights (Benjamin, 1999, pp. 562–70); the city's reflective surfaces (Benjamin, 1999, pp. 537–42); and public transport, the trams, which, like Benjamin's Paris Metro, carve new routes through the city, and create new ways to dream (Benjamin,1999 [C1a, 2]). Yet, the possibilities of a mobile modernity, the passage of the urban traveller from one state of consciousness to another as she or he passes from one part of the fragmented metropolis to another, is something that Marxist critics have felt is denied in Gissing's texts.

To re-engage with the city in Gissing we need to think in terms of a different constellation. We need to respond to the uncertainty of modernity, what Ulrich Beck calls the risk society (Beck, 1992), with some of the panache of one of Benjamin's urban types, the gambler:

> Hasn't his eternal vagabondage everywhere accustomed him to reintepreting the image of the city? And doesn't he transform the arcade into a casino, into a gambling den, where now and again he stakes the red, blue, yellow *jetons* of feeling on women, on a face that suddenly surfaces (will it return his look?), on a mute mouth (will it speak?) What, on the baize cloth, looks out at the gambler from every number – luck, that is-, here, from the bodies of all the women, winks at him as the chimera of sexuality: as his type. This is nothing other than the number, the cipher, in which just at that moment luck will be called by another name, in order to jump immediately to another number. (Benjamin, 1999, p. 489[O1, 1])

Here Benjamin is not advocating the limited belief-system of the gambler on its own terms, but the kind of creative confusion, what he calls *Zerstreutheit* (an idea developed from Proust's *désagrégation* (Proust, 1988)), that exceeds the immediate goals of money or sex and offers moments of transformation that only urban modernity can bring about.

But that is enough pleasure for the time being, get out your red flags and eventually, I promise, we will arrive at the imperial city, not Peking, but a different, stranger and more exotic nineteenth-century London than the dismal town most often associated with George Gissing. Before we go, however, let us roll the die one more time and see what the game of chance has given us in terms of the improbabilities of literary anniversaries, as arbitrary as any game of chance, but always an opportunity for an academic event.

The year 2003 has given us one literary anniversary already: the birth of George Orwell, né Eric Blair on the 25 June 1903. There are six months to go before the anniversary of George Gissing's death on 28 December in the same year, but the coincidence of that brief overlap of lives is suggestive – not least because the first of my Marxist critics, Raymond Williams, links them in *Culture and Society*. In 1958 he wrote of Gissing: 'he is...the spokeman of...despair: the despair born of social and political disillusion. In this he is a figure exactly like Orwell in our own day, and for much the same reasons. Whether one calls this honesty or not will depend on experience' (Williams, 1963, p. 177). Later in the same work, Williams argues that 'Gissing found the London poor repulsive, in the mass; his descriptions have all the gener-alising squalor of a Dickens or an Orwell' (Williams, 1963, p. 179). Williams' judgement is dismissive in a way that gives pain to those Gissing scholars sensitive to their subject's tangential relationship to the canon, and who are apt to forget that in Williams' first major work of criticism few of the Victorian greats escape some kind of censure: Dickens, Gaskell, Carlyle amongst them. What is more interesting, at a conference where our task is to look back at the development of a critical reputation over a hundred years, is Williams' positioning of Gissing both historically and politically.

Historically, he places him in the transition between the nineteenth and the twentieth centuries which he calls the 'interregnum'. Politically, he marks him out with Orwell (with whom *Culture and Society* concludes) as an exile. Orwell was 'one of a significant number of men who, deprived of a settled way of living, or of a faith, or having rejected those which were inherited, find virtue in a kind of improvised living and an assertion of independence' (Williams, 1963, p. 279). His self-imposed isolation echoes Gissing's 'proper study' which was 'the condition of exile and loneliness' (Williams, 1963, p. 181). With this definition, Williams sets the terms for later left-wing criticism of Gissing: he was a maverick, not particularly sympathetic to the Left, yet his novels offer the opportunity for a reading against the grain. The refusal in his fiction to accept the morality or the social palliatives offered by Victorian society allows us to see its truth.

Williams' conclusions about his subject seem at first to be marked by the tendency to biography that is the bane of so much Gissing criticism. He was, Williams remarks, a 'deeply sensitive, deeply lonely man' (Williams, 1963, p. 181). Yet a comparison with his Orwell essay makes it clear that, for Williams in the proper mode of the historical materialist, the politics of both men were a reaction to what each, in his own way, saw as the impossible contradictions of modernity – rather than, on the one hand, the trauma of Gissing's expulsion and imprisonment, and, on the other, Orwell's deep-seated psychological complexes. For Williams the lesson to be drawn is that:

> We have to understand, in the detail of experience, how the instincts of humanity can break down under pressure into an inhuman paradox; how a great and humane tradition can seem at times, to all of us, to disintegrate into a caustic dust. (Williams, 1963, p. 284)

The reference to dust is, of course, an allusion to the opening of 1984, where it signifies, as so often in realist fiction, the urban in all its material grittiness. But the image of the city as caustic dust also indicates the objection Williams has to both authors' representations of the urban masses. He sees their novels as dismissive, condescending, belittling, as putting the working class in their place. Their texts cap or limit the potential of the new industrial cities. This view became the orthodoxy on Gissing and yet, despite its limitations, the period after the publication of *Culture and Society* in 1958 and the publication of Fredric Jameson's *The Political Unconscious* in 1983 constituted, at one and the same time, one of the most fruitful periods of both cultural Marxism and of Gissing criticism. It is one of the many paradoxes in a century of literary criticism that while Gissing's politics – whether of class or gender – lack easy definition, it was, by and large, left-wing critics who kept his reputation alive and latterly, and perhaps more surprisingly feminist critics, like Sally Ledger, who have continued to find him of interest (Ledger, 1997, pp. 162–9).

A key figure in this process was John Goode, who wrote some of his key essays in the 1960s, but whose monograph, *Ideology and Fiction*, now recognised as amongst the best works on Gissing, was not published until 1978. Goode claims two of the most fashionable Marxists of the 1970s as key influences: Antonio Gramsci and Walter Benjamin. Reading *Ideology and Fiction* now, it is also clear that his acknowledgement of the 'pervasive influence' (Goode, 1978, p. 9) of these two is partly an attempt to distance the book from two other currents, the older influence of Georg Lukács' treatment of nineteenth-century realism and the iron grip of Althusser's theory of ideology on literary studies at the time.

Goode specifically compares Gissing to Lukács, broadly following Lukács' periodisation of European realism to the extent that he sees Gissing as 'having a place in the large aesthetic disruption which takes place in European literature from the late fifties on' (Goode, 1978, p. 39). As Goode implies, the process was more gradual in England. But Goode attributes to Gissing a better grasp of ideology than Lukács. Gissing is able to see that (what was then called) 'classic realism' was 'a product of the particular possibilities released not by a general historical situation but by the specific determinations of the relationship between the writer and his public' (Goode, 1978, p. 35). It was the change in that relationship at the end of the century that propelled Gissing into the a new mode of realism, a realism that had limitations of which he was highly conscious.

In fact, Goode argues, it was a consciousness of limitations that makes his work so significant (Goode, 1978, pp. 45–6). Gissing was aware of the ideological boundaries of both the forms of middle-class culture of earlier realists, like Dickens, and their own selection of a particular kind of scientific realism. Goode, and as we shall see, this is also true of Fredric Jameson, finds Gissing's value as a writer in the reading strategies his texts offer to see through the late nineteenth-century's ideologies of class. The theory of ideology here is developed within a broadly Althusserian framework, more, I suspect, because Goode is in a dialogic relationship with the theoretical debates of the time than because he espouses a fully-fledged Althusserianism. This is apparent not just in terms of his understanding of ideology as an imaginative relationship to the real, but also in the pessimism he articulates about the ideological function of the institution of literature itself. The conclusion to *Ideology and Fiction* defines the most radical element of Gissing's texts as their refusal to conform to literature's ideological function. Instead, they operate a kind of negative dialectic against literature itself as bourgeois form.

Gissing's work resisted identification with a comfortable, middle-class view of Victorian society, even if his fallback position was often reactionary – in Adorno's terms, a different kind of identity thinking. Goode's negative dialectic results in a kind of circular argument, in which literary criticism itself shores up the dominant ideology:

> The most important institutional function of literature is its making of ideology. In fact, most teachers of literature would claim that the close analysis of literary texts liberates the student from ideological conditioning – frees him from the stock response. It is this claim which precisely constitutes the ideological function of literature, because it creates the very important illusion that choice is still theoretically possible... The most revolutionary text can be immunised in this way, the conditions of its production are obscured by its canonisation; it becomes a kind of gospel ripe for commentary – it reflects, represents, mobilises itself as an object. What it ceases to do is to intervene in the world of social action. Reading is a private affair and literature calls into being a group, a élite, a specialised section of traditional intellectuals who can convince themselves that they are not conquered by the dominant ideology (which is an important condition of its conquest). (Goode, 1978, p. 201)

Traditional intellectuals here are implicitly opposed to Gramsci's organic intellectuals, the agents of social and political change (Gramsci, 1971, pp. 5–23), but without them this truly is a nether world, a circle of hell from which there is no escape. Gissing's success is in writing novels that cannot be recuperated by the institution. Not because they are bad novels, although the worst aspect of his work involves his weak attempts to reimpose a cultural hierarchy against the commercial age, but because Gissing insists on concentrating on what Goode calls the 'urbanisation of the unclassed' (Goode, 1978, p. 201). In effect, his texts operate an anti-aesthetic, where the poetic does not allow the reader-critic to be distracted from the real, class-based conditions of production: 'Gissing wrote novels to make a living, and he wrote them about the struggle to make a living in the remote respectable corners of urban society: the motive and the representation are at one, and because they are at one, we can never feel that we ignore the conditions of production' (Goode, 1978, p. 201).

Few people these days, I imagine, get that worked up about the intricacies of Marxist literary criticism of the 1970s. The significance of Goode's book for this conference is the way in which his theoretical conclusions are founded on his understanding of Gissing's relationship with the city. Because, although I have focused on Goode's conclusions about the ideological function of the institution of literature, those conclusions are arrived at via his reading of Gissing's London. In that reading, there is a close fit between

Gissing's textual mapping of the city and Charles Booth's cartography in his *Inquiry into the Life and Labour of the People in London* (1969). Just as the colour coding of Booth's maps implies rigid boundaries between zones defined by class, so Gissing's characters inhabit particular zones which break up a conception of the city as a totality. In his analysis of Gissing's London, Goode returns to Lukács and his understanding of naturalism as part of an aesthetic disruption caused by a working-class threat to the bourgeois world-view, so that the representation of a social totality is no longer possible. Instead, Gissing's London is made up of distinct locations: 'not "the city" as a conceptualised response, as a totality', but 'delimited spaces that have to be lived in or crossed' (Goode, 1978, p. 74). Although Waymark in *The Unclassed* is described as a *flâneur*, moving at will through the city's different spaces, Goode argues that 'the hustle of the city streets with its random contingencies is London, but only part of Gissing's London. Mostly, the novel is based on areas with contained social structures which hold even the unclassed within them – the West End is a specific location within the city, not the city itself' (Goode, 1978, p. 77). The city's meaning is constructed from motifs that are attached to specific domains of these delimited spaces (Goode, 1978, p. 80); and Goode goes further to argue that working-class domains offer a privileged view of the city: 'Only London could create the unclassed, but only the unclassed can see London' (Goode, 1978, p. 107).

Goode, like Williams, prefers the novels of urban deprivation over the later suburban novels. But, I would argue, this is not just a dubious selection between novels, but also within novels. Goode is choosing to understand the city on only one level, on the level of what might be called 'real material processes'. He stands on one side of a dividing line in cultural studies: on the one side, those who hold to an understanding of modernity in terms of such processes and who then perform an ideology critique to get at those processes (or real worlds); and on the other, those who argue that the saturation of modernity with images and symbols, what Benjamin calls the return of myth in the midst of modernity (Buck-Morss, 1989, pp. 78–80), means that those dreamworlds offer quite different versions of the city. Thus, in his analysis of *In the Year of Jubilee*, the novel which offers the most panoramic vision of the city and which, above all others, is concerned with the city streets, Goode limits that vision to the aspirations of suburbia, which appears as just another delimited zone of the city, the preoccupation of Gissing's later period.

If we turn to the other most influential Marxist critic on Gissing, Fredric Jameson, we find that Jameson too makes the city central to his understanding of Gissing's work. But Jameson's approach to the real is, as one might expect given the pages of mediations that constitute the theoretical first chapter of *The Political Unconscious* (Jameson, 1981, pp. 17–102), more complex than that of Goode – although that complexity does not always lead to better readings of the novels. On *The Nether World* he writes that it is best read, not for its documentary information on the conditions of Victorian slum life, but as testimony about the narrative paradigms that organize middle-class fantasies about those slums and about 'solutions' that might resolve, manage, or repress the evident class anxieties aroused by the existence of an industrial working class and an urban lumpenproletariat. (Jameson, 1981, p. 186)

Nonetheless, when it comes to the city, Lukács on classic realism is again the reference point:

> In Gissing...the Dickensian city is little by little drained of its vitality and reduced to the empty grid of calls by one character to another, visits to oppressive rooms and apartments, and intervals of random strolls through the poorer quarters. (p. 190)

How easy, one might comment, it would be to substitute Kafka's *The Trial* for *The Nether World* in that description. A comparison that can also be made between Kafka's three spheres of interiors, city streets and a green space, and Gissing's urban trinity of the slums (in the novels of the 1880s), the suburbs (in the novels of the 1890s) and the rural (in *The Private Papers of Henry Ryecroft*). But such a comparison is not usually made because Gissing is thought of as a realist or, in Jameson's Lukácsian categorisation, a naturalist writer rather than a modernist.

Instead, Jameson, like Goode, chooses to focus on the scientific discourse of classification in Gissing's texts: 'a form of high naturalist specialization that seeks to pass itself off as a map of the social totality...the characters of the novel will be reduced to nothing more than illustrations of their preexistent presences' (Jameson, 1981, 190–1). This analysis, which corresponds with Williams and Goode to the extent that it finds the core of Gissing's value in a negative aesthetic, is, however, supplemented with an account of how desire is dealt with in the novels, an account that offers Jameson's most influential contribution to critical discussions of Gissing: the concept of *ressentiment*, whereby the humiliation of the subaltern class is turned upon the ruling class through a morality that itself glorifies self-abasement. Desire in the novels is classified, as in the case of Richard Mutimer in *Demos*, as a kind of class envy. Unusually amongst Gissing critics, Jameson is alert to the later novels' wit, but he too commits the cardinal sin of Gissing criticism, the biographical impulse, referring us back to the the youthful misdemeanour and imprisonment as 'an incurable wound' in order to offer an original account of Gissing's use of language as that of a thwarted classicist who uses English as 'if it were a dead language like Latin' or:

> Better still Gissing's language offers perhaps an early example of what Roland Barthes has called *écriture blanche*, white or bleached

writing...this linguistic practice seeks through radical depersonalization – as though a kind of preventive suicide – to neutralize the social conflicts immediately evoked and regenerated by any living use of speech. (Jameson, 1981, pp. 203–4)

Thus, desire is neutralised: 'universal commodification of desire stamps any achieved desire or wish as inauthentic' (Jameson, 1981, p. 204). What this does is to make Gissing into a modernist, a writer who is in many ways closer to Kafka or Beckett, than Balzac or Dickens. What it leaves out is the opportunity for play that such processes of defamiliarisation or strategic alienation allow. However, if we accept that Gissing is a modernist, a position I think is defensible, then his relationship to the city becomes more not less important because, as Williams reminded us in his late work, the city is the place where modernism is born. Yet Jameson follows earlier Marxist critics and leaves his subject in a cul-de-sac, imprisoned, this time as symbol of 'unhappy consciousness', when a different understanding of Gissing's city might lead us back to the streets.

Such an understanding is now offered to English-speaking scholars by the translation of Walter Benjamin's *Arcades Project* a work, which, although unfinished, suggests in much more detail the relationship between the urban and modernity Benjamin had in mind in the Baudelaire essays that influenced John Goode. At over a thousand pages of notes, quotations and commentaries, Benjamin's work, even in its incomplete form, amounts to the literary montage he envisaged. Almost, but not quite, a work constructed entirely from citations, these are organised and juxtaposed in ways that generate unexpected constellations that – even if they do not always speak for themselves in the ways Benjamin hoped – produce, like the thought processes of the gambler, new and unexpected perspectives.

If, as I have suggested elsewhere, the playful aspects of Gissing's prose have been almost universally and systematically downplayed in favour of the image of the lonely and embittered man, nursing that 'incurable wound', the city that has been built up to house the man has been mapped onto the biography (McCracken, 2001). Gissing's irony, the satirical elements that abound in the novels of the 1890s, but which are by no means absent in the 1880s are matched by his acute observations of the emergent public culture of a new commercial age. One aspect of this is his exploration of London's food cultures, an exploration which extends from the scientific to the anthropological to the carnivalesque (McCracken, 2005). Another, most prominent in *In the Year of Jubilee*, but equally to the fore in *The Town Traveller*, is the extension of commodification into every aspect of everyday life, but not just in a way that drains city-living of its vitality. As David Glover has pointed out, the panoramic visions of the city in *In the Year of Jubilee* configure a new experience of urban modernity (Glover, in Postmus, 2001). All of this raises the question of whether

Gissing's mapping of the city into delimited spaces, and hence his politics as a politics of paralysis or stasis, has been read too quickly as a kind of negative aesthetic. What happens, one might ask, and what justification might there be for reading these spaces as a kind of urban montage, closer perhaps to Robert Delaunay's proto-cubist deconstruction of the Eiffel Tower than to Booth's dry mapping of social class?

There is not the space here to offer the comprehensive survey that these questions call for, so instead I am going to put forward the view that the well-known chapter of *The Nether World*, 'Io Saturnalia', suggests that even in the texts of the 1880s, sometimes called the proletarian novels, Gissing's novels move consciously between the different levels of reality covered by Benjamin in *The Arcades Project*. The chapter figures at least three kinds of dreamworlds.

The first dreamworld, already present in this early novel, is the emergent commodity culture of the late Victorian period. Crystal Palace – once the showcase for mid-Victorian wealth – has, along with the great international exhibitions of the nineteenth century, a central place in Benjamin's work. This massive structure made of the new industrial technologies of iron and glass was an arcade on a huge scale. Like the arcades it confused exterior and interior, inside and outside, nature and culture. Built tall enough to include the trees of Hyde Park, it absorbed not just the whole of London, but, in its displays, the whole world, offering a phantasmagoria of commodities (Richards, 1991, pp. 17–92).

The city produces dreamscapes. If it was the arcades that gave the project its working title, they were not, according to Benjamin, the only city spaces that gave rise to the surreal dreamworld of the nineteenth century: 'arcades, winter gardens, panoramas, factories, wax museums, casinos, railroad stations' are all 'dream houses of the collective' (Benjamin, 1999[L1, 3]). This sense is reflected in Adela's experience of the railway station in *Demos*, where that space, far from being delimited, is as much a state of mind as a grounded experience: 'It impressed her as if all the world had become homeless, and had nothing to do but to journey hither and thither in vain search of a resting place' (Gissing, 1986, p. 349).

According to Benjamin, the concept of 'phantasmagoria' that describes these dream spaces is a product of the new commodity culture that emerged after the French Revolution: 'Capitalism was a natural phenomenon with which a new dream-filled sleep came over Europe, and, through it, a reactivation of mythic forces' (Benjamin, 1999[K1a, 8]). If the opening of the nineteenth century marks the threshold of this new era, its first and most enduring expression in the nineteenth century were the great exhibitions. These events – Benjamin dates the first as 1798 – juxtaposed commodities from across the globe, wrenching them out of their original context and into a new arrangement or constellation. Torn from their cultural traditions, they were reassembled like the found objects of a surrealist work of art. In the unlikely, and perhaps still underestimated, culture of nineteenth-century commercialism, Benjamin discovers the poetics of the modern in a 'premature synthesis' (Benjamin, 1999[G2, 3]). He argues that the experience closest to that of nineteenth-century urban life is the drug experience. By contrast, when he writes that the 'history that showed things "as they really are" was the strongest narcotic of the century', the distinction between lived experience and dependency is clear (Benjamin, 1999[N3, 4]).

In the 'Saturnalia' chapter, Gissing explores the ways in which the dream-worlds cut across the boundaries erected by social class and the delimited spaces of the city. In this he is, as usual, historically accurate. By the 1880s, Crystal Palace, now moved to South London, had become a holiday destination for London's working class, a role that echoed an earlier characteristic of the great exhibitions. From their beginnings, they had been a workers' destination, both in order to wonder at the riches on display, and also a point at which international political links might be made. French delegations to the London exhibitions of 1851 and 1862 were met by parties of English workers and the rendezvous marked a milestone in co-operation between French and English workers' organisations (Benjamin, 1999[G5, 2], [G5a, 1]). Benjamin cites Georgi Plekhanov, the Russian Marxist:

> The world exhibition has given the proletariat an excellent idea of the unprecedented level of development which the means of production have reached in all civilized lands – a development far exceeding the boldest utopian fantasies of the century preceding this one...

He goes on:

> The exhibition has further demonstrated that modern development of the forces of production must of necessity lead to industrial crises that, given the anarchy currently reigning in production, will only grow more acute with the passage of time, and hence more destructive to the course of the world economy. (Benjamin, 1999[G4a, 1])

If, on the one hand, this latter statement seems of a piece with the mechanistic form of scientific Marxism for which Plekhanov is best known, on the other, anarchy is exactly the state of affairs Gissing depicts as the day degenerates from festival to fist fight:

> Near St James's Church Jack Bartley made a stand and defied his enemy to come on. Bob responded with furious eagerness; amid a press of delighted spectators swelled by people just turned out of the public-houses, the two lads fought like wild animals. Nor were they the only combatants. Exasperated by the certainty that her hat and dolman were ruined, Pennyloaf flew with erected nails at Clem Peckover. It was just what the latter desired. In an instant she had rent half Pennyloaf's garments off her back. (Gissing, 1974, p. 112)

Here a defined space is exceeded by the energy of the combatants as are the constraints of the law: 'There was no question of making arrests...it was the night of the Bank holiday and the capacity of police cells is limited' (p. 112).

At a different level to Plekhanov, and envisaging a different outcome, Gissing suggests that anarchy is the converse of commodity culture, that the riot of goods and pleasures offered by Crystal Palace is met by a breakdown in social order. For Gissing, the violence is internal to the working class, not directed towards its masters, but towards part of the cycle of despair of the nether world that is working-class life. But, as becomes clearer in the novels of the 1890s, there is contradiction between plot and the novel's textuality. If the failure of philanthropy condemns the novels' characters to further circuits of their particular circle of hell, the language of the novel invokes a further set of subsidiary dreamworlds, including those of John Hewett's feverish political speeches on Clerkenwell Green.

The second dreamworld concerns Gissing's historical approach to modernity, usually characterised by Marxist critics as ahistorical. If we return to Jameson's point about Gissing's language as dead or bleached of all life, we find that not only does it rely on the suspect biographical reading, it underestimates the dialectic of modernity that takes place in Gissing's texts, including his diary where, in his trips to Italy and Greece, the overwhelming impression is of the ancient world as still present in the contemporary. As always the acute social observer, in his diary, Gissing constantly picks out customs, forms of speech and even burial practices that echo the Roman or Greek past: for example, the entry for 3 December 1888, 'Strange to see everywhere about the streets – on public proclamations, offices, even dust-carts, the letters "S.P.Q.R." ' (*Diary*, 1978, p. 87); or for 11 December on the same trip, 'An interesting feature of the by-streets are the splendid teams of oxen bringing in loads of straw etc. from the country. These fine beasts, with their immense horns, always make me think of the antique. Such animals Virgil saw, and Homer, I suppose' (*Diary*, p. 93).

Gissing's own movements in the late 1880s, despite the image of the lonely and embittered man, are not confined to London, let alone its poorer areas. Far from being static, by the end of the 1880s Gissing was making annual trips to the continent on the proceeds of his novels. In the porous zone, that is Naples, Gissing and Benjamin meet not, of course, in time, but in a common space in which modernity is understood to absorb earlier epochs, rendering them trivial by reducing them to the ephemerality and forgetfulness of fashion, so that history itself becomes an exhibition or an arcade. Gissing describes Naples as a space in which past and present interpenetrate:

> Let me see if I can put down some of the points which seem most characteristic of Naples to one who has just arrived. The amount of buying and selling, especially in poor streets; the fanciful harness of horses; the

multitudes of donkeys; the hard and excellent paving, squares placed diamond-wise; the enormous houses, vast doorways, great rooms, thick walls; the madonna faces among the lower classes; the elegant appearance of officers; the abundances of clerics in the street and their leisurely walk,- including monks of medieval appearance; the gradoni; the soft note of the street-organs; the saints with lamps before them;the long musical cry of the sellers going about the streets at night. (*Diary*, Entry for 31 October 1888, p. 61)

This is a description that conforms to Benjamin's view that in Naples ancient myth and superstition mingle with the modern, a process that is enabled by the material structure of the city itself:

The architecture is as porous as [the] stone. Building and action interpenetrate in the courtyards, arcades and stairways. In everything they preserve the scope to become a theater of new, unforseen constellations. The stamp of the definitive is avoided. No situation appears intended forever, no figure asserts its 'thus and not otherwise'. This is how architecture, the most binding part of the communal rhythm, comes into being here: civilized private, and ordered only in the great hotel and warehouse buildings on the quays; anarchical, embroiled, villagelike in the centre, into which large networks of streets were hacked only forty years ago. And only in these streets is the house, in the Nordic sense, the cell of the city's architecture. In contrast, within the tenement blocks, it seems held together at the corners, as if by iron clamps, by the murals of the Madonna. (Benjamin, 1986, pp. 165–6)

Better than Jameson's suggestion of Barthes for an understanding of Gissing's relationship with the past is Benjamin's favourite poet, Charles Baudelaire. In Baudelaire, Benjamin found an understanding of modernity's dynamic relationship with the past; although Baudelaire's conception of the relationship between the modern and the past is governed by the opposition between modernity and classical antiquity, 'the modern, with Baudelaire, appears not only as the signature of an epoch but as an energy by which this epoch immediately transforms and appropriates antiquity. Among all the relations into which modernity enters, its relation to antiquity is critical' (Benjamin, 1999[J5, 1]).

In Baudelaire's aesthetic, Benjamin found a methodology by which that relationship could be represented, allegory: 'the stamp of time that imprints itself on antiquity presses out of it the allegorical configuration' (Benjamin, 1999[J6a, 2]). But, while Baudelaire's method opened up the possibility of the dialectical relationship between past and present that for Benjamin might unleash the full potential of the modern, Baudelaire's method of correspondences between the modern and antiquity was too rigid: 'The correspondence between antiquity and modernity is the sole constructive conception of history in Baudelaire. With its rigid armature, it excludes every dialectical conception' (Benjamin, 1999[J59a, 5]). Benjamin's own 'dialectical conception' was facilitated by his engagement with Baudelaire's partial account of modernity, which he understood not in terms of an aesthetic truth but as itself a kind of historical remnant or ruin: 'The experience of allegory, which holds fast to ruins, is properly the experience of eternal transience' ([J67, 4]).

This then is the historical understanding that underpins the satire of the 'Saturnalia' chapter. It is not a straightforward degeneration narrative, where the modern is a travesty of the classical past. Instead, antiquity and the present co-exist in what Benjamin calls *Jetztzeit*, the time of now, and nowhere is that co-temporality, more concentrated than in the spaces created by the great exhibitions, themselves spaces that are only enabled by the modern city.

The third and final dreamworld is that of mobility, the train journey across the city, from North to South. Trains and trams in the novel make the connections between different parts of the city and are associated with labour mobility and, crucially, the New Woman's mobility; for example Clara's employment as a barmaid and later an actress. New routes or passages through the city create the possibility of crossing boundaries and thresholds and of experiencing the different states of consciousness those crossings engender. It is this mobility and its psychic consequences that give Gissing's texts their energy, even if it is an energy that the plot then closes down.

If we return from Crystal Palace to the Angel Islington and the passage with which I started, we find all of these aspects of the phantasmagoric city – the reflective surfaces of Victorian commodity culture, a dynamic, if conservative, approach to modernity, a city divided yet navigable – and we find them not just as content, but also in the form and language of the text, which offers the jumble of images as a list that represents the simultaneity of their impact.

Re-reading Gissing's London after *The Arcades Project* might lead us to conclude that Williams was premature and perhaps too optimistic in his judgement on Gissing. Capitalism has not proved so easy to overcome that the contradictions Gissing grapples with could be so easily surpassed. Similarly, Goode's conclusions about both Gissing and the possibilities of literary criticism, while not without some merit, close down the argument too soon; while Jameson does not take the implications of his reading as far as they might go. A century after Gissing's death, it is possible to read all three critics in terms of the epoch in which they were writing: the period of the Cold War between 1945 and 1989. It might now be argued that the political paralysis induced by the Cold War irrupts in their reading of late nineteenth-century fiction. In fact, there is a whole other argument to be had about the history of cultural marxism and its sudden decline in the

1980s, but this is not the place for it. For today, it is enough to say something which does not, I think, detract from the achievements of Gissing criticism or from cultural Marxism's contributions to that criticism in the twentieth century: when it comes to the cities of Gissing's imagination, there is a lot left to explore.

Bibliography

Adorno, T.W. *Negative Dialectics*, trans. Ashton, E.B. (London: Routledge, Kegan, Paul, 1973).

Beck, U. *Risk Society: Towards A New Modernity* (London: Sage, 1992).

Benjamin, W. 'Naples', in *Reflections: Essays, Aphorisms, Autobiographical Writings*, trans. Jephcott, E. (New York: Schocken, 1986).

——. *The Arcades Project* (trans.) Eiland, H. and McLaughlin, K. (Cambridge, MA.: Belknap Press of Harvard University Press, 1999).

Booth, C. *Inquiry into the Life and Labour of the People in London* [1892] (New York: Augustus M. Kelley, 1969).

Buck-Morss, S. *Dialectics of Seeing: Walter Benjamin and the Arcades Project* (Cambridge, MA.: MIT Press, 1989).

Coustillas, P. ed., *London and the Life of Literature in Late Victorian England: The Diary of George Gissing, Novelist* (Hassocks, Sussex: The Harvester Press, 1978).

Gissing, G. *The Nether World* [1889] (Brighton: The Harvester Press, 1974).

——. *Demos: A Story of English Socialism* [1886] (Brighton: The Harvester Press, 1986).

Glover, D. ' "This spectacle of a world's wonder": Commercial Culture and Urban Space in Gissing's *In the Year of the Jubilee*', in Postmus, Bouwe, ed., *A Garland for Gissing* (Amsterdam: Rodopi, 2001), pp. 137–151.

Goode, J. *Ideology and Fiction* (London: Vision, 1978).

Gramsci, A. *Prison Notebooks* (London: Lawrence and Wishart, 1971).

James, S.J. *Unsettled Accounts: Money and Narrative in the Novels of George Gissing* (London: Anthem, 2003).

Jameson, F. *The Political Unconscious: Narrative as Socially Symbolic Act* (London: Methuen, 1981).

Ledger, S. *The New Woman: Fiction and Feminism at the* fin de siècle (Manchester: Manchester University Press, 1997).

Lukács, G. *Studies in European Realism* (New York: Grosset and Dunlap, 1964).

McCracken, S. 'From Performance to Public Sphere: The production of modernist masculinities', *Textual Practice*, 15, 1 (Spring 2001), 47–65.

——. 'Just a Morsel to Stay Your Appetite: George Gissing and the Cultural Politics of Food', in Ryle, Martin and Bourne Taylor, Jenny, eds, *Voices of the Unclassed* (Aldershot: Ashgate, 2005).

Proust, M. *A La Recherche du Temps Perdu, tome 1 : Du Côté de chez Swan* (Paris : Gallimard, 1988).

Richards, T. *The Commodity Culture of Victorian England: Advertising and Spectacle, 1851–1914* (London: Verso, 1991).

Ryle, M. and Soper, K. *To Relish the Sublime: Cultural Self-realization in Postmodern Times* (London: Verso, 2002).

Thacker, A. *Moving Through Modernity* (Manchester: Manchester University Press, 2003).

Williams, R. *Culture and Society* (Harmondsworth: Penguin, 1963).

6

'Citizens of London?' Working Women, Leisure and Urban Space in Gissing's 1880s Fiction

Emma Liggins

In a letter to his sister Ellen in 1885, during a period of intensive teaching and writing, Gissing complained, 'I no longer feel like a citizen of London. Libraries, book-shops, museums, theatres, all are strange to me – even the very streets' (*Letters*, 2, 1991, p. 285). Lacking both the time and the money to participate fully in urban culture, his position mirrors that of a dominant figure from 1880s fiction, the East-End work-girl frustrated by her limited and controlled access to public space. In her feminist account of women's historical exclusion from citizenship, Ruth Lister has argued that 'women enter public space as *embodied* individuals... if women cannot move or act freely in the public sphere... then their ability to act as citizens is curtailed' (Lister, 1997, pp. 71, 113). Gissing's portrayal of female alcoholism and women's occupation of public houses demonstrates that the threat of female sexuality tends to disqualify women from citizenship, though he also protests against their 'restricted access to the public life of the city' (Parsons, 2000, p. 5). In this chapter, I will explore his participation in current debates about working-class leisure, the constraints on women's behaviour in public houses and on Bank Holiday excursions. Whilst ostensibly denouncing working-class amusement as vulgar and excessive, the 1880s novels also reveal his sympathies with the work-girl's right to leisure.

Debates about working-class leisure

In an article on 'The Amusements of the People' in the *Contemporary Review* in 1884, the novelist Walter Besant's list of amusements included 'the theatre, the music-hall, the public house, the Sunday excursion' plus parks and tea-gardens, with the public house functioning as the workman's equivalent of the gentleman's club because 'his employers have found him no better place and no better amusement' (1884, pp. 345, 344). Despite confessing his ignorance of women's amusements, Besant recognises that their participation in leisure is generally limited, observing of married mothers, 'one does not see how they can get any holiday or recreation at all'. His fictional manifesto for a People's Palace, *All Sorts and Conditions of Men* (1882) is typical of the plots of the new East-End fiction addressing both the difficulties of and the necessity for enticing the workers into such alternative spaces as clubs, lecture rooms and libraries. The middle-class proviso that 'the only condition of admission [to the Palace] will be good behaviour, with exclusion as a penalty' (p. 71) can only be achieved by downplaying the question of whether alcohol would be served, an issue which divided reformers before the opening of the actual Palace in the Mile End Road in 1887 (Small, 1997, p. xxii). As Besant noted in his 1897 Preface, the novel satisfied popular demands in 'catch[ing] and represent[ing] the ideas of the day', the need for 'recreation time' and the improvement of public spaces to enjoy it. It is interesting to note that Gissing objected to being bracketed with Besant as a 'philanthropic novelist' in an 1888 review by Edith Sichel (*Letters*, 4, p. 75). Sichel knowingly perceived Gissing's pessimistic narratives of the failures of philanthropy as a more authentic vision of the East End, an important modification to Besant's 'bowdlerised Whitechapel' (Coustillas and Partridge, 1973, pp. 114, 126).

Feminist social investigators expressed their concern that women's occupation of the streets led to their frequenting 'the music hall, the cheap theatres, the gin-palaces, the dancing saloons and the wine shop', spaces associated primarily with drinking and casual sexuality (Stanley, 1889, p. 76). In Gissing's fiction men's awareness of the dangers of urban culture for women are shown in the recurring scenes in which fathers, brothers and husbands join policemen in patrolling the streets, subjecting women to various forms of street harassment. In his first novel *Workers in the Dawn* (1880) Arthur Golding waits for hours outside Carrie Mitchell's lodgings for her return from a music hall because 'it was agony to him to think of her walking about the streets without his company and protection' (Gissing, 1880, Vol. 2, p. 340). In her 1885 discussion of how to prevent prostitution, Mary Jeune stressed that girls needed to be 'controlled and supervised' on public holidays and after work, claiming that 'very much is being done in England to guard young women . . . from the perils of our streets at night' (Jeune, 1885, p. 348). Concerns about the drunken revelry of the working classes on Bank Holiday excursions surfaced in a number of accounts. An article on the need to provide forms of 'legitimate and desirable pleasure' for young working women confirmed the 'well-known' fact that 'public holidays are a terrible danger to girls . . . In 1882, in one London police-court there were 240 convictions of women against 301 of men' (Greville, 1884, p. 22). It also reinforced the point that more respectable spaces tended to be 'inaccessible to women and children', encouraging 'the fatal habit of frequenting public-houses' (Greville, 1884, p. 23).

Women's restricted access to public space

Although it would be misleading to claim that working women had no experience of leisure, domestic responsibilities ensured that 'freedom of movement for married women was severely restricted' (Davies, 1992, p. 55). Andrew August makes the crucial point that 'women's claims to leisure were weaker than those of their husbands', not least because 'women's access to time and money for their own leisure depended on conditions in the family economy' (1999, p. 128). Feminist research has also revealed that 'the established definition of leisure as a reward for paid labour both ignores and distorts the experiences of [women] performing unpaid labour' (Langhamer, 2000, p. 190). Married women were not the only ones for whom leisure was a luxury, as the expenses of female homeworkers also made it practically impossible to set aside money for entertainment. Gissing's more refined working heroines are rarely shown enjoying themselves in public places: the seamstress Emma Vine in *Demos* (1886) turns down a proposed Bank Holiday excursion in order to continue sewing, preferring to combine childcare and socialising within the home. According to Lister, her 'time poverty' detracts from her citizenship, as 'formal equality for women in the public sphere . . . is undermined by the weight of their responsibilities in the private' (1997, p. 133). An alternative explanation is provided in Claire Langhamer's discussion of 'gendered notions of leisure entitlement'. She argues for a conceptualisation of leisure as separate from the public sphere, whereby adult women increasingly 'carve out' opportunities for leisure by alternative uses of domestic space (Langhamer, 2000, pp. 18, 138).

Gissing's views on access to leisure were typically contradictory and fluctuated according to his material circumstances. In his letters and diary he expresses mixed feelings about space, gender and respectability, not least in his descriptions of public amusements recorded on his European tour of 1888–89. He is particularly impressed by the Italian work-girls' enjoyment of art galleries. Parisian café culture is to be admired for its 'restfulness' after London and the people's capacity for enjoyment without vulgarity (*Letters*, 3, p. 21) but his own 'calm enjoyment in the Louvre' has been marred by a 'clash with a great crowd in the Place du Carrousel, gaping at a lot of balloons going up' outside the gallery (*Diary*, 1978, p. 56). He hesitates between the terms *caffé* and *brasserie* for a Florentine space which admits men, women and children when 'in England, or in France, no decent woman would be able to go to a place of this kind' and marvels that they consume coffee and ices, rather than alcohol (*Letters*, 4, p. 20). Woman-friendly spaces such as the museums and galleries which Gissing himself enjoyed might hope to offer the required combination of recreation and culture for the respectable work-girl. In *The Nether World* Bob Hewett's attempts to point out 'objects more likely to supply her with amusement' to Clem Snowdon in the British Museum gesture to the possibility of cultural engagement, and the topical point that 'had [the Museum] been open to visitors in the hours of the evening, or on Sundays, [he] would possibly have been employing his leisure nowadays in more profitable pursuits' (p. 220). But the socially inferior Clem, who has no aspirations to respectability and is more at ease showing off her finery in the crowded pit at the theatre, only takes advantage of the Museum as a free public space in which to engage in extramarital flirtation; 'much [she] cared for antiquities'. Such scenes are intended as a satire on the workers' limited appreciation for high culture.

However, Gissing can also be seen to empathise with working women denied leisure opportunities because of their limited earning power. On his walks round London in 1889, he is 'more and more appalled' by the regions around Regent Street and the Strand, proclaiming 'I stand aghast at the expenditure of such men as frequent the restaurants etc. Without one penny to spend on pleasures, I am entirely shut out from the new theatres and places that I should like to see' (*Diary*, 1978, p. 143). This envy of the spending power of West-End consumers is rather puzzling given the restaurants, cafés and theatres he has enjoyed in Europe, but clearly testifies to a sense of exclusion from certain public spaces which aligns him with the working woman. The choice of leisure is of course determined by disposable income, which puts women with their meagre salaries at a disadvantage and encourages male control. Arthur Golding sneers at his wife Carrie's vulgarity for visiting the music hall, 'a place in which no woman who valued her reputation would care to be seen' (Vol. 2, p. 349), but refuses to take her to the theatre, arguing 'I can't afford to pay for a good place, and I don't choose that you should crowd in with a lot of vulgar people; it isn't nice' (Vol. 2, p. 358). However, the London work-girl's 'fondness' for the theatre, generally perceived to be dangerous and vulgar, prevails in the fiction. In an attempt to account for lower-middle-class male authors' 'sensitiv[ity] to the plight of women' at the turn of the century, Arlene Young concludes that it was 'most probably their own marginality... [which made them] anxious to champion the cause of a subjugated group, but free of the peculiar social and ideological constraints that hampered women themselves' (1999, p. 156).

An account of how these constraints might operate is provided in one of Gissing's earliest short stories 'Phoebe' (1884) about an out-of-work Hoxton flowermaker faced with the 'limitless possibilities' (p. 28) of spending a fantasy disposable income she discovers hidden in her lodgings. The 15-year-old Phoebe imagines the City as a 'crowded, roaring place' with grand shops, 'whither no doubt everybody repaired who had money to spend, and wanted the best' (p. 32). However, the 'sense of her shabbiness' and inferiority prevents her from buying gloves alongside West-End shopping ladies and it seems 'beyond all possibilities' to approach the counter in a large confectioner's, as 'her mind recurred to those humbler shops in Hoxton, where she would feel much less timid' (p. 33). Displaced and inexperienced as a consumer, she buys nothing until she has to resort to the 'humiliat[ion]' of eating in 'a dirty little eating-house' (p. 34). The work-girl's unfamiliarity with the West End is then coupled with her inability to make choices as a consumer and to manage her own entertainment. Hesitating in the crowds outside the theatre she falls prey not to the jostling 'rough lads' who 'alarm' her but to the 'envious glances' of another girl, who is only too happy to take charge of her spending and to steal the change. Phoebe's vulnerability stems from her confusion in the face of 'such a variety of goods and prices' in the metropolis; she struggles to cultivate 'the new urban female style of being "at home" in the city' noted by Judith Walkowitz (1992, p. 46), as her financial naivete and 'timidity' in urban space constrain her enjoyment in the public sphere.

Female drinking and the public house

The harnessing of women's city pleasures to the dangers of drink further jeopardises the legitimacy of their occupation of certain places of entertainment, such as public houses and music halls. Zola's narrative of the alcoholic laundress Gervaise, *L'Assommoir* (1877), both condemns and applauds women when they go 'out on the loose', associating them with disorder and lack of control. Although Gissing's serious reading of Zola did not begin until the early 1890s, it is hard to believe that he was unaware of this popular representation of female drinking; he may have read a cheap translation or seen one of the many stage versions in London or Paris (Brown, 1995, pp. 489–90). The immorality of laundresses was seen as inseparable from their drinking habits – according to one of Clementina Black's investigators in the early 1910s, 'they all drink more or less – many of them a great deal' (Black, 1915, p. 120). Patricia Malcolmson contends that as the traditional breadwinner the laundress exercised a rare right of entry to such a space, arguing that 'her economic power enabled [her] to do her drinking openly rather than joining the "stair-head drinking clubs" of women excluded from the public house' (Malcolmson, 1981, p. 461). At first Gervaise is afraid to enter old Colombe's bar to collect her drunken husband, reinforcing August's view that 'male drinking or other leisure [had] a protected status' (August, 1999, p. 128). Her later belief in her 'perfect right' to enter the bar to remind her husband of his promise to take her to the circus effectively signals her loss of respectability rather than her economic power; her fear that 'it wasn't really the right place for a respectable woman' (p. 335) is only abated after 'she was putting it down like a fish' (p. 339). Women can only access such spaces by sacrificing their respectability and risking degeneration into 'a sottish mess among all the bawling men' (p. 358). Drinking punch in the hot, crowded saloons of Montmartre, the laundress is 'in a daze' (p. 368), symbolically on a level with the half-naked dancers, recalling 'that slut of a Clemence, who kicked up her skirts at the dance-halls, screeching like a banshee' (p. 185).

At a time when the 'considerable barriers' against women's drinking were reinforced in the lay-out of British pubs, which often relegated women to separate rooms (Davies, 1992, pp. 65, 63), women who drink or frequent pubs in Gissing's fiction similarly risk their respectability and femininity. Like Gervaise, they are liable to participate in or enjoy watching violence: the Zolaesque work-girl Clem Peckover in *The Nether World* is renowned for her brutality. The bestial creatures 'mad with liquor' who tear each other 'with their claws' (p. 65) in the gin-palaces of Gissing's first novel are seen as unfeminine; a key scene shows Golding horrified at the vision of 'his wife a drunkard, engaging in a low brawl before a public-house' (Vol. 3, p. 41). The marital status of these women supports Carl Chinn's claim that it was only acceptable for older, married women to frequent such spaces (Chinn, 1988, p. 120), as the author tends to avoid positioning his single work-girls in such a dangerous environment. Although historians suggest that married couples often went to pubs and music halls together around the turn of the century, Gissing's female drinkers tend to socialise with other women rather than their spouses. Indeed, Harriet Smale in *The Unclassed*, who keeps late hours in Mrs Sprowl's East-End pub, has chosen her own form of public amusement against her husband's wishes. In the later novel *Demos*, Gissing continues to endorse women's right to such a choice as the widowed Kate Vine's drinking is alternatively explained as another telling sign of the 'process of degradation' brought on by 'extreme poverty' (p. 391), and a flight from the responsibilities of motherhood. The diverse representations of female drinkers seems to bear out Davies' assertion that 'patterns of pub attendance among women were more complex than any simple contrast between male indulgence and female exclusion might suggest' (Davies, 1992, p. 61).

The Bank Holiday excursion

After a series of Acts in the early 1870s served to increase public holidays (Bailey, 1978, pp. 80–1), the Bank Holiday excursion of the masses was promptly seized on by the press as a showcase for drunken excess. For Gissing, British 'rowdiness' was always annexed to the vulgarity he affected to despise. In a letter to his sister Margaret in May 1882, he spluttered 'Never is so clearly to be seen the vulgarity of the people as at these holiday-times. There [sic] notion of a holiday is to rush in crowds to some sweltering place, such as the Crystal Palace, and there eat and drink and quarrel themselves into stupidity' (*Letters*, 2, p. 87). The 'Io Saturnalia!' chapter of *The Nether World*, with its descriptions of the 'imbecile joviality' (p. 108) of the people, realises what Peter Bailey has categorised as 'the bourgeois fear of the vulgarisation of leisure' (Bailey, 1998, p. 29). The chapter opens with the view that a Bank Holiday is 'a day gravely set apart for the repose and recreation of multitudes who neither know how to rest nor how to refresh themselves with pastime' (p. 104). The 'perpetual rush of people for the trains to the "Paliss"' (p. 105) shows a desperate desire for enjoyment, intensified by the steady drinking of the 'multitudes' released from their labour. There seem to be no sexual divisions of leisure here as both men and women indulge in dancing, drinking, gorging and fighting. Gissing also hints at the imbalance between work and leisure in the lives of the workers, as the women's enjoyment in particular is marred by their exhaustion: he notes 'See how worn-out the poor girls are becoming... the stoop in the shoulders so universal among them merely means over-toil in the workroom' (p. 109). In his letters he characterised 'this idea of setting aside single days for great public holidays' as 'absurd', calling for 'a general shortening of working-hours all the year round' (*Letters*, 2, p. 87). But representing work-girls as being incapable of calm enjoyment would effectively be counterproductive. The newly married Pennyloaf is singled out from the 'pert' and shrieking women who surround her by her attempts at respectable behaviour, primarily through refusing drink. However, on the crowded train home she struggles to free herself from the 'jovial embrace' of a man and ultimately she too is provoked into violence by the malicious behaviour of her rival Clem Peckover. Returning home with 'her pretty face... all blood and dirt' (p. 113), the work-girl's tears testify to her frustration at being out of control of her own limited leisure experiences.

The disorderly Bank Holiday scene was clearly perceived to be appealing to middle-class readers, as the editor of the *English Illustrated Magazine* later commissioned Gissing to write the short story 'Lou and Liz' (1893) on a similar theme. The eponymous work-girls, who barely earn enough to support Liz's child between them, have 'somehow managed' (p. 2) to save up in order to afford a day's entertainment. Despite the constant restrictions on leisure in the form of inadequate earnings and maternal duties, they are determined to have a good time:

> They... drank beer when they could afford it, tea when they couldn't, starved themselves occasionally to have an evening at the Canterbury or at the Surrey (the baby, drugged if he were troublesome, sleeping now on his mother's lap, now on Lou's) and on a Bank-holiday mingled with the noisiest crowd they could discover. (p. 3)

Adopting the common practice of taking children to public venues, the girls risk their femininity by drugging the baby. At Rostherne Gardens the screaming child, who does not respond well to sweet food and beer, and is a heavy burden to be carried amongst the crowds, is more 'troublesome', as child-care blurs work into leisure for women. The dancing and drunken flirtations of the women are kept in check by the duties of motherhood: "Ow can y'expect to enjoy yerself when you 'ave to tike babbies out!' (p. 12). The day is then 'hopelessly spoilt' by Lou's fight with the husband who deserted her, shaming them into leaving early as 'people were pointing at them' (p. 12). Liz's enjoyment is also marred by the 'personal anxieties' that Lou will abandon her either for a man or for a less restrictive lifestyle, another sobering reminder of the difficulties of single motherhood. The story significantly ends with the return to 'the week's labour'. Such Bank Holiday scenes suggest the shortfalls of a gender-neutral concept of citizenship, in which women might 'participate as [men's] equals in the public sphere' (Lister, 1997, p. 92), and demonstrates Gissing's enduring belief in the desperate need for the people to 'learn to make some sensible use of [their hours of leisure]' (*Letters*, 2, p. 87).

An examination of the urban freedoms of the East-End work-girl then reveals what Langhamer refers to as 'the ambiguities of "work" and "leisure" in women's lives' (Langhamer, 2000, p. 18). In East-End fiction women always risk their respectabilities by drinking and enjoying themselves in public, suggesting that equality with men in the public sphere is not easily achievable. Gissing's writing reflects current debates about the need for regulation of leisure activities, and the desire to find alternative public spaces than the public house whilst endorsing women's right to leisure. His sympathetic account of the constraints which limit the work-girl's enjoyment may parallel his own sense of marginalisation as a citizen of London, struggling to pay his way in the newly commercialised city.

Bibliography

August, A., *Poor Women's Lives: Gender, Work and Poverty* (London: Associated University Presses, 1999).

Bailey, P., *Leisure and Class in Victorian England: Rational Recreation and the Contest for Control, 1830–1885* (London: Routledge & Kegan Paul, 1978).

——, *Popular Culture and Performance in the Victorian City* (Cambridge: Cambridge University Press, 1998).

Besant, W., 'The Amusements of the People', *Contemporary Review*, 45 (1884), 344–53.

——, 'The People's Palace', *Contemporary Review*, 47 (1887), 226–33.

——, *All Sorts and Conditions of Men: An Impossible Story* (1882; London: Chatto & Windus, 1903).

Black, C., 'The Organization of Working Women', *Fortnightly Review*, 52 (1889), 695–704.

Brown, F., *Zola: A Life* (New York: Farrar, Strauss & Giroux, 1995).

Chinn, C., *They Worked all their Lives: Women of the Urban Poor in England, 1880–1939* (Manchester: Manchester University Press, 1988).

Coustillas, P., ed., *London and the Life of Literature in Late-Victorian England: The Diary of George Gissing, Novelist* (Hassocks: The Harvester Press, 1978).

Coustillas, P., and Partridge, C., eds, *Gissing: The Critical Heritage* (London: Routledge and Kegan Paul, 1972).

Davies, A., *Leisure, Gender and Poverty: Working-Class Culture in Salford and Manchester, 1900–1939* (Buckingham: Open University Press, 1992).

Gissing, G., 'Lou and Liz' in *The Day of Silence and other Stories*, ed. Coustillas, P. (London: J.M. Dent, 1993). First published in *English Illustrated Magazine* (August 1893).

——, 'Phoebe' in *Stories and Sketches* (London: Michael Joseph, 1938). First published in *Temple Bar* (March 1884).

——, *Demos: A Story of English Socialism*, ed. Coustillas, P. (1886; Brighton: The Harvester Press, 1972).

——, *The Nether World*, ed. Gill, S. (1889; Oxford: Oxford University Press, 1992).

——, *Workers in the Dawn* (1880; New York and London: Garland, 1976).

Greville, V., 'The Need of Recreation', in 'Social Reforms of the London Poor', *Fortnightly Review*, N.S. 35 (1884), 21–36.

Jeune, M., 'Saving the Innocents', *Fortnightly Review*, 44 (1885), 345–56.

Jones, Rev H., 'The Homes of the Town Poor', *Cornhill Magazine*, 13/60 (1889), 452–63.

L.D., 'A London Slum', in Black, C., ed. *Married Women's Work* ed. Alexander, S. (1915; London: Virago, 1987).

Langhamer, C., *Women's Leisure in England, 1920–1960* (Manchester: Manchester University Press, 2000).

Lister, R., *Citizenship: Feminist Perspectives* (Houndmills: Macmillan, 1997).

Malcolmson, P., 'Laundresses and the Laundry Trade in Victorian England', *Victorian Studies*, 24:4 (1981), 439–62.

Mattheisen, P.F., Young, A.C. and Coustillas, P., eds, *Collected Letters of George Gissing*, 6 volumes (Athens: Ohio University Press, 1990–6).

Parsons, D.L., *Streetwalking the Metropolis: Women, the City and Modernity* (Oxford: Oxford University Press, 2000).

Sichel, E., 'Two Philanthropic Novelists: Mr Walter Besant & Mr George Gissing', *Murray's Magazine* (April 1888), 506–18. Quoted in Coustillas, P. and Partridge, C., eds, *Gissing: The Critical Heritage* (London: Routledge & Kegan Paul, 1973).

Small, H., ed., Introduction to Besant, W., *All Sorts and Conditions of Men* (1882; Oxford: Oxford University Press, 1997).

Stanley, M., 'Clubs for Working Girls', *Nineteenth Century*, 25 (1889), 73–83.

Walkowitz, J.R., *City of Dreadful Delight: Narratives of Sexual Danger in late-Victorian London* (London: Virago, 1992).

Young, A., *Culture, Class and Gender in the Victorian Novel: Gentlemen, Gents and Working Women* (Houndmills: Macmillan, 1999).

Zola, É., *L'Assommoir* trans. and ed. Tancock, L. (1877; Harmondsworth: Penguin, 1972).

7

'Counter-jumpers' and 'Queens of the Street': The Shop Girl of Gissing and his Contemporaries

Elizabeth F. Evans

In Gissing's London, women employed in shops had a variety of names: 'women in business,' 'queens of the street,' 'counter-jumpers,' and, most commonly, 'shop girls.' This constellation of names indicates the range of responses the female shop assistant elicited, and also points to a number of anxieties that surrounded her and her place of employment.[1] At once a victim of commercialism and an aspiring social climber, the woman behind the counter was associated variously with the New Woman, the slave worker, the prostitute, and the modern commerce itself. As Sally Ledger has convincingly argued in her essay on Gissing's *The Odd Women*, it was the shop girl rather than the New Woman that was the more problematic figure of modern urban life. I build upon Ledger's recognition that the shop girl was a figure of fascination and discomfort for both Gissing and his contemporaries by reading Gissing's *The Odd Women* (1893) and *In the Year of Jubilee* (1894) side by side with contemporary discourse about the shop girl in the periodical press. This comparative reading not only confirms that Gissing's conflicted attitudes toward these emblems of modernity were shared by his contemporaries, but also suggests his use of a prevalent narrative: the shop girl, who may be morally tainted by her exposure to the public sphere, will marry perhaps into a higher social circle, and is liable to corrupt the sanctity of the private sphere. Whether shop work is an indicator or an exasperator of female social and sexual radicalism is left unresolved in Gissing's work. What is clear is that the space of the shop is a microcosm of the metropolis and that the danger of and to women who walk the shop floor is to be found in their corresponding walking of the city streets.

In *The Odd Women* and *In the Year of Jubilee*, the shop girl represents both modern life's ominous commodification and women's dangerous new accessibility to public spaces. Gissing associates a shop girl's identity with knowledge of urban byways, a knowledge that is affiliated with sexual proclivity. His concern with the physical and moral challenges faced by young women employed in shops was shared with his contemporaries. But whereas periodical articles often focus on her suitability as a wife, a role that she is assumed to covet, Gissing's shop girl seems desirous of a more independent existence. Though Gissing remains critical of modern commercialism and women's involvement in the public sphere, and deeply worried by the shop girl's liability to sexual and social transgression, he is often sympathetic in his portrayals of his female protagonists' love of the city and desire for urban experience.

Female shop assistants are among the new social actors Judith Walkowitz identifies, women whose presence 'challenged the spatial boundaries – of East and West, of public and private – that Victorian writers on the metropolis had imaginatively constructed to fix gender and class difference in the city' (Walkowitz, 1992, p. 68). Shop girls became known for their use of public transportation and their self-confident navigations of the city and the figure of the shop girl became a salient emblem for women's new involvement in public urban life. Periodicals of the day not only recognize the increasing number of women working in shops,[2] but also reveal the uncertainty of the shop girl's class and geographic origins and her social status as a shop worker. One writer finds that 'every kind of girl, drawn from every class and strata of society, is found behind the counters of the modern emporium and in the comfortless barracks where its servers are housed – the daughters of artisans, of agricultural labourers, of skilled mechanics, of struggling and of prosperous shopkeepers, of clerks and of professional men' (Bird, 1911, p. 65). Their diverse social backgrounds are also evoked by a former shop girl as she enjoins shopping ladies to treat girls behind the counter with more kindness. She writes, 'Many young ladies at home have little or no sympathy with the "common shop-girls," as they often term them. . . . In many cases they are girls suited to a higher sphere, but, through force of circumstances, have been obliged to go early into the world' ('Sympathy', 1888, p. 351). Both of these descriptions attempt to correct a prevalent stereotype of 'the shop girl' and express the popular apprehension of her as ambiguous and contradictory.

Gissing's portrayals of Monica Madden (*The Odd Women*) and Nancy Lord (*In the Year of Jubilee*) reflect this interest in the shop girl's ambiguous class status. Neither girl was born to a station in which she expected to have to earn a living, but each finds she must do so because of her father's inadequate provisions. Monica, an uneducated daughter of an educated man takes work at a draper's, though to 'serve behind a counter would not have been [her] choice if any more liberal employment had seemed within her reach' (p. 40). She is, as her future husband is quick to recognize, 'no representative shopgirl' and is ill-at-ease with her co-workers (p. 247). Nancy comes later to the work force and, without any marketable skills, owes her job as superintendent at the South London Dress Supply Association to luck and her well-bred airs. As her employer says, 'You can learn all you need to know [about fashions] in an hour. It's the ladylike appearance and talk more than anything else' (p. 277). Gissing's characterizations draw from popular conceptions that girls from middle-class families were the more successful shop assistants. Descriptions of a shop girl's duties nearly always reference the need for tact and polite manners, particularly in dealing with irritable lady shoppers. Nancy's ladylike airs help her to a better position in the hierarchy of shop labor.

And yet, while Gissing's shop girls are said to be atypical of 'the common shop girl,' they both are also identified with unsavory aspects of the shop-girl identity. Monica discovers herself behaving no differently from other 'women in business' in 'mak[ing] chance friendships with men in highways and byways' (p. 138). And long before Nancy ever thinks of having to find employment – a turn of events that shocks all who know her – the narrator explicitly likens her to a shop girl. Excited by 'physical contact' with the crowds walking the streets on Jubilee Day, Nancy's 'emotions differed little from those of any shop-girl let loose. . . . Could she have seen her face, its look of vulgar abandonment would have horrified her' (p. 58). Gissing's conjuncture here of 'vulgar abandonment' with the behavior of a shop girl in her free time is an association also addressed in the periodical literature, as I will discuss shortly.

Along with trying to classify who or what she was, the periodical press demonstrated concern with her work conditions, a concern that Gissing shared. Though commentators were motivated by diverse ideological concerns, including labor rights, equitable treatment of women, and social morality, they could agree that the conditions of shop labor were physically and morally dangerous. As the writers of *Women's Work* ruefully acknowledge in the section on 'Shop Assistants,' an 'account of the labour of men and women in shops . . . must, if truthfully given, be little else than a recital of their grievances' (Bulley and Whitley, 1894, p. 49). Gissing's attention to the hardships of Monica's experiences echo contemporary periodicals' discussions of shop girls' lengthy workday, spent on their feet, and the living-in system. Gissing's depictions of Monica's 13- to 16-hour work day are supported by various investigations during the last decades of the century that estimate that most shop assistants worked between 75 and 90 hours a week (Holcombe, 1973, p. 109). The majority, if not all, of these long work days were spent standing, as employers frowned on the use of chairs, even after these became legally required. Monica tells of girls sent to hospital with varicose veins and of her own feet losing all feeling at the end of a long day.

The system of living-in, which required employees to live in housing provided by their employer, was frequently criticized, in part for the expectation that young women would leave the premises on Sunday. Gissing's ironic description of Monica's employers who 'acted like conscientious men in driving [their employees] forth immediately after breakfast and enjoining upon them not to return until bedtime' (p. 53) evokes the problem, described by another writer, 'of young girls obliged to spend all Sunday in the Park because they had no place to go' ('Young,' Women in Business, 1897, pp. 82–3). Gissing also shares many contemporary observers' disapproval of the liberty allowed to young female employees, including the provision of latchkeys to let themselves in late at night.

According to social observers, the moral dangers resulting from the living-in system, the absence of parental surveillance, and the freedom to wander the streets were compounded by the low salaries shop girls received. As one writer for *The Cosmopolitan* asks, 'Is it possible to live pure, upright lives under such conditions? . . . It is possible, as is attested by the thousands who maintain their integrity in spite of all hindrances; but it is more than hard. It has been well said that, while men's wages cannot fall below the starvation line women's can, since the paths of shame are always open to her' (Woods, 1890, p. 103). Low wages meant that if shop girls were to enjoy commercial entertainment, most had to depend upon being 'treated' by male acquaintances. As Gissing's description of one of Monica's colleagues infers, accepting money or gifts from men was a slippery slope. Monica shares a room with 'a young woman with a morally unenviable reputation, though some of her colleagues certainly envied her. Money came to her with remarkable readiness whenever she had need of it' (p. 74). One writer for *The Independent* reports that some 'superintendents on engaging girls plainly advise them to secure "friends" to help defray their expenses' ('A Salesgirl's Story,' 1902, p. 1821).[3] Amateur prostitution, in other words, was sometimes necessary to supplement a shop girl's meager income, as is implied in this sardonic joke: 'A girl asking for a rise is told, "No, miss, we cannot give you a rise, but we can give you a latchkey"' (Holcombe, 1973, p. 135).

The concern about the shop girl's moral status stemmed from the sexual availability her employment implied. Her involvement in commerce was itself a problem. As Walkowitz puts it, 'if she sold things, did she not sell herself?' (Walkowitz, 1992, p. 46). The more successful shop assistant modeled the clothes that she sold, like Nancy (*In the Year of Jubilee*), who speaks of her job to 'exhibit myself as a walking fashion-plate' (p. 307). In a sense, the shop girl's body is involved in the commercial exchange: this money for the clothes to produce that image. Like the prostitute, the shop girl is subject to the desires of the market place, and the successful shop girl markets herself as well as her wares. Gissing depicts the shop girl's commodification and ambiguous correlation with the prostitute most strikingly in *The Odd Women*. While discussing the hardships of Christmas shopping hours, Monica relates how one girl fainted every night but, after a shot of brandy, would come back to continue work because her ' "book of takings" wasn't very good, poor thing, and if it didn't come up to a certain figure at the end of the week she would lose her place' (pp. 61–2). That this problematic employment took place in a heterosocial public space, along with the host of difficulties already described, meant that economic and sexual exchanges threatened to merge. As Walkowitz argues, 'the shopgirl . . . and other service workers occupied the "middle" ground of sexuality,' as neither 'ladies' nor 'prostitutes' (Walkowitz, 1992, p. 46).

Gissing draws connections between shop work and prostitution throughout *The Odd Women*, most explicitly through the character of Miss Eade. Monica's fellow shop assistant is depicted 'loitering about' the streets 'showily dressed,' exhibiting the love of finery for which streetwalkers were known (p. 72). When Monica encounters her at the Victoria station 18 months later, 'cheap finery' of the 'loudest description' and 'thin cheeks...artificially reddened' are appropriate, for she is in the process of soliciting (p. 298). Miss Eade, whose 'voice could not have been more distinctive of a London shop-girl' in the earlier scene (p. 72), now 'snarled in the true voice of the pavement' (p. 299). With a voice archetypal of both the shop girl and the prostitute, she implies how little separates the two professions. Their closeness is suggested spatially as well, for the streets around the shop are redolent with the selling of female bodies; Monica talks with her sisters after work one evening while, 'Only a few yards away, a girl to whom the pavement was a place of commerce stood laughing with two men' (p. 88). In Gissing's portrayal of the life of a shop girl in *The Odd Women*, there seems little difference between using the pavement as 'a place of commerce' and being 'girls in business.'

The periodical press suggests that much of the discomfort with the shop girl's hardships and problematic moral status are related to the perception that she will – if she has anything to do with it – marry. As was widely recognized, most shop girls were eager to escape the trade through marriage. Indeed, social critics who urged unionization to achieve improvements in work conditions and remuneration recognized that few shop assistants were willing to risk their jobs because few believed that they would be long at work. Rather, work in a shop was imagined as a temporary stopgap between childhood and wifehood. The likelihood of marriage could only heighten concerns that the shop girl's work conditions were damaging to her moral state, for they might compromise her suitability as a wife and mother. The periodical articles exhibit a preoccupation with this domestic suitability. One writer worries that, considering the 'disorderly,' 'barrack-like,' and 'inexpressibly dreary' living-in system, 'What woman, after this environment, would know how to make a home pleasant?' (Rowe, 1896, p. 397). But, says another writer, many 'make good marriages...and they must find the habits of patience, good temper, courtesy, and self-control learnt by them in business serve them in good stead in their after married life' (Belloc, 1895, p. 16).

The issue of whether a woman so associated with the market place could really make a good wife is also evoked in the confusion surrounding the shop girl's identity. Much of the periodical literature references her illegibility. Not only was her class status uncertain, but the manners she acquired in the shop, along with the clothing she purchased, made her liable to misclassification. On the street, girls employed in fine shops could be mistaken for their social betters. Financial investment in their public image meant, in the words of one contemporary, that, complete with 'hats, gloves, and fine boots,' they 'seem the queens of the street' (Quoted, McBride, 1978, p. 681). This interest in superficial attainments was seen as a moral danger. At least one commentator finds a shop girl's 'great temptation to an excessive love of dress,' an occupational hazard equivalent to 'the danger of making undesirable acquaintances' (Hamilton, 1893, p. 129). The social confusion caused by the better class of shop girls' appearance exacerbated the public concern with the physical and moral dangers of their labor, and with their potential to corrupt the domestic sphere.

While the middle and upper classes tended to see shop assistants as at the level of the servant class, members of the working class saw them as aspirers to middle-class respectability, calling them 'counter-jumpers' (Holcombe, 1973, p. 107). Periodical literature frequently makes reference to shop girls' perceived ambition to marry above their station. The same article that argued that many shop girls are, by birth, 'suited to a higher sphere,' also claims, 'Many of these shop-girls have attended private classes for self-improvement so that they may acquit themselves properly should fortune favour them with a step higher in life' ('Sympathy', With Shop-Girls, 1888, p. 351).

Mass entertainment suggested that this ambition to marry 'up' was often fulfilled. Shop-girl musicals were enormously popular in the 1890s and 1910s and, as Erica Rappaport observes, 'the shop girl never remains a worker in these stories. At some point in the play she usually changes places with an upper-class shopper' through marriage or unexpected inheritance (Rappaport, 2000, p. 198). Monica's marriage to a wealthy man may evoke this mythos, though Gissing makes her regret her choice.

In *The Odd Women* Gissing most reveals his skepticism that a once 'public' woman can fully enter or return to the private sphere by making Miss Eade, the shop girl turned prostitute, a double for Monica in her marriage to Widdowson. Repeatedly, Miss Eade figures into crucial points in Monica's relationship with Widdowson: she meets him due to Miss Eade's failure to meet her for a steamboat outing; soon after her first arranged meeting with Widdowson, she encounters Miss Eade loitering near the shop; and, following her removal from Widdowson's home, when she wishes she had never married him and even 'thought with envy of the shop-girls in Walworth Road [and] wished herself back there,' she encounters Miss Eade soliciting in Victoria station (p. 212). A spectral presence on the periphery of Monica's story, Miss Eade is not just a cautionary figure, but a parallel identity, for Gissing suggests that Monica's marriage is itself a form of prostitution.

As the chapter titled 'At Nature's Bidding' makes clear, Monica's engagement is not the result of 'natural' passion or love, but the social system. As she explains to Widdowson, once they had met without conventional introduction, they were required to keep their courtship from their friends until their engagement. Conducting their entire courtship out-of-doors and in secret, Monica is pressed to decide quickly whether to continue this dubious arrangement or engage to be married. The shame she feels in this unconventional meeting and courtship evolves into the shame of marrying and living with a man she does not love. As she later acknowledges, she married for a home and to escape from shop work. Monica very nearly sinks to the final step of adultery, so great is her desire to escape from this new imprisonment.

In *In the Year of Jubilee*, Nancy's fall occurs long before she finds employment in a shop. Her sexual fall in fact takes place in a pastoral setting, though it occurs after her saturation with the populist and commercial influences of Jubilee. Her desire to support herself and her child is, moreover, a sign of her growing maturity, not a danger to her morality. And while it is tempting to see Nancy's shop work as her most radical step – for it is that which gets the most response from her friends – her work is nothing to her wanderings, scandalous in part because they are unknown to those who would protect her. Nancy searches for, and finds, pleasure in solitary walks through the streets of London. She is described dining alone in a restaurant, 'saunter[ing] along' window shopping, and with a sound knowledge of London transport. Most surprising of all, 'Walking alone at night was a pleasure in which she...indulged herself pretty frequently' (p. 158). Monica Madden, who has a thorough knowledge of public transportation to the disgruntlement of her husband, also enjoys London's public spaces. If Gissing condemns Monica's actions, disapproval is tempered by his sympathetic portrayal of the hardships of shop life and by a suggestion that an impulse to experience urban life is a nearly inevitable result for young people in London.

Gissing dramatizes the threats of ambiguous class status, morality, and femininity represented by women's new participation in the public sphere. The uncertainty of what it means to be a shop girl is suggested in this brief dialogue between Nancy and her estranged husband as he questions her on her employment:

> Why have you made yourself a shop-girl?
> I didn't know that I had.
> I am told you go daily to some shop or other.
> I am engaged at a place of business... (p. 304)

Nancy resists being labeled a 'shop girl' and insists on the respectability of being 'engaged at a place of business.' But unwholesome associations that Nancy rejects nonetheless persist. In this interaction, Gissing draws attention to the uncertainty of what it means to be a 'shop girl' – a 'counter-jumper' or 'lady assistant' – and leaves that uncertainty unresolved.

I have discussed how Gissing draws upon periodical discourse concerning the figure of the shop girl. But his portrayals also differ in significant ways from those in contemporary journals. Certainly, these differences are related in part to generic distinctions. With their limited space, periodical articles tended to expose the problems of shop work and to suggest remedies, not to explore the problems of the shop as an *effect* or manifestation of new modes of commercial exchange and relationships between the sexes, rather than as a *cause* of those changes. Developing his shop girl characters at novel's length, Gissing was able to discuss the ambivalence she embodied. More than simply having more space, however, Gissing's interest in the ways that the shop girl's sexual respectability was compromised and codified by class connotations reveals the danger by association present for any woman navigating public streets – or engaging in the market-place. Gissing's exploration of the shop girl reveals the increasing challenges to the separateness of 'public' and 'private,' and to the legibility of class and gender, embodied in the New Public Woman. Gissing is rather like the protagonist of his *Eve's Ransom* (1895) who finds in Eve not the ideal of submissive femininity he had expected, but a woman who is confident in her enjoyment of the city. He spies upon 'Eve's movements without scruple,' for his interest in her had 'kindled and fanned' (1980, p. 25).[4]

Notes

1. I follow the late-nineteenth-century convention of calling all these female workers 'shop girls,' though this categorization often obscured dramatic differences in relative economic prosperity and work conditions.
2. By 1914 there were nearly half a million female shop-assistants, making this by far the largest group of middle-class women workers in the country (Holcombe, 1973, p. 103).
3. Although *The Cosmopolitan* and *The Independent* were published in New York, I have included these American periodicals because they voice concerns also present in their British counterparts.
4. I would like to express my appreciation to the American Association of University Women, with whose generous support I researched and drafted this chapter.

Bibliography

'A Salesgirl's Story.' *The Independent* 54 (1902) 1818–21.
Belloc, M.A. 'The Shop-Girl.' *The Idler* 8.43 (1895) 12–17.
Bird, M. Mostyn. *Woman at Work: A Study of the Different Ways of Earning a Living Open to Women* (London: Chapman & Hall, 1911).
Bulley, Miss A. Amy and Miss Margaret Whitley. Preface by Lady Dilke. *Women's Work* (London: Methuen, 1894).
Gissing, George. *Eve's Ransom*. 1895 (New York: Dover, 1980).
——. *The Odd Women*. 1893., ed. Young, Arlene, (London: Broadview, 1998).
——. *In the Year of Jubilee*. 1894., eds Delany, Paul and Henry, Jon Paul (London: Everyman, 1994).

Hamilton, C.J. 'Shop Girls-Life Behind the Counter.' *The Young Woman* (1893) 128–30.

Holcome, Lee. *Victorian Ladies at Work: Middle-Class Working Women in England and Wales 1850–1914* (Hamden, Conn.: Archon Books, 1973).

Ledger, Sally. 'Gissing, the Shopgirl and the New Woman.' *Women: A Cultural Review* 6 (1995) 263–74.

McBride, Theresa M. 'A Woman's World: Department Stores and the Evolution of Women's Employment, 1870–1920.' *French Historical Studies* 10 (1978) 664–83.

Rappaport, Erika Diane. *Shopping for Pleasure: Women in the Making of London's West End* (Princeton and Oxford: Princeton University Press, 2000).

Rowe, O.M.E. 'London Shop-Girls.' *Outlook* 53 (1896) 397–98.

'Sympathy with Shop-Girls [By One of Them].' *Chambers's Journal of Popular Literature, Science and Arts* 65 (1888) 351–52.

Walkowitz, Judith. *City of Dreadful Delight: Narratives of Sexual Danger in London* (London: Virago, 1992).

Woods, Katharine Pearson. 'Queens of the Shop, the Workroom and the Tenement.' *The Cosmopolitan* 10 (1890) 99–105.

'Young Women in Business.' *Englishwoman's Review* (1897) 77–84.

8
Rebellion in the Metropolis: George Gissing's New Woman Musician

Laura Vorachek

In his depiction of Alma Frothingham, the female protagonist of *The Whirlpool*, George Gissing intersects two cultural debates of the *fin de siècle*: the New Woman and female musical genius. Setting his novel against the backdrop of the specular economy of late nineteenth-century London, Gissing's engagement with these debates sheds light on the vexed question of his feminism. His New Woman's increased autonomy and sexual freedom is evident in her pursuit of a professional musical career. Alma believes she has control over her own sexuality and the sexual response her performances elicit in others. However, she does not recognize that by marketing her talent, and thereby commodifying herself, she loses the very agency in the public marketplace which she believes she has.

As several modern critics have noted, the figure of the New Woman was established in the periodical press, a product of journalistic discourse.[1] The New Woman symbolized greater social, economic and sexual freedom for women, reflecting women's increased demand for education, employment and travel. Drawing on this image from the popular press, New Woman fiction responded to the social changes occurring at the end of the nineteenth century. Two points of contest engaged by several New Woman novelists are the relationship between gender and genius and the tension between women's domestic responsibilities and their ambition to become professional musicians.

The female musician had an affinity with the New Woman, paralleling this increased independence in her choice of instrument and even musical careers. Most notably women began to take up the violin and art music composition (as opposed to popular drawing-room ballads), two 'masculine' musical occupations that were not grounded in the drawing room like the piano, women's instrument of choice for most of the century. No longer confined to the home, or to traditional circumscriptions of women's roles, women began to act on desires for professional careers. Female professional musicians were seen as feminists regardless of their political views. Thus, the *fin de siècle* female musician embodied women's social advancements.

The issue of women's musical ability was hotly contested in the musical periodicals of the day (and this continues into the twenty-first century). The question asked again and again was 'Where is there a female Beethoven?' A correspondent to *The Monthly Musical Record* in 1877 felt that women's deficiency in the creation of music was biological:

> a woman endowed with a lively, excitable imagination, rarely possesses that enormous perseverance and energy necessary for a composer.... It is an established maxim that 'a woman can never be a great composer,' and I do not mean to dispute its truth; certainly no female Beethoven has appeared as yet, nor do I think that such will ever be the case; setting aside everything else, no woman has the *physical* strength without which such a genius could not exist. (Artiste, 108, original emphasis)

Thus a woman's physical constitution – her lack of 'perseverance,' 'energy' and 'strength' – impede her success.

German music critic Hans von Bulow voiced similar sentiments in an article reprinted from the Leipzig *Signale* in *The Musical World* on 6 March 1880. After praising the violin-playing of Wilma Norman-Neruda by calling her a genius, he qualifies his statement by terming it 'receptive genius.' 'We may allow that the fair sex possess *reproductive* genius, just as we unconditionally deny that they possess *productive* genius...' (p. 155, original emphasis). He then relates a story in which he refuses to look at a friend's wife's compositions because ' "I do not believe in the feminine of the notion: Creator. Furthermore, everything with the flavour of woman's emancipation about it is utterly hateful to me. I consider ladies who *compose* far more objectionable than those who would like to be elected *deputies*" ' (p. 155). He connects women's advancement in the musical arena with women's political agitation, indicating that women's attempts to engage in this 'masculine' activity are a threat to a larger male cultural dominance. The biological basis for his objection to both women's creation and women's suffrage is evident in the ending of his anecdote. He reports telling this male friend, ' "I promise most solemnly that, on the *lendemain* of the day that you announce your (own) happy accouchement of a healthy baby, I will make the first serious attempt at converting myself to a belief in the vocation of the female sex for musical productivity" ' (p. 155). For von Bulow, women's creation is limited to the reproduction of music and children, reflecting broader cultural notions about a woman's place in the private sphere. When men birth babies, then he will believe women are capable of 'productive genius.'

Von Bulow was not alone in his opinion of women's capabilities. In an 1882 article entitled 'The Feminine in Music' in *The Musical Times*, the author argues that women have failed as creative musicians because they have been emulating men, but might be more successful if they 'approach[ed] their art as women' (p. 522). Claiming that a woman is de-sexed by her attempts at 'masculine' creation, the author states, 'The woman artist should always regard her art from a woman's point of view. Were this done, distinctiveness would follow. The result may not compare with the work of men for strength and comprehensiveness, but that is neither necessary nor desired. What we regard as both necessary and desirable is the emancipation of woman *within her own musical domain*' (p. 522, emphasis added). Thus this author both limits what women can achieve in 'strength and comprehensiveness' and circumscribes them to a gendered province, maintaining separate spheres of ideology and excluding women from the possibility of creating a great work.

In opposition to these arguments, others stressed women's unequal opportunities. Stephen S. Stratton counters in his address to the Musical Association (later the Royal Musical Association) in 1883 that women's 'defective education' and the formerly degraded position of music and the musician have impeded women's success (p. 130). Ethel Smyth, the first British composer to achieve in the 1890s the kind of musical status normally reserved for men, argued that the 'boy's club' atmosphere and lack of performance opportunities for women were to blame (Smyth, 1933, p. 4). American concert pianist Amy Fay responded to the debate in an article in *Music* (October 1900), reasoning that 'If it has required 50,000 years to produce a male Beethoven, surely one little century ought to be vouchsafed to create a female one!' (p. 506). But, as musicologist Paula Higgins contends, 'the proliferation of tracts in the late nineteenth and early twentieth centuries dealing with the "woman composer" question arose precisely because women had proved themselves to be competent composers' (Higgins, 1993, p. 189).

The discourses employed by critics of women's musical ability reflected larger discussions of women's intellectual and artistic capabilities, but the focus on female sexuality and physiology presented unique problems for champions of women's musical genius. The long-standing association of music with female sexual desire only reinforced the delimitation of female creativity to reproduction – of children and of others' art. Gissing enters this debate with *The Whirlpool*, revealing what he sees as the consequences of giving women's musical aspirations free reign – the erosion of the private sphere. Gissing reinforces gender biases about female creativity, countering that women's control over their sexuality is illusory once they enter the public marketplace.

When women's ambitions tend toward the public arena, they enter a late nineteenth-century economy based on speculation, as evident in the rise and fall of Bennet Frothingham's company at the start of the novel. But whereas men bring financial capital into this economy, women bring themselves and, as such, they bank on the visual spectacle of their bodies. Since women must figuratively prostitute themselves, female sexuality is inextricably linked in this novel to female aspirations. This association has fatal consequences for aspiring female professional musician Alma Frothingham. Indeed, it is only the women with no ambition outside the domestic arena, like Mrs. Basil Morton, who survive this economy untainted.

Gissing undermines Alma's ambition from the start. She is introduced to the protagonist, Harvey Rolfe, when 'not quite twenty-one, [she] was studying at the Royal Academy of Music, and, according to her friends, promised to excel alike on the piano and the violin, having at the same time a "really remarkable" contralto voice. Of late the young lady had abandoned singing, rarely used the pianoforte, and seemed satisfied to achieve distinction as a violinist' (p. 31). She is established as a 'promis[ing]' musician but we get our first hint of the limits of her talent in this passage. While the Royal Academy of Music accepted female students from its inception, and female violin students from 1872, it was not a terribly prestigious institution and many serious musicians went abroad to study.[2] Alma's decision to concentrate on the violin also indicates that music is more about 'distinction' than art for her, since her choice marks her apart from most musically accomplished middle-class women; she 'abandon[s]' those staples of drawing-room entertainment – the piano and singing. The piano was losing its cache at this time as it became more affordable to the working classes, making the violin a more distinctive choice.

The standing posture in performance also distinguishes the violinist, and Alma's choice may be due to this effect as well. Paula Gillett argues that the violinist's relationship with her audience was very different from that of traditional female musicians because the violinist faced the audience, unlike the pianist, but was intent on the music, 'oblivious to [the audience's] existence,' unlike the singer (p. 115). The sexual allure of this pose is evident in Harvey's observation of Alma playing at a party at the Frothingham's.

> Alma's countenance shone—possibly with the joy of the artist, perhaps only with gratified vanity. As she grew warm, the rosy blood mantled in her cheeks and flushed her neck. Every muscle and nerve tense as the strings from which she struck music, she presently swayed forward on the points of her feet, and seemed to gain in stature, to become a more commanding type....She stood a fascination, an allurement, to the masculine sense. (p. 32)

The description belies earlier cultural prejudice against female violinists as ungraceful and recalls American violinist Camilla Urso's argument in her 1894 paper presented at a musical congress that a woman is 'more picturesque and possesses more attraction than the male performer' (reprinted, Kagan, 1997, p. 732). This is certainly the case for Harvey, whose attention is drawn to the sight of her body in performance rather than the music. He notices that her body is 'warm' and 'tense,' her face and neck 'flushed,' and that she is 'an allurement to the masculine sense.' Alma's performance is a sensual, sexual spectacle for Harvey who 'only had eyes for [her]' (p. 32).

Her artistry is subverted by the lack of notice given to her music and by the narrator's suggestion that it is only 'gratified vanity' which makes her shine. In fact, we later learn that 'Alma had no profound love of the art.... [W]hen at length, with advancing social prospects, the thought took hold of her that, by means of her violin, she might maintain a place of distinction above ordinary handsome girls and heiresses, it sufficed to overcome her indolence and lack of the true temper' (p. 228). For Alma, lazy and deficient in the temperament of an artist, music is a means of making herself more marketable, a way to stand out in a field crowded with beautiful and monied women.

Alma claims to want to be a professional musician and after her father's death goes to Germany to study. However, she romanticizes the labor required of an artist and is naive about the consequences of identifying herself as such. She does not realize that her ambition puts her in a socially and sexually liminal space. When Felix Dymes visits her in Germany, he meets her with 'very frank admiration.' His greeting was 'that of a very old and intimate friend, rather than of a drawing-room acquaintance,' signaling a new familiarity due to her changed social and economic circumstances (p. 66). His disregard of propriety is then manifested in an abrupt marriage proposal. He takes advantage of their equal footing as 'artists' to ask, ' "Do you think people who go in for music, art, and that kind of thing, ought to marry?" ' Alma puts the question aside, but

> With audacity so incredible that it all but made her laugh, Dymes... jerked out the personal application of his abstract remarks. Yes, it was a proposal of marriage—marriage on the new plan, without cares or encumbrance; a suggestion rather than a petition; off-hand, unsentimental, yet perfectly serious, as look and tone proclaimed. (p. 69)

Alma, not recognizing her liminal position in society now that she is an aspiring professional artist, free from the protection as well as the restraints of domestic life, is surprised and amused at Dymes' proposal, which is not as 'audaci[ous]' as she believes. Positioning herself as a New Woman, pursuing a musical education in order to support herself, she has signaled that she is open to 'marriage on the new plan.' That this plan is more of a business proposal – 'off-hand,' 'unsentimental' and 'without cares' – than a declaration of love indicates that she is now considered a player in the market economy by the other characters in the novel.

Alma receives another unconventional proposal while in Germany, although this one is decidedly less humorous. She meets Cyrus Redgrave, who encourages her in her artistic pursuits. He tells her, 'There are so many things to be said about going in for music as a profession. You have the talent, you have the physical strength, I think.' His eye flattered her from head to foot. 'But, to be a great artist, one must have more than technical qualifications' (p. 77). He continues,

> I have seen much of artists; known them intimately, and studied their lives. One and all, they date their success from some passionate experience. From a cold and conventional existence can come nothing but cold and conventional art. You left England, broke away from the common routine, from the artificial and the respectable. That was an indispensable first step, and I have told you how I applauded it. But you cannot stop at this. I begin to fear for you. There is a convention of unconventionality: poor quarters, hard life, stinted pleasures—all that kind of thing. I fear its effect upon you. (p. 78)

He counsels her to travel and seek variety and pleasures, all of which she cannot afford in her present position, leaving her to think that he might, like Dymes, intend to propose to her. What Redgrave actually has in mind is hinted at in his repeated emphasis on her need to break away from 'conventional existence' and 'the respectable,' his recommendation that she have 'passionate experience,' and his praise of her body. Drawing attention to her 'physical strength' could imply her artistic capabilities since, as we have seen, many commentators felt that this was a necessary component of genius, but Redgrave's 'flatter[ing]' gaze indicates he is referring to her attractive figure. Preying on her claims to artistry and flattering her ambition, he does propose – that she be his mistress.

Alma's reaction highlights her naiveté about the social position of an artist. She thinks:

> So this was his meaning?—made plain enough at last, though with the most graceful phrasing...none the less did she imagine herself still illumined by the social halo, guarded by the divinity which doth hedge a member of the upper middle-class. Was she not a lady? And who had ever dared to offer a lady an insult such as this? Shop-girls, minor actresses, the inferior sort of governess, must naturally be on their guard; their insecurity was traditional; novel and drama represented their moral vicissitudes. But a lady, who had lived in a great house with many servants, who had founded an Amateur Quartet Society, the hem of whose garment had never been touched with irreverent finger—could *she* stand in peril of such indignity? (pp. 80–1)

Even after this second proposal she does not recognize that she has placed herself on the level of 'shop-girls, minor actresses, the inferior sort of governess' – all subject to sexual propositions in the workplace – by leaving the ranks of amateur musicians firmly lodged in the middle class. She resigned her 'halo' and 'the divinity' of her gender and class upon positioning herself as a professional in the public sphere. Her indignation and reliance on 'novel and drama' for information indicate that despite her independence, it is she who is 'traditional,' she who clings to conventionality and the precepts of the private sphere she has left. Awakened to the connection between female ambition and a perception of sexual availability, Alma will later trade on this to achieve her goals.

Shortly thereafter Alma returns to England and the protection of the domestic arena, accepting Harvey's marriage proposal. For Alma, and Gissing too, women's artistic goals and domesticity are not compatible. Alma uses music to avoid her domestic duties, especially mothering her child. She thinks, 'Of course, she was not a model of the home-keeping virtues; who expected an artist to be that?' (p. 226). Gissing's female musician's artistic pretensions are an excuse for being an uninterested mother; the family suffers at the expense of women's ambition.

Dissatisfied with her social opportunities, Alma decides to launch her professional career with a public recital, a venture in the marketplace that requires capital and the backing of investors. Some capital she brings with her, in the form of her physical appearance. Mrs Strangeways indicates this when she encourages Alma's ambition. ' "[T]here is room just now for a lady violinist—don't you think? One has to take into account other things besides mastery of the instrument; with the public naturally, a beautiful face and a perfect figure—" ' (p. 185). Mrs Strangeways judges that the market requires more of a 'lady violinist' than 'mastery of the instrument,' and that the view of Alma's 'beautiful face' and 'perfect figure' while she performs will contribute to her success. Alma is fully aware that making a spectacle of herself is an important component of her bid for distinction. Reflecting on Mrs Strangeways's 'allusion to her personal advantages', she thinks, 'She was not ill-looking; on that point there needed no flatterer's assurance.... For all that, she must pay grave attention to the subject of dress.... [H]er attire must be nothing short of perfection in its kind' (p. 215). Alma is indeed an astute self-marketer, carefully considering the effect of her beauty and dress, as well as the notoriety of her maiden name in generating a large turnout for her recital. As she is selling herself rather than her artistic abilities, Gissing aligns her with prostitution regardless of her sexual activity.

While her husband does not encourage her in this enterprise, Alma does find support in Dymes and Redgrave, both of whom, as we have seen earlier, hope that her musical ambition will pay sexual dividends. With both men Alma recognizes the sexual implications of their 'business' relationship, but is confident that her allurement will enable her to reap the benefit of fame with minimal expenditure on her part. However, employing her sexuality to manipulate these men has its consequences:

> Not with impunity could her thought accustom itself to stray in regions forbidden, how firm soever her resolve to hold bodily aloof. Alma's

imagination was beginning to show the inevitable taint. With Cyrus Redgrave she had passed from disdainful resentment, through phases of tolerance, to an interested flirtation, perilous on every side. In Felix Dymes she easily, perhaps not unwillingly, detected a motive like to Redgrave's, and already, for her own purposes, she was permitting him to regard her as a woman not too sensitive, not too scrupulous. These tactics might not be pleasant or strictly honorable, but she fancied they were forced upon her.... [S]he was going forth to conquer the world by her mere talents, and can a woman disregard the auxiliary weapons of beauty? (pp. 222–3)

Gissing conflates ambition and sexuality with a musician who feels flirtation and overlooking impropriety are necessary 'to conquer the world.' As a result, Alma is mentally compromised or 'taint[ed],' despite 'her resolve to hold bodily aloof,' by entertaining thoughts 'forbidden' to a proper, married, middle-class woman. Thus, her artistic ambition has become infected with sexual desire.

Harvey senses the *general* impropriety of Alma's public career, if not the specific acts she has committed to achieve it. He decides not to attend Alma's recital because '[her] name, exhibited in staring letters at the entrance of the public building, had oppressed him with a sense of degradation; he felt ignoble, much as a man might feel who had consented to his own dishonour' (pp. 285–6). Although Harvey is unaware of Alma's flirtation with Dymes and assignations with Redgrave, her name on the marquee of the recital hall is enough to make him feel cuckolded.

Alma's name is 'exhibited' in public through gossip as well. Mrs Rayner Mann, a 'friend' and supporter of Alma's, tells a guest:

I do so hope she will be a success. I'm afraid so much depends upon it. Of course, you know that she is the daughter of Bennet Frothingham? Didn't you know? Yes, and left without a farthing. I suppose it was natural she should catch at an offer of marriage, poor girl, but it seems to have been *most* ill-advised. One never sees her husband, and I'm afraid he is anything but kind to her. He *may* have calculated on her chances as a musician. I am told they have little or nothing to depend on. (p. 238)

Mrs Rayner Mann's speculation about Harvey and his financial motives in marrying Alma are false, but Alma's impending performance excites public interest in the state of her marriage and places her husband in a negative light, destabilizing the sanctity of the private sphere.

Despite considerable build-up to the event, the spectacle of Alma's public debut is withheld from the reader. In addition to the sensual responses evoked by her violin-playing, her extramarital flirtations and the speculation about the state of her marriage that her public recital arouses imbue this performance with sexuality. We do not see it – in keeping with Victorian conventions of sexual acts occurring off stage – but a paying audience does, thereby cementing Alma's self-prostitution.

However, we do see the toll it takes on her person. Alma suffers a breakdown after the recital, her body as well as her mind 'show[ing] the inevitable taint' of sexuality and ambition. Thus, Gissing affirms the connection of women with the body. William Greenslade argues that Gissing was drawing on contemporary degenerationist discourses on women's 'nature' and the effects of urban life for his portrait of Alma. I would suggest that Gissing is participating in cultural debates about women's musical genius as well. Alma does not, in fact, have the physical strength necessary for genius.

Alma's public ambitions are contrasted with a woman who remains firmly in the private sphere – Mrs Basil Morton. She is described hyperbolically as the ideal woman with no ambitions other than motherhood: 'Into her pure and healthy mind had never entered a thought at conflict with motherhood. Her breasts were the fountain of life; her babies clung to them, and grew large of limb' (p. 303). In contrast, Alma finds motherhood and domestic duties 'obstacle[s]' to her ambitions, her son Hughie is sickly and her daughter dies, and her mind is not 'pure and healthy' but tainted by her lustful passions. Mrs. Morton is the novel's final portrait of a female musician. Her children and Hughie sing 'the songs they had newly learnt with Mrs Morton, she accompanying them on the piano' (p. 419). She is engaged in the 'appropriate' *amateur* musical career for women – nurturing children and making the home a haven from 'the whirlpool' of the public sphere.

Mrs Morton is an over-idealized figure, perhaps because Gissing fears that her type is disappearing at the end of the nineteenth century. Harvey tells Basil Morton, who would rather his daughters stay at home than get jobs: ' "Don't lose sight of the possibility that by when they are grown up there may be no such thing as 'home'. The word is dying out" ' (p. 320). He worries that the private sphere is disappearing with women's entrance into the public workforce. With women literally or metaphorically prostituting themselves to achieve their goals, the separate spheres collapse and all relationships between men and women become based on sexual exchange, as evident in Alma's relationships with Dymes and Redgrave. Therefore, Harvey is cuckolded in spirit, if not in fact, by her public ambitions.

Gissing thus reinforces gender biases about creativity in *The Whirlpool*, problematizing women's desires to move beyond the private sphere and leaving no possibility for female creative ability outside of Mrs Morton's childbearing. He undercuts Alma's artistry and associates women's aspirations with sexual desire, which disrupts the stability and sanctity of the private sphere with gossip and sexual intrigue. Having thoroughly discredited Alma's ambition, Gissing then shows her efforts taxing her physically, demonstrating that, were she serious about music, this woman does not have the strength necessary for genius. He removes any external obstacles to Alma's ambitions, placing only internal or 'natural' barriers in the path of his female musician. As a result, the absence of women's musical genius is figured as an inherent deficiency, rather than due to cultural prohibitions to women's success in this field.

The Whirlpool illustrates a feminism limited by anxieties about the encroachment of the increasingly commodified culture of the *fin de siècle* on the home. Work that takes women into the public arena – that is spectacularly visible, such as Alma's recital – is shown to undermine and erode the domestic sphere. Because her product, music, is intangible, and yet requires self-display, her professional ambitions highlight that for Gissing there is a fine line for women between employment and commodification.

Notes

1. See, for example, Cunningham (1978), Jordan (1983), Ledger (1997), Stetz (2001) and Tusan (1998).
2. Gillett (2000, pp. 79–80); Bernstein (1986, p. 307).

Bibliography

Artiste. 'Women a Composers.' *The Monthly Musical Record* (July 1, 1887): 108.

Bernstein, Jane A. ' "Shout, Shout, Up with Your Song!" Dame Ethel Smyth and the Changing Role of the British Woman Composer.' *Women Making Music: The Western Art Tradition 1150–1950*. Eds Bowers, Jane, and Tick, Judith (Urbana: Indiana University Press, 1986), pp. 304–24.

Cunningham, Gail. *The New Woman and the Victorian Novel* (New York: Barnes & Noble, 1978).

Fay, Amy. 'Women and Music.' *Music* 18 (1900): 505–7.

Gillett, Paula. *Musical Women in England, 1870–1814: 'Encroaching on All Man's Privileges.'* (New York: St Martin's Press, 2000).

Gissing, George. *The Whirlpool* (1897) (London: Everyman, 1994).

Greenslade, William. *Degeneration, Culture and the Novel: 1880–1940* (Cambridge: Cambridge University Press, 1994).

Higgins, Paula. 'Women in Music, Feminist Criticism, and Guerrilla Musicology: Reflections on Recent Polemics.' *Nineteenth-Century Music* 17.2 (1993): 174–192.

Jordan, Ellen. 'The Christening of the New Woman: May 1894.' *The Victorian Newsletter* 63 (1983): 19–21.

Kagan, Susan. 'Camilla Urso: A Nineteenth-Century Violinist's View.' *Signs* 2.3 (1977): 727–34.

Ledger, Sally. *The New Woman: Fiction and Feminism at the Fin de Siècle* (Manchester: Manchester University Press, 1997).

The Musical Times 'The Feminine in Music.' (October 1, 1882): 521–22.

Smyth, Ethel. 'Female Pipings in Eden.' *Female Pipings in Eden* (Edinburgh: Peter Davies, 1933), pp. 1–56.

Stetz, Margaret Diane. 'The New Woman and the British Periodical Press of the 1890s.' *Journal of Victorian Culture* 6.2 (2001): 272–85.

Stratton, Stephen S. 'Woman in Relation to Musical Art.' *Proceedings of the Musical Association* (May 7, 1883): 115–46.

Tusan, Michelle Elizabeth. 'Inventing the New Woman: Print Culture and Identity Politics During the Fin-de-Siècle.' *Victorian Periodicals Review* 3102 (1998): 169–82.

Von Bulow, Hans. 'The Violin-Fairy.' *The Musical World* (March 6, 1880): 154–55.

9
'Children of the Street': Reconfiguring Gender in Gissing's London

Margaret E. Mitchell

Gissing's representations of London are inevitably caught up in representations of gender. As always, with Gissing, this relationship is fraught with tension, even contradictions: at times the city seems to impose rigid boundaries on the lives of its fictional inhabitants and the conventions of gender that shape their identity, while at other times it seems to grant a kind of freedom that has profound implications for gender and for social progress in general. Focusing on *The Nether World* (1889) and *The Unclassed* (1884), I explore these very different visions of the city and its relationship to its inhabitants. Juxtaposing these two particular novels – positioning Gissing the pessimist alongside Gissing the idealist, and the figure of the Victorian angel alongside the streetwalker – generates a curious observation: the city defeats the angel, in the bleak conclusion of *The Nether World*, while the prostitute in *The Unclassed* not only secures a happy ending but is endowed with a kind of power to transform the city. But my essay is less concerned with Gissing's representations of women, a subject which has been productively explored by a number of feminist critics in recent years, than with the way gender itself operates in these novels – that is, the ideological work that it performs.[1] I contend that gender is central to the resolution of the social conflicts Gissing explores in these works. Ultimately, the question of whether the city is ruthlessly determinative or whether it may be shaped in accordance with human ideals is embedded in two extremes of Victorian femininity, the domestic angel and the prostitute. In both cases, Gissing implies that gender, for better or worse, is constructed by the city, and is at the same time central to the city's imagined possibilities.

In *The Nether World*, Gissing forces upon his readers a consciousness of what the narrator refers to as the 'pest-stricken regions of East London,' 'a city of the damned,' where there are 'streets swarming with a nameless populace' (1889, p. 164). The novel seeks to name the 'nameless populace,' and part of this process, inevitably, is the construction of gendered characters. Gender is an important element of the novel's attempt to register the effect of urban poverty on human subjectivity; it is also a crucial component of the scheme of human relationships onto which the novel's major ideas are projected. John Goode writes that '[t]he named streets of London map the fate of [Gissing's] protagonists' (Goode, 1979, p. 105); I would like to make the related claim that the city 'maps' the protagonists' gender, and their gender, to a considerable extent, maps their fate. The very possibility of social change is caught up in the question of gender, and controlling all versions of possibility – possibilities for human development, social mobility, gender identity, philanthropy, political change, and plot itself – is the city.

The city imprints its stamp on every character in Gissing's nether world. Clerkenwell bounds the lives of this novel's characters, and the particularly urban poverty that prevails there shapes their intellects, outlooks, physiques, and possibilities. An early description of Clem Peckover articulates this relationship between urban environment and human development: '[O]ne would have compared her, not to some piece of exuberant normal vegetation, but rather to a rank, evilly fostered growth. The putrid soil of that nether world yields other forms besides the obviously blighted and sapless' (1889, p. 8). Clerkenwell is the 'soil' out of which these characters grow. 'Nature' is repeatedly perverted in this urban context; 'natural' development is thwarted.

Gender is by no means automatic in Gissing's nether world; certainly it is not presented as an attribute conferred at birth. When the narrator introduces the Hewett family, for instance, while the older children are identified as girls or boys respectively the most recent addition to the household is simply 'an infant,' who is assigned neither a name nor a gendered pronoun, but referred to as 'it' (1889, p. 15). Later, after Pennyloaf's ill-advised marriage to Bob Hewett, we encounter her sitting drearily on her step; 'on her lap was one more specimen of the infinitely multiplied baby, and a child of two years sprawled behind her on the landing' (1889, p. 130). Bob and Pennyloaf's offspring, even as they grow older, remain insistently without gender. Pennyloaf herself, as a wife and mother, remains indistinctly gendered in spite of her 'poor prettiness': 'Pennyloaf was not a bit more womanly in figure than on the day of her marriage'; she is 'wasted under the disfigurement of pains and cares' (1889, p. 130). Gender, by implication, is a latent quality, one which can be thwarted or distorted.

In this light, an early description of Jane Snowdon is striking; Jane is exceptional in part because 'she had features that were not merely human, but girl-like.' Tellingly, the narrator remarks that Jane does not look like a child who has been 'put out to nurse upon the pavement' (1889, p. 4); the city streets, this image suggests, are an inadequate mother, under whose influence such basic traits as gender may fail to develop. Later in the sentence, the phrase 'children of the street' (1889, p. 4) strengthens the image of the city as mother. The fact that Jane is 'girl-like' suggests that other influences are at work in her. An improvement in her economic situation further eliminates impediments to 'nature,' and has a transformative effect on Jane. When her grandfather rescues her from the Peckovers and establishes her in circumstances that are at once more comfortable and more domestic, she becomes still more 'girl-like'; her neat, quiet appearance establishes her not only as distinctly feminine, but as a particular version of Victorian femininity. 'A woman's soul,' we are told, 'had begun to manifest itself under the shadow of those gently falling lids' (1889, p. 98). Under improved material conditions, that is, Jane becomes what Pennyloaf does not: womanly. She also acquires an attribute which manifests itself in no other character in the novel, and which Ruskin identifies as a quintessentially feminine power.[2] Its effect is most noticeable on Sidney Kirkwood: '[I]t was but one manifestation of a moral force which made itself nobly felt in many another way. In himself Sidney was experiencing its pure effects [. . .]' (1889, p. 139).

At the other end of the feminine spectrum from Jane is Clem Peckover, who presents a curious contradiction. She is at once a pure product of her urban environment, which usually implies a thwarting of nature's aims, and, in another sense, the character most insistently linked to 'nature': she is compared to 'a barbarian in ambush' (1989, p. 120), 'a cunning as well as fierce animal', 'a beast about to spring' (1889, p. 144), a 'noble savage running wild in woods' (1989, p. 6). She is presented as a throwback to an earlier stage of evolution. The conditions of urban life, it is implied, have brought about this reversion; have divorced Clem from 'civilization' itself (1889, p. 6). There is more than a hint of masculinity in this construct of femininity; the predatory and warlike images are more closely linked with conventional notions of masculinity than femininity. Thus Clem is both 'naturally' and ambiguously feminine. When nature 'has its way' with Jane, she becomes an embodiment of the Victorian domestic angel, demure, submissive, and self-sacrificing; a construct of gender that is a product of culture and ideology. In Clem, who is 'not at all disposed to occupy herself in domestic activity' (1889, p. 259), nature bypasses the developments of centuries, and produces a 'barbarian.'

While Jane and Clem are, in their own ways, recognizable types, Gissing insists upon Clara Hewett's anomalousness. Clara has features 'of very uncommon type, at once sensually attractive and bearing the stamp of intellectual vigour'; she combines 'the temper of an ambitious woman with the forces of a man's brain' (1889, pp. 25–6). Her curious blend of sexuality and intellect suggests both feminine and masculine qualities; she is noticeably devoid, however, of Jane's domestic virtues. Her unconventional gender is further destabilized by her decision to accept the attentions of Scawthorne; 'from that day,' we are told, her suffering 'became less womanly. [. . .] The disease inherent in her being, that deadly outcome of social tyranny which perverts the generous elements of youth into mere seeds of destruction, developed day by day, blighting her heart [. . .]' (1889,

p. 86). In Clara, nature is at odds with the 'social tyranny' which has prevented nature's expression and her healthy development. The sexual transgression that diminishes her 'womanly' qualities may be attributed to the 'unrelenting forces' that compel her to take a drastic step; in that sense, her gender, linked to disease, is both shaped and blighted by the poverty that limits her possibilities.

Sidney Kirkwood's masculinity, too, remains in flux until the final chapter. Until he comes under Jane's influence, his life is characterized by thwarted promise. But the impact of Jane's improving femininity upon his conflicting impulses is striking:

> To Jane he owed the gradual transition from tumultuous politics and social bitterness to the mood which could find pleasure as of old in nature and art. This was his truer self, emancipated from the distorting effect of the evil amid which he perforce lived. He was recovering somewhat of his spontaneous boyhood; at the same time, reaching after a new ideal of existence which only ripened manhood could appreciate. (1889, p. 143)

The phrase 'ripened manhood' indicates the extent to which these changes are linked to a particular manifestation of masculinity. To Jane's particular version of femininity, then, Gissing ascribes the power to overcome the effects of the city, to allow the emergence of a 'truer' kind of man, linked to a period of natural or 'spontaneous boyhood'. Crucially, however, this 'truer self,' this superior model of masculinity, is explicitly apolitical, involving a retreat form 'tumultuous politics' in favour of the pleasures of 'nature and art.'

In an important sense, the emergence of these precarious yet conventional gendered ideals in Jane and Sidney ultimately defeats Michael Snowdon's plan involving Jane, which is the central reform scheme of the novel. Snowdon's intention regarding Jane has been 'to raise up for the poor and the untaught a friend out of their own midst' (1889, p. 178) and eventually to endow her with 'the power to put an end to ever so little of the want and wretchedness about her' (1889, pp. 177–8). When he learns of Sidney's love for Jane, he temporarily revises his vision to accommodate Sidney and Jane working together in the service of his dream. Two main factors conspire to thwart his aims: one, at the level of plot, is the scheming and interference of other characters. More subtly, the gendered ideals Jane and Sidney have come to embody are incompatible with the altruistic ideals Snowdon is promoting. We are told of Jane that 'Her nature was homekeeping; to force her into alliance with conscious philanthropists was to set her in the falsest position conceivable [...]' (1889, pp. 234–5). Jane's pleasure in the plan is not abstract, but personal: 'Consecration to a great idea, endowment with the means of wide beneficence – this not only left her cold, but weighed upon her, afflicted her beyond her strength. [...] Jane rejoiced simply because she loved a poor man, and had riches that she could lay at his feet' (1889, p. 226). While Jane embodies a construct of femininity that is essentially domestic and individualistic and functions most effectively within marriage, Snowdon wishes to redirect her 'self-forgetful virtues' toward the public good.

Sidney, too, is conflicted. Though he is initially inspired by Michael's vision, his 'ardour' is eventually reined in by the 'thought of his personal relations to Jane' (1889, p. 179). Also at work is Jane's influence, which has fostered in him a particular version of masculinity: 'I am a man in love, and in proportion as my love has strengthened, so has my old artist-self revived in me, until now I can imagine no bliss so perfect as to marry Jane Snowdon and go off to live with her amid fields and trees, where no echo of the suffering world should ever reach us' (1889, p. 233). The ideal forms of gender that Sidney and Jane represent at this point in the novel privilege domesticity, nature, and art, and are therefore utterly at odds with Michael Snowdon's vision of a life devoted to the service of others – specifically, to easing the effects of urban poverty, from which Sidney now wishes to retreat altogether.

Partly as a result of this impasse, the novel ends in stalemate. Possibilities for domestic contentment are thwarted along with broader schemes for social reform. By the novel's conclusion, Sidney is miserably married to Clara Hewett and Jane remains alone, having lost even her inheritance. None of the variations of gender entertained by the novel, whether determined by the city or defined against it, leads to happiness or fulfillment in any form: not Jane and Sidney's traditional Victorian ideals, nor Clem's regressive savagery, nor Clara's fusion of feminine beauty with masculine intellect and daring.

Represented as a regression to an earlier 'strain' of human development, Clem Peckover indicates that the city will determine the course of evolution, not vice versa. Clara Hewett, perhaps the novel's most radically gendered figure, is destroyed when she attempts to defy the urban boundaries that define the lives of the characters in *The Nether World*. At the point when she is at last on the verge of her first success as an actress, a jealous friend throws acid in her face, ruining her hopes. Thus the one character who attempts to achieve mobility – in terms of both class and geography – is destroyed by her daring. Ultimately, she is contained within the confines of Crouch End, an outlying region of the growing city, where 'whatever you touch is at once found to be a sham' (p. 364).[3] None of the configurations of gender offered by the novel create the conditions for positive change, whether personal or social. Thus the city in *The Nether World* polices possibility, violently resisting both change and mobility.

In an earlier novel, Gissing presents a more hopeful vision of the city. Unlike the characters in *The Nether World*, Ida Starr of *The Unclassed* moves through the streets of London with remarkable freedom – a physical mobility that is ultimately echoed by her social mobility.[4] In *The Unclassed*, Gissing ultimately fuses seemingly contradictory elements of Victorian femininity in order to shape a new feminine ideal, one that incorporates wifely domesticity, reformist zeal, and the prostitute's sexuality and freedom. In a sense, Ida Starr combines the most positive qualities of the various women in *The Nether World*; she also enables Gissing to forge a very different conclusion to a novel which shares similar social concerns: the poverty and alienation of urban life. Many critics have objected to *The Unclassed* precisely because of its uncharacteristic optimism, and in a sense their views are reinforced by the fact that Gissing is known to have altered the ending at the insistence of his publisher. As Jacob Korg points out, it is likely that he originally had something more bleak in mind.[5] But I contend that there is another way to read *The Unclassed*, one that locates meaning both in its surprisingly happy ending and in the very lack of verisimilitude for which the novel has so often been criticized. Frederic Jameson has influentially asserted that narrative creates 'imaginary or formal "solutions" to unresolvable social contradictions' (Jameson, 1981, p. 79), while Rosemarie Bodenheimer adds that 'a "private" plot may be a writer's most revealing account of a public problem: it traces out a model of imaginable action within an implicit construct of social life, creating a fantasy about the manner and direction of social change' (Bodenheimer, 1988, p. 7). Specifically, the uncharacteristically optimistic conclusion of *The Unclassed* posits an imaginary solution to urban poverty and suffering that turns upon a reconfiguration of gender; Gissing constructs a fantasy whereby social change may be accomplished by radically transforming the Victorian ideal of femininity.[6] Crucially, this transformation takes place in the character of Ida Starr, a prostitute, whose history and profession link her inextricably to the city itself.

Ida's radical literary function distinguishes her from other nineteenth-century fictional prostitutes and fallen women, frequently agents of containment whose narrative expulsion permits the reestablishment of order, the perpetuation of existing social hierarchies. Gissing exploits what Lynda Nead has described as the disruptive and unstable nature of the prostitute to forge a conclusion that arguably inverts the social order, systematically eliminating more conventionally gendered characters from the novel and installing a former prostitute, representative of the streets, at the head of the middle-class household. In *The Unclassed*, Gissing presents a social fantasy in which the conventionally rigid boundaries of both class and gender become permeable, creating the conditions for a new and more just social order.

Like the characters in *The Nether World*, Ida Starr in *The Unclassed* may be seen as a child of the streets, although in a slightly different sense. Her mother, Lotty, is a prostitute, and Ida's parentage makes her the unwitting agent of disruption in the novel's opening scene: 'There was strange disorder in Miss Rutherford's schoolroom' (1884, p. 1). Ida, in this scene, has reacted violently to the taunt that her mother 'got her living in the streets' (1884, p. 5); she is expelled from school, banished at the age of 10 from respectability, doomed by her mother's association with the streets. Already the fictional prostitute's ability to destabilize class boundaries is evident. Gender boundaries, too, are quickly called into question: the disorderly young Ida early expresses dissatisfaction with gendered possibilities, remarking to her mother, 'And then I often wish I was a boy [...]. They're stronger than girls, and they know more. Don't you wish I was a boy, mother?' Lotty promptly agrees, for the practical reason that boys 'can go out and shift for themselves' (1884, p. 13).

When we first encounter the adult Ida, she is on the streets herself; the need to 'shift for herself' has led her to adopt her mother's profession. The ensuing scene with Waymark, the novel's hero, takes place on the street – where Ida, presumably, has been plying her trade – immediately giving Ida an indisputable authority as well as the upper hand in their initial encounter. Although she later entreats Waymark to be her friend 'as if [...he] had got to know [her] in a respectable house, and not in the street at midnight' (1884, p. 91), it is precisely the street, of course, that enables their otherwise improbable relationship. Ida's ease on the streets of London gives her an assurance, a kind of mastery, that is far more often represented as a masculine characteristic. For the characters in *The Nether World*, the streets are purely a blighting influence, an inadequate parent, imposing only limits and unnatural constraints on the lives they foster. In contrast, Ida's association with the streets confers upon her an extraordinary freedom, not only to move about the city but to shape her own life and character.[7]

In this sense it is precisely Ida's status as a prostitute, free of the restraints and obligations that characterize most Victorian heroines, that permits Gissing to shape a radically different model of ideal femininity. In marked contrast to Clara Hewett, whose urban mobility and unconventional gender are linked to disease and disfigurement, Ida's experience as a prostitute appears to coexist with a feminine purity more often associated with the domestic realm; for Gissing, as for Waymark himself, this seeming paradox in fact defines Ida's status as an ideal: 'My ideal woman,' Waymark notes, 'is the one who, knowing every darkest secret of life, keeps yet a pure mind – as you do, Ida' (1884, p. 131). Ida's purity links her undeniably to the figure of the angel in the house, but her experience on the streets and her acquaintance with life's 'darkest secret[s]' significantly revises the angel's chaste domesticity.[8]

The social fantasy embodied by Ida and Waymark's happy ending does not extend to the other characters. Emphasizing the successful reconfiguration of gender that Ida represents, Gissing repeatedly suggests that the gloomy fates of the novel's peripheral characters are inextricably linked to gender. Julian Casti, a poet possessed of 'effeminate beauty' and a 'terror' of 'speaking out with manly firmness' (1884, pp. 288–9), dies young, his ideals thwarted. His wife Harriet's coarse femininity is similar in some ways to Clem Peckover's, and leads to her early and violent death. Maud Enderby stands at the other end of the spectrum of femininity, ethereal and disembodied; Gissing spares her a tragic death, but relegates her instead to a religious sisterhood, effectively ejecting her from the social realm of the novel.

When the angel, her savage and beastly antithesis, and the insufficiently masculine man have all been purged from the landscape of the novel, the prostitute remains along with the figure of the writer. Upon the death of Ida's slumlord grandfather, Ida and Waymark inherit his fortune – derived, significantly, from precisely the urban injustice and exploitation Gissing exposes in both novels – and leave the ranks of the 'unclassed' for the comfortable middle class, in a narrative twist that may be read as a conservative ideological maneuver. As Jacob Korg asserts, Ida and Waymark now become 'free to detach themselves from social problems and to find happiness within conventional limits' (Korg, 1963, p. 67). And yet this is not, in fact, what they do: there is no suggestion that they will abandon the city for suburban comfort or pastoral nostalgia, and no indication that Ida will give up her work. Significantly, Ida brings her 'old sense of the world's injustice' – acquired on the streets – to the task of filling her grandfather's position as landlord. Undeniably, Ida's philanthropic endeavours are vulnerable to critique, inviting charges of both sentimentality and paternalism. What I wish to emphasize, however, is the significance of the transformative power Gissing attributes to Ida, not despite her complex and contradictory identity and history but precisely because of it.[9] Ida feels herself more closely linked to urban poverty than ever; and while her history of prostitution might invite us to see her as a pure victim of the city, instead it confers upon her the 'power' to bring about change (however minor, however problematic) within that city. The fact that the children see her as a 'sorceress' emphasizes the transformative powers with which this social fantasy endows her. The children's question – 'what limit could there be to her powers?' (1884, p. 272) – becomes the novel's question as well. By combining in Ida Starr elements of the angel, the streetwalker, and the reforming New Woman, Gissing collapses the oppositions generally assumed to structure these very different versions of Victorian femininity, proposing both a revised feminine ideal and a newly imagined relationship to the city.

In both novels, gender is an unstable category, one that is shaped but not irrevocably determined by social and economic forces as well as evolution – and, most importantly, by the city. In *The Nether World*, this instability is simply a part of the characters' quiet tragedies. Neither conventional Victorian concepts of gender nor radical challenges to those conventions lead to personal happiness or social progress: the city defeats the angel and the savage alike. *The Unclassed*, less realistically but perhaps more adventurously, exploits the instability of gender to forge, in Ida Starr, a sort of urban sorceress, while collapsing the opposition between domestic happiness and social progress established in *The Nether World*. In the later novel, characters are ultimately at the mercy of their urban environment, powerless to alter it or transcend its confining boundaries. In *The Unclassed*, Gissing envisions a more dynamic relationship between the city and its inhabitants, one that is mutually constitutive: the city may shape its children, but they in turn have the potential to transform the city.

Notes

1. Here I am influenced by Mary Poovey's (1988) formulation of the ideological work of gender.
2. According to Ruskin, the ideal woman's talent is for 'sweet ordering, arrangement, and decision' (Ruskin, 1887, p. 136), while the home over which she presides is 'the Place of Peace' (Ruskin, 1887, p. 137).
3. Asa Briggs observes that '[b]y the end of the century it was beginning to be difficult to tell where London ended' (Briggs, 1963, p. 80). Gissing describes Crouch End as pushing at the boundaries of the city.
4. My analysis of *The Unclassed* refers to the 1895 revised edition.
5. Jacob Korg speculates that 'it would have been very like Gissing to end by showing the lovers separated, their lives blighted by destructive social forces' (Korg, 1963, p. 67). But I think it is only fair to Gissing to assume that, whatever changes he made to the final volume, his fundamental intentions and the ideas underlying them remained intact.
6. I make a related argument about Ida's transformative function elsewhere. See 'Gissing's Moral Mischief: Prostitutes and Narrative Resolution.'
7. See Judith Walkowitz, who points out that 'seasoned prostitutes were capable of independent and assertive behavior rarely found among women of their own social class' (Walkowitz, 1980, p. 20).
8. Similarly, Patricia Ingham argues that 'for most of the narrative, Ida steps out of her gender and class as conventionally constructed, by being pure but not chaste, working-class but refined, independent but not unfeminine, an agent but not masculine or middle class' (Ingham, 1996, p. 159).
9. Constance Harsh (1992) argues that Ida has been reduced to a 'conventional benefactress' by the novel's end. While I agree that Ida remains problematic, I contend that her transformation has a socially symbolic resonance that extends beyond her character to the city itself.

Bibliography

Bodenheimer, R. *The Politics of Story in Victorian Social Fiction* (London: Cornell University Press, 1988).

Briggs, A. *Victorian Cities* (New York: Harper & Row, 1963).

Gissing, G. *The Nether World*. 1889. (Oxford: Oxford University Press, 1992).

——. *The Unclassed*. 1884. (Brighton: The Harvester Press, 1976).

Goode, J. *George Gissing: Ideology and Fiction* (New York: Barnes & Noble, 1979).

Harsh, C. 'Gissing's *The Unclassed* and the Perils of Naturalism.' *ELH*, 59 (1992) 911–38.

Ingham, P. *The Language of Gender and Class: Transformation in the Victorian Novel* (New York: Routledge, 1996).

Jameson, F. *The Political Unconscious: Narrative as a Socially Symbolic Act* (Ithaca: Cornell University Press, 1981).

Korg, J. *George Gissing: A Critical Biography* (Seattle: University of Washington Press, 1963).

Nead, L. *Myths of Sexuality. Representations of Women in Victorian Britain* (Oxford: Blackwell, 1988).

Poovey, M. *Uneven Developments: The Ideological Work of Gender in Mid-Victorian England* (Chicago: University of Chicago Press, 1988).

Ruskin, J. *Sesame and Lilies* (Orpington, Kent, England: George Allen, 1887).

Walkowitz, J.R. *Prostitution and Victorian Society: Women, Class, and the State* (Cambridge: Cambridge University Press, 1980).

10

'Woman as an Invader': Travel and Travail in George Gissing's *The Odd Women*

Josephine A. McQuail

" 'Woman as an Invader' "; such was the title of Mary Barfoot's lecture in *The Odd Women* (1893) to the young girls in her " 'old maid factory' " (pp. 55, 151), as one of her new recruits, Monica, calls it, or her training place for young women entering new professions in office work. *The Odd Women*, the novel by George Gissing detailing the ascendancy of this "new" or "odd" woman who in all likelihood would remain single and hence must make her own living, is even today a remarkable consideration of the "war" between the sexes. Yet, despite the portrayal of remarkable women in this novel, Gissing comes off both as an advocate for women's rights and as a misogynist. This mixed view is justified by his ambiguous attitude toward women. There are women like Rhoda Nunn and Mary Barfoot of *The Odd Women* and Amy Reardon of *New Grub Street* whose upstart feminism causes problems in their relationships to men; then there is the pliant Nancy Lord from *In the Year of Jubilee* who is contrasted with the violent Ada Peachey (modelled on Gissing's then wife Edith), who finally acquiesces to her husband. As the title to Mary's talk implies, Gissing examines the modern male's resentful view of women who are becoming increasingly powerful with newly won opportunities and freedoms. Some of these were legal, like the Married Woman's Property Acts that provide Amy with the right to control her own fortune, and some were technological, like the typewriter that allowed Rhoda and Mary Barfoot to train a new fleet of working women. Another invention that allowed women much more mobility at this time than previously was the railway system itself. The railway and the underground system, as well as other organized public transport, gave women mobility and liberated them from old constraints, like strict notions of chaperoning and paternalism generally.

Like almost everything else in British Victorian society, there was a class structure at work in rail travel. Daniel Pool points out that "The railroad, like many technological innovations, was not immediately seen as radically different from its predecessor modes of transportation, with the consequence that just about everything about it was initially modeled on the stage-coach"

(Pool, 1993, p. 148). Originally, Pool points out, there were only two classes on the "carriages" corresponding to the inside and outside of the stage-coach; even the compartments ("coaches") on the first-class carriages were modelled on the six-person capacity of the interior of the stage-coach (Pool, 1993, p. 148). Third-class carriages were added later, and were, as described in a meeting in 1838, "'open boxes – no roofs'" (Quoted, Pool, 1993, p. 148). These new class divisions in the novel transit system caused consternation, as is implied by a satirical volume called *The Railway Moral Class Book*, purported to be by the Bishop of London. According to this sage, who, among other things, prescribed etiquette for Sunday travel by class status, under "Morals for the Second Class": "they may be permitted to travel on Sundays, but as they are to understand this permission as a sufferance merely, and their conduct in availing themselves of it is by no means approved of" (Quoted, Andrews, 1937, p. 26). Some difference is shown for "Morals for the First Class": "Moreover, being accustomed to amuse themselves all the six days of the week, it would be cruel to deprive them of their recreation on the seventh; and having little or no business on any day, they have as much business to travel on Sunday as any other" (Quoted, Andrews, 1937, p. 26). Under "Morals for the Third Class" is the comment: "For this class of people to travel on Sundays is a heinous crime. They are meanly clad, and live upon a coarse kind of food.... The Legislature therefore, has acted very improperly in compelling Sunday trains to run Third class carriages" (Quoted, Andrews, 1937, p. 26). In Daumier's "First Class" and "Third Class" carriage illustrations (pp. 1–2), the contrast between the classes can be observed clearly: the first-class carriage is well lit, and its four occupants (perfectly balanced as to gender) look out the windows or read. In contrast, in the third-class carriage innumerable people are crowded together; no one looks out the windows, and a woman nurses a baby in the foreground, something that would be unheard of in the first-class carriage because of its indecorousness.

In addition to the anxiety caused by the mixing of classes, public transport also caused unease because of the way it exposed women to public scrutiny and public intercourse, and the very carnality of "Third Class Carriage" is what would be repulsive to the print's intended middle-class viewing public. Another print by Daumier (dated 1841) "Interior of an Omnibus" shows a proper young woman, clutching shawl and umbrella close and shrinking from a boorish-looking butcher and an inebriated drunk, both of whom pen her in as she rides on a bus. In Daumier's print the woman's bodily proximity to the men would have caused anxiety in a contemporary viewer. Both the employment of women in public enterprises like shops and factories, and the ability of women to travel on the newly available transportation systems like tubes, trains and omnibuses had the same effect on conservative social commentators, to induce an extreme unease and the suspicion that female sexuality would be let loose in these situations. Here, Helena Michie's analysis of the suspicion and erasure of the female body in Victorian fiction in her *The Flesh Made Word: Female Figures and Women's Bodies* comes to mind: the mortification of the flesh tames the forces of female sexuality, for if the female body were not chastised it would break the bounds of propriety.

Monica Madden in *The Odd Women* brings both anxieties to the fore in her story. Monica, when we meet her as a young woman, must work at a draper's every day except Sunday. On this day she herself takes her excursions, not taking a day of rest as the "Bishop of London" would advise to both second- and third-class travellers. Her unchaperoned travels leave her open to male admiration: first, Mr. Bullivant, who insists on accompanying her on the omnibus, then Widdowson.[1] Her excursions are detailed with precision by Gissing. Monica goes for a ride on a steam boat and meets Widdowson. For their second meeting and first deliberate assignation, they met at Battersea Park and Albert Bridge (and that very Sunday Monica *had* attended church upon leaving her sisters). Parting, Monica reveals her voluminous knowledge of public transport, to Widdowson's chagrin:

Now I must go quickly home.
But how?
By train – from York Rd. to Walworth Rd.
   Widdowson cast a curious glance at her. One would have imagined that he found something to disapprove in this ready knowledge of London Transit. (1893, p. 51)

Indeed, for other characters – Amy Drake and Monica's sister Virginia – knowledge of London transit and the habits of the public in conjunction with transit do prove fatal to their status as gentlewomen (and again, the proximity between a gentlewoman and some less than savoury male characters in Daumier's "Interior of an Omnibus" evokes this anxiety as well). Amy is a kind of foil to Monica, and in fact later occurrences will apparently point to a similar affair between Monica and Barfoot. Barfoot explains his liaison with Amy thus:

The girl had no parents, and she was on the point of going to London to live with a married sister.
   It happened that by the very train which took me back to London, when my visit was over, this girl also travelled, and alone. I saw her at Upchurch Station, but we didn't speak, and I got into a smoking carriage. We had to change at Oxford, and there, as I walked about the platform, Amy put herself in my way, so that I was obliged to begin talking with her. This behaviour rather surprised me. I wondered what Mrs. Goodall would think of it. But perhaps it was a sign of innocent freedom in the intercourse of men and women. At all events, Amy managed to get me into the same carriage with herself, and on the way to London we were alone. You

> foresee the end of it. At Paddington Station the girl and I went off together, and she didn't get to her sister's till the evening. (1893, p. 107)

Barfoot's ironic tone tells us that Mrs. Goodall (who incidentally has a philanthropic scheme for the elevation of women similar to that of his cousin Mary's) would be right in questioning the propriety of Amy's behaviour and that far from a sign of "innocent freedom" Amy had in mind another kind of "intercourse" all along. Mrs. Goodall's good intentions involve the mixing of classes: " 'Mrs. Goodall always had a lot of Upchurch girls about her, educated and not; her idea was to civilize one class by means of the other, and to give a new spirit to both' " (1893, p. 107), as Barfoot explains to his friend. Amy's lower class and fallen status entirely justify his behaviour in Barfoot's mind. In Barfoot, Gissing projects society's paranoia about the effect of the free mingling of the sexes – and classes – on public transport: that the woman's voracious sexual appetite will be unloosed.[2]

Monica does not entirely "fall" like Amy, but Monica herself, in explaining how her acquaintance with Widdowson came about to her roommate Mildred, betrays a consciousness that her behaviour was questionable from the first:

> Throughout, her manner was that of defence; she seemed doubtful of herself, and anxious to represent the case as favourably as possible; not for a moment had her voice the ring of courageous passion, nor the softness of tender feeling. The narrative hung together but awkwardly, and in truth gave a very indistinct notion of how she had comported herself at the various stages of the irregular courtship. Her behaviour had been marked by far more delicacy and scruple than she succeeded in representing. Painfully conscious of this, she exclaimed at length, –
> 'I see your opinion of me has suffered. You don't like this story. You wonder how I could do such things.
> "Well, dear, I certainly wonder how you could begin,' Mildred made answer, with her natural directness, but gently.' Afterwards, of course, it was different. When you had once got to be sure that he was a gentleman –
> "I was sure of that so soon,' exclaimed Monica, her cheeks still red.' You will understand it much better when you have seen him." (1893, p. 123)

Both Widdowson and Monica look a bit askance at her behaviour. Widdowson seems to blame Monica for even taking the position at the draper's. But Monica herself explains the apparent lack of propriety in their continued meetings:

> I have behaved very imprudently, continued the girl. But I don't see – I can't see – what else I could have done. Things are so badly arranged. It

wasn't possible for us to be introduced by anyone who knew us both, so I had either to break off your acquaintance after that first conversation, or conduct myself as I have been doing. I think it's a very hard position. My sisters would call mean immodest girl, but I don't think it is true. I may perhaps come to feel you as a girl ought to when she marries, and how else can I tell unless I meet you and talk with you? And your position is just the same. I don't blame you for a moment; I think it would be ridiculous to blame you. Yet we have gone against the ordinary rule, and people would make us suffer for it – or me, at all events. (1893, p. 83)

All of the novel's characters are indeed painfully conscious of propriety. Later, Monica will try to persuade Bevis, who she thinks she loves, to elope with her to France, where his employment is taking him. This plot parallels the unconventional "free union" which Barfoot proposes to Rhoda. Ironically, Monica seems ready to finally defy convention while Rhoda does not. Though Rhoda tells herself she prefers the open defiance of the convention of marriage, she does so out of pride, as the feminist in her would prefer being a bold rebel – fallen woman in the eyes of society – to a hypocrite. Finally she asks Barfoot to make their marriage a legal one, though what shakes her confidence in the proposed "free union" is his production of a wedding ring which he says he intends her to wear. She views this as a sham, as a pretense of marriage taken up to fool their friends and acquaintances, an inconsistency in moral principles. And the obstacle to a successful free union between Rhoda and Barfoot is their respective egotism. Rhoda refuses to believe that Everard has not had a dalliance with Monica, who indeed has been thrown in his path while she attempted to rendezvous one last time with Bevis; just as Widdowson refuses to believe in his wife's innocence (at least when it comes to a dalliance with Barfoot) after a private detective observes her in front of Barfoot's door (afraid of a possible encounter with Bevis's sisters, Monica knocks on Barfoot's door, coincidentally one floor below Bevis's, knowing Barfoot to be away with Rhoda in the Cumberland). Just as Bevis is incapable of ultimately defying convention by eloping with Monica whom he has enjoyed flirting with, so Barfoot plans on actually marrying Rhoda after first "testing" her by getting her to accept the idea of a free union.

Of course, what ultimately makes the contemplated elopements of the doomed couples possible is also public transportation: Monica desperately proposes an escape route for herself, but Bevis objects:

"You are sure you can leave home to-morrow – without being suspected?"

"Yes, I am sure I can. He is going to the City in the morning. Appoint some place where I can meet you. I will come in a cab, and then you can take me on to the – "

"But you are forgetting the risks. If you take a cab from Herne Hill, with your luggage, he will be able to find out the driver afterwards, and learn where you went."

"Then I will drive only as far as the station, and come to Victoria, and you shall meet me there." (1893, p. 265)

Just as Monica's mobility early in the novel allows her to escape the confines of work and her companions there, access to public transportation gives her the means, at least, of escaping her unhappy marriage.

Public transport and the railways also widened the circle of social acquaintance. It is in passing through a railway station that Rhoda Nunn is apprised that her old friends, the Madden sisters, now reside in London. As Rhoda explains in her letter to Virginia:

'DEAR Miss MADDEN, – This morning I chanced to meet with Mrs.Darby, who was passing through London on her way home from the seaside. We had only five minutes' talk (it was at a railway station), but she mentioned that you were at present in London, and gave me your address. After all these years, how glad I should be to see you! (1893, p. 18)

All their lives might have been very different if not for this chance encounter. The fatal mixing of people and classes also occurs in *Denzil Quarrier*, where Denzil and Glazzard coincidentally meet in Kew station. Rhoda, too, is predisposed to believe that Barfoot and Monica are having some sort of clandestine affair because of her chance observation of their coincidental encounter on the way to the railway station.

As he entered Sloane Square he saw Mrs Widdowson, who was coming toward the railway; she walked rather wearily, with her eyes on the ground, and did not become aware of him until he addressed her.

"Are we traveling the same way?" he asked. "Westward?"

"Yes. I am going all the way round to Portland Road."

They entered the station, Barfoot chatting humorously. And, so intent was he on the expression of his companions' downcast face, that he allowed an acquaintance to pass close by him unobserved. It was Rhoda Nunn, returning sooner than Miss Barfoot had expected. She saw the pair, regarded them with a moment's keen attentiveness, and went on, out into the street. (1893, p. 220)

And again, the privacy of the railroad carriage does indeed allow for an inappropriate intimacy between Everard and Monica to be assumed:

In the first-class carriage which they entered there was no other passenger as far as Barfoot's station. He could not resist the temptation to use rather an intimate tone, though one that was quite conventional, in the hope that he might discover something of Mrs. Widdowson's mind.... (1893, p. 220)

Barfoot, conscious of the impropriety of their conversation but desiring her advice, next engineers an encounter with her at an Exhibition at the Royal Academy, and wonders "how much intelligence he might attribute to Mrs Widdowson. Obviously her level was much below that of Rhoda. Yet she seemed to possess delicate sensibilities, and a refinement of thought not often met with in women of her position" (1893, pp. 222–3). Again, the condescension of his attitude toward Monica is obvious, and justifies the liberties he takes with her, though he credits her with delicacy and refinement.

Virginia, in making her way to Rhoda's, has recourse to another convenience provided by railways, but her journey is by foot (presumably she is too poor to purchase a ticket for public transportation, but she also wants to buy a book for Monica from the Strand):

Past Battersea Park, over Chelsea Bridge, then the weary stretch to Victoria Station, and the upward labour to Charing Cross. Five miles, at least, measured by pavement.... In front of Charing Cross Station she stopped, looking vaguely about her. Perhaps she had it in her mind to return home by omnibus, and was dreading the expense. Yet of a sudden she turned and went up the approach to the railway. At the entrance again she stopped. Her features were now working in the strangest way, as though a difficulty of breathing had assailed her. In her eyes was an eager yet frightened look; her lips stood apart. Another quick movement, and she entered the station. She went straight to the door of the refreshment room, and looked in through the glass. Two or three people were standing inside. She drew back, a tremor passing through her. A lady came out. Then again Virginia approached the door. Two men only were within, talking together. With a hurried, nervous movement, she pushed the door open and went up to a part of the counter as far as possible from the two customers. Bending forward, she said to the barmaid in a voice just above a whisper, – "Kindly give me a little brandy." Beads of perspiration were on her face, which had turned to a ghastly pallor. The barmaid, concluding that she was ill, served her promptly and with a sympathetic look. Virginia added to the spirit twice its quantity of water, standing, as she did so, half turned from the bar. Then she sipped hurriedly two or three times, and at length took a draught. Colour flowed to her cheeks; her eyes lost their frightened glare. Another draught finished the stimulant. She hastily wiped her lips, and walked away with firm step. (1893, pp. 19–20)

Virginia's (and surely Gissing's choice of name is ironic here) and Amy's degradation are both tied to the railway. The great anonymous compiler (known only as "Walter") of his erotic interludes, author of *My Secret Life*, is a source of more explicit detailings of assaults on female virtue in public transport. "Walter" is almost as obsessive in amassing details in his descriptions of his meanderings as Gissing. And we see an overlap in the defiant and careless attitude of "Everard Barfoot" and Walter in their descriptions of the seduction of these girls, but Walter can be more forthcoming:

> So one morning I set off for London. Just as the train started Molly and her mother appeared; she put the girl into a third-class carriage. At the first station the train stopped at I got into the carriage with Molly, who opened her eyes wide when she saw me. We were soon in conversation. Molly was going to an aunt's in London who was to meet her at the Terminus. You may guess which way my talk ran. I kept whispering lewed [sic] things in her ear....
>
> There are tunnels on that line. There were no lights then in third-class carriages. In one tunnel I kissed her, and on my kiss being returned, got my fingers on her cunt, and kept them there till approaching light made me withdraw them. It was a cold, foggy day. I sat close to her wrapped in a traveling-cloak, and partially covered her with it and with my rug. I got her hand under my cloak with the pretence of warming it, gradually introduced my prick into her hand, and there I kept it a quarter of an hour, she looking in such a fright all round at the people every now and then, but enjoying the warmth of the feel. Just before entering London is another tunnel, I had another grope at her warm quim, and arranged my clothes. (Anonymous, 1996, pp. 311–12).

Though Gissing cannot be as explicit as the author of *My Secret Life* is, his account of the erotic lives of Rhoda, Barfoot and Monica is remarkably frank, and as Michie perceptively observed, Barfoot's attraction to Rhoda is expressed in physical terms that do eroticize the usual anaemic Victorian literary portrayals of women:

> In a reversal of the traditional Victorian theme, her strength is in turn eroticized, so that Evrard [sic] feels the movement of Rhoda's well-developed hand muscles with intense sexual pleasure. He is equally attracted to her stamina in their walking tour of the lake country. Feminine asexuality, delicacy, and a lack of appetite are exposed as sham when Virginia falls eagerly on a piece of beef at Rhoda's house after explaining that she is a vegetarian. (Michie, 1987, p. 52)

The railways made life easier for people, simply by making their journeys less arduous, as Virginia's would have been if she had not walked. Rail travel expedited people's ability to move from country to city to take jobs or find better opportunities in the cities, which of course was the reason Monica came to London. Richard Altick in *Victorian People and Ideas* notes that "Cheap fares enabled common people, few of whom had ever been more than a few miles from their birthplace, to move considerable distances at will. Their horizons were broadened beyond the narrow confines of the parish and the town marketplace" (Altick, 1973, p. 80). Monica shows reluctance in signing up for Rhoda and Edith's typewriting course, but the Madden sisters' ability to travel makes the potential employment possible: " 'I don't know whether it's worth while,' she said, after a long silence, as they drew near to York Road Station, when they were to take [a] train for Clapham Junction" (1893, p. 69). This mobility itself, of course, was fatal to female virtue in some cases, which is perhaps implied in Widdowson's remarks to Monica: " 'I am glad you have relatives here, and friends. So many young ladies come up from the country who are quite alone' " (1893, p. 44) – and seen in the story of Amy's "fall." However, if rail travel and all associated with it was risky to women's characters, work itself was, too. Widdowson says to Monica, while deprecating the very street she worked on as abhorrent to him because of her sufferings there, " 'Why did you ever come to such a place?' " (1893, p. 81) and "There was severity rather than sympathy in his voice" (1893, p. 81). Monica's response is revealing: " 'I was tired of the dull country life ... And then I didn't know what the shops and the people were like' " (1893, p. 80).

Widdowson's disapproval is obvious. As Wanda Fraikan Neff points out in *Victorian Working Women*, "Women as workers did not harmonize with the philosophy of the Victorians, their deification of the home. Women ought to marry. There ought to be husbands for them. Women were potential mothers..." (Neff, 1919, p. 14). The extent of Monica's improprieties with Widdowson is shown by the fact that even in education women were strictly chaperoned. At Queen's College, for example, lady visitors were to chaperone the girls during the lectures by male professors. Occupations for middle-class females were extremely limited in themselves, and reformers like the fictional Rhoda Nunn tried to invent suitable positions for such women in jobs like bookkeeping, housekeeping, clerk, with appropriate training proposed in government schools (Neff, 1919, p. 180). Monica's older sisters had carefully considered Monica's options, and, Alice being a governess and Virginia a companion to a gentlewoman, decided "Monica would be better off 'in business' than in a more strictly genteel position" (1893, p. 12). Ironically, other jobs commonly available to women were even worse for the morals of the female workers than Monica's experience in the draper's establishment proved it to be. For instance, women commonly worked in the textile industry, and because wages for such workers were low, "social evils" were worse (Neff, 1919, p. 103), as women accepted offers of money from people like "Walter," the author of *My Secret Life*, to grant them sexual favours, or sought escape from their misery in substance abuse. Government investigators of women's working conditions heard accounts of the "prostitution of young girls, the general immorality, the drunkenness, and the use of laudanum among women" (Neff, 1919, p. 103). Gissing hints at prostitution in the draper's establishment where Monica works in the portrayal of "a young woman with a morally unenviable reputation, though some of her colleagues certainly envied her. Money came to her with remarkable readiness whenever she had need of it" (Gissing, 1893, p. 54). Indeed, the seamy underside of life in London intersects with the action of the novel on more than this one occasion; for instance, in the neighborhood of Monica's job, where her older sisters come one day just after Monica has given notice to quit her job to tell her the good news that Alice had found a position:

> Both clapped their hands like children. It was an odd little scene on the London pavement at ten o'clock at night; so intimately domestic amid surroundings the very antithesis of domesticity. Only a few yards away, a girl to whom the pavement was a place of commerce, stood laughing with two men. The sound of her voice hinted to Monica the advisability of walking as they conversed, and they moved towards Walworth Road Station. (Gissing, 1893, p. 72)

Monica certainly finds the clerical work that Rhoda and Edith offer her preferable to the shop, which would seem not to be an onerous job, but standing long hours at the counter and meagre meals take their toll on health. Indeed, the way Monica describes the shop differs little from descriptions of the sweatshops of the needletrade at the time. Neff in *The Victorian Working Woman* described it: "During the busy season there was no fixed time for meals. Ten minutes were allowed for breakfast, fifteen or twenty for dinner, fifteen for tea, and supper was postponed until the work was finished, at eleven, twelve, or even later" (Neff, 1919, p. 120). Rhoda Nunn quizzes Monica on her work, and Monica explains: "There's twenty minutes for each meal... but at dinner and tea one is very likely to be called into the shop before finishing. If you are long away you find the table cleared" (1893, p. 38). The shop floor is as bad as the worst factory in Monica's description: "A girl has just gone to the hospital with varicose veins, and two or three others have the same thing in a less troublesome form. Sometimes, on Saturday night, I lose all feeling in my feet; I have to stamp on the floor to be sure it's still under me" (1893, p. 38). As Neff points out: "To the Victorians belongs the discovery of the woman worker as the object of pity, and in the literature of the early nineteenth century one first finds her portrayed as a victim of long hours, unfavourable conditions, and general injustice, for whom something ought to be done" (Neff, 1919, p. 11). In this sense, Gissing's novel is rather conventional. But Michie sees Rhoda's declaration that she wished the girls who collapsed in private, in "their garrets and the hospitals" because of miserable working conditions but yet were eager to get any work situation, no matter how arduous, would have "their dead bodies collected together in some open place for the crowd to stare at" (Michie, 1987, p. 38) as a rebellion against the code of female oppression. The private sufferings of the female body should become public spectacle. Yet the female characters still shrink from the idea of public notoriety. Monica and Rhoda both contemplate the negative effects of defying society's sexual code by eloping with their lovers without the benefit that marriage will have on their and their partner's reputations.

In Gissing's general skepticism about technology, however, he is rather unconventional. For many Victorians, the railway was the symbol of the progress of their age. But Altick captures its dual nature in his description of the city: "The city, like the railroad, had a profound impact upon the sensibilities. It was at once the supreme triumph of civilization and civilization's most catastrophic mistake" (Altick, 1973, p. 77). In descriptions of Rhoda Nunn, both women's work and rail travel have more positive spin on them. Gissing was capable of utter condemnation of the city. In *The Year of Jubilee*, for instance, King's Cross underground station is described:

> They descended and stood together upon the platform, among hurrying crowds, in black fumes that poisoned the palate with sulphur. This way and that sped the demon engines, whirling lighted waggons full of people. Shrill whistles, the hiss and roar of steam, the bang, clap, bang of carriage-doors, the clatter of feet on wood and stone – all echoed and reverberated from a huge cloudy vault above them. High and low, on every available yard of wall, advertisements clamoured to the eye: theatres, journals, soaps, medicines, concerts, furniture, wines, prayer-meetings – all the produce and refuse of civilisation announced in staring letters, in daubed effigies, base, paltry, grotesque. A battleground of advertisements, fitly chosen amid subterranean din and reek; a symbol to the gaze of that relentless warfare which ceases not night and day, in the world above. (1894, pp. 280–1)

Escape from the city offers hope, though. In *The Nether World* city and country are contrasted:

> Over the pest-stricken regions of East London, sweltering in sunshine which served only to reveal the intimacies of abomination; across miles of a city of the damned, such as thought never conceived before this age of ours; above streets swarming with a nameless populace, cruelly exposed by the unwonted light of heaven; stopping at stations which it crushes the heart to think should be the destination of any mortal; the train made its way ... beyond the outmost limits of dread, and entered upon a land of level meadows, of hedges and trees, of crops and cattle. (1889, p. 164)

In *The Odd Women* Rhoda, though neither she nor Barfoot prove equal to their ideal of romance, has both meaningful work and right values. Barfoot asks her what her work is: " 'What is your work? Copying with a type-machine and teaching others to do the same – isn't that it' "; Rhoda replies: " 'The work by which I earn money, yes. But if it were no more than that –' " (1893, p. 208). Rhoda undertakes her journey to Seascale by the Cumberland, using the train to escape the city. Monica's wretched and unfulfilled life, society's judgements and expectations, come between Rhoda and Barfoot. But they both use train travel to broaden and enjoy themselves: Everard in his exotic journeys (including the Orient Express) and Rhoda in her walking holiday. Gissing, at least in *The Odd Women*, does seem to show that technology *can* enhance human life, rather than simply make it more miserable. But it is perhaps the exceptional individual, like Rhoda and Everard, that may employ it thus positively.

In their encounter in the Lake District, Rhoda and Everard to some extent re-enact the courtship between Monica and Widdowson. They take a miniature steam railway to the top of Eskdale where they walk; Monica and Widdowson had met on the excursion steamboat. If Rhoda and Everard could have kept to themselves, perhaps they could have had the ideal relationship; this is more than can be said for Monica and Widdowson. As Everard says to Rhoda: " 'We are in an ideal world remember. We care nothing about the sons and daughters of men. You and I will spend this one day together between cloudless heaven and silent earth – a memory for a lifetime. At nightfall you will come out again, and meet me down by the sea, where you stood when I first saw you yesterday' " (1893, p. 297). In the paradise of the Cumberlands, there are no societal obligations, distressing coincidental encounters, or alienating technologies. Rhoda has no need of exercising her calling, to help the "Odd Women" be useful. But the happiness of a marriage between Rhoda and Barfoot is really inconceivable. Despite Everard's apparent sincerity in his wooing of Rhoda, it seems her very unavailability is what is attractive. Early on in his attraction by her, Barfoot thinks: "he was tempted to make love to her as an interesting pastime, to observe how so strong-minded a woman would conduct herself under such circumstances. Had she or not a vein of sentiment in her character? Was it impossible to move her as other women are moved?" (1893, p. 143). To Gissing's credit, he resists the conventional ending of marriage (though Everard finally marries a far more conventional woman than Rhoda). Monica dies after giving birth to a daughter, and Rhoda's last words while holding the infant girl tell us that the struggles of the "Odd Women" are not at an end: " 'Poor little child!' " (1893, p. 386). Yet there is much hope for the "Odd Women" in the ending of the novel; Monica's sisters Virginia and Alice, who had seemed so hopeless, are determined to open a school when Monica's baby gets a little older. Rhoda's efforts have paid off for the most unlikely of the dispossessed women, and her work must go on.

Notes

1. Monica's predilection for public transport was not unique: the anonymous author of *My Secret Life* reports of one of his sexual conquests less innocent than Monica: "She spent her money on fruit, sugar candy and bull's eyes and riding in omnibuses.... A girl of fifteen riding in an omnibus by herself for pleasure, and gorging herself with sweets out of money got by feeling a man's prick in a street, seems an amusing fact" (Vol. VII, pp. 1474–5).
2. With Everard, there is a possibility that Gissing had in mind the anonymous author of *My Secret Life*, or at least the collector of erotica that Legman, in his introduction to the book, speculates is the author of the erotic account. Like Henry Spencer Ashbee, Barfoot travelled to the Orient. And his relentless catalogues of female looks imply a constant state of sexual arousal, as does the possible vulgar connotation of his name as "Ever Hard." The author of *My Secret Life* certainly explodes the notion that Victorian women were sexually unresponsive, though he tends to exploit the servant class, rather than middle- or upper-class women.

Bibliography

Altick, Richard D. *Victorian People and Ideas: A Companion for the Modern Reader of Victorian Literature* (New York: Norton, 1973).
Andrews, Cyril Bruyn. *The Railway Age* (London: Country Life, 1937).
Anonymous. *My Secret Life*. Vol. I–XI (in two volumes) (New York: Grove, 1966).
Gissing, George. *Denzil Quarrier* (London: Lawrence & Bullen, 1892).
——. *In the Year of Jubilee* (1894) (New York: Appleton, 1895).
——. *The Nether World*. (1889). Ed. Gill, Stephen (London: Oxford University Press, 1999).
——. *Odd Women* (1893). Intro. by Elaine Showalter (New York: Penguin, 1995).
Legman, G. "Introduction." *My Secret Life*. By Anonymous. Vol. I–XI (in two volumes) (New York: Grove, 1966). xxi–lxiii.
Michie, Helena. *The Flesh Made Word: Female Figures and Women's Bodies* (New York and Oxford: Oxford University Press, 1987).
Neff, Wanda Fraiken. *Victorian Working Women* (New York: Columbia University Press, 1919).
Pool, Daniel. *What Jane Austen Ate and Charles Dickens Knew: From Fox Hunting to Whist – the Facts of Daily Life in 19th Century England* (New York: Touchstone, 1993).

11

The Clash of Space and Culture: Gissing and the Rise of the 'New' Suburban

Lara Baker Whelan

Far from insignificant sidelines of an urban landscape, suburban spaces have their own place in the body of criticism dedicated to the impact of nineteenth-century urbanization on literature and culture. Books specifically about the Victorian and, later, Edwardian suburb were published through to the end of the Edwardian period, including George and Weedon Grossmith's *Diary of a Nobody* (1888–89), two sections of the first volume of Charles Booth's landmark work, *Life and Labour of the People in London* (1892), T.W.H. Crosland's *The Suburbans* (1905), Howard Keble's *The Smiths of Surbiton* (1906), and C.F.G. Masterman's *The Condition of England* (1909), which dedicates an entire chapter to 'The Suburbans.' Beyond these specifically suburban works, there are also many novels that take the suburban phenomenon at least partially as their subject, such as E.M. Forster's *Howard's End* (1910) and George Gissing's *In the Year of Jubilee* (1894). But after about 1880, writing about the suburbs is different from that of the previous 30 years. Overall, the picture of the suburbs that emerges from 1880 through the First World War is the image with which modern readers are more familiar – the suburb as trivial, dull, bourgeois, pretentious; an object of mockery by those who considered themselves above the petty concerns of the world of mid-level clerks and accountants.

In particular, George Gissing's writing about the middle class in the last decade of the nineteenth century reflects a wider cultural shift in Victorian conceptions of the ways in which class was defined, especially in reference to the cultural significance of suburban space. Gissing, along with many of his contemporaries, describes a gradual change in perceptions of class identification, from possession of a home in a particular district or housing estate to possession of a more modern aesthetic sensibility located in the individual rather than in the environment. As this emphasis on aesthetic education as a class marker develops, we begin to see some authors, including Gissing, positing the existence of two distinct forms of a broadly conceived middle class, one 'naturally' inferior to the other intellectually, incapable of sustained attention or serious mental effort while perfectly capable of earning a yearly income that would place them, economically, on a par with the other subset of the class. I will call this 'inferior' class, for reasons I hope to make clear, the 'new suburbans.' In fiction of the period, characters who attempt to transcend their 'natural' abilities by acquiring the trappings of middle-class identity are placed in the suburbs, which come to represent not the earlier-century ideal of privacy, quiet and respectability, but social climbing, camouflaged poverty (of mind and pocket) and sexual impropriety.

The shape of London had changed significantly since the first stirrings of suburban development, when it was still possible to combine a fairly large portion of space and privacy with reasonable rents. The last 30 years of the nineteenth century saw some of the highest growth rates for London, but this growth was not constant. The biggest boom in suburban building happened after 1875, when a new spate of homes and suburban railway lines began to spring up (Jones, 1971, p. 207). This new building was significantly less expensive than previous suburban housing options. Martin Gaskell estimates that 'new property within a mile of a suburban railway station offered accommodation...within the rental range of 35...to 120 pounds,' as opposed to the previous standard of approximately 100 pounds per year (Gaskell, 1977, p. 166). The houses got even cheaper after 1881, when speculative builders discovered they had built more houses than anyone seemed to want (Jahn, 1982, p. 126). Additionally, wages continued to increase, although this rate of growth slowed to about 7 per cent in 1895, down from 107 per cent in the 30 years prior to that (Rodger, 1989, p. 63). Taken together, this set of circumstances meant that after 1875 there was more housing available to people with wider ranges of income than had previously existed. The steady wage increases also meant that anyone earning a regular pay cheque could afford 'more house' than someone in a parallel position 30 years earlier. Hence, there were more people in the lower income brackets who could afford to become suburbanites, and there were plenty of suburban homes and trains to town to accommodate them. There was simply no way to keep suburban space as the exclusive territory of the upper reaches of the middle class.

For better or worse, the suburb had triumphed over the landscape of London. However, despite the vast numbers of those in the working and lower middle classes who achieved the new version of the suburban dream, the upper reaches of the Victorian middle-class continued to hold on to their position as the dominant form of culture. This segment of society set the standard for what was considered a morally and socially 'decent' lifestyle. The physical embodiment of those values in the suburban ideal had failed; a suburban residence with a respectable façade no longer guaranteed anything in particular about the inhabitants of that space. As the suburb's usefulness for distinguishing among classes faded, there was a general shift towards emphasizing taste, or aesthetic sensibility, as ways of recognizing and dividing the new species of middle class from the old. No longer focused on physical space, class markers at the end of the nineteenth century and beginning of the twentieth shifted to intellectual 'space,' which was thought to be less subject to 'misuse' or appropriation by lower-class groups. Along with Culture (in Matthew Arnold's sense) came a new perspective on the urban lifestyle, and an opposition developed in literature of this period between the cultured city dweller and the suburban Philistine.

Matthew Arnold's terminology – Philistine, Culture, and 'Sweetness and Light' – had a significant influence on the way late-century commentators framed the discussion surrounding Culture and the suburbs. Arnold first published his influential *Culture and Anarchy* as a series of articles in 1867 and 1868 in an early attempt to address the impact of the 'new' class of suburbans on Victorian society, and to define some of the problems he foresaw in the overemphasis on the 'forms' of class. In the preface, he defines Culture as 'the best which has been thought and said in the world' (Arnold, 1994, p. 5). The opposite of Culture is what he calls 'our stock notions and habits, which we now follow staunchly but mechanically, vainly imagining that there is a virtue in following them staunchly which makes up for the mischief of following them mechanically' (Arnold, 1994, p. 5).

This opposition, between an emphasis on 'the best' thoughts (resulting in vitality and new ideas) and 'mechanical' habit (resulting in stagnation), impacted on much of the thinking about class and the suburbs for the next 30 years. Gareth Stedman Jones notes that in the 1870s many of those in 'professional' careers were aware that it was not their income but their education that gave them prestige (Jones, 1971, p. 269). Another commentator remarks that 'an interest in art was by [the 1870s] a great leveller, an instrument of a new kind of class fusion' (Metcalf, 1972, p. 129).

A primary example of this shift is the late-century attitude towards Hampstead. It is one of only three suburbs that T.W.H. Crosland in *The Suburbans* (1905) finds acceptable, and is mentioned by several other commentators on the suburban scene as a highlight of the middle-class lifestyle. Hampstead's desirability originates in what Crosland calls its emphasis on 'taste':

> Over above its gates you shall read, 'Please refrain from entering unless you are possessed of some taste and at least five hundred a year.' You may be a stockbroker, or a lawyer, or an editor, or a dentist, or something in Mincing Lane, or a minister of religion, or a retired blacking manufacturer, but we shall insist upon your being in receipt of a decent income, and upon your possession of sufficient taste to know the difference between Shakespeare and the musical glasses. (Crosland, 1905, p. 104)

Jesse Argyle, in recommending Hampstead, notes that the region gains its desirability from its 'influential colony of workers in art, science and literature' (Argyle, 1892, p. 295). Note that here the potential suburbanite's profession no longer matters; lawyers may mix with retired tradesmen as long as their income is high and, most importantly, their education has been sufficient to develop a taste for 'the best which has been thought and said in the world.' The presence of 'artistic types' is no longer worrisome. Instead, those who pursue Culture add that which distinguishes Hampstead from the dreary regions of the Philistine, a term which Arnold uses to designate both the middle classes and those members of the working class who '[look] forward to the happy day when it will sit on thrones with commercial members of Parliament and other middle-class potentates' (Arnold, 1994, p. 68).

Judging by its numerous starring roles in turn-of-the-century literature, the 'new class' inhabiting these suburbs was problematic for those who watched it develop precisely because it lacked any emphasis on 'the best' either in thought or in action. One such writer was Crosland, who had published his vicious condemnation of turn-of-the-century suburbia in *The Suburbans* (1905). The primary problem Crosland had with the suburbs was the class affiliation of those who lived there and their impact on suburban space. He characterizes the typical suburb as a place '...where everybody's portion is soot and grime and slush; where the only streams are sewers, and the gardens are all black, and the principal population appears to consist of milkmen, postmen, busguards, scavengers, butchers' boys, nursemaids, drapers' assistants (male and female), policemen, railway-porters, Methodist ministers, and sluttish little girls who clean doorsteps' (Crosland, 1905, p. 16). Crosland speaks not of one particular instance, but of the whole of suburbia. The image of the suburb that made earlier-century readers anxious about suburban space, with the dirt and the working-class 'invaders,' has here become the norm, not the exception. Geoffrey Crossick, commenting on *The Suburbans* from a twentieth-century perspective, notes that '[d]islike of the self-righteous superiority that pervades Crosland's book can not prevent agreement that mass suburbia was *a creation of the lower middle class*' (Crossick, 1977, p. 33, emphasis mine). The suburb as a 'creation of the lower middle class' represents a considerable shift from the original conception of the suburb as a respectable retreat from urban living for the high-wage-earning individuals from the worlds of finance and business.

In fact, much of the writing about the suburbs after 1880 is so similar to earlier writing about the 'residuum,' or the lowest levels of British society, that authors often have to remind us that they are no longer describing Seven Dials or the East End, and drop names like Streatham, Clapham, and Camberwell as they construct their scenes. Crosland compares the typical suburbanite to 'uncivilized' Native Americans: '...when it comes to speech and manners, one is constrained to admit that the young of the suburbans are but slightly differentiated from the young of the Kickapoo tribe of

Indians' (Crosland, 1905, p. 63). It was not unusual, mid century, to see depictions of the urban poor as tribal, or even animalistic, but to see this association made specifically suburban is new to British literature. And it was not only Crosland who made this connection. Sir Arthur Conan Doyle, in 'The Sign of Four' (1890), describes Watson and Holmes' journey through South London in this way:

> We had during this time been following the guidance of Toby down the half-rural villa-lined roads which lead to the metropolis. Now, however, we were beginning to come among continuous streets, where labourers and dockmen were already astir, and slatternly women were taking down shutters and brushing doorsteps. At the square-topped corner public-houses business was just beginning, and rough-looking men were emerging, rubbing their sleeves across their beards after their morning wet. Strange dogs sauntered up and stared wonderingly at us as we passed... (Doyle, 1986, p. I: 153)

Reading this for the first time, one might think that by 'continuous streets' Doyle is referring to areas near the City proper, such as Lambeth or one of the other notoriously 'run-down' districts on the south side of the Thames. This puts the 'slatternly women,' the early-morning drinking, and the 'rough-looking men' in the context of urban figures, typical of, for example, Dickens' portraits of working-class London life. But the next paragraph gives us a new context for these behaviours – a specific location for the scene: 'We had traversed Streatham, Brixton, Camberwell, and now found ourselves in Kennington Lane, having borne away through the side streets to the east of the Oval' (Doyle, 1986, p. I: 153). It is not in Lambeth that we find the slatternly women and rough men, but in the mid-range southern suburbs, including Camberwell, the epitome of the 'new' suburb of lower-middle-class clerks and low-level officer workers. Indeed, it seems this new suburb, inhabited by the 'lower' classes, became a force to contend with as the century drew to its close. As Gareth Stedman Jones explains, 'Working-class London now stretched from West Ham to Notting Hill, from Tottenham to Wandsworth' (Jones, 1971, p. 326); it was inescapable and difficult to ignore.

Albert Grosch, writing his autobiography in the twentieth century, argued that this 'new' suburb represented the Victorian era more than anything else. He writes:

> They [these suburban neighbourhoods] have to be seen to be believed, and though jerry-building in the main was responsible for their existence they remain as a symbol of their age.... It is not Dickens, it is not Galsworthy, indeed I know of only one writer who put Victorianism absolutely and completely in print, and that was George Gissing. (Grosch, 1947, pp. 5–6)

Grosch is right about Gissing. He, above all other late Victorian novelists, concerned himself with the suburbs as they were in the 1880s and 1890s. In particular, his novels *New Grub Street* (1891) and *In the Year of Jubilee* (1894) focus on the plight of the suburban family aiming for a lifestyle beyond their income and social position. These families struggle and scrape, spending money they do not have on keeping up appearances for no other reason beyond that 'it's expected.' They are colourless and dull, pathetic, and certainly not intended to be objects of admiration.

In the Year of Jubilee follows the fortunes of several suburban families, including the Morgans, who typify the new suburban, where the boundary between solvency and insolvency is enormously permeable. Mr Morgan's work as a debt collector requires proximity to London neighbourhoods very similar to the Morgan's own. Mrs Morgan keeps Mr Morgan's work from the neighbours, concerned about its effect on their 'gentility,' a word Gissing uses with irony in regard to the Morgans and others like them. Mrs Morgan focuses on her children's prospects instead of her husband's; she brags about her son 'in an office,' her elder daughter who writes fiction, and her second daughter trying to pass an exam for which she has no aptitude and the family no funds. That having a son in an office can be considered 'genteel' shows how far things have come; 'genteel' as it is used by Mrs Morgan appears to mean essentially the same thing as 'respectable,' although the two words were not used interchangeably 20 years earlier, when 'genteel' meant that one was of good family, steeped in upper-class culture.

Characters in Gissing's novels make observations about the effects of education and culture on this new class of suburbanite. In *New Grub Street* (1891), John Yule remarks:

> Do you call it civilising men to make them weak, flabby creatures, with ruined eyes and dyspepsic stomachs? Who is it that reads most of the stuff that's poured out daily by the ton from the printing-press? Just the men and women who ought to spend their leisure hours in open-air exercise; the people who earn their bread by sedentary pursuits, and who need to *live* as soon as they are free from desk or counter, not to moon over small print. Your board schools, your popular press, your spread of education! Machinery for ruining the country, that's what I call it. (Gissing, 1993, p. 24)

Note, the speaker does not include himself in the group that needs to 'live' in the open air; he is of a different quality, and he can stand the 'strain' of intellectual pursuits. The implication here is that there are certain levels of human society that are better off left to their 'natural' pursuits than in trying to acquire a civilized veneer. Of course, without education, the new suburbans could not exist, to the extent that education results in the ability to read and write, a necessary function for many clerk-level jobs. Clearly, Yule means education beyond the 'three Rs' – a finer distinction reflected in acquiring the trappings of Culture.

In the same novel, a similarly cynical young man, Whelpdale, proposes to take advantage of this 'natural' difference by exploiting the lower class's inability to really appreciate Culture, here in the form of good literature. He argues for a newspaper that

> address[es] itself to the quarter-educated, that is to say, the great new generation that is being turned out by the Board schools, the young men and women who can just read, but are *incapable of sustained attention*. *People of this kind* want something to occupy them in trains and on 'buses and trams. As a rule they care for no information – bits of stories, bits of description, bits of scandal, bits of jokes, bits of statistics, bits of foolery.... Everything must be very short, two inches at the utmost; their attention can't sustain itself beyond two inches. (Gissing, 1993, p. 460, emphasis mine)

His listeners at first object to this idea, feeling that this kind of material would not do the target audience any 'good,' or that it would encourage 'bad habits' in them, but they are all eventually brought round to his way of thinking by the argument that the only time 'these people' really read anything is on trains when one cannot concentrate very well anyway. In fact, Gissing's argument throughout this novel seems to be that it is nearly impossible to acquire the trappings of 'class,' either in manner or in education, although he then goes on to question the value of such distinctions in a culture that prioritises money and material success over all else.

Gissing depicts new suburbans struggling to attain education and culture at great expense both to their health and to their bankbook, a struggle that is ultimately futile. He explicitly states in *New Grub Street* that '[t]he London work-girl is rarely capable of raising herself, or being raised, to a place in life above that to which she was born; she cannot learn how to stand and sit and move like a woman bred to refinement, any more than she can fashion her tongue to graceful speech' (1993, p. 85). In *In the Year of Jubilee*, Jessica Morgan works herself almost to death to pass an examination she is apparently simply not smart enough to pass. In the same novel, Horace and Nancy Lord's aping of cultural attainments they do not actually possess leads them both into dire trouble. In fact, Gissing's attitude towards education for this class is that it damaged their prospects for a happy life. Gissing remarks in *New Grub* Street with all apparent sincerity that

> Had they been born twenty years earlier, the children of that veterinary surgeon would have grown up to a very different, and in all probability a much happier existence, for their education would have been limited

to the strictly needful, and – certainly in the case of the girls – nothing would have encouraged them to look beyond the simple life possible to a poor man's offspring.... To the relatively poor... education is in most cases a mocking cruelty'. (1993, p. 40)

This sentiment is echoed in *In the Year of Jubilee*, as Nancy Lord's father questions his decision to educate his children. He looks instead to the example of his long-dead mother, a simple country woman who happily fulfilled her domestic duties. At the end of his life and as he has watched his children develop questionable values and vague social discontents, Lord comes to the conclusion that his children would have been happier if they had not been encouraged to think above their 'natural,' and class-linked, abilities.

Around the same time that authors begin to wonder whether all humans are equally suited to the pursuit of Culture (a question very likely driven by the dominant culture's desire to say, definitively, '*Here* lies the mark of class'), a problem also arises regarding the 'culture of the suburbs.' Here I refer not to the working and lower middle-classes characterized as unsuited to a higher position by Gissing, but to the group defined by Arnold's Philistine, who focused on material success. The 'right kind' of person had Culture; the 'jumped-up' middle and lower middle classes had the suburbs and material goods – these latter kinds of characters tend to populate the majority of Gissing's novels of the 1890s: Luckworth Crewe, Horace Lord, Beatrice French and her sisters, and Jasper Milvain, to name just a few.

Interestingly, around this time a desire for urban life begins to revive, and we also see a new-found admiration for the working-class figures emerging. The 'natural' child of the city, the Cockney or factory boy, if left to his own devices, can now be depicted with a sense of admiration. Doyle, in 'The Stock-Broker's Clerk' (1892–3), celebrates the 'smart young City man, of the class who have been labelled cockneys, but who give us our crack volunteer regiments, and who turn out more fine athletes and sportsmen than any body of men in these islands' (Doyle, 1986, p. I: 496). This particular specimen is a 'well-built, fresh-complexioned young fellow, with a frank, honest face and a slight, crisp, yellow moustache' (Doyle, 1986, p. I: 496), a far cry from the Cockneys described by Mayhew or Dickens at mid-century. C.F.G. Masterman also celebrates this class, or, in his terms, this 'new race' as a product of the city and of Victorian progress:

Cellars have vanished into homes, wages have risen, hours of labour diminished, temperance and thrift increased, manners improved. The new civilisation of the Crowd has become possible, with some capacity of endurance, instead of (as before) an offence which was rank and smelling to heaven. (Masterman, 1909, p. 133)

This description of the urban working class contrasts in almost every significant detail with Engels' horrifying portrait of the same class 50 years earlier in *The Condition of the Working Class in England* (1847). Indeed, Masterman is optimistic about the future for this class, 'small, wiry, incredibly nimble and agile in splicing thread or adjusting machinery, earning high wages in the factories, slowly advancing (one may justly hope) in intelligence and sobriety, and the qualities which go to make the good citizen' (Masterman, 1909, p. 134). Masterman ties this 'new race' directly to urban culture, arguing that in their ultimate fulfillment of their potential, 'The "Crowd" is then complete. The City civilisation is established. Progress pauses – exhausted, satisfied' (Masterman, 1909, p. 134).

The City as the pinnacle of civilization – this sentiment would have been unthinkable even 20 years earlier. And this is where I suspect that a parallel shift is occurring in Victorian culture in regard to the definition and value of work. Previously, the working classes had been objects of concern, philanthropy, pity, and certainly prejudice, but their work had been granted a degree of grudging respect, which in some ways reappears magnified at the turn of the century. But the work of the new suburban is not similarly valued – it is seen as meaningless, empty, mindless and more of a burden to the surrounding culture than a necessity. To what extent were Victorian conceptions of the meaning and value of work shifting between c.1850 and the 1890s, when more women were entering the work force, which was also dealing with larger numbers of men and women from the working classes who had been taught to read and write 'a good hand?' To what extent was the opportunity for leisure re-entering class definitions, or even being redefined itself, and what impact might that have on the kinds of work that were valued by the dominant culture at the end of the Victorian era? These are questions that deserve attention, and will shed further light on the connections between education, income, employment, and class affiliation, and the ways in which they are represented in literature of the period.

Bibliography

Argyle, J. 'Outlying London – North of the Thames.' *Life and Labour of the People in London*. Vol. 1. 1889. Charles Booth, ed. (London: Macmillan and Co., 1892).

Arnold, M. *Culture and Anarchy*. Lipman, Samuel, ed. (New Haven and London: Yale University Press, 1994).

Booth, C., ed. *Life and Labour of the People in London*. Vol. 1 (London: Macmillan, 1892).

Crosland, T.W.H. *The Suburbans* (London: John Long, 1905).

Crossick, G. 'The Emergence of the Lower Middle Class in Britain: A Discussion.' *The Lower Middle Class in Britain 1870–1914*. Crossick, Geoffrey, ed. (New York: St Martin's Press, 1977).

Doyle, A.C. *Sherlock Holmes: The Complete Novels and Stories*. 2 vols. (New York: Bantam Books, 1986).

Engels, F. *The Condition of the Working Class in England*. 1847 (London: Allen and Unwin, 1950).

Forster, E.M. *Howard's End*. 1910. Duckworth, Alistair, M. ed. (Boston and New York: Bedford Books, 1997).

Gaskell, S.M. 'Housing and the Lower Middle Class, 1870–1914.' *The Lower Middle Class in Britain 1870–1914*. Crossick, Geoffrey, ed. (New York: St Martin's Press, 1977).

Gissing, G. *In the Year of Jubilee*. 1894 (London: Everyman, 1994).

——. *New Grub Street*. 1891 (Oxford: Oxford University Press, 1993).

Grosch, A. *St Pancras Pavements: An Autobiography* (London: Catholic Book Club, 1947).

Grossmith, G. and W. Grossmith. *Diary of a Nobody*. 1888–89 (Ware, Herts.: Wordsworth Editions, 1994).

Jahn, M. 'Suburban Development in Outer West London, 1850–1900.' *The Rise of Suburbia*. Thompson, F.M.L. ed. (Leicester: Leicester University Press, 1982).

Jones, G.S. *Outcast London: A Study in the Relationship Between Classes in Victorian Society* (Oxford: Clarendon Press, 1971).

Keble, H. *The Smiths of Surbiton*. 1906 (London: T. Fisher Unwin, 1925).

Masterman, C.F.G. *The Condition of England* (London: Methuen, 1909).

Metcalf, P. *Victorian London* (New York and Washington: Praeger, 1972).

Rodger, R. *Housing in Urban Britain 1780–1914* (London: Macmillan, 1989).

Thompson, F.M.L., ed. *The Rise of Suburbia* (Leicester: Leicester University Press, 1982).

12
'Muddy depths': The Thames in Gissing's Fiction

Christine Huguet

Although Gissing's work certainly does not signal the literary discovery of the Thames, his fictional river, at once a static and a dynamic feature, a natural and an urban sign, a legible environment and a symbolically charged milieu, testifies to the author's abiding concern with London, the world capital. Because Gissing posits the metropolis overwhelmingly as the main locale of his novels of contemporary life, the river is given the place of honour as a centring device and an adequate emblem. Will Warburton proudly settles in 'the city on the Thames', the periphrasis intimating that (a) London, the hub of the British Empire, is first and foremost a great port, the world's trade focus, the Thames epitomising its brisk commercial activity; (b) the river is also London's structural backbone and spatial core. More exactly the city's heart is located on Westminster Bridge, as indicated by the milestone in Sutton where the Mumfords live in *The Paying Guest*, the bridge also being London's great meeting-point, for parties of 'jubilants' to start public rejoicings from, for instance.

Gissing the physiognomist and sociologist of the river

The reportage elements in Gissing's vision of the river as a significant section of the metropolis bear witness to his lifelong allegiance to realist art. His persuasive large-scale map of the river, of its banks and its bridges, helps to establish the veridictory modalities that constitute the referential illusion. In particular the inclusion of real toponyms into the topography of make-believe and the accurate tracing out of a character's route across the river and back (in *In the Year of Jubilee* and *Will Warburton* for instance) coax the reader into acceptance of the mimesis. Gissing's conscientious empiricism even leads him to use historical dating – thus in *Isabel Clarendon* Battersea Bridge, described as a condemned bridge, 'perhaps already gone' (*Isabel Clarendon*, 1969, II, p. 121) and the effigy of Thomas Carlyle that has 'just been set up' (*Isabel Clarendon*, II, p. 302) ensure the story's contemporaneity. The realist artist also makes the most of technicalities of the tide. Indeed, if steamboat passengers can be indifferent to it amateur rowers should watch warily how the tide allows their boat to drift onwards. Billy's death in Gissing's story 'The Day of Silence' is partly caused by his father's failure to realise that the tidal range falls off rapidly to the west and that the tide has actually begun to run down beyond Battersea Bridge.

If as reality effects such data have striking verisimilitude, to Gissing scholars they are also of interest as so many relevant details patiently gleamed from the life. Gissing's figurative representation of the river necessarily includes memory and subjectivity, and first-hand knowledge of particular sections of the Thames certainly accounts for oxymoronic treatment of the river. All the likes and dislikes of the characters are lifted straight from the life and richly documented by Gissing's personal writings. The sheer disgust at the now moribund Regent's Canal (then linking the Thames to northern England by way of the Grand Union Canal and over which Gissing's Hanover Street windows looked in 1879–81) is duly registered in *Demos* and years later in *The Private Papers of Henry Ryecroft*. On the other hand, touching, almost naïve delight in the Thames at Chelsea, the flowing breadth of stream, the dancing and gleaming 'wind-stirred waverlets' (*Isabel Clarendon*, II, pp. 120–21) under the Suspension Bridge, is a feeling shared by Gissing and Ada Warren in *Isabel Clarendon*. Gissing's narrators also audibly voice their creator's preferences for particular bridges, expertly assessing their architectural interest. Interestingly, however ambivalent Gissing's emotional response to the Thames proves to have been, he retained his professional interest in it all along. In her recollections of the artist, Gabrielle Fleury mentions his clinical observation of the river in his quest for adequate material to feed into his fiction. His risky night walks near the Thames directly inspired scenes in the early novels, he told her (*Letters*, IX, pp. 289–90). The embankments were indeed dangerous spots for night strollers, as Hilliard, the hero of *Eve's Ransom*, soon finds out when he wakes up on a bench near the river with empty pockets. Gissing himself noted in his diary how he 'got ideas for a story' (*Diary*, 1978, p. 312), namely 'A Lodger in Maze Pond,' on a morning spent in London Bridge district in August 1893. And the long spell of 'maddening' heat (*Diary*, p. 312) through much of that summer probably prompted him to write 'The Day of Silence' as well a week later, unless the tragedy be a fictional rendering of some real-life boat accident Gissing would have heard or read about.

While the river provides multifarious reality effects, it also functions in the representation of the relationship between the physical and the social aspects of urbanism. It helps Gissing to develop a sophisticated sociological eye for the metropolis – indeed his fiction consistently underlines the function of the river in the delineation of class-linked areas. In particular the double right-angle bend of the Thames through the city's heart forms a natural barrier-like boundary between North and South, between the literally South-East 'down-and-out' and that other nation dominantly present in the West End. The townscape on either bank, which is reflected in the water, is socially heavily connoted. Gissing's fictional pockets of abject poverty seemingly corroborate the colour scheme employed by Charles Booth in his social maps of London, the colour of East-End streets darkening noticeably whenever the river is approached. But they also stand in more significant isolation thanks to repeated emphasis on London's shameful paradox – geographical proximity and urban unity effectively defeated by class hierarchy and residential segregation. The East-End districts are mere 'compass points of the huge metropolis' ('The Prize Lodger,' in *Human Odds and Ends*, 1977, p. 133) and eventually Queer Street constitutes an altogether foreign region within the city, the Thames acting as a well-nigh impassable line of severance. Lambeth, for instance, is evoked in an 1886 letter as 'a strange world, so remote from our civilization' (*Letters*, III, p. 47) while Gissing similarly allows Gresham in *Workers in the Dawn* to enquire ironically about 'the Oriental regions' and 'clime' (*Workers in the Dawn*, 1985, pp. 40 and 227). In the later story 'The Prize Lodger' the narrator again wonders at the practical 'obliteration in the map of a world capital' ('The Prize Lodger,' p. 133) of the East-End districts and at the ordinary West-End dweller's blissful unawareness of them. At best opposite banks watch each other with curiosity, sometimes tinged with awe or suspicion. Walkers on the Chelsea Embankment like young Ada Warren contemplate Lambeth as 'a mysterious region of toil and trouble' (*Isabel Clarendon*, II, p. 196) safely over to the south. On the contrary Southwark or Lambeth girls like Thyrza and Lydia Trent have but a misty knowledge of 'that happy London on the other side of Thames' (*Thyrza*, 1984, p. 51). Thyrza simply has no idea what there is to see inside Westminster Abbey. So if Gissing focuses on several bridges in his observation of intra-urban transit, it is mostly to expose their pretended unifying function. Southbound moves obey such varied but equally invalid and pernicious motives as philanthropy, self-interest or simply idle curiosity. Thus in *Workers in the Dawn* Gresham objects to Helen Norman that the East End is a fit place for Bible-readers only, in *Thyrza* cynical MP Dalmaine surveys from the comfortable height of Westminster the doings of the ordinary mortals inhabiting his borough across the water, thus combining pleasure with business. As for Will Warburton rashly crossing the river to explore nearby Battersea, he is only mistakenly hunting for picturesqueness amidst squalor. None of these characters ever consider settling for good on the other side. Northbound transit over the water, on the other hand, clearly highlights the distinction between the day and the night populations of one district since no East-Ender legitimately crosses the river if not to gain his place of toil. Old Mr Boddy painfully stumps his way across Westminster Bridge with his blacking-brushes in *Thyrza*, and in Gissing's short story 'The Salt of the Earth' opens up with an evocation of the march of the commercial clerks streaming daily across Blackfriars Bridge, magnetically attracted to the emporium of finance, the City. In *The Town Traveller*

Christopher Parish is another resigned character joining in 'the great morning procession' (*The Town Traveller*, 1981, p. 36).

The river not only efficiently divides off the haves and the have-nots, the employers and their employees vertically; but it also makes up a line of horizontal separation between two further entities whenever it is treated as a natural highway for human traffic. Gissing's fiction documents in great detail most of the holiday-making mores of Victorian London's strata, including bathing, rowing, riverside walking, going on a steamboat, picnicking even (mentioned in *The Unclassed*), and it does so with keen attention to their class-based specificity. His socio-cultural interest in the differential class attitudes towards the river as a place of amusement manifests itself through frequent references to up- and down-stream locations. The Thames makes up a kind of street sprawling over an enormous area, and as one moves along the banks to the west, it becomes an increasingly adequate place of recreation, democratically available to all. As soon as it gets warm enough, many a Gissing character, whatever their class, talks of going up the river – Julian Casti in *The Unclassed*, Luke Ackroyd in *Thyrza*, Scawthorne in *The Nether World*, the employees of the drapery establishment in which Monica Madden has been placed in *The Odd Women*, Will Warburton's favourite westward destinations (then in their prime) include Battersea Park, Kew and Richmond. Significantly the narrative voice never disapproves so conspicuously of the crowds along and on the river as of those swarming at cheap seaside resorts or in suburban amusement grounds of the Rosherville type in Gissing's story 'Lou and Liz.' Landing-stages and craft, either 'nimble skiffs in which persons of a higher class take their pleasure upon the Thames' or 'ungainly old tub[s]' ('The Day of Silence,' p. 20), sufficiently signify the sabbatarian's social status; so does the degree of merriness and/or intoxicated expansiveness displayed. In 'The Day of Silence' Gissing introduces one further damning distinction between left and right bank – only from people on the Battersea side could help be forthcoming in case of danger on the water: 'from the other side no aid could be expected' ('The Day of Silence,' p. 22).

Plot utility: Specificity of the river

Of the elemental forces represented in the novels of George Gissing water comes first, the reason probably being the river's uniqueness. Better than any other London natural locus (such as a garden or a park) establishing links between man and urbanised matter, the Thames becomes relevant in the plot mechanism for its triple specificity – it is deep, it is wide, and it is a reflector.

Depth is perhaps its greatest asset because of the hackneyed yet ever attractive ballad motifs and other imaginative potentialities afforded by the dumping of things into the river (such as Isabel Clarendon's letter dropped into the water by Kingcote) and especially by drowning, whether it be suicide, murder or accident. Gissing's earlier fiction ('The Last Half-Crown'; 'Cain and Abel'; *Workers in the Dawn*) caters to contemporary demand for sensational endings, in particular melodramatic suicides with, occasionally, added complications – double drowning as suicide and crime in 'The Sins of the Fathers,' as crime and punishment in 'Brownie', or else drowning and subsequent madness in 'A Quarry in the Heath.' Although the water Gissing drowns these early characters in is not always Thames water, still such immature stories look forward to his great London tales of woe with the river as sombre backcloth. The riverside attracts many a passive Gissing hero wandering aimlessly about the streets, longing for 'the rest which the river always offers to the despairing' (*Workers in the Dawn*, p. 422), wishing 'that the dread tide could whelm him' (*Thyrza*, p. 113), but interestingly gross sentimentality finds itself in abeyance after 1881. Not a single character actually takes the plunge, allowing the river instead to function as some sort of mute confidant. The typical Gissing loser is depicted in sorrowful isola-tion, staring hard at the flowing tide, 'sunk in miserable reflections upon [his] wasted life' (*Workers in the Dawn*, p. 421), reviewing his past in solitary musing. Such communing with oneself distinctly forwards characterisation – Arthur Golding's alternate moods of passive desperation and active rebellion work themselves out by the waterside in *Workers in the Dawn*. As for Kingcote's shifting response to outer pressure, it is also voiced in terms of his reaction to the river in *Isabel Clarendon*. In *Thyrza* the numerous introspective pauses establish dramatic contrasts between past and present (Gilbert Grail revisits the same spot in widely differing circumstances) as well as between antagonistic characters. Egremont and Grail being driven to the very same standing place on Lambeth Bridge is emblematic of similarity and profound division at once between the two men. Lionel Tarrant in *In the Year of Jubilee* does not quit 'his musing-station' (*In the Year of Jubilee*, 1976, p. 342) on Westminster Bridge before he has wrought himself to a point of cynical unscrupulousness. But such self-contemplating stances away from the throng can be ironically undermined too, as when Mr Filmer's wandering steps bring him to the riverside to make the wrong reading of the situation in Gissing's story 'In Honour Bound' or again when meek Christopher Parish watches the flood, wonders what the use of life may be and talks of accepting the river's invitation to die in a mock-tragic scene. In earnest or not, the pensive Gissing hero contemplating the stream and possibly suicide is invariably portrayed leaning on the damp parapet of the bridge dictated by the storyline, gazing blankly at the dark stream, shut out in his gloomy journey-in, only to be recalled to reality by the sound of a voice, of the piercing wind or else by his benumbed arms. Mechanical contemplation of nearby riverfronts from this midway station brings no clearer vision of one's fate. Only the flood rushing under the bridge seems to penetrate the hero's consciousness. Then the Thames waters are evoked in insulting epithets throughout – 'black', 'gloomy', 'gross', 'muddy', 'sullen', 'solid'. To the hero looking down into the sombre stream beneath the dull surface, black depths even seem to be 'made blacker by the reflection ... of the lights upon the banks' (*Workers in the Dawn*, p. 421), hence Gissing's fondness for night scenes of introspection. The objectionable silt boiled up by the current still allows ink-black water to act as a reflector of the soul (except when it becomes a matter for curiosity, either Godwin Peak's scientific curiosity in *Born in Exile* or the real-life, illusion-breaking curiosity of Gissing's companion on Battersea Bridge in 1883). Imaginative response to the substantial constancy of the turbid stream, to the familiar, silent mystery of the heavy-flowing tide does not merely create pathetic fallacy of a crude kind. At his best Gissing intuitively touches on the complex cosmic reverie studied by Gaston Bachelard in his essay on imagination of matter, especially in *Thyrza* when sight is coupled with hearing: 'Gilbert bent his head and listened to the rush of the water, voiceful, mysterious' (*Thyrza*, p. 113). Technically speaking, scenes of riverside introspection sometimes call forth the most felicitous devices. Thus treacherous Lionel Tarrant's walk towards the river and subsequent meditation upon Westminster Bridge open up a long analeptic parenthesis breaking narrative linearity. Solitary musing sometimes also ensures change of perspective. The narrator's voice then becomes mute and the text invariably shifts out to the hero's consciousness, often in free indirect speech, as in 'Why could he not be free to expand his nature to the uttermost, to develop all his faculties to that rich fulness of which he felt he were capable?' (*Workers in the Dawn*, p. 422).

If Gissing superbly exploits black depths, he does not fail for all that to capitalise upon another attribute of the river – its breadth. Thanks to it his fictional Londoners, especially his working-class people, get 'their only chance of privacy ... in the open air' (*The Town Traveller*, p. 58) and nowhere better than on the riverbanks. As locales for intimate conversations the embankments are put to various uses; they enable the two potential rivals Snowdon and Mutimer in 'Mutimer's Choice' to discuss Bella in a 'quiet spot' with no eavesdropper around, 'no traffic near at hand' and 'the wash of the river below ... almost the only sound' ('Mutimer's Choice,' *Essays & Fiction*, 1970, p. 246). Similarly the two girlfriends in *Isabel Clarendon* take advantage of the deserted Chelsea Embankment to exchange confidences about marriage; and in *The Town Traveller* brazen Polly Sparkes twice chooses the Embankment below Waterloo Bridge for her business talks. Men and women in love are of course those in greatest need of privacy and the river's romantic potentialities quite make up for its gloominess. Gissing's fiction contains its load of far-fetched chance meetings or carefully planned appointments. The Monica Madden subplot in *The Odd Women* rests entirely on that acquaintance Edmund Widdowson picks up with the unfortunate shopgirl. Even if Monica has refused hard flirtation in a cosy tête-à-tête on the river with Mr. Bullivant, she has actually 'picked up some feller'

(*The Odd Women*, 1980, p. 48) that day, to use her companion's crude language. What Monica prefers to refer to as her adventure at Richmond only has the appearance of one and leads to a formal and conventional appointment and to genteel love-making in a rowing-boat the next week. Thus both the riverside and the midstream provide the setting for mock-romantic love scenes in which stage-directions about rowing and tilling become ironical outward manifestations of the couple's supposedly complex emotions. The Thames similarly activates the sexual game in *Will Warburton*, with chance meetings fast transforming into downright, if unavowed, appointments. Following 'nature's prime impulse' (*Will Warburton*, p. 233) the hero plays his foolish part in the little drama imagined by Rosamund Elvan on the stage of Battersea Park Embankment. Reasons why the disillusioned Gissing hardly ever indulges in a genuine love scene by the Thames would perhaps not be hard to find. In *Demos*, Rodman stands his first wife up on Westminster Bridge after a cynical scene of sham affection; in *In the Year of Jubilee* Nancy Lord obviously makes the wrong decision in agreeing to meet Luckworth Crewe at London Bridge. And Christopher Parish blackmailing Polly – 'I will be standing at the south end of Westminster Bridge. The *river* will be near if *you* are not; remember that' (*The Town Traveller*, p. 144) – is only slightly less ludicrous than another fellow-clerk of unprepossessing appearance, Jonas Warbrick, pleading his empty cause before shedding solitary tears on the dark embankment of 'Under an Umbrella.'

Finally one more specific trait of the river is made much of by Gissing – its gleaming surface, especially when the broadening sheet of water reflects the rays of the setting sun and enhances the beauty of the flushed sky. Whenever its muddy depths cease to be probed into and it is treated instead as a watery mirror, the waterscape becomes 'far from unlovely' (a litotes found in *Isabel Clarendon*, II, p. 121), and even a doomed character like Biffen in *New Grub Street* may still watch the river 'with a quiet smile' (*New Grub Street*, 1978, p. 528) and enjoy for the last time the eternal splendour of the dusky sky. Unsurprisingly Thames scenery, especially at dusk, ever inspires Gissing's fictional artists. If logically painting is the first art involved, with Arthur Golding's 'excursions to spots some miles up the Thames' (*Workers in the Dawn*, p. 251), Ada Warren's metamorphosis into a talented writer establishes for the first time in Gissing's work a central parallelism between pictorial and verbal representation. Ada first emerges as a fledgling writer with her 'River Twilight' prose sketch published in *The Tattler*. Instead of finding 'bits for her pencil' about Chelsea Embankment, she has discovered that she could 'picture in words that which had so impressed her' (*Isabel Clarendon*, II, p. 195) and she passes henceforth from literal, idle sketching to liberating, paid writing. Leaning upon the parapet of a bridge then ceases to be a gender-specific posture. The water, rich with the reflection of the western sky, acts as a powerful catalyst in the heroine's *Bildung*. Authorship suddenly lifts Ada out of her insignificance and endows her with a compensatory new 'noble type of beauty' (*Isabel Clarendon*, II, p. 296). Gissing's own partiality for river sunsets even urges him to utilise Ada's experience of urban beauty to engineer the final romance. But such a hopeful portrait of the artist in his/her natural environment reads too much like wishful thinking not to find ironical counterparts in the later texts. Ada Warren's rival Chelsea artist turns out to be scheming, amateurish Rosamund in *Will Warburton* whose pseudo-aesthetic 'quest for a good subject for a water-colour' and rapturous interest in the sunset and 'a certain effect of sky and water' (*Will Warburton*, p. 209) are nothing but the gross amorous device of a coquette. Debunking of the artistic stance is brief but more cruel in *Ryecroft* where the mature enunciator condescendingly looks back on his starved but inspired younger self gazing at the rosy sky from Battersea Bridge and then speeding home to write a description of the glorious sunset. 'How proud I was of that little bit of writing! I should not much like to see it again, for I thought it then so good that I am sure it would give me an unpleasant sensation now,' Ryecroft comments wistfully (*Ryecroft*, 1982, p. 212). Both Ada Warren and Ryecroft are to be understood as contrasting (semi-)fictional versions of the author himself, Ada being the one unironical female palimpsest, probably because Gissing imagined her shortly after writing his own essay. So if location and posture vary slightly (Ada is not actually leaning on the parapet like Gissing or Ryecroft but walking along the embankment) emotional distance is not yet to be felt. Twenty years later, on the other hand, autobiographical *mise en abyme* becomes merciless. Nevertheless, irony in *Ryecroft* is levelled at the character alone, the elder narrating 'I' significantly never trying to sneer at 'the beauties of earth and heavens' ('On Battersea Bridge,' *Selections*, 1925, p. 58) the broad sweep of the river allows the display of.

Conclusion

In Gissing's picture of his time the metropolis and, within the metropolis, the Thames, certainly have a key role to play. The river becomes a privileged urban sign contributing to the creation of the sense of place his fiction is convincingly imbued with. It is also particularly well sign-posted in order to illustrate the centrality of class in urban organisation. Gissing's river-image has a protean character and triggers off varying responses – from plain disgust at the offensive sewage effluents (euphemistically called 'mud') implicitly drifting with the tide in his novels, to grateful acknowledgment of the river attractions and beauties. Gissing's view of the Thames is certainly less fascinating and more restrictive than Charles Dickens's since, in an attempt to withstand the encroachments of commercial civilisation Gissing carefully avoids either having a good look downstream towards the estuary, for instance, or making use of the teeming docks and bulk wharves, thus missing fascinating narrative possibilities. But despite partial representation the river Thames not infrequently grows, as under the pen of Dickens, into a symbolic and/or mythical stream whose flow archetypally runs parallel with the course of human life itself – a fact which should give Gissing scholars additional food for thought.

Bibliography

Coustillas, Pierre, ed. *George Gissing. Essays & Fiction* (Baltimore and London: Johns Hopkins Press, 1970).

——. *London and the Life of Literature in Late Victorian England. The Diary of George Gissing, Novelist* (Hassocks: The Harvester Press, 1978).

Gissing, George. 'The Day of Silence', *The Day of Silence and Other Stories* (London: J.M. Dent; Rutland, Vermont: Charles E. Tuttle, 1993).

——. 'The Prize Lodger', *Human Odds and Ends* (New York & London: Garland, 1977).

——. *In the Year of Jubilee* (Hassocks: Harvester Press, 1976).

——. *Isabel Clarendon*, 2 vols. (Brighton: Harvester Press, 1969).

——. *New Grub Street* (Harmondsworth: Penguin Books, 1978).

——. *The Odd Women* (London: Virago, 1980).

——. *The Private Papers of Henry Ryecroft* (Brighton: Harvester Press, 1982).

——. 'On Battersea Bridge', *Selections Autobiographical and Imaginative from the Works of George Gissing. With Biographical and Critical Notes by his Son* (New York: Jonathan Cape and Harnon Smith, 1925).

——. *Thyrza* (Brighton: Harvester Press, 1984).

——. *The Town Traveller* (Brighton: Harvester Press, 1981).

——. *Will Warburton* (London: Hogarth Press, 1985).

——. *Workers in the Dawn* (Brighton: Harvester Press, 1985).

Mattheisen, Paul F., Young, Arthur C. and Coustillas, Pierre, eds *The Collected Letters of George Gissing*, 9 vols. (Athens, Ohio: Ohio University Press, 1990–97).

13
'Amid the Dear Old Horrors': Memory, London, and Literary Labour in *The Private Papers of Henry Ryecroft*

Mary Hammond

In 1912, an anthology called *The Charm of London* was published in Britain by Chatto and Windus. Compiled by Alfred H. Hyatt, it included several romantic watercolours of city views and short contributions from a range of authors from Dickens and Tennyson to George Gissing and Walter Besant. It is an upbeat, self-congratulatory volume; all of the contributors are either full of praise for Britain's capital or, at the very worst, charmed by its idiosyncrasies.

Such books were neither unusual nor new at the beginning of the twentieth century, and the idea of London as a unique social space worthy of investigation has of course continued unabated. Perhaps unsurprisingly, George Gissing – London author *par excellence* – has occupied an important place in many of these recent explorations. They have tended, however, to seize almost exclusively upon his gloomy representations of the individual alienated by the modern world and his portrayals of the doomed writer of integrity drowning in a world of mass-produced pulp. For Judith Walkowitz, for example, 'Gissing's novels represent an embattled, defensive self, contending with an anomic social environment lacking coherence, meaning, or direction' (Walkowitz, 1992, p. 38), while for Peter Keating, 'neither Reardon nor Gissing provided an attractive alternative model of how to live by literature in an age of unprecedented opportunities' (Keating, 1989, p. 32). For most recent critics, in fact, Gissing exemplifies the modern author's moral and creative dilemmas, and London – the centre of the publishing industry – is the stage on which these struggles can be most effectively enacted. Even Peter Ackroyd, who cites Gissing several times, does so most frequently in terms of his weariness of the metropolis (Ackroyd, 2000).

In the light of this critical consensus it is somewhat surprising to revisit the extract from Gissing's work as it appeared in *The Charm of London*, which unashamedly celebrates the capital, and to find in it an unaccustomed fondness for the place. The extract's presence there prompts us to ask whether he has been quoted out of context, or whether the recent critics are just wrong. The answer, in fact, is both. Fondness for London was certainly not his habitual mode, but there is evidence to suggest that Gissing was extraordinarily ambivalent about London and, more importantly, about what it meant for the future of writing. It is not difficult to take a passage or even a whole novel out of the body of realist work spanning Gissing's career and find a rabid hatred for the vulgar, greedy capital with its quick-fix reading habits. But seeping through the hatred and the realism there is also an undeniable fascination with modernity's greatest achievement, the city, which tends at times to hint at realism's inadequacy as a modern representative mode. It is worth considering some of the nuances of Gissing's opinions of London, for they have something to add to our understanding of the relationships between the modern psyche, the city, and literary representation not only in Gissing's own time, but also in the literary movements which followed him.

I have found it useful here to go back to a late essay by Raymond Williams. While in much of his writing he, too, has tended to treat Gissing as one of modernity's lonely victims, he does provide us in the later works with a way of thinking through some of the links between realism and modernism, locating at least one of these in the modern city. In 'When was Modernism?' Williams suggests that the ground-breaking literary movements of the early twentieth century relied heavily both on the city as 'the most appropriate locale for art made by the restlessly immobile émigré or exile', and on the mid-nineteenth century authors who had mapped it. As he puts it, 'without Dickens, no Joyce' (Williams, 1989, p. 34). As he also points out though, we have tended to ignore the contributions made by later realists to this mapping, rather too conveniently preferring breaks to continuities. But in privileging Freud over Zola, the hidden over the surface of *fin-de-siècle* urban existence, we have tended to write out of modernism's history one of the main schools of thought that formed it.

For many pre-modernist authors, the city is important in terms of a feeling of isolation which it engenders in the individual. Williams traces this trope as far back as Wordsworth's *Prelude*, begun in 1798 (Williams, 1989, p. 39). But for later nineteenth-century authors it is crucial, also, in terms of the sense of strangeness which it engenders in the writing subject. The experience of urban alienation is linguistic as well as physical in this period. It is a result of increasing immigration and the drift from country to town which stirred up but failed to integrate different linguistic communities. It is also, for writers, a result of the bewildering growth and diversification in the market for books after the Education Acts of the 1870s, and the disturbing fluidity of national borders within the book trade prior to the first effective International Copyright Act in 1909. Arriving in London in 1876, Henry James noted that: '[London] is the single place in which most readers, most possible lovers, are gathered together ... It is the most inclusive public and the largest social incarnation of the language, of the tradition' (James, 1905, pp. 6–7). But while he saw literary associations everywhere he looked these encompassed Harriet Beecher Stowe as well as *Punch*, Thackeray, and the *Illustrated London News*. London's literary scene is clearly by this time an increasingly global one, the 'English literary tradition' no longer comfortably recognisable, but rapidly evolving beyond national boundaries (James, 1905, p. 14).

From a quintessential mode of communication central to England's public sphere since the eighteenth century, writing becomes in this period a powerful symbol for the contradictions of modern city life, part of a mode of production which for the first time in history alienates its participants from one another, and from themselves. What Williams calls 'this intense, singular narrative of unsettlement, homelessness, solitude and impoverished independence' is embodied in 'the lonely writer gazing down on an unknowable city from his shabby apartment' (Williams, 1989, p. 32). Ford Madox Ford summed this up in 1905, echoing not only Marx but also Gissing's *New Grub Street*:

> all work in modern London is almost of necessity routine work: the tendency to specialise in small articles, in small parts of a whole, insures that ... there is no call at all made upon the special craftsman's intellect that is in all the human race. It is a ceaseless strain upon the nerves and upon the muscles. It crushes out the individuality ... this tendency is most observable in the periodical press, that most enormous and most modern of industries. Here upon the whole the aesthetically intrinsic quality of the work offered by a young man does not matter much. The employer sits as it were in an office chair between the great public and the young men who besiege him. (Madox Ford, 1905, pp. 87–94)

This horrified recoil from mass publishing and a huge, half-literate urban readership unites many writers in this period, of course. But I want here to draw out some more important links between Gissing, the city and proto-modernists such as Ford. Williams himself sees in Gissing's work a fusion and confusion between social and psychological alienation which points ahead to 'observable tendencies in twentieth-century avant-garde art' (Williams, 1989, p. 41). He does not, however, explore how this is achieved, and therefore misses some of the key reasons for reading Gissing alongside the proto-modernists.

Gissing does not disrupt his narratives in the same way as the modernists, who made linguistic alienation one of the governing principles of their experiments with form. But he does repeatedly use the circumstances of modernity to disrupt the lives of his characters and, more importantly, for him language is central to this disruption. *New Grub Street* abounds with poignant images of misplaced linguistic exchange. Biffen and Reardon stand, ragged and starving, on an icy street corner which will make them both ill, discussing one of the fragments of Euripides (1891, p. 412). Biffen risks his life to save from a house-fire a manuscript that he knows will never be read (1891, pp. 465–71). A stubborn adherence to outmoded linguistic forms in a modern world kills both of them. Words, in Gissing's novels, are misplaced, misused, and misunderstood. The idea of an irreversible social breakdown both mirrored and in part created by the art-world works in direct opposition to many other nineteenth-century city novels such as Elizabeth Gaskell's *Mary Barton* (1848) and *North and South* (1855), and Walter Besant's *All Sorts and Conditions of Men* (1882), in which class is unproblematic and innate. These narratives are often driven by the search for a rightful place for a temporarily troubled community. But there *is* almost always a community. Gissing, however, disrupts all notions of social or linguistic communities in his depictions of the rootless realities of city life, and the bitterness of *New Grub Street* is largely driven by this disruption. Emotional bonds are financial, dutiful, sometimes circumstantial, but seldom genuine and lasting. Families and even friends are incapable of co-existing indefinitely in any sort of harmony or comfort. The educated can no longer live by disseminating their learning. The half-educated hack can get rich writing ephemera which appeals to the lowest common denom-inator. Besant's successful crusade in this period to achieve professional recognition for writers through the establishment of a Society of Authors with London as its base strikes no chord with Gissing. He finds in profes-sionalism only an increase of the confusion between qualitative categories. 'Yes, yes,' he writes towards the end of his life, in *The Private Papers of Henry Ryecroft*, 'I know as well as any man that reforms were needed in the rela-tions between author and publisher ... nonetheless do I loathe and sicken at the manifold baseness, the vulgarity unutterable, which, as a result of the new order, is blighting our literary life. It is not easy to see how, in such an atmosphere, great and noble books can ever again come into being' (Gissing, 1903, pp. 214–15).

Gissing also works in opposition to the attempts at classification of the city's inhabitants made by social commentators such as Charles Booth, whose *Life and Labour of the People of London* was begun in the 1880s. Booth writes of the city of London that its inhabitants 'live in darkness, with doubting hearts and ignorant unnecessary fears' (Booth, 1889, p. 18) and then spends seventeen volumes trying to dispel the darkness with colour-coded maps. But in *New Grub Street* Gissing is content to let the dissolving traditional subject founder and die, and the dissolute modern one prosper in a status quo that only needs to last for a day. In this sense, as early as 1891 Gissing is among the most modern of writers.

While *New Grub Street* might be the most famous of Gissing's novels, it is far from being his last word on the subjects of language and the city. It would be difficult to pull a passage from that novel and transplant it into the 1912 *Charm of London* volume. Edwin Reardon's assessment of the city is pessimistic to say the least: 'it's a huge misfortune, this will-o'-the-wisp attraction exercised by London on young brains. They come here to be degraded, or to perish, when their true sphere is a life of peaceful remoteness' (Gissing, 1891, pp. 473–4). Reardon, the embodiment of outmoded artistic integrity, is offered this chance of peaceful remoteness, not in this book, but in one of the last of Gissing's career, *The Private Papers of Henry Ryecroft*. Written during 1901, published in serial form in 1902 under the title 'An Author at Grass' then in book form in 1903, *The Ryecroft Papers* was described by Gissing as 'in style...better than anything I have yet done' (Coustillas, 1978, p. 533) and hailed by at least one reviewer as his 'masterpiece' (Coustillas and Partridge, 1995, p. 419). The character of Henry Ryecroft can be read as a version of Gissing himself – indeed, John Halperin has provided a detailed and convincing reading of the book which demonstrates how closely the published reminiscences resemble Gissing's own life, arguing that 'what we have [in this book] is the "novel" as spiritual confession, as private memoir. It is perhaps the fullest artistic expression of the close connection between Gissing's work and his life' (Halperin, 1982, p. 315).

The autobiographical elements are undeniable. But Ryecroft is also a revised version of Edwin Reardon, a Reardon given a different type of marriage and a surprise legacy which has rescued him from London, a failing literary career, and an untimely death. In this sense he is as unlike the real Gissing (who managed to make a living from writing) as Reardon (who did not). More important than the autobiography/fiction debate, though, is Gissing's unusual manner in this novel of *writing* the writer's life. From a position of relative ease, free from monetary cares in a cottage in Devon, Ryecroft/Reardon is able to reflect on the life – and the city – to which he devoted his youth. And writing from a twice-removed position as the fictional editor of a fictional dead author's journal, Gissing is able to be more honest about writing and the city than ever before. Now, at the beginning of the twentieth century, he found that the resurrection of dead voices, the privileging of the private over the public sphere, the emphasis on self over society, and the juxtaposition of city and country as extremes of experience articulated a fragmenting modern consciousness more fully than the safely colour-coded maps of the nineteenth century had been able to do. These stylistic devices are, of course, part of the book's fantasy of cloistered, comfortable middle age reflecting on hungry public youth. But Ryecroft is a writer as well as an ageing lower middle-class misanthrope, and he chooses to write rather than to remain silent. The abdication of Victorian social-realist responsibility in favour of the novel of the self augurs a new literary phase as much as a personal one, whether Gissing was aware of it or not.

The idea of the city as a place of darkness and decay goes back at least as far as the eighteenth century, but it achieved particular prominence in the nineteenth. By the middle of the century it already had an intimate relation to art. Ruskin, for example, found the introduction of beauty into urban architecture finally pointless, 'inconsistent alike with the reckless luxury, the deforming mechanism, and the squalid misery of modern cities' (Davis, 1995, p. 336). In many works later in the century, country-living is posited as the antidote for city life. Charles Booth suggests that: 'it is not in the country but in town that "terra incognita" needs to be written on our social map. In the country the machinery of human life is plainly to be seen and easily recognised: personal relations bind the whole together. The equipoise on which existing order rests, whether satisfactory or not, is palpable and evident' (Booth, 1889, p. 18). But while Gissing devotes pages to the joys of the countryside in *The Ryecroft Papers*, and Henry states emphatically that 'the last thought in my brain as I lie dying will be that of sunshine upon an English meadow' (1902, p. 84), he returns obsessively to London in these memoirs. Walking in the summer countryside he suddenly remembers 'an August bank-holiday when, having for some reason to walk all across London, I unexpectedly found myself enjoying the strange desertion of the great streets, and from that passed to surprise in the sense of something beautiful' (p. 98). Walking along a road after nightfall he is reminded of London streets and 'by a freak of mind wished I were there ... Not seldom I have a sudden vision of a London street, perhaps the dreariest and ugliest, which for a moment gives me a feeling of homesickness' (p. 234).

Why the nostalgia? Why, after the horrors depicted in *New Grub Street*, is Gissing/Ryecroft homesick for them? The answer lies in a particularly important modern paradox. *The Ryecroft Papers* does not just represent a physical retreat from the city to the country, from barbaric darkness to the noble pastoral. That would be an easy solution, as it was to many of Gissing's near-contemporaries. The book also signals a political retreat, from the public to the private realm implied by its title; a moral retreat, from active social engagement to lonely self-exploration; and an artistic retreat, from writing for an audience to writing for oneself. *The Ryecroft Papers* is a clear signal that for those writers who abhorred mass education, a writer's task should be to spurn the crowd-pleaser for mass publication and, for the good of art, turn inward. All this should sound very familiar to modernist scholars.

In *Ryecroft* this inward turn takes two forms which should sound equally familiar. First, the book is 'introduced' by Gissing himself in a fictional but mock-factual 'preface' which states that the late author's journals came to him disordered and fragmented, apparently needing both editing and ordering. This the fictionalised Gissing accomplished, he tells us, by dividing the journals into four sections, each named after one of the seasons. Publication, ordering, a 'Natural Law' is thus forced upon Gissing's idealised author after his death, beating into submission a work that, as the preface puts it, was in its original form 'irregular ... in fragmentary pieces' (p. xiii), written 'without restraint'. In this 'mere incondite miscellany' of 'disconnected passages', Gissing tells us, Ryecroft 'spoke of himself, and told the truth as far as mortal could tell it' (p. xiv). This is an important signal that the scientific, almost obsessive cataloguing of details on which realism depends is becoming inadequate as a form, that its ordering principles are incapable of telling the truth about the modern human mind. The novel needs 'disconnecting' from traditional language systems – and from the contemporary publishing industry – if it is to express consciousness adequately.

Second, this fragmentary collection slips back and forth in time and place and addresses no audience in particular. Like Proust, it meanders after memories called up by the smell of a book or a cup of tea. It ruminates on topics from politics to classical mythology to English cookery with no pretence at authority except that of the thinking, writing self. There are no facts, statistics or attempts to be persuasive. There is, in fact, no dialogue whatsoever. Ryecroft is done with human interaction; for him all speech has become meaningless. When he does invoke the sound of people, he describes it merely as noise – as bellow, clamour, scream, shout or yell (p. 71). This book marks a move away from the surface plurality of realism, and towards a landscape of the mind. It suggests that true realism is actually all about individual perception, that the mind has an intensely personal relationship with time and space. Remembering a peaceful hour spent under a tree in the country and wondering whether he will ever be able to repeat it, he writes: 'No, no; what I remember is just one moment of my earlier life, linked by accident with that picture of the Suffolk landscape. The place no longer exists; it never existed save for me' (p. 106). This, it seems to me, is an extraordinarily modern statement, and it is worth investigating its importance.

In his seminal work *A Genealogy of Modernism*, Michael Levenson devotes an entire chapter to Ford Madox Ford, reading back into Ford's early work the seeds of the innovator he was to become. 'Ford insisted on realism and self-expression concurrently ... civic realism thus collapses into an egoism which no longer attempts to establish shared norms of reality ... the Impressionist, in Ford's view, is entitled, even obliged, to be personal in the presentation of reality – since there must be no pretence of a neutral body of knowledge. To render reality then *is* to manifest individuality. Since they are necessarily personal, perceptions of the real are expressions of the self' (Levenson, 1984, pp. 115–16).

Levenson is right, I think, to insist on the importance of a genealogy of modernism. Ford's view of the great Victorian thinkers as moral crusaders for whom there is no longer a place is crucial in marking the move from social conscience to individual consciousness. But where Levenson is slightly more limited in his analysis, perhaps, is in his emphasis on Ford as a proto-modernist who somehow managed to see what others did not. Modernism's famed 'breaks with the past' are formal, not ideological. Ford was a contemporary of Gissing's, and they shared more than a historical moment: Gissing, too, argued for a move from civic realism to egoism – and he did it not in essays, but in a novel, prefiguring the shape of literature to come. After all, as we have seen, in 1905 Ford was still harping on the theme of the isolated, exploited London artist at the mercy of the mass periodical market (Ford, 1905, p. 94), something that had been thoroughly explored by Gissing back in 1891. By 1901 Gissing had moved on, and he had done so in exactly the manner that Levenson attributes to Ford: by abandoning the social and political for the individual and autonomous.

It would be stretching the point to claim a place for Gissing among proto-modernists such as Conrad and James. The style that pleased him so much in *Ryecroft* looks back to the eighteenth century as much as forward to the twentieth. But the *Ryecroft Papers* is worth re-evaluating as a contributor to the politics of modernism. This contribution becomes apparent in the passage quoted in the *Charm of London* volume with which I began:

> Some day I will go to London, and spend a day or two amid the dear old horrors...I think most of my haunts are still in existence: to tread again those pavements, to look at those grimy doorways and purblind windows, would affect me strangely...Oh my ambitions, my hopes! How surprised and indignant I should have felt had I known of any one who pitied me...What a poor feeble wretch I now seem to myself, when I remember thirty years ago! (Gissing, 1903, pp. 27–32)

Ryecroft's obsessive return to 'the dear old horrors' of London indicates an important moment of confusion and even division in the writing self. It marks on the one hand a triumphant sense of having survived trial by fire in the urban literary marketplace; there is a sense of excitement over the possibilities offered by the crowd, and by what had become by this period an extremely sophisticated publishing industry. But on the other hand there is the opacity and horror of a metropolis created by the Victorians, a sense that art, like the individual, must turn inward if it is to rescue itself from the grinding mediocrity which is democracy's by-product. These two contradictory impulses – the progressive and the conservative – were to emerge ever more strongly in the work of the writers now described as modernists, but they have one of their first incarnations here, in the work of George Gissing. To write that a return to the city would 'affect me strangely' is to articulate the quintessential turn-of-the-century urban experience of a dissolving and confused subjectivity. For Gissing, the future of psychologically truthful literature lies not in spurning the city, but in understanding it. As Williams suggests, late realists like Gissing 'devised and organized a whole vocabulary and its structure of figures of speech with which to grasp the unprecedented social forms of the industrial city' (Williams, 1989, p. 32). We ignore these writers at our peril.

Bibliography

Ackroyd, P. *London: the Biography* (London: Chatto and Windus, 2000).
Besant, W. *All Sorts and Conditions of Men* (1882; Oxford: Oxford University Press, 1997).
Booth, C. *Inquiry into the Life and Labour of the People in London*, 2nd Series, Vol. 1 (London: Macmillan, 1889).
Coustillas, P. ed., *London and the Life of Literature in Late Victorian England: The Diary of George Gissing, Novelist* (Hassocks: The Harvester Press, 1978).
Coustillas, P. and Partridge, C. *George Gissing the Critical Heritage* (London: Routledge, 1995).
Davis, P. ed., *Selected Writings of John Ruskin* (London: Everyman, 1995).
Ford Madox, F. *The Soul of London: A Survey of a Modern City* (London: Alston Rivers, 1905).
Gaskell, E. *North and South* (1855; London: Penguin, 1995).
——. *Mary Barton* (1848; London: Penguin, 1996).
Gissing, G. *New Grub Sreet* (1891; London: Penguin, 1985).
——. *The Private Papers of Henry Ryecroft* (London: Constable, 1903).
Halperin, J. *Gissing: A Life in Books* (Oxford: Oxford University Press, 1982).
Hyatt, A.H. *The Charm of London* (London: Chatto and Windus, 1912).
James, H. *English Hours* (Boston and New York: Houghton, Mifflin, 1905).
Keating, P. *The Haunted Study: A Social History of the English Novel 1875–1914* (London: Secker and Warburg, 1989).
Levenson, M.H. *A Genealogy of Modernism: A Study of English Literary Doctrine 1908–1922* (Cambridge: Cambridge University Press, 1984).
Walkowitz, J.R. *City of Dreadful Delight: Narratives of Sexual Danger in Late-Victorian London* (London: Virago, 1992).
Williams, R. *The Politics of Modernism*, Pinkney, Tony, ed. (London: Verso, 1989).

14

Gissing's Urban Neurasthenia

John Halperin

It is typical of Gissing's life that he spent most of it living in places that he hated. Wakefield, as Russell Kirk once commented, is "ingeniously designed for the torment of any man who cares for beauty and tradition." (Coustillas, 1968, p. 3). From *Workers in the Dawn* (1880), his first published novel, to *Will Warburton* (1905), the last one he completed, and almost everywhere in between, Gissing's repugnance to city life is vividly articulated. He always wished to live amidst what is soft and gentle; by necessity, until his last years, he was condemned to live amidst, and have constantly in front of him as subject-matter for his books, only what he loathed.

> Arthur Golding, the hero of *Workers in the Dawn*, already at seventeen feels within himself the stirrings of a double life, the one, due to his natural gifts, comprehending all the instincts, the hopes, the ambitions of an artist; the other, originating in the outward circumstances of his childhood...showing him...the ever-multiplying miseries of the poor amongst whom he lived. (I, p. 237)

Arthur compares the art he yearns to produce with that of Hogarth:

> The art to which he was devoted was not the same in which Hogarth had excelled. He felt that it would be impossible for him to take up his pencil for the delineation of such varieties of hideousness. Beauty was the goddess that he worshipped at the inmost shrine of his being, and to the bodying forth of visible shapes of beauty his life must be devoted, or he must cast aside the pencil for ever...how should he go for his models to the slums and the hovels amidst which his wretched childhood had been passed? (I, pp. 255–6)

Gissing's friend Morley Roberts commented after the novelist's death that his "very repugnance to his early subjects led him to choose them. He showed what he wished the world to be by declaring and proving that it possessed every conceivable opposite to his desires" (Roberts, 1912, p. 306). In this spirit, *Workers in the Dawn* describes London as a nineteenth-century waste land, an awful place in which, for the sake of peace and an end of suffering, it is better to be dead than alive. Here is Gissing's description of Whitecross Street in the East End on Christmas eve:

> Out of the very depths of human depravity bubbled up the foulest miasmata which the rottenness of the human heart can breed... stifling a whole city with their infernal reek. The very curs that had followed their masters into the gin-palaces shrank out into the street again, affrighted by the brutal din. (I, p. 106)

A quarter of a century later had Gissing grown more tolerant of the metropolis in which he spent most of his life? *Will Warburton*, like *The Ryecroft Papers* (1902–3), compares urban to country life and informs us, in case we did not know, that it is better to go to work every day "through lanes overhung with fruit-tree blossoms" than through "the filth and stench and gloom and uproar" of London (p. 145). The city's streets are characterized in *Will Warburton* as a "vast slaughter-strewn field of battle" (p. 22). The sounds of the city are "cries of pain or of misery, shouts savage or bestial; over and through all, that low, far-off rumble or roar, which never for a moment ceases, the groan... of suffering multitudes" (pp. 160–61). At the end of his life London and Paris, Rome and Athens, no longer beckoned to Gissing. He yearned only for Henry Ryecroft's country cottage.

That country-cottage fantasy begins as early as *Isabel Clarendon* (1886), written in 1884–85 when Gissing had been in London only a few years. The neurasthenic hero Bernard Kingcote, after some months in a country cabin, arrives in London; "the roaring crowd" makes him "wish for deafness... Every sensitive chord of his frame was smitten into agony... and stirred him to a passion of loathing. His very senses rebelled; he felt sick, faint" (I, p. 174; II, p. 91 and pp. 95–6).

In *A Life's Morning* (1888), written in 1885, Gissing sounds his earliest note of environmentalism. He hated industry's rape of the landscape, having seen a good deal of it growing up in Yorkshire in the 1860s. We get the taste of an ecological theme in this novel in the description of the country around Dunfield as "blighted by the curse of... industrialism." The grass has "absorbed too much mill-smoke to exhibit wholesome verdure." "Take in your fingers a spray from one of the trees... and its touch left a soil" (p. 64). The river is described as "foul... with the refuse of manufactures" (p. 73). Smoke from the local coal-pits has a habit of blowing in the open windows of train-carriages, "giving a special flavour to bread and meat," and making sandwiches "smoky" (p. 195). A local colliery town is characterized as "vomiting blackness" and as a "region of blight and squalor... [and] smoke-fouled streets" (p. 133). The industrial theme combines Gissing's love of the country with his hatred of "progress," a note sounded even more loudly in *Demos* (1886).

Written in 1885–86, *Demos* reveals its author as an enemy of, among other things, the industrial plutocracy. While it often betrays contempt for industrial workers, *Demos* never defends their masters. On the contrary, the new class of industrialists and the political Establishment that coddles it are attacked with special bitterness here. "Men with large aims cannot afford to be scrupulous in small details," snarls the narrator (p. 244). The environmentalist theme touched on in *A Life's Morning* is taken much further in *Demos* – into a remarkably sustained and prophetic condemnation of the rape of the countryside by heavy industry. Long before novels like *Howards End* and *Lady Chatterley's Lover* made this theme famous, we find Gissing in the mid-1880s absorbed with it. The very first paragraph of *Demos* describes the town of Bealwick, "with its hundred and fifty fire-vomiting blast furnaces," as a hell in the middle of "greenery" (p. 1). Hoxton, the neighbouring town, is delineated in language reserved for Gissing's most emotional outbursts. It is

> a region of malodorous market streets, of factories, timber yards, grimy warehouses of alleys swarming with small trades and crafts, of filthy courts and passages leading into pestilential gloom; everywhere toil in its most degrading forms...working folk of the coarsest type, the corners and lurking-holes showing destitution at its ugliest. (p. 26)

Hubert Eldon, the middle-class manager who often speaks with Gissing's voice in *Demos*, tries, while at the works at Wanley, to preserve the surrounding areas from ecological disaster, to keep the countryside unsullied by industry. But Richard Mutimer, the new working-class boss without taste, wants to construct an "ideal" community of workers in the middle of a green valley. As a result of this misguided "progress," there is a good deal of tearing-up of the countryside, and of authorial commentary on how spurious the interests of "progress" are. "It used to be all fields and gardens over there," says Mutimer proudly to his sister as they stand on the churned-up site of New Wanley. "See what money and energy can do!" (p. 201). Exactly. Gissing was unimpressed by the examples of Robert Owen, Charles Fourier, Thomas Hughes (the author of *Tom Brown's Schooldays*), and others who had attempted to establish communities of workers along socialist lines. The working classes, he thought, were beyond help. The novelist goes on to describe in these terms Mutimer's rape of the land:

> Building of various kinds was in progress in the heart of the vale; a great massive chimney was rising to completion, and about it stood a number of sheds. Beyond was to be seen the commencement of a street of small houses, promising infinite ugliness in a little space; the soil over a

considerable area was torn up and trodden into mud...the benighted valley was waking up and donning the true nineteenth-century livery. (pp. 67–8)

At the end of *Demos*, when Mutimer is disinherited and Eldon returns to power, New Wanley is joyously destroyed. Mutimer's awful project, the novel decries, "has ruined one of the loveliest valleys in England" (p. 281). Eldon vows to "sweep away every trace of the mines and the works and the houses, and...restore the valley to its former state" (pp. 338–39). There will be peace in the valley after all. "It may be inevitable that the green and beautiful spots of the world shall give place to furnaces and mechanics' dwellings," Eldon tells Adele, but he will have no part in such "desolation and defilement."

"Then you think grass and trees of more importance than human lives?" Adele asks him.

"I had rather say that I see no value in human lives in a world from which grass and trees have vanished," Eldon replies (p. 77).

"A world from which grass and trees have vanished" aptly characterizes the urban settings of *Thyrza* (1887) and *The Nether World* (1889), written between 1886 and 1888.

Thyrza is one of Gissing's most neurasthenic novels. We can see the writer's visceral hatred of the metropolis in his description of Gilbert Grail's route to work, in the course of which Grail is almost overcome by the inimical physical environment.

He went to work through a fog so dense that it was with difficulty he followed the familiar way. Lamps were mere lurid blotches in the foul air, perceptible only when close at hand; the footfall of invisible men and women hurrying to factories made a muffled, ghastly sound; harsh bells summoned through the darkness, the voice of pitiless taskmasters...Gilbert was racked with headache...he longed for nothing more than to lie down and lose consciousness of the burden of life. (p. 108)

The physical properties of London – described here in terms reminiscent of *Bleak House* – are responsible for Gilbert's headache and desire for unconsciousness, a neurasthenic response. *Thyrza* contains a sustained commentary on the qualities of urban life.

Windows glimmered at noon with the sickly ray of gas or lamp; the roads were trodden into viscid foulness; all night the droppings of a pestilent rain were doleful...and only the change from a black to a yellow sky told that the sun was risen. (p. 98)

Gissing's characterization of the Caledonian Road is of a waste land.

> It is doubtful whether London can show any thoroughfare...more
> offensive to eye and ear and nostril. You stand at the entrance to it,
> and gaze into a region of supreme ugliness; every house front is
> marked with meanness and inveterate grime; every shop seems
> breaking forth with mould or dry-rot; the people who walk here
> appear...to be employed in labour that soils body and spirit. Journey
> on the top of a tram-car from King's Cross to Holloway, and civilisa-
> tion has taught you its ultimate achievement in ignoble hideousness.
> You look off into narrow side-channels where unconscious degrada-
> tion has made its inexpugnable home, the region with black-breathing
> fissure. You see the pavements half occupied with the...most sordid
> wares...the public-houses look and reek more intolerably than in
> other places. (p. 319)

As we shall see, we are not finished with King's Cross. The novel goes on
here to describe another section of Lambeth as "redolent with oleaginous
matter; the clothing of men was penetrated with the same nauseous odour"
(p. 73) – suggested perhaps by the sections of *Bleak House* which conjure up
Krook's oily neighbourhood.

The waste-land motif so noticeable in *Demos* and *Thyrza* comes back with
a vengeance in *The Nether World*, the greatest slum-life novel in English. The
setting is penurious Clerkenwell; descriptions of an inner city in the clutch
of alien forces are, even for Gissing, unprecedentedly vivid and violent. The
London streets are full of "thin clouds of unsavoury dust," (p. 2) the air has
a "stifling smell and a bitter taste" (p. 344). When it rains, along with the
water descends "the smut and grime" that characterize the neighborhood;
"the pavement was speedily over-smeared with sticky mud...Odours of oil
and shoddy...grew more pungent" (p. 203). In Shooter's Gardens, which is
rock-bottom Clerkenwell,

> the walls stood in a perpetual black sweat; a mouldy reek came from
> the open door-ways; the beings that passed in and out seemed soaked
> with grimy moisture, puffed into distortions, hung about with rotting
> garments. (p. 248)

When, after weeks of fog, darkness and rain, the sun momentarily appears,
Clerkenwell, like a shy tramp peering into the beam of a torch, cringes in all
of its ugliness from the unfamiliar illumination.

Gissing in *The Nether World* cannot resist putting some characters on
a train travelling from the city to the country in order to underline
once again the contrast between the urban slums and what lies beyond
them.

Over the pest-stricken regions of East London, sweltering in sunshine
which served only to reveal the intimacies of abomination; across
miles of a city of the damned, such as thought never conceived before
this age of ours; above streets swarming with a nameless populace,
cruelly exposed by the unwonted light of heaven; stopping at stations
which it crushes the heart to think should be the destination of any
mortal; the train made its way ... beyond the outmost limits of dread,
and entered upon a land of level meadows, of hedges and trees, of
crops and cattle. (p. 74)

The novelist's urban neurasthenia may also be glimpsed in his hatred of
another phenomenon concomitant with the growth of cities in the later
years of the nineteenth century. In both *In the Year of Jubilee* (1894) and *The
Crown of Life* (1899) – especially in the earlier novel – advertising has a lot to
answer for.

In *The Crown of Life* the chief proponent of advertising is an Italian named
Florio, who declares that it is "the triumph of the century, the supreme
outcome of civilisation!" (p. 261). In *In the Year of Jubilee* there is a more
leisurely and detailed commentary on advertising, whose chief advocate,
Luckworth Crewe, also happens to be a developer of land. Predictably, he is
the novel's prize booby. The ecology theme of *In the Year of Jubilee* is carried
forward here in the account of the spreading suburbs and Crewe's greedy
passion for "developing" the countryside (p. 218). Suburban Camberwell
and Brixton are described as simultaneously remote from London and yet
firmly within its grubby grasp. Did E.M. Forster read *In the Year of Jubilee*?
The following passage about land speculation could well have inspired
several chapters of *Howards End*:

London, devourer of rural limits, of a sudden made hidden encroachments upon the old estate, now held by a speculative builder; of many
streets to be constructed, three or four had already come into being, and
others were mapped out, in mud and inchoate masonry, athwart the
ravaged field. Great elms, the pride of generations, passed away, fell
before the speculative axe, or were left standing in mournful isolation to
please a speculative architect; bits of wayside hedge still shivered in fog
and wind, amid hoardings variegated with placards and scaffolding black
against the sky. The very earth had lost its wholesome odour; trampled
into mire, fouled with builders' refuse and the noisome drift from adjacent streets, it sent forth, under the sooty rain, a smell of corruption, of
all the town's uncleanliness. (p. 60)

Advertising, a new phenomenon of the nineties hated by Gissing with
one of his most singular passions, is violently attacked in *In the Year of
Jubilee* as the most visible and obnoxious sign of modern triviality and

decay. Posters for "somebody's 'Blue'; somebody's 'Soap'; somebody's 'High-class Jams'" (p. 114) fill the city of London in this novel; advertisements for soap and pills ring the piers along the Thames. All that is hateful about the present, all that is destructive of beauty and taste, is symbolized for Gissing in the defacements of advertising. The bathing-machines at Crewe's resort are plastered with advertisements. "Nay, the very pleasure-boats on the sunny waves declared the glory of somebody's soap, of somebody's purgatives" (p. 424). Crewe plans to put his advertisements even on the walls of caves. To Nancy Tarrant he expounds – with tongue perhaps slightly in cheek – the credo so detested by the author of *In the Year of Jubilee*:

> How could we have become what we are without the modern science of advertising? Till advertising sprang up, the world was barbarous. Do you suppose people kept themselves clean before they were reminded at every corner of the benefits of soap? Do you suppose they were healthy before every wall and hoarding told them what medicine to take for their ailments? (p. 74)

Today's paradise of advertising might have surprised Thackeray or Trollope or George Eliot, but it would not have surprised Gissing.

Perhaps no passage in this novel so uncannily strikes the modern note as this description of King's Cross underground station:

> They descended and stood together upon the platform, among hungry crowds, in black fumes that poisoned the palate with sulphur. This way and that sped the demon engines, whirling lighted waggons full of people. Shrill whistles, the hiss and roar of steam, the bang, clap, bang of carriage-doors, the clatter of feet on wood and stone – all echoed and reverberated from a huge cloudy vault above them. High and low, on every available yard of wall, advertisements clamoured to the eye; theatres, journals, soaps, medicine, concerts, furniture, wines, prayer-meetings – all the produce and refuse of civilisation announced in staring letters, in daubed effigies, base, paltry, grotesque. A battle-ground of advertisements, fully chosen amid subterranean din and reek; a symbol to the gaze of that relentless warfare which ceases not, night and day, in the world above. (p. 74)

Advertising assaults the eye as dirty slums, a filthy climate, and the industrialization of the countryside assault the ear and nose and mouth. For Gissing in London, neurasthenia can be visual too.

In his largely neglected masterpiece *The Whirlpool* (1897), written in 1896, the novelist pleads for the preservation of rural life and values and attacks London as the venue of noise and tension. The peace and quiet of the scenes in Basil Morton's country home articulate Gissing's longing for peace and quiet in his urban one. *The Whirlpool*, like *In the Year of Jubilee*, is particularly unfriendly to commuter trains, which make much of the novel's noise: they are depicted as a source "of roar and crash and shriek" inimical to sanity (III, ii). London is the whirlpool, the vortex of urban chaos. Hugh Carnaby speaks of "this damned London" (II, ix): "Great God! When there is so much of the world clean and sweet, here we pack and swelter together, a million to the square mile! What eternal fools we are!" (III, vii). Gissing in *The Whirlpool* even takes the extraordinary step of having one of his characters killed by bad drains: outside of the novels of Charles Kingsley, who developed a sort of theology of drains, poor Henrietta Winter must be the only character in English literature to suffer such a fate (See III, viii.). By contrast, at the Mortons' country place, "No tramp of sooty smother hung above the house-tops and smirched the garden leafage; no tramp of crowds, clatter of hot-wheel traffic sounded from the streets hard by" (III, i).

In *The Whirlpool*, as in *Demos, In the Year of Jubilee*, and some of the other novels, there is a prophetic sense of what "improvements" and developers are doing to the countryside. Harvey Rolfe predicts sadly that it is "the destiny of every beautiful spot in Britain" to be "developed" (II, ii). Gissing probably was not an admirer of Jane Austen, but to any reader of *Sanditon* the sentiments as well as the duplicities of land developers may seem familiar.

The neurasthenic aspect of Gissing's response to the noise, dirt, and visual assaults of contemporary life is what perhaps makes him the most "modern" of Victorian novelists. It seems impossible that he has been dead for a hundred years; he speaks in the tones of the twentieth century, not the nineteenth. His nervous response to and hatred of the trivialities of his world also indicate a temperamental preference for everything that is dead, dying, and gone. As he wished always to be somewhere other than where he was, so he recoiled from his own time with a passion consistent and unflinching. His phobia is reflected in his writings from all the periods of his life, from early to late, private as well as published. "In a big advt. on the walls," he notes in his Commonplace Book (Korg, 1962, p. 45), "it is stated that 60,000 bullocks are slaughtered yearly to make somebody's beef-tea. Another announced that, every minute, 7 of Beecham's pills 'reach their destination.'" We think of Gissing as an urban novelist, a novelist *par excellence* of city life. He was, but we sometimes forget how much he hated it.

Bibliography

Coustillas, Pierre, ed., *Collected Articles on George Gissing* (London: Frank Cass, 1968).
Gissing, George, *The Crown of Life* (London: Methuen, 1899).
——, *Demos: A Story of English Socialism* (London: Smith, Elder, 1886).
——, *In the Year of Jubilee* (London: Lawrence and Bullen, 1894).

——, *Isabel Clarendon* (London: Chapman and Hall, 1886).

——, *A Life's Morning* (London: Smith, Elder, 1888).

——, *The Nether World* (London: Smith, Elder, 1889).

——, *Thyrza* (London: Smith, Elder, 1887).

——, *The Whirlpool* (London: Lawrence and Bullen, 1897).

——, *Will Warburton* (London: Constable, 1905).

——, *Workers in the Dawn* (London: Remington, 1880).

Korg, Jacob, ed., *George Gissing's Commonplace Book. A Manuscript in the New York Public Library* (New York: NYPL, 1962).

Roberts, Morley, *The Private Life of Henry Maitland* (London: Eveleigh Nash, 1912).

15

In Public: George Gissing, Newspapers and the City

Simon J. James

The city, notoriously in its nineteenth-century representations, is an entity whose meanings are numerous and irreducible. The experience of modernity is of consciousness being surrounded by more sensory stimuli than it can comfortably or even sufficiently process (Benjamin, 1989, pp. 57–66; Freud, 1959). Georg Simmel wrote in *The Metropolis and Mental Life* in 1902 of:

> the rapid crowding of changing images, the sharp discontinuity in the grasp of single glance, and the unexpectedness of onrushing impressions. These are the psychological conditions which the metropolis creates. With each crossing of the street, with the tempo and multiplicity of economic, occupational and social life, the city sets up a deep contrast with small town and rural life with reference to the sensory foundations of psychic life. (Simmel, 1950, p. 410.)

For Simmel this condition is imposed by the hold of money on social life, which is, of course, the predominant theme of the work of George Gissing. During *In the Year of Jubilee* (1895), Nancy Lord experiences a sense of dissolution as both a consumer and as a part of the commercial spectacle of a crowded London street:

> Nancy forgot her identity, lost sight of herself as an individual. Her blood was heated by close air and physical contact. She did not think, and her emotions differed little from those of any shop-girl let loose. The "culture," to which she laid claim, evanesced in this atmosphere of exhalations. (Gissing, 1976, pp. 68–9)

In order to avoid such a condition, the modern consciousness, and in particular that of the artist, should for Gissing be in a constant state not of openness but of resistance to the meanings of the external world. This threat is specific to modern city-living; particularly in a culture underlaid by the green myth such as English culture, in which the self can supposedly only achieve its freest expression in a rural environment. Gissing articulates this position in *The Private Papers of Henry Ryecroft* (1903); and also in the short story 'The Capitalist' (1894). Ireton's name is traduced by newspaper 'penny-a-liners' (Gissing, 1906, p. 29) following a divorce case (in which, typically for Gissing's representation of the modern urban woman, his wife proves at fault, not he) and subsequently retires to the country to pursue a healthy interest in naturalism, eventually even marrying into the aristocracy.

The association between modernity, the city, and violation of the self is common throughout Gissing's work; indeed it is the central theme of *The Whirlpool* (1897). Gissing's city novels of the 1890s – from *The Odd Women*, through *In the Year of Jubilee* and *Eve's Ransom* to *The Crown of Life* – are usually structured around a marriage or, at least, a romantic attachment; at the same time, however, the manifold stimuli of urban modernity enforce a condition of isolation upon the self. (Loneliness, however, is not an experience unique to the city: Bernard Kingcote in *Isabel Clarendon* (1886) is lonely both in the country and in London; Ryecroft's isolation also has a peculiar pathos.) London's means of transmitting information nonetheless offer at least the chance of connection, however, rare or unlikely: the story of *The Crown of Life* (1899) turns on chance meetings in public spaces. The plot of *Eve's Ransom* (1895) is generated by a chance encounter in a railway carriage and by Maurice Hilliard seeing a photograph of a friend of his landlady's daughter – a characteristic combination of an enforced conditions of urban living, rented lodgings, and of a new technology of representation, the cheap photographic reproduction. Adrian Poole places Gissing's London:

> at the heart of a communications industry, that with the advent of the telegraph and linotype, and the backing of increasing concentrations of capital, is expanding and co-ordinating the resources of the written world to cover the globe. London [. . .] is now a focal point not just for world trade and finance, but for world news, fashions and cultural attitudes. (Poole, 1975, p. 139)

One medium of transmission, in particular, seems to dominate attempts to establish connection. Although *The Times* and *The Daily Telegraph* are national media, newspapers are imaginatively constructed in Gissing as an urban phenomenon (see, for instance, his short story 'The Prize Lodger', 1896). Newspapers can be a means of disseminating information across the city, occasionally serving the purpose of bringing an association to light: think, for instance, of both Gissing himself and Waymark in *The Unclassed* (1884) advertising for friendship in a newspaper. This benefit is only an accidental consequence of newspapers' transmission of knowledge into the public space, however, since the purpose of these disposable media is to make money for their owners. In *The Crown of Life*, as newspapers create the climate for war, politicians gain popularity by beginning and supporting wars; newspapers sell more copies during wartime. 'I'm a journalist, Piers, and let me tell you that we English newspaper men have the destiny of the world in our hands,' boasts Alexander Otway. 'It makes me proud when I think of it. We guard the national honour.' In consequence, his brother Piers presciently fears the worst:

> When the next great war comes, newspapers will be the chief cause of it. And for mere profit, that's the worst. There are newspaper proprietors in every country, who would slaughter half mankind for the pennies of the half who were left, without caring a fraction of a penny whether they had preached war for a truth or a lie. [...]
> But doesn't a newspaper simply echo the opinions and feelings of its public?
> I'm afraid it manufactures opinion, and stirs up feeling. Consider how very few people know or care anything about most subjects of inter-national quarrel. A mere handful at the noisy centre of things who make the quarrel. The business of newspapers, in general, is to give a show of importance to what has no real importance at all – to prevent the world from living quietly-to arouse bitterness when the natural man would be quite different. (Gissing, 1899, p.158)

The proof of newspapers' status as a commodity above being a means of conveying information accurately is their carrying of advertisements (until as recently as 1966 the front page of *The Times* was composed almost entirely of advertisements). For Gissing, the publicity of the medium compromises its claim to accuracy: newspapers' representations are avail-able for sale. Usually as a result, people only read newspapers when lacking something that the newspaper might provide – usually money, but also friendship, self-fulfilment, or merely entertainment. In his story 'Spellbound', 'all the women and a few of the men, were genuinely eager to search columns of advertisements, on the chances of finding employment; the rest came for betting news, or a murder trial, or some such matter of popular interest' (Gissing, 1927, p. 257). Association with newspapers means contagion by the most vulgar of humanity: in the free library's newspaper room in this story, 'the scent of newspapers, mingled with the odour of filthy garments and unwashed humanity' (p. 269). *Isabel Clarendon*'s Kingcote 'bought newspapers, it is true, and sickened his soul with the reading of advertisements': his need to read advertisements 'sickens' because it is a symptom of his unemployment and poverty-induced degradation (Gissing, 1886, II, p. 175). In *The Whirlpool*, once the value of Harvey Rolfe's investments begins to decline, he neglects the disinterested cultural leisure-time reading of his bachelorhood at the beginning of the novel for 'the money article in his daily paper' and 'financial newspapers' (Gissing, 1897, pp. 21–2, 208). Parrish in *The Town Traveller* (1898) lacks the money to marry Polly and so enters a newspaper missing-word competition, eventually gaining her hand when he wins the prize of £550. William Greenslade draws attention to the 'combination of ideological combativeness and sociological insight' in Gissing's analysis of newspaper advertisement columns in *The Unclassed*: newspapers are both representation and evidence of city-dwellers' 'brutal fight for livelihood', of 'all the meanness, ruthlessness, anguish and degradation which such a system implies' (Gissing, 1884, I, pp. 106–7; Greenslade, 2001, p. 272).

In *New Grub Street* (1891), the magazine of fragments of information *Chit-Chat* is commercially successful because it is virtually empty of content, hence easier to read. While even the cultured may read newspapers because they lack something, the uncultured read them because they lack culture. The French sisters' living-room is evidence of their superficial education:

> The only books in the room were a few show-volumes, which belonged to Arthur Peachey, and half-a-dozen novels of the meaner kind, wherewith Ada sometimes beguiled her infinite leisure. But on tables and chairs lay scattered a multitude of papers: illustrated weeklies, journals of society, cheap miscellanies, penny novelettes, and the like. At the end of the week, when new numbers came in, Ada Peachey passed many hours upon her sofa, reading instalments of a dozen serial stories, paragraphs relating to fashion, sport, the theatre, answers to correspondents (wherein she especially delighted), columns of facetiae, and gossip about notorious people. Through a great deal of this matter Beatrice followed her, and read much besides in which Ada took no interest; she studied a daily newspaper, with special note of law suits, police intelligence, wills, bankruptcies, and any concern, great or small, wherein money played a part. (Gissing, 1895, p. 5)

The proliferation of printed commodities is both evidence of a healthy if ugly Darwinian competition between different species of reading-matter, and proof of the vulgarity of majority taste (Benjamin, pp. 27–9). Schopenhauer, a significant influence on Gissing, complained that, 'more than nine-tenths of all literate men and women certainly read nothing but newspapers. [. . .] Young people of the unlearned professions in general regard the newspaper as an authority simply because it is something printed' (Schopenhauer, 1970, p. 205). Thyrza's Egremont complains to Grail that:

> 'The working man's Bible,' he said, 'is his Sunday newspaper.'
>   And what does he get out of it? The newspaper is the very voice of all that is worst in our civilisation. If ever there is in one column a pretence of higher teaching, it is made laughable by the base tendency

of all the rest. The newspaper has supplanted the book; every gross-minded scribbler who gets a square inch of space in the morning journal has a more respectful hearing than Shakespeare. These writers are tradesmen, and with all their power they cry up the spirit of trade. Till the influence of the newspaper declines – the newspaper as we now know it – our state will grow worse. (Gissing, 1892, p. 93; see also Delany, 2002, p. 119)

The newly literate masses might choose to read Tennyson; but, as Gissing asserted in a correspondence with Edmund Gosse, since Tennyson did not publish in *The Referee*, a sporting paper, they do not (*Letters*, V, p. 701; cf. Gissing, 1962, p. 44). The characters of *In the Year of Jubilee* seem especially prone to lacking the sufficient culture to read and appreciate more solid matter. In a telling phrase (repeated later in *The Whirlpool*), Nancy has 'no mind' to read her new book, which is 'something about Evolution'; Peachey, on the other hand, is worried about his son after having 'had the misfortune about this time to read in paper or magazine something on the subject of heredity, the idle verbiage of some half-informed scribbler' (Gissing, 1895, pp. 13, 379). Uneducated choice in reading puts its possessor in a typical Gissing double-bind: better taste can only be acquired by a more elevated type of reading, which requires education in order to be palatable (Grylls, 1986, pp. 76–7). Percy Dunn in 'Spellbound' is even rendered unable to maintain regular employment by his habit of reading newspapers, 'stupefying himself with a drug which lulled his anxieties' (Gissing, 1927, p. 263). Samuel Barmby, lacking self-knowledge and overburdened with self-importance, champions the daily newspaper as an instrument of civilisation, and claims his own broad but unsystematic, shallow knowledge as evidence of the newspaper's superiority to the book:

> Quite uneducated, in any legitimate sense of the word, he had yet learnt that such a thing as education existed, and, by dint of busy perusal of penny popularities, had even become familiar with names and phrases, with modes of thought and of ambition, appertaining to a world for ever closed against him. He spoke of Culture, and imagined himself far on the way to attain it. His mind was packed with the oddest jumble of incongruities; Herbert Spencer jostled with Charles Bradlaugh, Matthew Arnold with Samuel Smiles; in one breath he lauded George Eliot, in the next was enthusiastic over a novel by Mrs. Henry Wood; from puerile facetiae he passed to speculations on the origin of being, and with equally light heart. Save for Pilgrim's Progress and Robinson Crusoe, he had read no English classic; since boyhood, indeed, he had probably read no book at all, for much diet of newspapers rendered him all but incapable of sustained attention. (Gissing, 1895, p. 214)

The chief occupation of Barmby's father is writing letters to the newspapers for the pleasure of seeing them printed. For Gissing one should read a newspaper, if at all, for the information it should convey, not for the vulgar pleasure of seeing one's name in it. Mr. Byles – in 'The Pessimist of Plato Road', suffering, according to the narrator, from 'sham education, and the poisonous atmosphere of everywhere diffused by newspapers, books and lectures' – declares the false intention to kill himself so that his suicide note will appear in the letters column of *The Daily Telegraph* (Gissing, 1927, p. 176). The vulgar consumers of the public, democratic medium of the newspapers crave to be a part of its subject, as described brilliantly by Barbara Leah Harman:

> Everyone in [*In the Year of Jubilee*] seems eager for affiliation with the press. Jessica Morgan is studying for her examinations, wasting her health and losing her hair, all to 'become B.A., to have her name in the newspapers' (18), and even Samuel Barmby Sr. regularly writes letters to the paper (though under a pseudonym) (179). Samuel Barmby Jr. is obsessed with the press and the publishing industry. He measures the level of a country's culture and civility by the number of newspapers it can support (China has only ten), and admires the sheer bulk of writing...
>
> Gissing might have focussed on Jessica's pursuit of education, but instead he concentrates on her desire to see her name published in the paper when she passes her examinations and compares her interest in self-publication with Barmby's. The public existence of the self is made possible by a medium that guarantees the loss of privacy, concretizes, reifies and multiplies the self, dooming it to a life of unregulated exposure, tainted by the political marketplace in which it appears. (Harman, 1998, p. 128)

Newspapers are a circulatory medium in their transmission of inform-ation into public spaces; when shared, they also physically circulate between readers in a public space (McCracken, 2001). This trope is liter-alized in Gissing when the surfaces of newspapers bear witness to having been read by more than one person. Gissing may have remembered this passage from late in *Great Expectations*, when Pip pretends in the Blue Boar:

> to read a smeary newspaper long out of date, which had nothing half so legible in its local news, as the foreign matter of coffee, pickles, fish-sauces, gravy, melted butter, and wine, with which it was sprin-kled all over, as if it had taken the measles in a highly irregular form. (Dickens, 1993, p. 353)

Two public forms of consumption, eating and reading, are also conflated around *The Town Traveller*'s vulgar Gammon, who eats heartily, takes three daily papers and enjoys the coffee-house's communal paper:

> Sweet to him were the rancid odours, delightfully familiar the dirty knives, the twisted forks, the battered teaspoons, not unwelcome the day's newspaper, splashed with brown coffee and spots of grease. (Gissing, 1898, p. 46)

In late nineteenth-century slang, a newspaper is a 'fish-wrapper': the value of its contents are so transitory that after only a day it will be good for nothing more than wrapping food (Green, 1998, p. 420). In *Thyrza* (1887), the newspaper is visibly only a commodity among many other commodities, and the distinction between them seems to blur: 'every article in the shop – groceries of all kinds, pastry, cooked meat, bloaters, newspapers, petty haberdashery, firewood, fruit, soap – seemed to exhale its essence distressfully under the heat' (Gissing, 1892, p. 176). Ryecroft, Edwin Reardon and many of Gissing's protagonists form an emotional attachment to the books they possess: the circulated newspaper is public property, and, uncared-for, it becomes marked by other matter. If one's name appears in a newspaper or magazine, therefore, dirt might stick to it; how Gissing must have winced when his own name was parodied as 'Gissing the Rod' in *Punch* (Coustillas and Partridge, 1972, pp. 72–3). In 'A Calamity at Tooting' (1895), Alma Dawson is mortified to discover that her name and a photograph of her as a baby had appeared in an advertisement for baby food. In *The Whirlpool*, Alma Rolfe is nervous that once she appears in public as a violinist, her maiden name might be discovered, and connected with her disgraced financier father. In Alma's quest to become famous as a musician, however, she fatally decides that all publicity is good publicity. Alma flirts with both Felix Dymes and Cyrus Redgrave in order to get her name publicized in advance of the concert, and is surprised that the mere mention of her name in the newspapers procures her numerous invitations even before she has played so much as a note in public. *The Whirlpool* repeatedly associates communication through newspapers with something going out of control: all news, in this novel, is bad news (Sloan, 1989, p. 140). Newspaper boys announce the suicide of Bennet Frothingham in the offices of the financial newspaper *Stock and Share*. Abbot dies of overwork when trying to buy shares in a provincial newspaper. Morphew is compromised when Tripcony persuades him to get a damaging paragraph printed in a newspaper. Sybil Carnaby misrepresents herself in the papers as a woman wronged; Alma's dalliance with Redgrave to gain newspaper publicity leads, indirectly, to his own death. Harvey Rolfe is forced from one public space, the concert-hall, to another, the restaurant, by his disgust at seeing his surname publicized; he then gains his first intimations of Redgrave's death from one further public space: the newspaper.

Harvey laid his hand upon an evening newspaper, just arrived, which the waiter had thrown on to the next table. He opened it, not with any intention of reading, but because he had no mind to talk; Alma's name, exhibited in staring letters at the entrance of the public building, had oppressed him with a sense of degradation; he felt ignoble, much as a man might feel who had consented to his own dishonour. As his eyes wandered over the freshly-printed sheet, they were arrested by a couple of bold headlines: "Sensational Affair at Wimbledon – Mysterious Death of a Gentleman." (Gissing, 1897, p. 308)

The review of Alma's performance, appearing in the same edition of the newspaper as the subsequent inquest into Redgrave's death, is rather luke-warm. The concert even fails to make a profit because of the amount of money which has been spent on the inflated representation of advertising. Alma retires after a breakdown, reported, of course, in the newspapers; and considers burning her archive of clippings, but seems to lack the courage to renounce publicity entirely. Later in the novel, she dies, as if her identity has become dissipated by the public circulation of her name.

Gissing shared Comte's disdain for texts that do not carry their author's name, such as newspapers and advertisements (Vogeler, 1984, p. 55). He copied into his American notebook the following passage from J.A. Froude's 'Leaves from a South African Journal':

We have a distinguished journalist on board. I scandalized him by saying that I thought in a hundred years newspapers would be abolished by general consent as nuisance. A gazette of authentic news would be published by authority, and that would be all. (Gissing, 1993, p. 28)

Nonetheless, Gissing does not recommend such censorship as advised by Schopenhauer and conducted by the Russian authorities in *The Crown of Life*. While most of the journalists in his fiction, such as Jasper Milvain, Lionel Tarrant and Alexander Otway, are untrustworthy, there are exceptions, such as Earwaker in *Born in Exile* (1892) and the Otways' father. Gissing's diary shows his own regular reading of newspapers: he advised his brother Algernon to purchase the weekly edition of *The Times*, and was pleased when *The Times* carried an advertisement of *The Unclassed* (*Letters*, II, p. 3, 227). Gissing wrote a letter to the same newspaper in 1891 (characteristically, on the subject of Greek pronunciation), and was gratified to see it published (*Letters*, IV, p. 272, p. 281). In 1893 *The Times* also published a letter in which Gissing drew attention to plagiarism of *The Nether World* by the Rev. Osborne Jay; Gissing was cheered that the reporting of the incident in other magazines provided 'a considerable advantage, in the way of advertisement' (*Letters*, V, pp. 136–7, p. 142). He was pleased but evidently found it incongruous when asked in 1902 to review F.G. Kitton's *Life* of

Dickens: 'amusing to think that *The Times* should request me to write for its columns!' (*Letters*, VIII, p. 382). Publicity, a part of the economics of mass society, is threatening to artistic authenticity. However, even the Gissing short stories critical of the mass medium of the newspaper appeared for the first time, of course, in the periodical press, in publications such as *The Illustrated London News, Harmsworth's Monthly Pictorial Magazine, T.P.'s Weekly* and many others, bringing Gissing much-needed recognition and money. Art in the modern world is unable to succeed unless consumers know of its existence, a characteristic Gissing irony: without publicity, there can be no publication.

Bibliography

Benjamin, Walter, *Charles Baudelaire: A Lyric Poet in the Era of High Capitalism*, trans. by Harry Zohn (London: Verso, 1989).

Coustillas, Pierre and Partridge, Colin, eds, *Gissing: The Critical Heritage* (London: Routledge and Kegan Paul, 1972).

Delany, Paul, *Literature, Money and the Market: From Trollope to Amis* (Basingstoke: Macmillan, 2002).

Dickens, Charles, *Great Expectations*, ed. Cardwell, Margaret (Oxford: Clarendon Press: 1993).

Freud, Sigmund, 'Civilization and its Discontents', *The Complete Psychological Works of Sigmund Freud*, 24 vols, trans. Strachey, James (London: Hogarth Press, 1959), XXI, pp. 64–145.

Gissing, George, *The Crown of Life* (London: Methuen, 1899).

——, *The Collected Letters of George Gissing*, ed. Coustillas, Pierre, Mattheisen, Paul F. and Young, Arthur C., 9 vols. (Athens: Ohio University Press, 1990–7).

——, *The Crown of Life*, edited by Ballard, Michel (London: Methuen, 1899; repr. Hassocks: Harvester Press, 1978).

——, *George Gissing's American Notebook: Notes – G.R.G. – 1877*, ed. Postmus, Bouwe (Lewiston: Edwin Mellen Press, 1993).

——, *George Gissing's Commonplace Book*, edited by Jacob Korg (New York: New York Public Library, 1962).

——, *The House of Cobwebs* (London: Constable, 1906).

——, *In the Year of Jubilee*, introduction by Tindall, Gillian (London: Lawrence and Bullen, 1895; repr. Hassocks: Harvester Press, 1976).

——, *Isabel Clarendon*, ed. Coustillas, Pierre, 2 vols. (London: Chapman and Hall, 1886; repr. Brighton: Harvester Press, 1969).

——, *New Grub Street*, edited by Bergonzi, Bernard (Harmondsworth: Penguin, 1985).

——, *Stories and Sketches* (London: Michael Joseph, 1938).

——, *Thyrza: A Tale*, ed. Korg, Jacob (London: Smith, Elder, 1892; repr. Hassocks: Harvester Press, 1976).

——, *The Town Traveller*, ed. Coustillas, Pierre (London: Methuen, 1898; repr. Brighton: Harvester Press, 1981).

——, *The Unclassed*, 3 vols. (London: Chapman and Hall, 1884).

——, *A Victim of Circumstances* (London: Constable, 1927).

——, *The Whirlpool*, ed. Parrinder, Patrick (London: Lawrence and Bullen, 1897; repr. Hassocks: Harvester Press, 1977).

Green, Jonathan, *The Cassell Dictionary of Slang* (London: Cassell, 1998).

Greenslade, William, 'Gissing and the Lure of Modernity', in Postmus, Bouwe, ed., *A Garland for Gissing* (Amsterdam: Rodopi, 2001), pp. 271–7.

Grylls, David, *The Paradox of Gissing* (London: Allen and Unwin, 1986).

Harman, Barbara Leah, *The Feminine Political Novel in Victorian England* (Charlottesville and London: University Press of Virginia, 1998).

McCracken, Scott, 'From Performance to Public Sphere: The Production of Modernist Masculinities', *Textual Practice*, XV (2001) 47–65.

Poole, Adrian, *Gissing in Context* (London: Macmillan, 1975).

Arthur Schopenhauer, *Essays and Aphorisms*, edited and trans. by Hollingdale, R.J. (Harmondsworth: Penguin, 1970).

Simmel, Georg, 'The Metropolis and Mental Life', in *The Sociology of Georg Simmel*, edited and trans. by Wolff, Kurt H. (New York: Free Press, 1950), 409–24.

Sloan, John, *George Gissing: The Cultural Challenge* (New York: St Martin's Press, 1989).

Trotter, *Cooking with Mud: The Idea of Mess in Nineteenth-Century Fiction* (Oxford: Clarendon Press, 2000).

Vogeler, Martha S, *Fredric Harrison: The Vocations of a Positivist* (Oxford: Clarendon Press, 1984).

16

George Gissing's *Scrapbook*: A Storehouse of 'Elements of Drama to be Fused and Minted in his Brain'

Bouwe Postmus

Compiling and collecting materials

On 29 April 1958 the Parke-Bernet Galleries at New York auctioned a lot that they described in their catalogue as 'a very interesting and important group of Gissing's writings in his autograph. Being manuscript notes written mainly in connection with his works and novels.' This material (defined as 'the property of a lady') was doubtless offered for sale by Alfred Gissing, the writer's younger son, into whose hands many of his father's miscellaneous papers had passed from his uncle Algernon by the mid-twenties of this century. Through the thirties Alfred Gissing had regularly been disposing of the manuscript material and valuable books and papers left by his father and he continued to add to his income in this way after he settled in Switzerland soon after the Second World War. In offering his father's literary documents and private papers for sale, he would often discreetly hide his identity behind that of an unspecified 'Continental lady', a ploy which seems to betray a slight sense of guilt as to the frittering away of his father's artistic inheritance.

The person who described lot 144 in the Parke-Bernet catalogue must be held responsible for some confusion as to the precise nature of the material, as a result of his use of the phrase 'in connection with.' Even a superficial examination of the collection will show that it would be more adequate to claim that most of these notes were made by way of preparation for future literary activity and as such they formed the indispensable raw material of Gissing's art. That he felt the need to introduce verifiable, realistic details into the worlds of his imagination, is perhaps more crucial to our under-standing of his art than the analysis of certain recurring structural and thematic concerns, which these notes invite.

The collection put up for sale in 1958 was acquired for the celebrated Carl H. and Lily Pforzheimer Foundation that remained its owner until 1992 when it moved west to end up on the shelves of the Lilly Library, at Bloomington, Indiana. In Quaritch's chronological catalogue of the

Pforzheimer [Gissing] collection, Arthur Freeman's admirable and detailed description (Freeman, 1992, p. 34) of lot 74 is a large improvement over the 1958 description. Under the heading 'An Evidential Goldmine' he states:

> The Pforzheimer Manuscript 'Scrapbook'. Twenty-five groups of MS comprising 70 leaves folio, 7 leaves 4to. (some blank, some written on recto and verso, some with newspaper clippings mounted), plus 8 leaves 8vo. and 12mo., in all about 25,000–30,000 words in Gissing's holograph, plus a large quantity of mounted and loose clippings, ephemera, etc. [Assembled c.1885–95.] (Freeman's square brackets.)

It was David Grylls who in 1991 claimed that the Pforzheimer *Scrapbook* 'is the single most important manuscript source that might be made available to Gissing scholars,' arguing that it would 'deepen our sense of Gissing's realism by exposing the broad social areas he researched... [and] how he processed raw materials' (Grylls, 1991, pp. 11–12). In preparing an edition of this unique document (Gissing, [n.d.] *Scrapbook*), the present writer has attempted, a century after Gissing's death, to make a contribution to the growing insight into the nature of his working methods.

Except for some of his early novels like *Workers in the Dawn* (1880), *The Unclassed* (1884) and *Isabel Clarendon* (1886), which he admitted were written with slight preparation and owed their existence to a form of spontaneous generation, the writing of the great majority of Gissing's later books was laborious, involving no little preliminary research, elaborate plot construction and endless rewriting. He was the first to admit that his powers of invention were 'the weakest of my various weak points,' (Gissing, 1993, p. 139) and he came to recognize increasingly that the collection and accumulation of materials derived from real life was the obvious remedy. But for someone like Gissing, who for long periods together was living a hermit's life, the acquisition of the prized raw material for his books was no easy matter. From the mid-1880s he made determined efforts to go in search of locations, people, vocabulary and language, situations and trades that he needed for the construction of the works of his imagination. Thus, he would wander at evening in the East End of London, rambling till midnight about filthy little courts, backyards and alleys, stumbling over strange specimens of humanity, which before very long found their way into such novels as *Thyrza* and *The Nether World*. Or, acting on a suggestion made by John Morley, the editor of *The Pall Mall Gazette*, he would frequent the various county courts in order to acquaint himself with some of the more extraordinary forms of human conduct. He found it very useful to observe strangers in public places, trying to imagine a life-history for them, as he had discovered that this might add a vividness to his as yet abstract ideas.

Of all the writers, poets and novelists in Gissing's fiction, very few have any great revelations to make about their profession, more specifically, about what is involved in the mysterious process of transforming the raw material of their art into the finished products of their imagination. But in Gissing's short story 'Comrades in Arms,' Wilfrid Langley, a successful popular novelist, is reflecting upon the nature of the creative process, as he sits in a London restaurant, enjoying an after-lunch cigarette:

> In this quiet half hour…he caught the flitting suggestion of many a story, sketch, gossipy paper. A woman's laugh, a man's surly visage, couples oddly assorted, scraps of dialogue heard amid the confused noises – everywhere the elements of drama, to be fused and minted in his brain. (Gissing, 1898, p. 1)

This seems to me quite an illuminating and attractive working definition of the novelist's art, and one, perhaps, not so far removed from Gissing's own practice, even if we take into account his serious reservations about the quality of his own shorter fiction, which he felt to be rather the product of market forces than of his artistic integrity. What Langley calls 'flitting suggestion[s]' for a story, Gissing was in the habit of calling 'hints.' To him the first stage in preparing for a new novel or short story was the 'getting of hints.' For example, on the day after completing *Thyrza* he writes to his sister Ellen: 'For a week or so [I] shall prowl about London, mostly with Roberts, "getting hints &c"' (Gissing, 1992, p. 77).

It is no exaggeration to claim that most of Gissing's peregrinations and removals were motivated by his artistic needs. If we find him travelling (e.g. to Birmingham), we may be sure that he has gone there to study the region for use in his next book. For the physical effort required – he thought nothing of dressing in workman's clothing and walking twelve miles a day about the dreary city streets – he would feel abundantly compensated by the host of precious details to flesh out the bare bones of *Eve's Ransom*. The move to Exeter in 1891, after 13 years in London, was not just due to his desire to make a fresh start after his second marriage to Edith Underwood, it was also necessitated by the demands of his art from the moment he had made up his mind that he wanted a provincial town for his next novel, *Born in Exile* (Gissing, 1993, p. 250). Similarly, his return to the metropolis (Brixton) was primarily inspired by the consideration that Tate's new public library would be just around the corner – easy access to a good library being essential to the type of writer who depended significantly on a wide assortment of literary sources as the basic material of his art.

In his *Commonplace Book* (Korg, 1962, p. 33) he recorded his astonishment at Dickens's failure to make the most of his vast opportunities as an extraordinarily gifted observer of the lower classes. He seems to be envious of Dickens's limitless fund of multiple experience and original observation and to be quite conscious that his own alternative sources of information such as local newspapers, attendance at magistrates' courts, and brief visits to potentially promising locations were merely second-best solutions. In letters to his brother Algernon, he was always urging him to keep notebooks and boasting that his own were becoming 'portentous' (Gissing, 1993, p. 218). And the same note of professional pride can be heard in a letter to his German friend Eduard Bertz: 'Yesterday I was looking all through my bundles of "notes". I have material for all the rest of my life' (Gissing, 1993, p. 276).

There is no doubt that the loose-leaved Gissing manuscripts that were sold in New York in 1958 and 1992, and since held by the Lilly Library, are the very same 'bundles' he mentions in his letter to Bertz. And today we are in a position to judge that they did indeed serve him until the end of his life. How precious these materials were to Gissing, may be concluded from the fact that he hung on to them through all the years of his, at times, desperate wanderings from one London garret to another, from England to France, Italy and Greece and back.

The earliest item from the *Scrapbook* that can be dated is a newspaper clipping of 5 September 1880, (typically) relating the granting of a free pardon to two men, after serving a term of two years' imprisonment, while they were innocent. The last document that can be dated with confidence is a review of the final volume of Charles Booth's *Life and Labour in London*, which appeared in the *Athenæum* on 22 August 1903, only four months before Gissing's death. Thus we are provided with proof positive that the contents of the *Scrapbook* were assembled over a period of 23 years, from 1880 to 1903, which significantly corrects and extends Freeman's briefer span of 10 years quoted above. In this context there is one additional point to be made about Gissing's handwriting as used in the *Scrapbook*. It is consistent throughout and resembles the mature, quite small hand he began to develop during his year in America and whose quality remained virtually unchanged from about 1882. However, some of his short stories dating from his first years in London (e.g. 'The Last Half-Crown') are in a larger hand, which one may be tempted to associate with the time Gissing began to build up this collection of data. It has been our assumption though that in the late seventies and early eighties there was still a degree of instability about Gissing's handwriting which led him to adopt different hands for different purposes. There is sufficient material evidence for the conclusion that by 1880 Gissing could and did write in the small hand that was to evolve into his characteristic trade mark.

There are among Gissing's surviving personal documents several other notebooks, whose contents are comparable to what is found in these 'bundles,' now better known as his *Scrapbook*, but none of these is as exclusively concerned with the nuts and bolts of the novelist's trade. In his edition of *George Gissing's Commonplace Book* Jacob Korg (Korg, 1962, p. 14) pointed out how closely it was related to *The Private Papers of Henry Ryecroft* and how many of its brief entries were later amplified into Ryecroft's meditations. At the same time quite a few of its entries are primarily passages quoted from his reading and his response to these. And it has long been recognized by the editors of another of Gissing's notebooks, *Extracts from My Reading* (Coustillas, 1988), that he was less concerned with noting particular quotations with a view to inserting them at a later date into his fiction, than with the delighted discovery that others had thought and expressed ideas similar to his own. In the *American Notebook* (Postmus, 1993) and the *Huntington Memorandum Book* (Postmus, 1996) as well, we find a mixture of literary and more mundane, domestic concerns: shopping lists, itineraries, addresses and train time-tables are jostling with snippets of conversation overheard, promising 'situations,' lists of names and surnames and thumbnail sketches of character. The last personal document that deserves to be mentioned in this context is Gissing's *Diary* (Coustillas, 1978), as he relied heavily on the detailed entries he made in it during his travels in Calabria in the autumn of 1897 for the writing of his travel book *By the Ionian Sea*. It is obvious that Gissing preferred to carry the more portable and convenient small notebooks whenever he was travelling, a practice that is confirmed by the fact that he would occasionally copy entries from one of his smaller repositories into the *Scrapbook* proper (Postmus, 1996, pp. iv–v).

The size and importance of the various sections differ greatly; the 'Education' section consists of a single page, whereas the 'Ideas' section comprises 41 printed pages, thus forming the backbone of the *Scrapbook*. It is easy to understand why Gissing should have turned to his 'Localities and Notes on Nature' dossier again and again. It is one of the sections that testifies most impressively to his remarkably acute powers of observation of natural phenomena. Many of the entries found in the 'Slang' section – limited though it may be – found their way into his books, adding greatly to the vivid linguistic colour of individual speech in his novels and stories. The two sections dealing with the public and private lives of the working classes demonstrate convincingly that originally Gissing was primarily interested rather in the classes below the one to which he belonged himself than the upper or upper middle classes to which he may have aspired. He knew full well that he should write of what he knew best. It was the vital principle underlying all his literary endeavours. Therefore, the conspicuous absence of a dossier with materials relating to the upper or professional (middle) classes may be interpreted as revealing a fundamental lack of knowledge of or even indifference to the sections of society that he attempted to portray in *Isabel Clarendon* and *The Emancipated*. If Gissing, like Ryecroft, may not have been a friend of the people, there is no doubt that he was profoundly and sympathetically interested in the substance and circumstances of their lives. Of his early, radical, political convictions there is little or no trace in these notes. What does surface is his disgust with the stupid credulity of the many-headed monster *Demos*, despite his heartfelt compassion for the oppressed and exploited, which remained the bass note of his art until the end of his life.

Inventing and writing the text: Gissing's use of the Scrapbook

Gissing himself distinguished three stages in the process that would eventually culminate in the finished artistic product, be it a novel or a short story. In the first or preparatory stage his work consisted in reading, making notes and reflecting. Apart from his apprentice work, which was written without relying on any notes at all and largely improvised, none of the later stories was ever written without the fearful toil and hard mental work of meditating daily for long hours after a promising idea had come to him. Rapid progress in the actual writing of the story could only be achieved through a full mapping out of his subject, and from his own dismal experience he knew that laborious and cumbersome (re)writing would inevitably result from subjects, settings or situations insufficiently clear to himself. A special kind of clarity was conditional upon his christening the as yet nameless creatures of his imagination and more often than not the preparatory stage was rounded off by this crucial giving of names (Gissing, 1992, p. 31).

In the second stage of his working method the largely mental preparation would be complemented by a deliberate and quite specific study of locations, trades, settings and habits of speech. This meant he must leave his rooms and walk the streets of Lambeth, Clerkenwell, or Camberwell in order to familiarize himself with scenes that he needed for *Thyrza*, *The Nether World* and *In the Year of Jubilee* respectively. It might involve him in temporary removals to boarding-houses, in journeys long or short to destinations far or near, for example into Essex for *The Nether World*, to Italy for *The Emancipated*, or to North Wales for *The Whirlpool*. 'Getting material,' 'filling my mind with pictures,' 'picking up matter' and 'roaming about the dark places of the country called London' are some of the terms he used in his letters for the indispensable encounter with a reality he had decided to portray in his work. He was absolutely convinced that only genuine and careful observation and accumulation of factual detail could lead to the preservation of the verisimilitude he regarded as essential to his art. This did not mean he was content with a literal transcription from life, or the mere handling of actual occurrences. That type of restricted realism was not what he was aiming at. His art was indeed firmly rooted in realistic elements, but these were always to be fused and minted in his imagination, whose powers of combination, construction and transformation were at the heart of Gissing's achievement.

Once he had completed the gathering of details from his encounter with reality – sometimes he had to resort to the consultation of books in the British Museum instead, or to consulting his brother Algernon (on legal questions) or his sister Ellen (for scholastic information) – the time had come to begin the actual writing of the story. Generally this was done when he had decided on the name of the book in hand, which appears to have been another highly significant act of christening by means of which he established the particular identity of his creation. Occasionally he would change the original title by the time he finished his manuscript, but often his clinging desperately to the title chosen would guide him over the treacherous shoals of lack of direction and inspiration.

To illustrate the workings of Gissing's creative faculty we shall proceed to a close examination of the genesis of 'The Fate of Humphrey Snell,' the story that to him seemed the best he had done in that genre (Gissing, 1994, p. 282). It was written in a week (11–18 October 1894), shortly after he had settled in Epsom, after spending the summer with his family at Clevedon on the Somerset coast. During his stay at Clevedon in August, he went on a walk from Cheddar to Wells, along the lower slope of the Mendips. In a lyrical letter to his brother Algernon he reported on the delightful day in the most glowing terms:

> Wells itself is ideally situated, amid the hills which break away from the windy Mendips to the great Somerset level. A peaceful village – little more; & at a turn of the street you come upon that glorious cathedral, set amid surely the most beautiful Close that exists, the entrance at each corner through the archways of grey crumbling stone. Anything like the Bishop's Palace I never saw. It is surrounded with a wall & a moat; the wall embattled & loop-holed, overgrown with ivy, & in places with peach & apricot; the entrance a draw-bridge & portcullis; the moat, very wide, supplied with water which rushes into it, foaming & roaring, from St Andrew's Well – a great spring coming somehow from the hidden depths of the Mendips. Swans & ducks swim about on the olive-green water. Close by is a walk shadowed by huge, dense elms, & all around are lawns, meadows, hills, rising to woodland & heath. A marvellous spot; civilized with the culture of centuries, yet quite unlike the trimness of other Cathedral towns.
>
> A rare place for botanizing. In a little wood hard by I found what I take to be the Great Mullein, some four feet high, in splendid flower. The walls of the lanes were covered with wall spleenwort & scale fern; harttongue everywhere. Astounding wealth of vegetation in all the ditches. There was a great purple-belled flower growing by the hedges; I never saw it before & wonder what it could be (Gissing, 1994, p. 224).

As so often before, all of Gissing's senses were reawakened by the change of environment and ready to drink in the marvellous scenery to be stored for later use. In his *Diary* entry for the day (3 August 1894) he confidently claimed to have been 'excogitating three short stories,' one of which being 'The Fate of Humphrey Snell' (Gissing, 1927, pp. 53–74). Its central incident is the fateful meeting in the Cathedral Close at Wells, under the light of the moon, of Humphrey, the young collector of herbs, and Annie Frost, an orphaned servant-girl turned out of the house of her sister. So many telling details of the setting were evidently inspired by Gissing's memories of his walk to Wells – memories still green when he returned to them years later in *The Private Papers of Henry Ryecroft* (Gissing, 1903, p. 81).

We must turn to the 'Occupations' dossier to see how the initial creative impulse was developed through a masterly exploitation and fusion of disparate materials previously collected and preserved in the *Scrapbook*. First of all there is a press-cutting taken from *Cassell's Saturday Journal* for 4 October 1893 (Appendix I), which consists of a lengthy interview with an old herbalist, who explains about the supply of plants and herbs by those who make it their trade to collect them. In passing we are reminded that these herb collectors are doing a good deal of their work at night time, working by moonlight. Then there is another newspaper cutting of a letter to the editor by an anonymous character signing himself 'One Who has Suffered' (Appendix II), about the sad fate of a telegraph messenger who fails his second medical examination for postman, and in consequence is dismissed from the service. The third and last press-cutting from the same dossier concerns an advertisement for a steward and stewardess to take charge of a workmen's club (Appendix III). Taking his cue from these sources Gissing 'invented' the character of the herb collector Humphrey Snell, his love of freedom and the simple, single life out of doors and his ultimate surrender of these prized possessions on account of his foolish infatuation with simple-minded, if pretty Annie Frost. 'Of all the paths lead to a woman's love / Pity's the straightest,' the adage that Gissing had entered into his *American Notebook* in 1877 apparently guided and directed the lives of not a few of his characters with equally disastrous consequences. His somewhat heavy-handed symbolism in the final paragraph of the story seems to hint at the possibility of Humphrey's early release from the prison-like constraints of his job in London through premature death, but we cannot be sure that even this mercy will be granted to the typical 'victim of circumstances' that Humphrey proves to be.

Another illuminating instance of how the creative process – from its inception to the finished product – can be helped along by external stimuli, begins with a letter (30 March 1893) to Gissing from Clement King Shorter, the editor of the *English Illustrated Magazine*, asking for a short story 'like the Bank Holiday scene in *Nether World*' (Coustillas, 1978, p. 300). Although he was just about to travel to London in search of a house in the Brixton region, Gissing replied that he would oblige, leaving Exeter on the same day. The glorious Easter week spent in abominable lodgings in Kennington Road, where he was kept awake by bugs, fleas, the crowing of cocks and a bestial row well into the night, nevertheless proved most profitable. On Easter Monday Gissing went to Rosherville Gardens, making many notes for the short story of low life he had promised to Shorter. No more than a week after his return from London he sat down to start work on the story called

'Lou and Liz', that owes its existence as much to the imaginative appeal of a particular location as to Gissing's judicious selection of items entered into the *Scrapbook*. Among them are references to a 'baby kept awake past midnight by a girl banging away on a piano,' a popular music hall song about the man who broke the bank at Monte Carlo, phrases of Cockney slang he had heard in the streets, and specific information about particular occupations (book folder, quill toothpick maker) and conditions of pay. Finally, he turned to good account a newspaper cutting from the 'Private Life of Working Classes' dossier, 'Polyandry at the East End,' which provided him with the pivotal plot feature of the story.

How much Gissing came to rely on his collection of notes is strikingly revealed too by the use he made of entries from the 'Localities and Notes on Nature' folder for passages of great emotional intensity. The decisive encounter of Piers Otway and Irene Derwent at Apedale Beck (Gissing, 1899, pp. 322–3, 325), where they pledge their love is a good example, Hilliard's celebration of his newfound freedom during an autumnal ramble that crowns *Eve's Ransom* is another (Gissing, 1895, pp. 378–9). Both passages derive their power primarily from the symbolical suggestiveness of real scenes observed by the author and preserved for future use in his *Scrapbook* (Appendixes IV.a. and IV.b.). Whether he was holidaying with his family in Yorkshire or visiting his brother Algernon at Willersey, he never missed an opportunity of adding to the large store of settings, natural and urban, that sooner or later would lend additional colour and verisimilitude to his fiction. There is an unmistakable increase in the affective and emotional temperature of such passages compared to other more conventional descriptions of nature and locations, wholly or largely the product of his imagination. His prose rises to a lyrical pitch, reinforced and maintained by felicities of rhythm and diction, which are often absent from scenes chiefly based upon literary models and precedents. For example, one feels that Robert Narramore's 'cozy quarters' owe their existence more to a rather vague and stereotype notion of the kind of residence fit for a well-to-do bachelor, than that it is based upon any real familiarity with such a place. By way of contrast, Eve Madeley's London address at Gower Place has an immediacy and actuality that must derive from the fact that it was a locality well-known to Gissing, who lodged there for a few months in the autumn of 1878.

As a final illustration of the gain in evocative power of passages based on *Scrapbook* entries we offer the opening paragraphs (Gissing, 1895, pp. 1–2) of *Eve's Ransom*: the precision of the descriptive details of the station platform and its vicinity is marshalled to create symbolic overtones suggestive of the primacy of a monstrous materialism at the expense of more humane and spiritual values. Gissing had travelled to Birmingham and the country around specifically in search of material, and though very few of his notes for the novel have been preserved, there is among the loose leaves of the

Scrapbook a tiny envelope (Gissing [n.d.] *Scrapbook*, p. 288) on which he recorded his impressions on the station platform at Barnt Green on the morning of 24 November 1892:

Barnt G[reen]. Station. End of Nov. Misty morn. after heavy rain. Dull white gleam of platform (concrete worn into holes, with pools) and of rails. Dull white distance, rails and hedges and hazy-coloured fields fading away at a few yards. Grey featureless vast of sky. Ghosts of trees. Air damp and cold. Smoke of a passing luggage train envelops everything for minute or two, unable to rise. Ring of signal for express. Luggage getting wet on platform.

Clearly he remembered the singular potential of that scene when he used it to open the first chapter of *Eve's Ransom* in January 1894.

Despite his evident and lasting love of the non-human world of nature, there is no question that the *Scrapbook* reveals that Gissing's principal interest was in the human world, especially the world of suffering humanity. His indignation at the heartless exploitation of workers by their capitalist masters and cruel bureaucrats alike may be inferred from the various newspaper clippings recording the dreadful events in the lives of those living on the edge of the abyss. His compassion with the working classes was the product of his hard-won familiarity with the circumstances of their lives, which he had begun to study seriously from his early years in London, when he was virtually living among them. Though he was tempted for a short period to embrace radical political theories, aimed at a reconstitution of society along socialist lines, as a recorder of the social customs of the London poor he soon developed the more objective stance of the sociologist, aiming to start with an adequate description of the status quo. Yet by the summer of 1888 the detailed notes he made of several meetings of workers do not try to conceal the exasperation and contempt he came to feel for their 'absolute lack of logic, absolute lack of relevance, [and] absolute lack of coherence' (Gissing [n.d.] *Scrapbook*, p. 92) in conducting a debate about social questions. It is as if Gissing by this time takes a greater interest in the external appearances and outward behaviour of the workers, their 'picturesque' qualities, than in their generally incoherent ideas.

In the 'Preface' to *A Writer's Notebook* Somerset Maugham expressed his indebtedness to the French novelist Renard, who into his *Journal* had entered a striking collection of disparate data to be used in the composition of his novels. 'As a writer no one could have been more conscientious. Jules Renard (1864–1910) jotted down neat retorts and clever phrases, epigrams, things seen, the sayings of people and the look of them, descriptions of scenery, effects of sunshine and shadow, everything, in short, that could be of use to him when he sat down to write for publication; and in several cases, as we know, when he had collected sufficient data he strung them together into a more or less connected narrative and made a book of them. To a writer this is the most interesting part of these volumes; you are taken into an author's workshop and shown what materials he thought worth gathering, and how he gathered them' (Maugham, 1951, p. x). For the Gissing reader of today similar discoveries are to be made through the study of the preliminary materials gathered in Gissing's indispensable *Scrapbook*.

Appendixes

I. [*Scrapbook*, 'Occupations (Men)', p. 222.]

What Becomes of Telegraph Messengers

SIR, – Pardon me for intruding upon your valuable space, but I should like to contra-dict the opinion generally expressed concerning Post-office telegraph messengers. The general idea prevails that when a boy enters the postal service he has secured a berth which is likely to carry him through life, but such is not the case. Now, take, for instance, a messenger on street delivery. At a given time he is sent to be examined by the doctor for night duty, for which work he is remunerated by the magnificent salary of 12s. per week. When he has served a period of perhaps four years he has to undergo a second examination for postman. And if he passes the doctor – which is not always the case – he receives 18s. per week, but in the event of failure has to resign the service, and, being at that time between the ages of 19 and 20, is turned adrift in the world, without knowledge of any trade, and at that age employment is most difficult to obtain. So the consequence is that many a poor fellow is ruined for life perhaps. – Yours, etc.,

ONE WHO HAS SUFFERED. [Crossed out].

II. [*Scrapbook*, 'Occupations (Men)', p. 219.]

[Press-cutting.]

Cassell's Saturday Journal. p. 59.   [October 4, 1893.]

A FEW WORDS WITH A HERBALIST

The Masses and Their Medicines

'There is a great deal of modern belief in ancient herb remedies, I am happy to say,' said a dealer in herbs and their compounds to a representative of CASSELL'S SATURDAY JOURNAL. 'I think I can tell you some facts not generally known, except to the doctors, who don't like 'em; for there are plenty of people who like the remedies of their ancestors. Of course, *I'm* very glad of it, and believe far more in what are called old women's recipes than in anything the doctors prescribe.
...

'How are the herbs and plants supplied? Oh, different ways. Sometimes old people in a small way collect 'em and send 'em to market. Then there are some who wander about the country for weeks, living in summer in the open air, and from time to time send their bundles of stuff up by train.'

'I know one man who enjoys his work, and is at it continually. He does a good deal at night, by moonlight. The old herbalists say some samples ought to be gathered at that time, but that isn't his reason. It's easier than under a hot sun. More than that, you're not so likely to be interfered with in the fields, copses, and so on. This chap takes his food with him, and there's plenty of water to drink in brooks, and so on, and, generally, a beer-shop handy on the main road. He knows over a big stretch of country the best places for all the herbs and plants we want, and some of the chemists. Some are much more valuable than others. He isn't particular about sleeping under a hedge, or in a shed'll do if nothing better's handy.'

'So he'll go on for weeks. From time to time he gets a postal order for his cash at some village inn. Everybody knows him, and he's often said he wouldn't change his free, open-air life, collecting his plants, with anybody.'

'I suppose he knows something of botany?'

'Never looked at a book about it in all his life, and wouldn't understand it if he did. But he's taught himself as much about English medical plants as any of those books could teach you. More than that, he knows all about wild flowers, and where to get the rarest ones, if you want 'em. He knows all the old women that the villagers go to for medicines – and they know a good deal of the old-fashioned remedies such as our ancestors used to have.'

'Some of 'em have given him recipes hundreds of years old, and he's sold 'em to me and I've made a little money out of 'em. Everything, as a rule, alters with time, but herbs and plants, of course, are just as good as they were a thousand years ago, when the only people as I've read who could make up medicines were the monks and the ladies in the country houses and castles.'

'I often think, when I'm sitting in my little shop in this noisy crowded street, and look at my stock, of the fields and woods all the different things come from, and what a waste there is from ignorance.'

'There's young nettles, for instance. As good as spinach when boiled, and a first-rate blood purifier. Then there's sorrel, and sainfoin, which our forefathers used for salads. Comfrey, again, used to be eaten as a substitute for asparagus. But there, I could go on all the evening talking about the plants and their virtues, which are all round country folk, to be had for the gathering.' [Crossed out].

III. [*Scrapbook*, 'Occupations (Men)', p. 223.]

[Press cutting]

STEWARD and Stewardess Wanted. To take Sole Charge of a Workmen's Club, members 400, keep the place throughout clean, and serve behind bar, wages £1 15s. per week, with rooms, coal, gas, and the profits of the eating department. Apply by letter only, 9, Whitfield-place, Tottenham-court-road. Cash security £30. [Crossed out].

IV. a. [*Scrapbook*, 'Localities and Notes on Nature. Science.' p. 284.]

Apedale Beck. The great tumbled white boulders, making a thousand tiny cataracts. The wooded glen, here sunny through tall pines and firs and rowans (berries red at end of August), these dark under branches. – The shallow ford. – Groups of tall purple loosestrife; ferns; meadowsweet. – Ever-present cool breeze, and music of waters, when around and above the moors blaze under cloudless sky. – Bell flowers. Brilliant yellow patches of ragwort. Strawberries. Great lichened hazel over whole beck. Tall grasses in moist corners. Thick moss on dry stones. Flash of sun on water through leaves. Dragonfly, now and then floating on water; or lies, half in, half out, on small stone. Then darts after midges on surface. Pools brown in sunshine, and greenish under branches. – The spate. Very brown.

IV. b. [*Scrapbook*, 'Localities and Notes on Nature. Science.' pp. 281–2.]

October 25th '92. White frost in the night. At nine o'clock walked from Willersey to Broadway. Sun shining brightly through a mist; cloudless sky; the paleness of shadows; beautiful effect of autumnal colours in trees and hedges, with abundant hawthorn berries and scarlet rose-hips. No wind, but the leaves falling in a steady shower, as if trees were being shaken, – the stalks of the ash descending thickly and heavily; thud of occasional crab-apple. The hawthorn leaves exquisitely silvered round the edge. Frequent spiders' webs in the hedges, glistening as the sun fell upon them. Blades of grass standing up frosted and gleaming.

Bibliography

Coustillas, Pierre, ed. *London and the Life of Literature in Late Victorian London: The Diary of George Gissing, Novelist* (Hassocks, Harvester Press; Lewisburg: Bucknell University Press, 1978).

Coustillas, Pierre and Bridgwater, Patrick *George Gissing at Work: A Study of His Notebook – 'Extracts from My Reading.'* (Greensboro, NC: ELT Press, 1988).

F.[reeman], A[rthur] *George Gissing 1857–1903, Books, Manuscripts and Letters: A Chronological Catalogue of the Pforzheimer Collection* (London: Bernard Quaritch, 1992).

Gissing, George *Eve's Ransom* (New York: D. Appleton, 1895).

—— 'Comrades in Arms.' *Human Odds and Ends: Stories and Sketches* (London: Lawrence & Bullen, 1898).

—— *The Crown of Life* (London: Methuen, 1899).

—— *The Private Papers of Henry Ryecroft* (London: Constable, 1903).

—— 'The Fate of Humphrey Snell' in *A Victim of Circumstances* (London: Constable, 1927).

—— *The Collected Letters of George Gissing*. Eds Mattheisen, Paul F., Young, Arthur C. and Coustillas, Pierre, Vols. III–V (Athens, Ohio: Ohio University Press, 1992–4).

—— [n.d.] *Scrapbook*. Ed. Postmus, Bouwe. Unpublished transcription of the MS in the Lilly Library, Bloomington, Indiana, USA.

Grylls, David. 'A Neglected Source in Gissing Scholarship: The Pforzheimer MS "Scrapbook."' *The Gissing Journal* XXVII, number 1: 11–12 (1991).

Korg, Jacob, ed. *George Gissing's Commonplace Book* (New York: New York Public Library, 1962).

Postmus, Bouwe, ed. *George Gissing's 'American Notebook': Notes – G.R.G. – 1877* (Leiston, New York/Salzburg, Austria: Edwin Mellen Press, 1993).

—— ed. *George Gissing's Memorandum Book: A Novelist's Notebook, 1895–1902* (Leiston, New York/Salzburg, Austria: Edwin Mellen Press, 1996).

Maugham, W. Somerset *A Writer's Notebook* (London: Readers Union/William Heinemann, 1951).

17

Gissing: A Life in Death – A Cavalcade of Gissing Criticism in the Last Hundred Years

Pierre Coustillas

Surveying the work which has been devoted to George Gissing and his achievement since his death in 1903 is bound to generate as much hope as disappointment, but temporal distance, while it blurs so many things, at least enables us to put in perspective the ups and downs of Gissing's reputation and the changing tastes of the reading public and the critics. For a long-vanished author perhaps more than for one still living, posthumous survival largely depends on the activity of his publishers, and it is significant that when Gissing temporarily ceased to be published, from 1940 to 1946, the hitherto steady flow of critical estimation of his work ran down to a trickle. As the latter half of the twentieth century was in sight, optimism about the fate of his work seemed to be rash. Very few people in England and America showed interest in him and they were not conspicuously articulate. Yet Gissing remained the man to whom, only a few weeks before death overtook him, H. G. Wells wrote: "Your fame in England grows steadily and you are the most respectable and respected of novelists next to Hardy, Meredith and James. You should come and savour it."[1] The success of *The Private Papers of Henry Ryecroft* had been immediate, and the book was to prove a steady seller on both sides of the Atlantic, and even more, as far away as Japan.

Any account of the variety of angles from which his personality and work have been viewed by successive generations must begin with a brief review of the dozens of obituaries that have been exhumed from the English-language press. They were much more personal than could be imagined. Obviously the broad lines of Gissing's life were by no means unknown to the majority of literati connected with the press. One often feels that obituarists refrained from being too explicit about such aspects of the writer's life as his expulsion from Owens College or his matrimonial misfortunes. The *Daily Chronicle*, for instance, wrote: "One cannot set out in cold print on the morrow of Gissing's death the pathos that lay behind a life of strenuous, sincere, and finally, and in the highest degree, successful literary effort."[2] C. F. G. Masterman exclaimed in the *Daily News*: "One's whole being revolts against such a bitter bludgeoning of fate."[3] Because he had found in the later novels a warmer outlook upon human development, Masterman resented the news of Gissing's death as a kind of personal outrage. In not a few London and provincial dailies, the event was made the subject of a leader, and editors occasionally grew prophetic. That of the *Bristol Times and Mirror* perceptively predicted that "the death of Mr George Gissing removes a great English writer who is likely to earn from future generations, when many of his more famous contemporaries are forgotten, the understanding and honour in life too sparingly accorded him."[4] The Yorkshire and Lancashire newspapers, for biographical reasons essentially, were as a rule both more prolific and specific in their reconstructions of Gissing's career. The article in the *Yorkshire Weekly Post* unexpectedly digressed, with remarkable accuracy, about his Wakefield relatives, announcing in its conclusion that it would soon serialize an (unspecified) novel from his pen.[5] "The two things that Gissing saw most clearly and emphasized with the greatest wealth of illustrations," the same newspaper observed in a later article, "are the vital importance of culture and the degrading effects of poverty [...] What Gissing meant by education was the development of the feeling for the beautiful, the cultivation of interest in the things of the mind for their own sake,"[6] a percipient statement to be bracketed with that of *The Times* obituarist, Harold Hannyngton Child, who deplored "the too early loss of one who valued his artistic conscience above popularity, and his purpose above his immediate reward."[7]

The wide spectrum of the press on 29 December 1903 reflected both knowledge and ignorance or at least tendentious views – Gissing was made the Apostle of Pessimism; he became the English Zola or a Disciple of Dickens; he was rightly yet alarmingly called a Famous Student of Owens College; an Eminent Novelist, a well-known Yorkshire novelist; his death was announced as his Farewell to Grub Street.[8] Most obituarists stressed the peculiar pathos that attached to his death, far from the land of his affection. Unsurprisingly a few notes rang false. Such inveterate and indelicate gossipers as William Robertson Nicoll and C. K. Shorter could not miss an opportunity to show their bad manners in the *British Weekly*, the *Sphere* and the *Tatler*.[9] Interestingly a number of friends and acquaintances of the deceased novelist wrote to the press, anxious to share their recollections with anonymous readers. G. W. Foote, a rationalist with whom Gissing had once been in touch, sided with Morley Roberts in the soul-snatching affair engineered by the *Church Times*;[10] former schoolfellows like Arthur Bowes and T. T. Sykes reminisced about their Cheshire days in Gissing's company at Lindow Grove School;[11] A. S. Wilkins, still a professor at Manchester, testified to Gissing's excellent results at Owens College.[12] No time was wasted by friendly critics whose names appear in critical anthologies on account of their early contributions to serious Gissing studies: Arthur Waugh, Nathaniel Wedd, Allan Monkhouse, Henry-D. Davray and Austin Harrison.[13]

Little by little the identifiable forms of interest in Gissing became more diversified. The publication of the posthumous works gave many opportunities for testifying, expanding and enquiring; the present-day bibliographer browsing in old periodicals or in volumes of personal recollections published by contemporaries of some repute keeps marvelling at the number of articles, reviews, notes and paragraphs he continually exhumes from oblivion. From the publication of *The House of Cobwebs*, with its quirky, error-ridden introductory survey by Thomas Seccombe, the movement developed fanwise. Gissing was anthologized as early as 1906 by Hesba Stretton,[14] it being already clear that *The Private Papers of Henry Ryecroft* was destined to become a favourite with compilers of thematic selections; miscellaneous Gissing letters to minor correspondents in the literary world and to admirers were regarded as choice bits by editors, notably that of *T. P.'s Weekly*. Mainly in central Europe, Gissing's work was quickly thought worthy of doctoral theses. A precursor in this field was August Schaefer, who as early as 1908 defended at the University of Marburg a dissertation on Gissing's life and novels.[15] His work was to be followed by a longish series of similar dissertations on social, political and cultural themes, culminating with Samuel Vogt Gapp's *George Gissing, Classicist* (1936). Encouraged by the as-yet still unmasked forger T. J. Wise, Clement Shorter and Edward Clodd published limited editions of selected letters they had received from Gissing, but the self-consciousness and aggressively defensive attitude of the family were obstacles in the way of a thorough knowledge of the man's personality and career.[16]

As early as 1904 there spread a feeling in the cultural world at large that, just as he had been unfortunate in his stormy life, Gissing was to be unlucky in death. The quarrel roused by H. G. Wells about his ill-considered introduction to *Veranilda*,[17] which was echoed as far as the United States and Australia, was only a prelude to the acrimonious discord that attended the appearance in 1912 of the fictionalized, condescending biography of Gissing by his old friend Morley Roberts, *The Private Life of Henry Maitland*. When a counter-fire of sorts was lit at the University of Manchester, Gissing's *alma mater*, by Percy Withers who collected funds for a public homage, an inconsequential local paper, the *Manchester City News*,[18] sullied his memory with indecent relish. Nor did Frank Swinnerton's critical study serve his subject's cause. "To write of Gissing is to write of one who failed," observed the young upstart with offensive aplomb.[19] Seccombe called the book an able deprecation and Lewis Horrox, when a second, toned down edition was issued in 1923, tore the volume to pieces, accusing Swinnerton of being "still as far as ever from apprehending the significance of Gissing," of being "blind to the tragedy and heroism" of his life.[20] When he later wrote shorter pieces on Gissing, Swinnerton somewhat relented, but his and Roberts's books did much harm to a novelist whose capacities and lasting relevance they were unable to grasp. The critics, English, American or Continental, who analysed Gissing's achievement in their wake, consciously wrote *against* Roberts and Swinnerton: May Yates, Anton Weber, Ruth Capers McKay, W. van Maanen and Robert Shafer are now viewed as worthy pioneers for that very reason.[21]

Soon after the early posthumous assessments of the whole *œuvre* Gissing, though rightly viewed essentially as a novelist, began to be appreciated as a fine short-story writer, and many compilers of anthologies of that medium thought it indispensable to include him in their volumes, the texts being usually reprinted from his most popular collection, *The House of Cobwebs* (1906).[22] The quality and originality of his work on Dickens, the *Critical Study* in particular, were fully recognized by specialists, although his introductions to the ill-fated Rochester and Autograph editions remained unknown outside the world of second-hand bookdealers.[23] Not so his only travel book, *By the Ionian Sea*, nowadays a compulsory item of luggage for all travellers to those shores, which continued to earn praise as an inspired vision of the ancient world and a graphic picture of daily life in the deep Italian South. The belletristic side of Gissing's works for a time threatened to put his social novels into the shade. Writers as diverse as Norman Douglas in *Siren Land* and *Old Calabria* and Christopher Morley in his many journalistic essays from the 1920s onward, let alone the American pirate publisher Thomas Bird Mosher, were leading figures in this evolution which was to be temporarily checked by the publication in 1927 of the deplorably edited *Letters of George Gissing to Members of His Family*. By that time the rising interest in both the life and works of the author was assuming a variety of new forms: collections of miscellaneous writings, most of which had first appeared in books, newspapers and periodicals (*The Immortal Dickens* and *Critical Studies of the Works of Charles Dickens, Selections Autobiographical and Imaginative*), essays and book chapters on his novels and view of life, or poems like those reprinted in *Manchester University Verses* in 1913. Other and better sustainers of his reputation were the chapters devoted to him in histories of English literature by Paul Elmer More, J. M. Kennedy, E. M. Chapman, Brewster and Burrell or Madeleine Cazamian.[24] Occasionally some hitherto unsuspected antagonist would raise his voice or sharpen his pen and deliver himself of his long-nursed hatred of a writer he did not in the least understand. Douglas Goldring, in his *Reputations* (1920), was one of them.

To hostile criticism book and autograph collectors were indifferent; they focused their attention on auction and secondhand booksellers' catalogues offering items which still rivet the attention of collectors of later generations. Those pioneers played an important and possibly unconscious role in that they were to prove auxiliaries of research once their treasures, after a new transit in salerooms, found permanent homes in the great institutional libraries where serious research is done. Evidence of their admiration for Gissing is reflected in some limited editions of short stories like *An Heiress on*

Condition (1923) and *A Yorkshire Lass* (1928); as well as in George Matthew Adams's article "Why I collect George Gissing" with its precious facsimiles of the author's account of books until 1898 in Part 18 of the *Colophon*. Slowly headway was being made towards a full knowledge of Gissing's writings, major and minor, but not of his life, or at least of the most secret areas of it. A volume like Walter T. Spencer's *Forty Years in my Bookshop* (1923), with its tantalizing descriptions of hitherto unrecorded manuscripts and presentation copies, made revelations that have scarcely aged in 80 years. Criticism of the works was then still largely elementary by late twentieth-century standards, partly because Gissing's correspondence was still mostly unknown; it could not fertilize a badly wanted full-length discussion of the works. The author's family published a few interesting articles which nonetheless partook of the nature of Victorian whitewashing. Alfred, Gissing's younger son, even wrote a biography based on the diary and the letters to his uncle Algernon and aunts Margaret and Ellen, but as it essentially consisted of lengthy quotations, he found no publisher desirous to bring out such an old-fashioned manuscript. Still, by the late 1930s, not a few scholars were anxious to break new ground. The American Stanley Alden had shown the way as early as September 1922 in his *North American Review* article "George Gissing, Humanist," and Robert Shafer, in his remarkable edition of *Workers in the Dawn* (1935) and elsewhere, perceptively enquired into the reasons for "the vitality of George Gissing." With him and other stimulating critics like Pelham Elgar, J. W. Cunliffe, Herbert J. Muller, H. V. Routh,[25] criticism, which was assisted by further valuable personal recollections by George A. Stearns, Austin Harrison and William Rothenstein among others, took a new step forward.[26]

In 1938, when Alfred Gissing, the sole member of the family who could still honour his father's work, made one more attempt to collect half-forgotten short stories, the general reader anxious not to miss a new Gissing book must have felt that his quest for uncollected material was completed and that dullness would henceforth be writ large across Gissing studies. However, we see in retrospect that only preliminary research had come to an end, and the outbreak of the Second World War apparently played havoc with all prospect of progress in the foreseeable future. Yet American university libraries were acquiring scarce material at low prices, and articles began to appear on the Gissing material in some special collections. For instance, the recently catalogued Adams Gissing collection at Yale was first described in the *Yale University Library Gazette* in January 1942. In October of the same year the *Classical Journal* offered its readers a carefully written article entitled "Some Reflections on the Scholarship of George Gissing." William C. Frierson, whose French thesis on English naturalism dated back to 1925, continued in 1942 his revaluation of Gissing in his volume, *The English Novel in Transition*. During the next year George Orwell published in *Tribune* his first article on Gissing, "Not enough money" (2 April), on the trail of an enquiry about Martha McCulloch McBarnes, a former pupil of Gissing at Waltham, Mass, who had renewed her acquaintance with him in the mid-nineties (*Waltham Tribune*, 1 March 1943). Specialized research was beginning, as the *Times Literary Supplement* occasionally reported.

After the war, fitful sympathetic efforts to launch a revival were made by Sidgwick and Jackson as well as by Home and Van Thal, but Gissing and his work had been relegated to the back of national consciousness; besides the attempts to give *A Life's Morning*, *In the Year of Jubilee* and *The Whirlpool* a new impetus were either awkwardly or half-heartedly made. The three novels and a fourth, *The Town Traveller*, reissued by Methuen in 1956, were all remaindered shortly after publication. Obviously Gissing's novels, with or without introductions, now had to find a new, younger audience. A number of major articles by William Plomer, V. S. Pritchett and Walter Allen in weeklies like the *New Statesman*, the *Listener* and the *Times Literary Supplement* drew public attention to the significance and specificity of Gissing's works, but his pessimism was rather crudely objected to and too frequently seen in a personal light.[27] In this respect Myfanwy Evans's article, with its unfortunate title "Cultivating Misery" (in *Time and Tide* for 7 March 1953), merely confirmed the tendency of most critics in those days to simplify Gissing's temperament and opinions in a way that discouraged readers from thinking of him with open minds. Various radio programmes of the 1940s and 1950s, including a recently discovered serialization of *In the Year of Jubilee* on the Regional Home Service for the North of England, contributed to enlarge the author's readership.[28] Collections of hitherto unknown letters flocked to the main Gissing repositories, Yale, the New York Public Library and the Carl H. Pforzheimer Library among others.

The year 1950 saw several publications which now strike us as more important than they must have seemed at that time. Jacob Korg published his first article on Gissing in the *American Scholar*, "George Gissing's Outcast Intellectuals," Russell Kirk asked in the Summer issue of the *Western Humanities Review* after a journey to Wakefield "Who Knows George Gissing ?", and an Italian journal, *Il Ponte*, offered its readers a chapter of *By the Ionian Sea* in translation, a prelude to the translation of the whole book by the poet and English scholar Margherita Guidacci on the centenary of Gissing's birth.[29] The revival of interest was slow, but it was favoured by two ground-breaking exhibitions held in the Berg Collection and in Wakefield to commemorate the author's death 50 years earlier. The catalogue of the former exhibition, the distinguished work of John D. Gordan, has proved to be a landmark in modern Gissing studies on account of the host of quotations from unpublished letters it contains. From the mid-1950s Korg and other American academics initiated punctual investigations of the growing collections in university libraries. His June 1955 article in *PMLA* on the novelist's division of purpose set the tone for various pieces by Royal A. Gettmann, A. C. Young, C. J. Francis and Harry Preble, but biographical research was to remain shallow for years because many hints supplied by Gissing's letters and diary were unwisely disregarded or left untapped.[30] When Gordon Haight tried his hand at elementary genealogical reconstruction in the June 1964 number of *Notes and Queries*, not a single suggestion he made was proved correct by later serious investigations. Textual studies were set in train by Joseph Wolff when he studied the two versions of *The Unclassed* (*Nineteenth Century Fiction*, June 1953) and Jacob Korg, some years later, showed how Gissing's *Commonplace Book* (1962) had been used in the published works. His main successors in this scholarly field were Bouwe Postmus and the present writer with such titles as *George Gissing at Work*, "Reminiscences of My Father," the so-called *American Notebook* and the *Memorandum Book*.[31]

But this is anticipating. If it is clearly established that the first period in the century of Gissing studies under review ended in 1939–1940, the second covers the years 1940–1958 or 1960 approximately. There were new developments in this middle period, noticeable for instance in all the articles, signed or anonymous, in the *Times Literary Supplement* and elsewhere, published by Anthony Curtis, John Middleton Murry, Richard Church and V. S. Pritchett, and more discreetly R. C. Churchill, who all kept Gissing's name alive in the years when Victorian studies were still only budding, and before his work came to be viewed more often than not in a political light. Raymond Williams, John Lucas, P. J. Keating and John Goode as well as Alan Swingewood and, more recently, Patrick Brantlinger waxed critical of Gissing because he was an independent analyst, who dared criticize the lower classes as well as the upper ones, and who of course did not respond positively to Marxism.[32] Criticism also came to be coloured for a few decades by the views of the so-called "literary" theorists, the latest of whom appears to be Gilles Deleuze,[33] but most readers viewed such political and methodological *rapprochements* as forced and unprofitable, also often suggested by ulterior motives. More useful from the biographical standpoint were the well-documented essays which were at first an offshoot of the centenary of Gissing's birth, for instance A. C. Young's detailed account of the relationship between the novelist and Eduard Bertz, C. J. Francis's study of Schopenhauerian ideas in the works, Orwell's seminal second article, posthumously published in 1960, Preble's exhumation of Gissing's contributions to the Russian periodical *Vyestnik Evropy*, and Shigeru Koike's overview of the extraordinary popularity of *The Private Papers of Henry Ryecroft* and the shorter fiction in Japan.[34]

Besides this highly diversified activity in which scholars of several nationalities were involved, what gave hitherto halting Gissing studies a fresh impetus was the publication of several important volumes of the writer's correspondence and private papers in the early 1960s: the letters to Wells, to Eduard Bertz and to Gabrielle Fleury, as well as Jacob Korg's edition of the *Commonplace Book*. *The Letters to Gabrielle Fleury*, while documenting retrospectively the failure of the marriage to Edith Underwood, revealed the ups and downs of a union hitherto only sketchily discussed by Morley Roberts. The biographical information they released was still unknown to Jacob Korg when he prepared his critical biography of Gissing (Seattle, 1963 and London, 1965), but it was complemented factually by the succession of books and booklets which appeared in the next 20-odd years – notably the catalogue/guide to the National Book League exhibition *The Rediscovery of George Gissing* (1971), by John Spiers and the present writer, the 10 Enitharmon Press titles, and the present writer's edition of Gissing's diary.

Meanwhile many other publications contributed to enlarge the novelist's audience. Practically all his works had been reprinted by 1987, often in critical editions, mainly by The Harvester Press, under the direction of its founder John Spiers, which reprinted 20 titles, and the Hogarth Press, which reprinted 5, as did Dent in Everyman's Library in the next decade. Critical anthologies were published by Pierre Coustillas (*Collected Articles*, 1968, and *Gissing: The Critical Heritage*, 1972, in collaboration with Colin Partridge), J.-P. Michaux (*George Gissing: Critical Essays*, 1981) and Francesco Badolato (*Antologia Critica*, 1984), whose work in Italian since the mid-1960s has been considerable. The Tragara Press of Edinburgh also drew public attention to Gissing's name in a way that was all its own with limited editions: *Brief Interlude* (1987) contained Gissing's letters to Edith Sichel with a commentary by the present writer, who also edited a half-forgotten short story, "A Freak of Nature" (1990), only known at the time in a bowdlerized form as "Mr. Brogden, City Clerk." The Tragara Press likewise published a tastefully produced anthology of Gissing's *Aphorisms and Reflections* selected by P. F. Kropholler (1989) and an *édition de luxe* of *By the Ionian Sea* (1992).

Critical discussion of the main works was conducted almost simultaneously with the reprinting of the novels in a series of volumes by Oswald Davis (a posthumous highly idiosyncratic publication), Gillian Tindall (a thematic exploration of the longer fiction in conjunction with the main events in Gissing's life), Adrian Poole (a reconsideration of Gissing in context), John Goode (a heavily didactic analysis of Gissing's fiction in the light of the critic's own ideology), John Halperin (a discussion of the principal works in relation with the author's life marked, it has been complained, by forced biographism), Robert Selig (a thorough, compact analysis of all the forms of Gissing's art), David Grylls (who concentrated fruitfully on Gissing's fascinating paradoxes), John Sloan (an analysis of Gissing's cultural protest throughout his career) and Christina Sjöholm (who focused her attention on Gissing's marriage portrayals). These by and large illuminating probings of the novelist's multiform artistry in no way duplicated – by anticipation or retrospection – the many enquiries which were conducted in less substantial, yet sometimes still more pertinent volumes, book chapters and articles of which the *Gissing Newsletter*, afterwards the *Gissing Journal*, have kept a full record since the mid-1960s (or, for that matter, in the contents of these two quarterlies). Nor could this summary critical survey afford to ignore P. J. Keating's pages on Gissing in his study of *The Working Classes in Victorian Fiction*, Patrick Bridgwater's monograph on Gissing and Germany, Rachel Bowlby's *Just Looking* or Gwyn Neale's well-researched booklet on Gissing and Wales, *All the Days were Glorious*, which bears comparison with other specialised studies like Clifford Brook's and W. J. West's small volumes on Gissing in Wakefield and Exeter.[35]

Along these volumes should be placed articles that made their mark in their day and that the passing of time has in no way rendered obsolescent: discussions of *In the Year of Jubilee* and *New Grub Street* by Robert Selig in *Studies in English Literature* and *Nineteenth-Century Fiction* respectively, an impressive essay by Charles Swann on *Born in Exile*, the two magisterial ones by Allan Atlas on Gissing and music, the very thorough investigations published by Martha Vogeler and Bouwe Postmus in the *Gissing Journal* or William Greenslade's anatomy of *The Whirlpool* as a period piece in *Victorian Studies*. But leaving the enumeration at this stage would mean overlooking the series of innovative articles by Janice Deledalle which have appeared in the *Gissing Journal*, notably on Henry James's pretentious, shapeless and unfair review of *The Whirlpool* and on the role played by Izoulet's *magnum opus* in *Our Friend the Charlatan*. Very few of the novels have failed to elicit from English, American or Italian critics important reassessments in the last two decades: *Thyrza* should be reread in the light offered by Francesco Marroni and *Will Warburton* with Luisa Villa's comment close at hand.[36]

The bulk of Gissing criticism increased to such a degree over the years that reviews of the progress achieved were thought necessary in volume form as well as in journals. This need was first felt by the Modern Language Association when it published *Victorian Fiction: A Guide to Research* (ed. Lionel Stevenson) in 1964 with a chapter on Gissing by Jacob Korg, then a *Second Guide* (ed. George H. Ford) in 1978 with an updated survey of Gissing studies again by Korg who, in between, had been commissioned to contribute a similar article to the *British Studies Monitor* for the summer of 1973, just before Joseph Wolff published his *George Gissing: An Annotated Bibliography of Writings about Him* (1974) and John Halperin "The Gissing Revival 1961–74" in *Studies in the Novel* for the spring of 1976. The latest survey seems to be "Recent Work and Close Prospects in Gissing Studies" by Pierre Coustillas in *English Literature in Transition 1880–1920*, Volume 32 (1989), Number 4. Also related to the subject is Volume IV of the third edition of the *Cambridge Bibliography of English Literature* (1999), with an entirely new entry on Gissing which supersedes the incompetent one by Bradford A. Booth in the 1969 edition. The two editions of Michael Collie's primary bibliography (1975 and 1985) have long been condemned as unusable by scholars with a sound knowledge of the subject. Conversely articles by collectors, booksellers and librarians, let alone the *Location Register of Twentieth-Century English Literary Manuscripts and Letters* (2 vols, 1988), have proved valuable auxiliaries.

In an altogether different manner which would have brought a wry smile of satisfaction on his face, Gissing has been celebrated in both his native town, Wakefield, and in southern Italy, two locations which for him were synonymous with exile, though in contrasting ways. A Gissing Centre was founded in 1990 in the house which had been briefly his father's property: a sanctuary full of Gissing books, mementoes and sundry domestic and cultural relics of the novelist and his relatives, it is now the starting-point of guided visits to the local places whose names are associated with him and his work. Wakefield has remained the place where he was born in geographical, social and cultural exile. To anyone desirous of investigating the problems connected with Gissing's roots, Clifford Brook's thoroughly researched booklet is essential reading, but Gissing's spiritual home was on the shores of the Ionian Sea, where Greek and Roman cultures mixed in what he called with emotion his land of romance. The book recently issued by the authorities of Catanzaro consisting of the proceedings of the symposium held locally in 1999 in honour of Gissing is another cultural landmark.[37] It is eminently appropriate that he should be commemorated on a tablet near the entrance of the former Albergo Centrale with his host, the world-famous Coriolano Paparazzo; and equally appropriate that in the nearby town of Crotone, the ancient Kroton, to which he devoted four chapters of *By the Ionian Sea*, he should be remembered on a plaque by the Albergo Concordia. A street was named after him in Wakefield, and homage was also paid to him with plaques in Chelsea and Paris, and various mementoes in the Old Reading Room of the British Museum which he immortalized in *New Grub Street*. As is only natural, nowhere is his travel narrative better loved than in Calabria, where the volume, aptly translated by Margherita Guidacci, is always referred to with admiration by educated people. Numberless references have been made to *By the Ionian Sea* since the 1950s in the Italian press, scholarly journals and books on travel literature, and Gissing's successors since 1897, from Norman Douglas to H. V. Morton and Paul Theroux, make of him a major figure among Anglo-American travellers along the Ionian shores. The new illustrated edition of the book, with its copious critical material, should encourage Gissing enthusiasts to venture south of Naples.[38] Literary tourists need not fear they might abruptly find themselves lost in a cultural desert when in view of Etna. Gissing has admirers along the Straits of Messina.

One more achievement in Gissing studies in the last hundred years cannot be passed over in silence, the *Collected Letters*, the editing of which was discussed publicly with gusto at the Amsterdam Conference in September 1999. The preparation of the nine volumes required a considerable amount of research, the fruits of which are not all visible in the introductions and the notes. A series of articles published in the *Gissing Newsletter* or *Journal* on the relationships between Gissing and John Northern Hilliard, Adolphus William Ward, Herbert Heaton Sturmer, Arthur Brownlow fforde and John Shortridge constitute the overflow, together with the volume devoted to BrianBorú Dunne, which was rightly seen as the coping stone of the whole edifice.[39]

New developments are shaping up. Not yet a tenth volume of collected letters, however; only a small gathering of miscellaneous notes, postcards and fragments of letters as well as a group of hitherto unknown or partly published letters, the originals of which had vanished in the 1930s, being converted into much needed money by Gissing's descendants. But other letters will sooner or later turn up, as will similar material recorded in old volumes of *Book Auction Records* or *Book Prices Current*. Meanwhile the full-length primary bibliography prepared by this writer will have appeared together with a badly needed collected edition of the short stories, probably in three volumes. If fate is kind, his biography of Gissing will follow. But the younger generations are at work in England, the United States, the Netherlands, Italy and Japan. There is no predicting what flowers will blossom in the great open spaces that extend before them.

Notes

1. *The Collected Letters of George Gissing*, ed. Paul F. Mattheisen, Arthur C. Young and Pierre Coustillas, Athens, Ohio: Ohio University Press, 1990–1997, Volume IV, letter of November 23, 1903, p. 161.
2. "Death of George Gissing," December 29, 1903, pp. 3–4.
3. "Death of Mr. Gissing," December 29, 1903, pp. 8–9, and "George Gissing," December 30, p. 5.
4. "George Gissing," December 30, 1903, pp. 4–5.
5. January 2, 1904, p. 2. The novel was *Will Warburton* (7 January–20 May 1905).
6. "Culture in Practice: George Gissing as a novelist," *Yorkshire Weekly Post*, February 13, 1904, p. 7.
7. "Obituary: Mr. George Gissing," December 29, 1903, p. 4.
8. See respectively *Daily Mail*, p. 3; *Yorkshire Daily Observer*, p. 4; *Echo*, p. 2; *Manchester Evening News*, p. 3; *Leeds and Yorkshire Mercury*, p. 5; *Leeds Daily News*, p. 3; *Daily Mirror*, p. 4.
9. A Man of Kent, "The Late Mr. George Gissing," *British Weekly*, December 31, 1903, p. 345; "A Literary Letter," *Sphere*, January 2, 1904, p. 4; also January 9, p. 48, January 23, p. 90 and January 30, p. 112; C. K. S., "Literary Gossip," *Tatler*, January 6, 1904, p. ix.
10. G. W. Foote, "Soul Snatchers," *Freethinker*, January 17, 1904, p. 33; "In Memoriam: George Robert Gissing," *Church Times*, January 8, 1904, p. 33; Morley Roberts, "The Late George Gissing," *Church Times*, January 15, 1904, p. 61. See also January 29, 1904, p. 130.
11. Arthur Bowes, "George Gissing's School-Days," *T. P.'s Weekly*, January 22, 1904, p. 100; T. T. Sykes, "The Early School Life of George Gissing," *Alderley and Wilmslow Advertiser*, January 29, 1904, p. 3.

12. "The Late Mr. George Gissing," *Manchester Guardian*, December 31, 1903, p. 10.
13. Respectively, "George Gissing," *Fortnightly Review*, February 1, 1904, pp. 244–56; "George Gissing," *Independent Review*, February 1904, pp. 280–82; "George Gissing," *Manchester Quarterly*, April 1905, pp. 106–23; "Causerie littéraire: George Gissing," *La Semaine Littéraire* (Geneva), August 4, 1906, pp. 361–63; "George Gissing," *Nineteenth Century*, September 1906, pp. 453–63. With the exception of Wedd, these writers were to comment on Gissing's life and works on various occasions in the following decades.
14. *Thoughts on Old Age* (London, 1906).
15. *George Gissing: Sein Leben und seine Romane*, Marburg, 1908.
16. Shorter published *Letters to an Editor* in 1915, while Clodd published *Letters to Edward Clodd from George Gissing* in 1914, and included some in his *Memories* (1916) and in *Autobiographical Notes with Comments upon Tennyson and Huxley by George Gissing* (1930).
17. See Pierre Coustillas, "The Stormy Publication of Gissing's *Veranilda*," *Bulletin of the New York Public Library*, November 1968, pp. 588–610.
18. From 8 to March 29, 1913, *passim*.
19. *George Gissing, a Critical Study* (1912), p. 42.
20. Seccombe's judgment occurs in his article "Gissing: A Sentiment," *New York Times Review of Books*, December 8, 1912, pp. 753–54, that of Lewis Horrox, "George Gissing and Mr. Swinnerton," in *Nation and Athenæum*, March 1, 1924, pp. 770–72.
21. See respectively, *George Gissing, An Appreciation* (Manchester, 1922); *George Gissing und die soziale Frage* (Leipzig, 1932); *George Gissing and his Critic Frank Swinnerton* (Philadelphia, 1933); "George Gissing's Life from his Letters," *Neophilologus*, January 1933, pp. 115–30, and "The Vitality of George Gissing," *American Review*, September 1935, pp. 459–87.
22. This was the first posthumous collection of his short stories. *A Victim of Circumstances* (1927) and *Stories and Sketches* (1938) were substantial additions to the canon.
23. For Gissing as critic of Dickens, see Pierre Coustillas, *Gissing's Writings on Dickens* (1969).
24. In *Shelburne Essays*, Fifth Series (1908), pp. 45–65; *English Literature 1880–1905* (1912); *English Literature in Account with Religion* (1910); *Adventure and Experience* (1930); *Le Roman et les Idées en Angleterre* (1923).
25. See *The Art of the Novel* (1933); *English Literature during the Last Half-Century* (1919); *Modern Values* (1937); *Towards the Twentieth Century* (1937).
26. In "George Gissing in America," *Bookman* (New York), August 1926, pp. 683–86; *Frederic Harrison: Thoughts and Memories* (1926); *Men and Memories* (1932).
27. Respectively, "Books in General," *New Statesman and Nation*, February 23, 1946, p. 140; "Books in General," *New Statesman and Nation*, November 8, 1947, p. 372 and "A Novelist Born Too Soon," *Listener*, November 28, 1946, pp. 760–61; [Walter Allen], "The Permanent Stranger," *Times Literary Supplement*, February 14, 1948, p.92.
28. See *Radio Times*, November 10 and 17, 1950.
29. Respectively Spring 1950, pp. 194–202; Summer 1950, pp. 213–22; Pietro De Logu, "La Calabria Vista da uno scrittore inglese: George Gissing in Viaggio da Paola a Cosenza," September-October 1950, pp. 1326–27 and *Sulla riva dello Jonio* (Cappelli, 1957).

30. See *PMLA*, pp. 323–36; "Bentley and Gissing," *Nineteenth-Century Fiction*, March 1957, pp. 306–14; "George Gissing's Friendship with Eduard Bertz," *Nineteenth-Century Fiction*, December 1958, pp. 227–37; "Gissing and Schopenhauer," *Nineteenth-Century Fiction*, June 1960, pp. 53–61; "Gissing's Articles for *Vyestnik Evropy*", *Victorian Newsletter*, Spring 1963, pp. 12–15.

31. The first two of these titles were published by Pierre Coustillas, the first in collaboration with Patrick Bridgwater (Greensboro NC, 1988), the second in a Gissing number of *English Literature in Transition*, Vol. 32 (1989), no. 4, pp. 419–30; the last two titles by Bouwe Postmus (Lewiston NY, 1993 and 1996).

32. Respectively in *Culture and Society* (1957); *Politics and Literature* (1971); *The Working Classes in Victorian Fiction* (1971); *George Gissing: Ideology and Fiction* (1978); *The Novel and Revolution* (1975); *The Reading Lesson: The Threat of Mass Literacy in Nineteenth-Century British Fiction* (1998).

33. *Lines of Flight: Reading Deleuze with Hardy, Gissing, Conrad and Woolf*, by John Hughes (1997).

34. For Young, Francis and Preble, see note 30. George Orwell, "George Gissing," *London Magazine*, June 1960, pp. 36–43, an article commissioned in the late 1940s but published only after the author's death. Shigeru Koike, "Gissing in Japan," *Bulletin of the New York Public Library*, November 1963, pp. 365–73.

35. The volumes concerned are: *A Study in Literary Leanings* (1966); *The Born Exile: George Gissing* (1974); *George Gissing in Context* (1975); *George Gissing: Ideology and Fiction* (1978); *George Gissing: A Life in Books* (1982); *George Gissing* (1983, revised 1995); *The Paradox of Gissing* (1986); *George Gissing: The Cultural Challenge* (1989); *"The Vice of Wedlock": The Theme of Marriage in George Gissing's Novels* (1994); *Gissing and Germany* (1981); *Just Looking: Consumer Culture: Dreiser, Gissing and Zola* (1985); *All the Days were Glorious* (1994); *George Gissing and Wakefield* (1980, revised 1992); *Gissing in Exeter* (1979).

36. See "A Sad Heart at the Late-Victorian Culture Market: George Gissing's *In the Year of Jubilee*," *Studies in English Literature 1500–1900*, Autumn 1969, pp. 703–20, and " 'The Valley of the Shadow of Books': Alienation in *New Grub Street*," *Nineteenth-Century Fiction*, September 1970, pp. 188–98; " 'Sincerity and Authenticity': The Problem of Identity in *Born in Exile*," *Literature and History*, Autumn 1984, pp. 165–88; "George Gissing's Concertina," *Journal of Musicology*, Spring 1999, pp. 304–18, and "George Gissing on Music: Italian Impressions," *Musical Times*, Summer 2001, pp. 27–38. For Martha Vogeler's and Bouwe Postmus's many valuable contributions to the *Gissing Newsletter*, afterwards the *Gissing Journal*, see the table of contents on Mitsuharu Matsuoka's website http://www.lang.nagoya-u.ac.jp/~matsuoka/Gissing.html. William Greenslade's article on *The Whirlpool* appeared in the Summer 1989 number of *Victorian Studies*, pp. 507–23. Major contributions to the *Gissing Journal* by Martha Vogeler will be found in the October 1993, January 1996 and October 1999 issues; by Bouwe Postmus in the January 1992, January and October 1995, July 1996 and April 1998 issues; by Janice Deledalle-Rhodes in the October 1997, April 1999 and October 2000 issues. Francesco Marroni's article, "*Thyrza*: Gissing, Darwin and the Destinies of Innocence," appeared in the *Gissing Journal*, July 1998, that of Luisa Villa, "The Grocer's Romance: Economic Transactions and Radical Individualism in *Will Warburton*," in the number for April 2000.

37. *George Gissing a Catanzaro*, ed. Mauro F. Minervino, Catanzaro: Città di Catanzaro [2002].

38. *By the Ionian Sea*. Introduction and Notes by Pierre Coustillas, Oxford: Signal Books (2004).
39. *The Collected Letters of George Gissing*, ed. Paul F. Mattheisen, Arthur C. Young and Pierre Coustillas (1990–1997). The articles on Gissing and Hilliard, Sturmer, Ward, fforde and Shortridge appeared in the *Gissing Journal* for January and October 1993, July 1994, April 1996, July and October 1999 respectively.